SHOT
ACROSS THE
BOW

THE DEEP SIX • Book 5

JULIE ANN WALKER

Shot Across the Bow
The Deep Six book 5
Copyright © 2021 by Limerence Publications LLC

Limerence Publications LLC
ISBN: 978-1-950100-10-1

To Megan, for your grace and perseverance. You've shown me that being vulnerable and being strong go together.

Take me to the ocean. Let me sail the open sea. To breathe the warm and salty air and dream of things to be.
~Erica Billups

PROLOGUE

July 16th, 1624...

Death is such an indignity.

Bartolome Vargas had always thought so. Thought the howls of pain and the flash of fear in formerly courageous eyes were some of life's greatest injustices. Yet nothing had prepared Spain's most famous sea captain for the horror of the illness that had fallen over the surviving members of his crew.

Granted, none of them had fared well in the long weeks since the Santa Cristina *succumbed to the early season hurricane. The small island upon which they had been marooned afforded them little in the way of sustenance, forcing them to survive solely on the rainwater they collected in the storage barrels washed ashore from the wreck and what fish and crustaceans they could harvest from the sea. But barring injury, infection, or battle with their enemies, they* had *survived.*

'Til this very morn...

The keening cry of the ship's surgeon—a man who had served under Bartolome for nigh on fifteen years—had wrenched Bartolome from a fitful sleep. In the twilight of dawn, he had spied the good doctor squatted at the edge of their squalid, slapdash campsite. The man had shaken with the effort to expel the demon inside him, his face mottled red, his wildly rolling eyes seemingly sunk deep into his skull.

Within five hours, the surgeon had succumbed, his last minutes plagued by convulsive spasms and a thirst no amount of water could quench. In that short amount of time from sunrise until the man's death, three more of Bartolome's brave crew had begun to show signs of the mysterious ailment.

He had sent a handful of his healthiest sailors to the beach to dig a grave for the surgeon, but he feared there would be more than one hole in the sand before the day's end.

"'Tis your fault we are dying here and not safe in Havana!" Alvaro yelled from his bedroll at the edge of the clearing.

The young helmsman had been growing more mutinous by the day.

Were they still aboard the Santa Cristina, *Bartolome would have long since had the headstrong sailor keelhauled for insubordination. But too many of his men had already been lost, and those that were left were suffering. The thought of meting out additional misery, even to one as defiant as Alvaro, did not sit well with Bartolome's conscience.*

"If you had not fired and scuttled that French ketch," Alvaro continued, "we would all be—"

2

"Dead!" Bartolome bellowed, feeling his face grow hot. He might not have the stomach to punish Alvaro for the sharpness of his tongue, but neither would he stand idly by while the youth callously sliced him with it. "We would all be dead by the hands of our enemies. And instead of the treasure remaining safe in her watery tomb, 'twould be in the hands of the British or the French or those bastardly Dutch!"

"Hold your tongue, Alvaro," Rosario, Bartolome's most trusted second-in-command, came to stand next to him as he surveyed those who were sick and those who eyed askance the sick and kept their distance lest they too fall ill. "'Tis not the capitán's *fault. We are cursed. We have been cursed since the day our good King Philip set us on this course."*

Is that true? *Bartolome wondered.* Are we cursed?

He had no time to ponder the answer before one of the afflicted, their cooper, lurched over to a water barrel and plunged his face into the tepid liquid, sucking in great gulps. The sick man came up with water sluicing down his shoulders. His voice was reed-thin when he wailed, "The thirst! It claws at me!"

A second later, the man grabbed his stomach and retched onto the sand at his feet. Like the surgeon, the flesh had hollowed over the cooper's cheeks and eyes. The skin on the backs of his hands was wrinkled like parchment, making him appear far older than his twenty-seven years.

Rosario crossed himself and whispered a desperate prayer.

In weeks past, Bartolome may have joined his midshipman in a plea to the Almighty. Of late, however, he had begun to lose faith that god cared one whit about any of them.

3

After watching the cooper crawl back to his bedroll and curl into a miserable ball, Bartolome closed his nose to the foul stench of illness and unwashed bodies, and made his way over to the afflicted man. He was determined to offer any aid he could.

After kneeling beside the cooper, however, he knew his ministrations would be for naught. The dark specter of Death was there in the cooper's eyes. 'Twould not be long now before the man's soul left his body to fly into the mystery of the afterlife.

Poor bastard, *Bartolome thought helplessly.*

He had been so certain if they were patient, if they remained stalwart and true to their cause, a Spanish ship would happen upon them. He had been convinced that with a prize as colossal as the one the Santa Cristina *had carried in her big belly, their good king would have every ship in the Spanish Navy scouring the waters of the Caribbean, looking for her remains.*

Yet...the days had stretched into weeks and the weeks had stretched into months. Not once from their various makeshift crow's nests built around the island had they spied a vessel flying the colors of home. Not once had their searching eyes detected even a glimmer of salvation.

'Twas as if their island had been enchanted by some terrible sea witch's spell, visible only to their enemies.

Mayhap Rosario is right, *Bartolome mused miserably.* Mayhap we are all doomed to die on this sorry spit of mangrove forest and sand.

But if their fate was to be forever entombed on the island, he took comfort in knowing the treasure remained hidden in its new home. Remained safe and secure from the light of day and the beady, covetous eyes of their numerous adversaries.

'Til a true son of Spain comes to claim it...

CHAPTER 1

Present Day
8:45 PM...

Tactical awareness...

It meant knowing all the exits in the bar. Having a close approximation of how many people were inside making merry. And recognizing the two guys in the corner drinking whiskey and wearing ten-gallon cowboy hats carried concealed weapons in calf holsters under their Wranglers—*Texans, ya gotta love 'em.*

For Spiro "Romeo" Delgado, tactical awareness also meant knowing the exact moment Mia Ennis walked into the place.

The hairs on his arms stood up. His stomach balled into a tight fist. And the oxygen in the room was reduced by half—which was something considering Schooner Warf Bar was open air along three whole sides.

These physical symptoms caused by her mere presence were nothing new. He'd been suffering from them ever since she'd been hired on to oversee the excavation he and his former SEAL Team members and current Deep Six Salvage partners were doing on the legendary *Santa Cristina.*

The state of Florida required a site with any sort of historic significance *must* contract a trained and certified professional to document the salvage process. And since there wasn't a *more* historic relic in all the Caribbean than the grand ghost galleon, enter Mia Ennis, acclaimed marine archeologist.

But back to the skitchy arm hair, mutinous stomach, and insufficient O_2 levels...

No two ways around it, they happened because Romeo had a thing for the brainy little strawberry blonde.

Nah. Not a *thing.* That word didn't come close to capturing what he felt.

It was more like he craved her like a drowning man craved air. Like a starving man craved an all-you-can-eat buffet. Like a poor man craved a winning lottery ticket.

It was a bone-deep hunger—*emphasis on the 'bone' and the 'deep.'*

Blame his insatiable appetite for her on her athletic figure, or her creamy skin that always held a hint of a blush, or her fascinating, amber-colored eyes that he was forever sinking into.

Lioness eyes was how he thought of them. And like those big cats that roamed the Serengeti, Mia moved with an innate grace that hinted at the kind of lover she would be.

The slow kind. The savoring kind. The *thorough* kind.

Sweet Mother Mary. Yeah, that *last* thing was surely the cause of his unprecedented preoccupation. Because while he was no stranger to attracting and being attracted *to* the opposite sex—his *nom de guerre* was 'Romeo' for shit's sake—never in his life had he found himself plagued by incessant thoughts of *one* woman.

Mia was an earworm that spun endlessly inside his head. Only instead of catching himself humming, he often caught himself dreaming about kissing her lips.

Those perfect lips that were so small and plush and pink. Like a rosebud just waiting to be plucked.

Dreaming about, but never daring to do it because even if she'd been interested in a little hunka chunka—which she'd assured him she was *not*—she was what was known in the dating world as *relationship material.*

*We're talking the kind of woman whose vocabulary doesn't include the word "fling." The kind of women who only has affairs that are chock-a-block full of potential and meaning. The kind of woman that expects a man to take a page from Beyoncé's book and...*put a ring on it.

And he? Well, he'd gotten his reputation as a straight-up skirt-hound because he liked his liaisons fun and dirty, with no holds barred and no expectations. Uncomplicated and... most importantly...*short-lived.*

When it came to romance, Mia Ennis was the heart-and-flowers yin to his one-night-stand yang. Which meant he'd be smart to stop wishing she was someone different, a good-time girl only out for a little fun in the sun, or that *he* was someone different, a man made to go the distance, and instead satisfy himself with what they *did* have. Which was a mutual like and respect for one another. A...friendship.

Never mind the look he sometimes thought he saw in her eyes. A look that, despite her words to the contrary, told him she might be curious what it would be like if they were ever to do the No Pants Dance.

As Wolf, their resident philosopher liked to say, *"Only a fool tests the water with both feet."* Which Romeo took to mean he should never jump into something he knew might end up drowning him or someone he cared about in heartbreak.

And hot damn, Mia's eyes are the deepest pools of all.

Glancing away from Doc and the black-haired woman sidled up next to him, Romeo watched Mia gracefully weave her way across the little dance floor to find an empty table under a palm tree. Mason and Alex followed close on her heels, but he barely spared them a glance.

As always, when Mia was present, he only had eyes for her. And suddenly, all he wanted was to be near her.

As a friend, he quickly reminded himself before tapping Doc on the shoulder. "Hey, bro. The others just showed up. Want to join them?"

Doc waved a distracted hand, keeping his attention on the dark-eyed Venus who rested her boobs on his arm like she was tired of holding them up on her own.

Doc was a man on a mission to drown his sorrows in a pitcher of beer and the willing ministrations of any woman who'd have him. Considering the guy stood nearly six and half feet tall, with shoulders that stretched about that wide, there were *plenty* of ladies to choose from. The buxom beauty who'd introduced herself as Candy had simply been the first to respond once Doc deployed his patented Dalton "Doc" Simmons sexual allure arsenal.

"You go on," Doc told Romeo over his shoulder before pulling the toothpick from his mouth and drawling to Candy, "That's an amazing dress." His scratchy voice made him sound like he smoked a pack a day even though Romeo had never seen him take so much as a puff. "What do you say to me taking it off you later?"

Romeo rolled his eyes, expecting Candy to either giggle and smack Doc on the arm, or get offended and stalk off in a huff. He was surprised when, instead, she came back with, "Funny. I was just thinking how good that shirt looks on you. Not as good as *I* would look on you, but still."

Doc sputtered and tugged his ear, a sure sign he'd been

caught off guard.

Romeo was a little surprised, too. In his experience, women with names like *Candy* weren't usually known for lightning-fast repartee.

The couple exchanged another volley of cringe-worthy pickup lines, and Romeo took that as his cue to vamoose himself. Of course, before he left, he gave himself an imaginary pat on the back for a wingman job well done.

Grabbing his glass of Don Julio straight up—because that's how his grandmother had taught him to drink it—he slipped off the barstool and made his way toward his friends.

Friends, friends, Mia and I are friends, he reminded himself for what was probably the fiftieth time that day.

The hot, humid air was ripe with the smell of spilled beer and the slightly fishy aroma wafting in from the nearby marina. A three-man band played sea shanties on the little stage in the corner. And outside, the stars sparkled like cut diamonds across the black underbelly of the night sky.

All around him, people danced drunkenly, conversed loudly, and laughed heartily despite sunburned noses and wind-chapped lips.

Key West...ain't she grand?

Never once could he remember having a bad time while visiting the island. The Conch Republic had a way of forcing a person to kick off their shoes, shove their toes in the sand, and slow way, *way* down—preferably with a drink in hand.

He took a sip of tequila while side-stepping a drunk who tried coaxing a recalcitrant woman out of her seat and onto the dance floor. If the look on the woman's face was anything to go by, the last thing she wanted was to cut a rug with a guy who couldn't pronounce his S's without sounding like a snake. But neither did she want to make a scene, so she was trying to *politely* tell the dude to go row, row, row his boat gently the hell on out of her line of sight.

9

Not your business, Romeo told himself because he had a bad habit of starting stuff with bombed-out barflies who thought downing five or six shooters gave them a good excuse to act like dickwads.

When he realized the harried woman had four friends with her—they'd been at the bar ordering drinks while she saved the table—he hastened his steps toward Mia and company, comforted by the thought that, *between the five of them, they can more than handle this annoying alcohooligan.*

Mia must've felt his approach.

She turned and the instant those fascinating eyes of hers collided with his, some invisible bastard slugged him in the gut. Like, for real though, he couldn't breathe, and the tequila threatened to return for an encore performance.

He managed what he hoped looked like a friendly smile—*we're friends; she's my friend.* And he was able to utter a hoarse "thanks" when she pulled out a chair in wordless invitation.

"You done playing Doc's support brah?" Alex quipped after he'd taken a seat.

Alexandra Merriweather was a diminutive historian and expert in *procesal*—the script used in the old Spanish Colonial documents. She'd been key in helping the Deep Six Salvage crew find the final resting place of the *Santa Cristina*. She was also a bookworm, a motor-mouth, and a wunderkind when it came to random bits of trivia.

Did you know only female mosquitoes bite? Did you know Aristotle had a stutter? Did you know 270 characters died in the series *Breaking Bad*?

Romeo had learned all of that from Alex. Which would have been more than enough to endear her to him, because he liked inane information as much as the next guy. That she'd also convinced Mason to take a second chance on romance when the man had sworn to live the rest of his life loveless and lonely? *That* had made Romeo absolutely *love* her.

"The key to being a great wingman," he told her with a wink, "is knowing when to fly away."

She snorted. Then her brow wrinkled as she glanced toward the bar and Doc's broad back. "What's up with him anyway? I've never seen him pass up dessert."

They'd been downing dinner at Pepe's Cafe—a hole-in-the-wall that was as popular with the locals as it was with the tourists because once you got past its ramshackle appearance, you realized the food was outstanding. But when their waiter came by to ask if they wanted slices of Key lime pie to finish off their meal, Doc had pushed back from the table and declared his intention to head to the bar to, quote, *"Find a lovely lady who'll want to add my banana to her fruit salad."*

Like so many of Romeo's former SEAL Team buddies and current business partners, Doc had a truly inventive way with words.

The look of disappointment on Mia's face when it seemed she'd have to skip dessert had nearly broken Romeo's heart. And since he'd needed a breath of fresh air after having spent the entire meal ignoring the fireworks going off in his groin because his knee had been touching hers under the snug little table, he'd volunteered to head out with Doc while she and the others indulged their sweet tooths.

Sweet teeth?

Whatever. The point was, he'd been happy to play the part of Doc's wingman not only because it meant Mia got her pie, but also because, "Today's an unhappy anniversary for Doc," he explained to Alex.

Her freckled nose wrinkled. "Is it? Nobody ever talks about—"

She was cut off when one of the women at the table behind them said in a strident voice, "Look, pal, she said she doesn't want to dance. Make like the insect you are and buzz off."

Romeo was stopped from turning to view the scene when Mia grumbled, "Someone should tell that guy that being a dick won't make what he's packing in his pants any bigger. It doesn't work that way."

As usual, her voice was soft and husky, barely rising above the noise of the bar. But there was nothing soft about her expression as she watched the table of ladies trying to dissuade Sir Slurs-a-Lot.

Romeo felt his lips curve into a wide grin. The thing about Mia Ennis was that she was incredibly circumspect. Some might even call her closed-mouthed. In fact, for the first few weeks she'd worked with Deep Six Salvage, he didn't think she'd uttered more than a dozen words.

Which meant discovering her salty wit and dry sense of humor had been more exciting than unearthing long lost treasure.

Or at least he *thought* it was more exciting. They hadn't found the *Santa Cristina's* mother lode, so he couldn't say for sure.

After carefully picking over the submerged remains of the galleon, they'd determined her cache of riches was missing. Turning their attention to searching Wayfarer Island with metal detectors had only proved that some of the *Santa Cristina's* crew had survived the wreck and spent some time marooned on the island. Finally, in a last-ditch effort, they'd used ground penetrating sonar and jackpot!

Uh, not *jackpot* jackpot. They hadn't found the riches, but they *had* stumbled across a plot of old, unmarked graves.

In one of those graves, they'd uncovered the remains of the *Santa Cristina's* famous captain. The metal buttons found alongside the bleached bones and stamped with the Vargas family crest had told them as much. But better than the bones or the buttons had been the captain's journal.

Someone had done their best to preserve the tome by

wrapping it in oilcloth before placing it inside an old lead box and burying it beside the man. The delicate ledger held the mundane reports of the ship's activities up until the day of the sinking, and then nothing. Except for one final entry on the very last page.

"Tell me again what the last journal entry read," Romeo said to her now, needing a distraction from the nearby drama.

He was *this close* to jumping into the fray and giving Señor Shitfaced a shiner. If anyone deserved five in the eye, it was that guy.

Alex cleared her throat. In a voice filled with portent, she quoted, "Alas, the mighty ship has gasped her final breath. But despair not. Her enormous life force remains. If you are a true son of Spain, you will know where to find it."

She shuddered and rubbed her arms to flatten the goose bumps there. Romeo felt a chill steal up his own spine. It was like Captain Bartolome Vargas himself whispered across the centuries, telling them they were close.

Below the words in the old journal had been printed a series of careful symbols. Alex had recognized them immediately. Although, to everyone's disappointment, she hadn't been able to decode them.

"It requires King Philip's encryption device," she'd told them while carefully closing the ancient ledger. *"I've read about the ciphers used between the king and his sea captains, but as far as I know, no samples of the code have ever been found. Until now..."* She'd rubbed a reverent, featherlight finger over the delicate leather cover.

"Please tell me the device is housed in a museum somewhere," LT had said while squatting beside the deep, sandy grave of the once-acclaimed sea captain. LT, otherwise known as Leo "The Lion" Anderson, was their former lieutenant. He'd been the one to convince them to join him in the hunt for the grand galleon after they bugged out of

the Navy.

Alex had shaken her head. *"I don't know. I need to check the Spanish Archives."*

The *Archivo General de Indias* in Seville, Spain—affectionately known as the Spanish Archives—was the somber repository of all the old documents dating back to the time of the *Santa Cristina's* wreck. If the cipher device still existed, clues to it whereabouts would be found there.

"What time does your flight leave in the morning?" Romeo asked Mason now. He'd agreed to fly Alex and Mason from Wayfarer Island to Key West in his prized single-engine amphibious plane so they could book a flight to the mainland in the morning and then skip across the pond to Spain. Mia had volunteered to tag along on the overnight trip because she'd wanted to file some paperwork regarding their findings with the state. As for Doc? He'd jumped at the chance to spend the night in a place that provided him with some diverting amusements.

"We catch a puddle jumper to Miami at oh-ten-hundred," Mason said in his thick, Boston accent that turned the word *jumper* into *jumpah*. "Our connecting flight to Madrid leaves at noon."

"Perfect." Romeo nodded. "That high-class attorney is supposed to land here at oh-ten-thirty, so we can all head to the airport together in the morning. We'll drop you and Alex off and pick up our lawyer without having to make two trips."

"Fuck The Man," Mason muttered. Talk of their lawyer had naturally brought to mind the certified letter they'd received direct from Uncle Sam.

After Mel Fisher, the most famous treasure hunter of all time, found and excavated the mighty *Atocha*, he'd spent years battling lawsuits brought by the state of Florida and the federal government regarding who had the rights to the sunken loot. Thanks to Mel's doggedness and determination, the courts had finally sided with him and determined that riches found both inside and outside state waters fell directly under the Admiralty Law. Which, without going into too much detail, basically meant *finders keepers*.

However, the federal government officially owned Wayfarer Island—they'd simply been leasing it to LT's family for the last hundred and fifty years. So as soon as the Deep Six crew moved their search from the waters *around* the island to the island itself, the government had been quick to point out that the question of whether Admiralty Law still applied was up for debate.

If Romeo and his partners found the *Santa Cristina's* mother lode on land, it was going to be a fight over who could lay claim to the wealth. And LT had decided to get out in front of the battle by hiring on an expert in the matter.

According to those in the know, no one came more highly recommended than one Camilla D'Angelo, Esq.

"Let's not get our boxers in a bunch just yet," Romeo cautioned Mason. "Hopefully you and Alex will find King Philip's cipher device and we'll decode the journal to discover the crew of the *Santa Cristina* brought up the treasure only to dump it in the sea somewhere else. All this posturing by the Feds will have been for nothing then, eh?"

Whatever Mason might have said in answer was cut off by the slurred voice of the drunk. "—gotta act like a bunch of bitchessss."

"Wow." Alex scowled. "That guy is the human version of period cramps."

Mia nodded. "Annoyingly painful and horribly unwelcome."

"You think he was born that way?" Alex scrunched up her nose. "Or did he take lessons?"

"It's usually a bit of both." Mia shrugged.

Alex grimaced. "Proof that human evolution can go in reverse."

"Okay." Romeo pushed up from his chair. "I tried to let it go. But I can't take it a second longer." Turning toward the drunk, he didn't attempt to keep the contemptuous edge from his voice when he said, "Look *cabron*, the ladies have asked you nicely to fuck off. *I*, on the other hand, won't be so friendly."

"Mind your businessss." The asshole rolled his eyes without even cutting Romeo a glance. The dude's ruddy cheeks matched the tip of his nose, letting Romeo know Mr. One-Too-Many was no stranger to getting cork high and bottle deep.

"Go on and keep rolling your eyes, *pendejo*," he snarled. "Maybe you'll find some brain cells back there somewhere."

That got the drunk's attention. He gave Romeo the once-over.

Romeo didn't spend ninety minutes each morning running on the beach, swimming in the lagoon, and lifting weights simply because he was health conscious. He also did it so that when he ran into jackoffs like Herr Half-in-the-Bag, he had the mass to back up his mouth.

Of course, when Mason, who was built like a shorter version of John Cena, stood from the table, the drunk's face drained of color. He proved he was smarter than he looked by stumbling out of the bar and onto the long, wooden dock that ran the length of the marina.

"May both sides of your pillow always be uncomfortably warm!" Alex called to the man's retreating back.

Romeo watched to make sure the bastard had thoroughly adiosed himself. Once he was satisfied, he touched a finger to his forehead, saluting the table of ladies who thanked him for intervening and asked him to join them.

"Some other time," he told them, and then blinked in

astonishment at how easily those three words had slid out of his mouth.

There'd been a time, not so long ago, when he'd have *jumped* at the chance to while away the hours with a group of beautiful tourists. Recently, however, his whole "sexit and exit" routine had lost its allure.

Because of Mia, he admitted to himself.

His intense desire to strip her naked had left him completely uninterested in doing the Devil's Disco with anyone else.

See? Earworm! A sexy, sensual, incessantly arousing earworm.

Who's my friend! Just my friend, damnit!

"And on that note..." Alex stood and wrapped a hand around Mason's bicep. "I think I'd like to skip the after-dinner drinks and head back to the hotel. I read somewhere that the tongue is the most powerful muscle in the human body." She pushed her tortoiseshell glasses higher on the bridge of her nose and grinned at Mason. "How's about you and me go find out whose is the strongest, huh?"

Mason frowned heavily—pretty much the guy's go-to expression—but Romeo could tell he was biting the inside of his cheek to keep from smiling. Putting a hand at the small of Alex's back, Mason bid Romeo and Mia a good night, and then quickly ushered his saucy little girlfriend out of the bar.

Shit, damn, and hell, Romeo thought. *Now it's just the two of us.*

It was easier to fake nonchalance and comradery toward Mia when they were surrounded by friends and colleagues. But it was almost impossible when he found himself alone with her. When there was nowhere to look but at her tempting mouth and no way to ignore the way her small waist flared dramatically to a pair of hips curved perfectly for the fit of a man's hand and—

Chronic masturbation.

That was *another* physical symptom caused by her mere presence.

Girding himself for the impact of her eyes when he retook his seat, he was relieved when she didn't look at him and instead kept her nose buried in her phone.

Wayfarer Island was smack-dab between Key West and Havana, Cuba. A small circle of sand and mangrove forest that grew out of the sea and boasted few modern conveniences, least of all cellular service.

Everyone who lived on the island had given up their phone plans—why pay for something they couldn't use? But not Mia. She'd kept hers active, and anytime she found herself in civilization, the device buzzed nonstop.

"Your cousin again?" He hitched his chin toward her lighted screen.

"He's asking what time we're leaving in the morning," she said and then pocketed her phone after shooting off a quick text.

And there they are, he thought, catching his breath. *Those eyes.*

As the band started in on their version of "The Drunken Sailor," an awkward silence stretched between them. He wasn't used to being awkward around women. In fact, he'd spent most of his adult life being the *opposite* of awkward around women. *Doc didn't dub me Rico Suave for nothing.* But something about Mia tied his tongue.

Searching his brain for a safe topic, something that *wouldn't* make him fantasize about running his lips from the point of her piquant chin down to the tips of her dainty toes, he seized on the first thing that came to mind. "You want something to drink? A gin and tonic?"

Yeah, he knew her usual. He also knew she loved avocados, fiddled with the diamond studs in her ears when she got nervous, and forgot to breathe anytime she was unsure or scared.

He'd made quite a study of Mia Ennis. It hadn't been intentional, of course. Just the natural result of him being unable to keep his eyes off her.

"No, thank you." She shook her head. "I think I'll follow Alex's lead, skip the after-dinner drink, and head back to the hotel. It's hot tonight, and the air-conditioning is calling my name."

She pulled out the collar of her soft-looking blouse and blew down the opening. The thought of her sweet-smelling breath drying the dampness of her skin had a heavy feeling settling behind his fly.

Tossing back the last of his tequila, he quickly rose to pull out her chair. "I'll walk you."

"It's only a couple of blocks. I'll be fine on my own."

"I'll walk you." His tone brooked no argument.

Typical of Mia, she merely smiled a closed-mouth smile and nodded her consent without saying another word.

They were outside, the warm sea breeze running gentle fingers through her wavy, shoulder-length hair, the next time she spoke. "You up for a couple chapters from *In Darkness and Dreams*?"

Recently, they'd discovered they shared a mutual love of P.J. Warren's Night Angels paranormal romance series. Ever since then, she'd been reading aloud to him from the newest novel.

The BUD/S O-Course, one of the training segments required to make it as a Navy SEAL, was a study in physical pain, intended to make anyone going through it suffer as much as humanly possible. But Romeo thought it was child's play compared to sitting beside Mia while she read aloud in that smoky, film-noir voice of hers.

"Sounds good," he was quick to answer, because

apparently he was a glutton for punishment.

Something his recruit division commander had said to him years before echoed through his head. *"When someone keeps doing the same self-destructive crap over and over again, it's no longer a bad decision. It's a bad habit."*

Mia Ennis had become a habit Romeo couldn't break.

Most troubling of all? He didn't want to.

CHAPTER 2

8:42 AM...

This is becoming a habit.

That was the first thought that ran through Mia's head when she was jolted awake by the feel of a hot, hard body stretched out beside her.

Or...beneath her?

Yes. Definitely *beneath* her.

It wasn't the *good* kind of habit either. Not the getting-eight-hours-of-sleep or including-a-retinol-into-her-skin-care-routine kind of habit. It was the good-way-to-get-her-pride-stomped-on-like-a-cigarette-butt kind of habit.

Spiro "Romeo" Delgado was so far out of her league it was like digging in the dirt with a stick as a kid compared to using advanced technologies to carbon date ancient bones. Like finding a penny on the beach compared to hauling up treasures of the deep. Like choking down Uncle John's tuna casserole compared to dining on one of Bran's homemade calzones.

Oh, she and Romeo might be well-matched in *some* areas. They both liked novels filled with angsty vampires, mischievous ghosts, and humorless werewolves. They'd both had less-than-ideal childhoods. And they'd both traveled the world—him on harrowing military missions and her on various hunts for sunken history.

So, sure, on paper they made a pretty good match. But people weren't paper. People were people, with arms and legs and bodies and faces, and that's where their similarities ended.

When it came to looks? To borrow one of her grandmother's favorite phrases...*my stars and garters!* In the case of Spiro "Romeo" Delgado and Mia Ennis, Romeo was the stars and Mia was the garters.

Not that she thought she should go around with a paper bag over her head or anything. She was capable of being seen in public without causing people to turn away in horror. You know, when she spent twenty minutes on her makeup and twice that long on her hair.

But Romeo? He had a face like a two-week paid vacation, a profile so beautiful that every woman from seven to seventy did a double take whenever he walked by.

And that's before they let their eyes travel down his body.

When that happened, their double takes turned into jaw drops. Seriously. They reminded Mia of that wolf in the old cartoons when his tongue unfurled across the table at the same time his eyes bulged from his head.

Romeo's physique was...well...art. Like Michelangelo's *David*, he was a study in sturdy bones, tough sinew, and meticulously defined muscle. In a word, yummy. In two words, holy crap! And in three words? *Homina, homina, homina.*

Not that Mia put much stock in looks. The most beautiful woman she'd ever known, her mother, was as vain and as selfish and as mean as they came. And Dr. Tamburro, her medieval history professor who had a severely disfiguring form of Muenke syndrome, was the nicest, gentlest, most generous person she'd ever met.

It was cliché, but she truly *did* believe that it was what was on the *inside* that counted. But there, too, Romeo outshined her.

You see, he was so much more than his movie star face and Olympian's body. He was also steady and considerate and capable. The man her mind landed on when she was looking for a little peace. And despite her heart's tendency to double-time it whenever he turned those melting chocolate eyes of his in her direction, she felt safer around him than she did around anyone.

Safe from everything.

Even the hurtful stuff that lived inside her.

And what had she done with this paragon of male perfection, you ask? Well, she'd slept with him.

Again.

Not the euphemistic slept with him unfortunately, but the *literal* slept with him. As in, they were still wearing their clothes from the night before. As in, she hadn't washed her face or brushed her teeth, so her mascara was clumpy and her tongue felt like it was wearing a sweater. As in, he'd nodded off before she'd finished reading one chapter of *In Darkness and Dreams* and she hadn't had the heart to wake him.

Okay, so that wasn't exactly true. It was more like she hadn't *wanted* to wake him.

When he was lying beside her, she was able to fall into a deep, dreamless sleep. Something that had alluded her since the day after her twenty-first birthday when she'd walked into her parents' condo in Chicago to find her father's face haggard and her mother crumpled into a wailing ball on the end of the sofa. When she'd been forced to realize she'd finally failed her younger brother completely, and that his blood was on her hands.

Yes. Before "sleeping with" Romeo, she'd thought a night without nightmares was a thing of her past. Which meant when she'd heard his soft snore while she'd been reading about the vampire Lazarus Luxido, her first instinct hadn't been to jostle him awake and encourage him to head to his own hotel room. Oh, no. Her first instinct had been to shoot an imaginary fist in the air, switch off the lamp, and snuggle onto her side with her back to him.

She'd been careful to keep a *platonic* distance between them, because he'd made it perfectly clear all he wanted from her was friendship. Except, just as she'd done the last time he'd conked out while she was reading, at some point during the hours between dark and dawn she'd rolled toward him.

Rolled *onto* him.

Her head was now pillowed on his chest. Her arm was thrown across his midsection. And she had one leg stretched over his hips.

Propriety told her she should move. The longing to luxuriate just a little longer kept her in place.

Keeping her eyes shut, she clocked the various sensations bombarding her senses. The steady *thud* of his big, healthy heart beneath her ear. The manly smell of his skin that reminded her of warm cedar and oiled leather. The feel of his erection pulsing insistently against her thigh.

For a moment, she allowed herself to pretend his unconscious reaction was meant for her. Allowed herself to fantasize about what it would be like to be wanted by him. To be *worthy* of him. To taste those wide, knowing lips. To feel those large, callused hands skating over her naked flesh. To see him rising above her, all dark goatee and white smile.

But pretend was all it was. A fantasy was all it would ever be.

"You're nothing I need, and I'm not anything you should want."

The words he'd spoken that rainy afternoon not so very long ago echoed through her head. And her lungs clenched tight because she was instantly reminded of the thought that had started her down this path the moment she woke up.

This is becoming a habit. The bad kind and—

Her thoughts screeched to a halt when his steady breaths turned shallow and the lovely, large pectoral muscle beneath her cheek tensed.

He was awake. Not the slow, sleepy sort of awake either. The *awake* sort of awake. The fully cognizant, zero mental cobwebs sort of awake.

And here I am clinging to him like maritime accretions cling to ancient underwater artifacts.

Aghast at her own audacity, she faked a long stretch and a big, dramatic yawn while rolling off him.

Nothing to see here. I haven't spent the last five minutes basking in your unconscious body. I, too, am just now waking up.

After blinking open her eyes, she found him on his side, watching her. A line had formed between his eyebrows. Something that looked like wariness glimmered in his eyes.

Oh, for the love of— Not again.

She didn't think she could live through a repeat of what happened the last time they'd shared a bed, when he'd worried she might misconstrue his intentions toward her and had felt obliged to tell her in no uncertain terms that he had absolutely *zero* interest in her *that way*.

Deciding a little humor was her best bet at dodging another of his humiliating Come-to-Jesus talks, she winked saucily. "Was that good for you?"

As she'd hoped, the tension drained from his big shoulders. "Mmm." He nodded, playing along. "Spectacular. You?"

"Best I've had since the last time we did it."

He chuckled and propped his head in his hand. When his eyes traveled over her face, she resisted the urge to check if she had creases on her cheek left by the material of his T-shirt. Instead, she forced herself to hold his gaze.

Easier said than done.

It was a heady thing to be this close to him. Headier still to be the sole focus of his dark, penetrating stare as the morning light streamed in through a break in the hotel curtains and highlighted the broad, tanned expanse of his brow, the wicked arch of his jet-black eyebrows, and the shadows his dimples created in his cheeks.

Those diabolical dimples that make him look sort of boyish when I know for a fact there isn't a single boyish thing about him.

Spiro "Romeo" Delgado was *all* man.

Her thigh still burned where a particularly manly part of him had touched her.

"I blame it on your voice." His tone was low and raspy from sleep.

"Blame what?" She felt her brow wrinkle.

"Me falling asleep when you read to me. Your voice is just so soothing. It's sort of throaty and raspy."

The unexpected compliment had her tensing. Not because it flustered her or flattered her. But because it reminded her of the mistake she'd made at seven years old, the mistake that'd ended with her committing the ultimate sin.

Some of what she was thinking must've projected itself into her expression. He pressed up on one elbow. "What? Did I say something wrong?"

She fiddled with a ball of lint stuck near the seam of the comforter. "My voice sounds like this because my vocal cords were damaged when I was a little girl."

"What happened to you?" His frown was so fierce, even his dimples couldn't make him look boyish now. Now, he was one-hundred percent, high-octane, former fighting man, and she knew how terrified his enemies must've been to face him across a battlefield.

She opened her mouth, but nothing came out. Her childhood—and all the sorrow and shame that'd sprung from it—had always made her feel separate from the world. Set apart. *Other.*

But amazingly, from the beginning, she hadn't felt separate from Romeo.

Quite the opposite; she felt a strange connection to him. As if, for the first time she'd found someone who could understand how her dark past continued to cast a long shadow into her present.

"Hey." He rubbed a finger between her eyebrows, smoothing the line she knew had formed there. "Breathe."

"I thought I was." She exhaled a windy sigh, her forehead tingling from the warmth left behind by his fingertip.

"It's okay if you don't want to tell me," he assured her.

"It's not that I don't *want* to tell you. It's just that..."

She let the sentence dangle, only finishing it in her head. *I can't.*

A soft knock sounded on the door. "Mia?" Doc's deep, raspy voice drifted in from the hallway. "You awake?"

Romeo's expression grew...she wasn't sure how to describe it. Purposefully blank, maybe? "You expecting company?" His voice sounded oddly neutral.

"No." She shook her head and glanced at the digital clock on the nightstand. The glowing red numbers had her bolting upright. "Oh my god! We're late!"

His gaze landed on the clock. He blinked as if the time displayed didn't compute.

She had a little trouble believing it herself.

He was usually up with the sun, getting in his workout. She, too, wasn't one for lingering in bed, but it was because sleep brought her little comfort. And yet, somehow that morning they'd missed Key West's wild rooster population crowing their wakeup tune. They'd missed their chance to have breakfast with the rest of the Deep Six crew. And they'd missed the opportunity to shower and change clothes.

"We need to leave for the airport in ten minutes," she hissed.

The reality of their situation galvanized Romeo into action. Tossing back the comforter, he catapulted out of bed and quickly crossed the room to throw open the door.

Doc stood on the threshold, looking worse for wear.

The uncombed hair. The unshaven face. The sunglasses that undoubtedly hid hideously bloodshot eyes. Mia knew all too well the signs of *brown bottle flu*—another of her grandmother's favorite phrases—and Doc sported each and every one.

His gruff tone matched his scruffy appearance when he looked over Romeo's shoulder, spied her still in bed, and quickly returned his attention to Romeo. "This isn't your room."

Romeo leaned a forearm against the doorjamb. "Wow. Nice investigating. You're like one of those CSI characters."

Doc ignored the wisecrack and again focused on Mia. "You okay?"

"Hey!" Romeo stood to his full height. "What the hell, bro? Who do you think I am?"

"Oh, pipe down," Doc grumbled. "For one, I have a splitting headache that a giant cup of coffee hasn't managed to put a dent in. For two, I'm not accusing you of coercing her. I'm just making sure those dreamy eyes, and that pirate smile, and those dastardly dimples didn't persuade her into doing something she regrets the morning after. So?" Doc stared hard at Mia. "You okay?"

"It's not what you think," she assured him, and then frowned.

Why did I say that?

Oh, right. Because she didn't want anyone thinking she was stupid enough to assume she stood a chance with the big, beautiful, Latin Lothario.

"I was reading *In Darkness and Dreams*, and we fell asleep." This last part she added almost entirely beneath her breath, hating her fair skin because she knew it showed her chagrin.

Doc lifted an eyebrow at Romeo. The toothpick that stuck out of his mouth wiggled as he worked it between his teeth. "You two are making a habit of that, huh?"

"Which part?" Romeo once again tipped his weight against the doorjamb. Except, there was something about the set of his shoulders that told Mia his casual stance was studied instead of sincere. "The reading romance together or the sleeping together?"

"Both."

"What's it to you?"

"Just...don't do anything stupid, okay? Either of you." Doc looked past Romeo again to include Mia in his warning. "I like you both too much to have to choose sides."

Romeo reached into the front pocket of his jeans and pulled out his hand, thrusting it at Doc, palm-up. "Oh, look. I found your nose. It was stuck all up in our business."

Doc cocked his head. "Why is it acceptable for you to be an idiot but not for me to point it out?"

"Why am *I* an idiot?" Romeo's chin jerked back.

Doc leveled a look on him. "You *know* why."

Romeo glanced over his shoulder at Mia. The expression on his face was one of resignation...and maybe a little regret?

Oh, for Pete's sake! Just once she'd like to wake up next to him and *not* see regret in his eyes. Was that too much to ask?

Turning back to Doc, Romeo adroitly changed the subject. "You know, it's really hard to take anything you say seriously when you smell like hot dog water and look like a freshly dug-up potato. Am I right in thinking last night was everything you hoped for?"

Doc snorted and adjusted his sunglasses. "Hardly. I'm embarrassed to admit it wasn't one of my better performances. Which is why I'm hoping you guys will hurry the hell up. I want to get out of here before Candy wakes up. I don't want to run into her in the lobby. I don't think I can face her in the light of day."

"Damn, bro." Romeo shook his head. "That bad, eh?"

"Worse." Doc grimaced. He added something else, but Mia didn't hear it because she got distracted by the *ding* of her cell phone.

Sighing heavily—she already knew who was texting her—she thumbed on the device.

Carter: *Still plan to head back to Wayfarer soon?*
Mia: *Yes. We fly out @ 10:30 ish.*

Her cousin kept her abreast of the happenings in Chicago. Each of her mother's stints in rehab. Every fall off the wagon. All the pleas for more money. Ad nauseum ad infinitum.

At first, Mia had wondered why he bothered to shoulder the responsibility of Jane Ennis. Sure, his mother and Mia's mother had been sisters. But Mia didn't remember Carter being particularly *close* to Jane while growing up. Then Carter had mentioned the stipend Jane paid him to, quote, "look after her" and it had all made sense.

The two things that were absolutely true about Mia's mother were that she liked other people to clean up after her messy life, and that she was willing to pay—though usually not more than pittance—for the convenience. And Carter? Well, he'd never seemed able to get his act together, always drifting from job to job, living hand-to-mouth. Any extra money coming in probably felt like a windfall to him.

Mia felt sorry for her cousin. Dealing with her mother was *far* from easy. In fact, a couple months earlier, Carter had texted her to say he was done, that Jane had pulled her last stunt. But Jane was nothing if not a master manipulator. And somehow, she'd convinced poor Carter to stay on.

Mia couldn't help but feel sorry for the poor guy. And it was her pity that kept her responding to his updates even though she'd stopped hoping for any sort of relationship with her mother years earlier.

Carter: Next time you're back in civilization, think about booking a flight to Chi-Town. Your mother would love to see you.

Jane Ennis loved many things, designer handbags, Chanel N°5, and anything that was pink. But Mia? No. Jane had never loved Mia. And Carter's text made her think of the last time she'd been in the same room with her mother.

It was right before she'd agreed to take the job overseeing the *Santa Cristina's* salvage. She'd booked a flight to Chicago to put flowers on her grandmother's grave. And when Carter heard she was in town, he'd set up a lunch date for Mia and Jane.

Against Mia's better judgment, she'd gone. She and her mother had barely put in their appetizer order at Gene and Georgetti's before Jane had turned to her with that look in her eye.

A look Mia had recognized all too well.

A look that had said her mother was itching for a fight...

"You still refuse to let your hair grow long." Jane pulled one luscious lock of scarlet hair over her shoulder, letting the ends curl around her manicured fingertip.

"I wasn't blessed with a mane like yours, Mom. I do the best I can with what I've got." Mia tried heading the confrontation off at the pass. Compliments had always been the best way to tame the beast that lived inside her mother.

As she'd hoped, Jane's mouth curved into a smile. Or, at least what passed as a smile on a face made mostly immobile by a gallon of Botox.

All too soon, however, the smile faded and her mother narrowed her emerald eyes. *"And why haven't you seen Dr. Johnson about your boobs? Heaven knows you have plenty of money to fix them."*

Mia would have been more plastic than flesh by the time she graduated high school had she not gone to live with her grandmother when she was seven years old. Even before Mia had learned to ride a bike, Jane had talked about the things they would *'get fixed'* once Mia came of age. Mia's brow, her nose, her chin, her lips... None of her natural features measured up to Jane's standards. Because none of her natural features were Jane's features.

Mia took after her father.

It had been her brother—beautiful, gentle Andy—who'd inherited Jane's flawless face.

"Please, Mom," she begged. *"Let's talk about something else. Anything else."*

Jane's nostrils flared, causing a sick sensation to swirl in the bottom of Mia's stomach. The smell of the shrimp cocktail the waiter placed in front of her made her want to retch.

"Okay." Jane folded her hands primly atop the white tablecloth, her eyes calculating as she stared at Mia. *"Let's talk about you giving me some money."*

"For what?"

Jane donned a saccharine expression that struck Mia as being patently false. "For another ninety days in the recovery center." Jane fluttered her false eyelashes. "I've just completed ninety days, and I'd like to do another round. I'm serious about getting sober this time."

Mia hoped her mother couldn't hear the suspicion in her voice when she said, "That's so great, Mom. But what about the money Dad set aside for just this reason?"

Hostility flared in Jane's eyes, but she tried to mask it with a sweet smile. "This place I'm going to isn't some run of the mill rehab, Mia. It's expensive. I used my yearly allotment on the first round. And that stingy lawyer that Richard has overseeing my trust refuses to let me dip into next year's cash."

Mia nodded. "Of course, I'd love to help. Just have the facility invoice me, and I'll be sure to pay the fee immediately."

One of Jane's eyelids twitched. "Why don't you just give me the money?"

That sick feeling in Mia's stomach become full-on nausea. She tried to keep her tone level when she replied, "You know why."

Mia's father, Richard Ennis, had been a brilliant man. His job as the city's most sought-after negotiator for corporate mergers meant that by the time he'd died of a massive heart-attack—no doubt brought on by years of steak dinners and high stress and topped off by the unbearable strain of losing a child—he'd amassed a not-so-small fortune.

A fortune he'd left to Mia with explicit instructions that he'd outlined in the letter attached to his will.

'My Mia,

If you're reading this, then I must apologize because it means I have left you alone in this world with no family to lean on. With Andy and your grandmother—and now me—

all gone, that leaves only your mother. And we both know she isn't fit to offer you any sort of support.

For what it's worth, she wasn't always this way. When I first met her, she was fun and vivacious, compassionate and good. Or...at least I *think* she was. Is it possible I was so blinded by her beauty that I only saw in her what I *wanted* to see?

For years I have asked myself that question. And it pains me to admit this, dear daughter, but I'm still not sure of the answer.

Regardless, I married her. And I have spent the last two and a half decades lying in the bed I made.

I don't regret honoring my vows to her even after it became clear she carried around a multitude of monkeys on her back. I promised to stand by her side through sickness and health, and that is what I have tried my best to do. What I *do* regret is that you and Andy suffered as a result of my decision.

My only excuse is that I kept thinking I would find a balance, a way to take care of *all* of you. Except in trying to take care of all of you, I fear I couldn't truly take care of *any* of you.

I hope, with this will, I can remedy that in some small way.

I have set up a trust in your mother's name that will provide her with enough money to live comfortably, but not so much money that she can live recklessly. And I have put aside additional funds that she may use only on therapy and rehabilitation.

The bulk of my estate, however, I am leaving to you. You have always had a kind and generous heart, Mia. I know you will use the money in good health and for good causes.

All my love, Daddy.'

"You selfish brat!" Hatred flamed so hot in her mother's

eyes that Mia felt like her own heart was burned to ash by it. "I cannot believe Richard left everything to you! It's not fair. It's not right!"

"He didn't leave everything to me, Mom." Mia struggled to keep the tremor that gripped her body from coming through in her voice. "He left plenty for you to—"

"Plenty? Plenty?" Jane snarled. "Are you kidding me? I can only afford to get a manicure every two weeks. I have to wait a whole month *between appointments to have my hair highlighted. And did you know the man at the Mercedes dealership told me I couldn't afford the payments on an S-Class? I had to get the E-Class this year, Mia. The E-class."*

Jane said this with the same derision others might use if they'd been forced to eat warm, worm-filled dirt.

"Is this truly the thanks I get after I spent twenty-five years of my life catering to your father's every whim?" Jane demanded.

Mia knew it was a rhetorical question, so she didn't bother answering. Although, in her head, she pointed out that never once had she seen Jane cater to anyone's whims but her own.

Jane pointed a pink-tipped finger at Mia's nose. "You want it all for yourself. Admit it."

"No." Mia shook her head. "I haven't touched a dime of that money. And I won't. I plan to donate it to charity once I find one I really like. One that helps kids in trouble."

Jane gasped. "It's a travesty to give all that money away when I need it. When it's rightfully mine!*" Her mother slammed her hand down on the table with enough force to make the silverware jump.*

Despite trying to add some volume behind it, Mia's voice came out as nothing more than a raw whisper. "I'm going to make the donation in Andy's name."

Jane recoiled. "How dare you even speak his name after what you did to him!"

It wasn't only Mia's heart that was ash then. Every inch of her skin burned. A terrible heat gathered behind her eyes.

"This was a mistake." She grabbed her purse and pushed up from the table. But she had to place a hand on the back of the chair to steady herself when the room spun.

Closing her eyes, she started counting to ten. It was something she'd learned to do as a child when her world spiraled out of control and felt helpless to do anything about it.

Eight...Nine...

Once she reached ten, she swallowed the bile burning the back of her throat, opened her eyes, and turned to leave.

"Don't you turn your back on me, you ungrateful little shit!" Jane yelled at her. "I'm your mother!"

Mia swung around. For the first time in her life, she told the woman who'd birthed her exactly what she thought.

"No, you aren't," she hissed, fully aware she was crossing a bridge and burning it behind her. "You never have been. I had nannies and housekeepers who showed me more affection than you ever did. Granny Susan, rest her soul, was the one who raised me. She was the one who loved me." She hated that her voice caught on a sob. "If anyone was ever my mother, it was her*!"*

"How was I supposed to love you after what you did?" Jane seethed.

Her mother's words ripped at the tattered remains of Mia's already shredded spirit. "I don't expect you to forgive me for anything. But I'm not the only one to blame for what happened to Andy. What about your role, Mother?"

Jane's eyes narrowed to bare slits. "What do you mean my *role? I never did anything to Andy!" she screeched her protest.*

Before Mia could sputter a response, their waiter scurried over, looking scandalized. Gene and Georgetti's was a classy place, and they expected their clientele to act accordingly. "Ladies!" he hissed. "Might I suggest you take this outside?"

"No." Mia lifted a shaky hand. "I'm done." She turned away before Jane could see the tears standing in her eyes.

"I'll take a glass of Chardonnay. And make it a big one," Mia heard her mother tell the waiter as she made her way to Gene and Georgetti's front door.

Her phone chimed, dragging her out of the horrible memory.

Carter: Still there?

Mia: Yeah. Sorry. Got distracted. Need to head to airport now. Take care.

Turning off her alerts because she didn't have the mental or emotional energy to answer Carter's question about making a trip to Chicago should he decide to reiterate it, she looked up from her phone to see Romeo and Doc still trading barbs.

"I *said*," Romeo stressed, "you have a face that would make onions cry."

"You don't have to repeat yourself, I ignored you the first time," Doc came back. "I was just being quiet because I was visualizing the duct tape I'd like to slap over your mouth."

Mia saw Romeo's shoulders quake and then both men were laughing and embracing, whacking each other on the back with hard blows that made her wince even as they made her smile.

After briefly falling into the rabbit hole that was the dysfunction of her family, it felt good to emerge back into a world where people were kind and honorable and loved each other freely.

When the men broke apart, Doc punched Romeo on the shoulder. "Now, hurry up. We've got cabs waiting to take us to the airport."

Romeo turned to Mia. "Meet you in the lobby in five?"

She nodded and hopped out of bed, needing to repack her toiletries into her overnight bag, and maybe, *hopefully*, steal away thirty seconds to do a quick pass over her teeth with her toothbrush.

After Romeo disappeared into the hall, headed for his own room, Doc stayed rooted in the doorway. She stopped on her way to the bathroom to tilt her head at the mountain of a man. "Something on your mind, Doc?"

He crossed his arms over his chest, and she could feel him studying her from behind the opaque lenses of his sunglasses. "Romeo speaks three languages," he said slowly. "And one of them is seduction. Problem is, sometimes he doesn't know he's speaking it. You take care of yourself. Okay, honey pie?"

If anyone else had used the endearment, Mia would have told him to take his *honey pie* and shove it straight up his misogynistic ass. But when Doc used it, it didn't feel condescending. Somehow—maybe it was Doc's tone or the concerned look on his face—it felt kind.

"Don't worry about me," she told him. "Romeo and I are just friends."

Even as she said the words, she wasn't sure who she was trying to convince more. Doc? Or herself?

CHAPTER 3

10:52 AM...

When are you going to invite *me* for a story time, huh?"
Romeo was in the middle of circling his pride and joy, the de Havilland Canada DHC-3 Otter, doing his pre-flight exterior inspection when he heard Doc ask the question. A quick peek under the belly of the plane showed Doc had an arm around Mia's shoulders. The sea breeze ruffled the big man's head of thick, messy hair. And there was a wry smile stretched wide over his scraggly face.

"You haven't read the first six books in the series. You can't jump in on book seven. You'd be completely lost." Mia beamed up at Doc.

And Romeo meant *beamed.*

Just like her words, Mia was judicious with her smiles. She might be quick with a closed-mouth grin, and many times he'd seen what looked like the shadow of an ornery smirk cross her face. But a full-on smile?

Those were rare.

Which, he supposed, was a good thing since he lost his head a little whenever he saw one, simply grinning like an idiot in return.

Except he wasn't grinning now.

Hell, no. He frowned so hard his jaw muscles ached and there was a definite twitch in his left eyelid.

The twitch only got worse when Doc chucked Mia under her chin. "Well maybe you'd be willing to go back to the beginning for me. What do you think?"

As if Doc wasn't charming enough, the bastard pulled down his sunglasses so he could add a seductive wink to his flirty talk.

Romeo didn't hear Mia's response over the sudden roaring in his ears. It wasn't the thunder of a plane engine touching down on the tarmac of Key West's little airport that'd rendered him momentarily deaf, however. It was the sound of his blood pounding through his veins.

He had the oddest urge to march over and whack Doc upside the head with a brick.

The moment after he had the thought, he reminded himself he shouldn't care that Mia was smiling at Doc or that Doc was doing his level best to woo her with that down-home, country-fried, cowboy charm of his. Romeo *shouldn't* care because...*she's my friend.* As such, he had absolutely zero claim over her romantically.

Plus, Doc was a brother to him in every way but blood. And if Mia could help heal Doc's bruised and broken heart, well...shouldn't Romeo want that for Doc?

He forced himself to give the idea of Doc and Mia some serious consideration and hoped it might be the kick in the pants he needed to let go of his silly, foolish, frickin' *irrational* preoccupation with the pretty little marine archeologist.

Doc and Mia. Mia and Doc...

Ignoring the fact that she was too short for the big Montanan, Romeo could admit they had a lot in common.

They were both college graduates with advanced degrees. They'd both been wounded by their pasts, in need of a little TLC. And they were both good people, conscientious and honorable—Doc's whole self-pitying act the night before notwithstanding.

Doc was strong enough to help shoulder the burdens Mia seemed to carry. And Mia had a tender and thoughtful heart that might be just the thing Doc needed to finally crawl out from under the mountain of his grief.

They could be perfect for each other, Romeo admitted.

So why did he feel serious chunkage coming on at the mere thought?

Because you want her for yourself, shit-for-brains, that annoying voice that lived at the back of his head insisted. *You have from the beginning.*

Yeah, he told the voice, *but I also want to eat my weight in tacos five times a week. Wanting something doesn't make it a good idea.*

Going back to his pre-flight inspection, he determinedly focused on his list.

Flaps? Free and secure.

Lights and wingtips? Working and in good order.

Leading edges? Check.

By the time he finished, he was feeling a little more like himself. Focusing on the fundamentals of aviation always put him in a good mood. But the moment he rounded the back of the plane and discovered Doc still had a muscled arm around Mia's shoulders, he was hit, once again, with the distinct urge to hunt up a brick.

A heavy one. With sharp edges.

Breaking news just in: You're a jealous asshat.

"The lawyer's late." He realized his words came out as

a snarl, so he made sure to keep his expression the picture of SoCal-surfer-dude cool when he glanced up from his watch. "LT said he gave her clear instructions to meet us on the tarmac after her flight landed. Which"—he pointed to the parked jet that'd gone wheels down twenty minutes earlier—"there it is. All landed and unloaded. Think she got turned around in the terminal?"

The toothpick hanging from the side of Doc's mouth jerked down. "That place is the size of a shoebox. If she got lost in there, she has the brainpower of a cockroach. Which doesn't bode well for us if she has to represent us in court."

"Someone should go in and look for her." Romeo stared meaningfully at Doc.

Doc removed his arm from around Mia's shoulders and Romeo ignored the relief that slammed into him like a wind shear. "Rock, paper, scissors you for it," Doc said.

"Fine." Romeo sighed and then grinned evilly when he beat Doc's rock with his paper.

A protracted groan issued from the depths of Doc's chest. "I'm the last one of us she should be meeting first, you realize. I hate lawyers. They're non-carbon-based life-forms sent here to suck out all that is good and wholesome from us Earthlings."

"Damn. Who told you that? Now someone will have to call the mother ship to have you abducted so all your orifices can be probed."

All three of them spun at the sound of a woman's voice. Doc sputtered, "Well...I...I'll be dipped in shit," at the same time Romeo called, "Good morning! Fancy seeing you here."

The black-haired woman inclined her head in a regal-looking nod. "Good to see you again too."

The night before, she'd been in vacation mode, wearing a sundress with her long hair cascading down her back. This morning, she was all business. Her hair was pulled back in a flawless bun, her figure was encased in a crisp, linen pantsuit, and her eyes were hidden behind a huge pair of black sunglasses.

"What are you doing here?" Doc demanded, looking more uncomfortable than Romeo had ever seen him.

Romeo coughed and stared hard at Doc, telling the man without words that his bald-faced question didn't exactly place him in the running for the role of Prince Charming.

"Sorry." Doc winced. "That was rude. How about I start with an apology for sneaking out on you this morning? I just figured after my lackluster performance last night, you'd probably prefer to wake up alone."

"Doesn't one actually have to *perform* in order for it to count as a performance?" Candy countered, her ruby-red lips twitching. "And you don't have to apologize again. I got your one-word note. *Sorry*," she quoted. "You're very succinct when you want to be."

Before Doc had a chance to answer, the woman let go of the handle of her rolling suitcase so she could thrust a hand toward Mia. "Hi. We haven't met. I'm Camilla D' Angelo. But you can call me Cami."

"Mia Ennis." Mia shook the hand offered to her, but her eyes were huge as she glanced between Doc and Romeo.

And there it was. That shadow of an ornery smirk.

"Very good to meet you, Mia." Cami smiled, and Romeo knew his own eyes were flying as wide as Mia's because the wind blowing across the tarmac had suddenly dried them out.

"I thought you said your name was *Candy*," he blurted.

"It was loud in the bar," she explained, shifting her purse to her opposite hand. "And since I didn't think I'd see either one of you again after last night, I figured it wasn't worth the effort of correcting you when you misheard me. But speaking of confused identities..." Her eyebrows puckered over the frames of her sunglasses, "I thought *you* said your name was Romeo. And was I crazy, or did you tell me your name was Doc?" She turned to frown at Doc.

"My name *is* Doc," Doc grumbled, and damned if Romeo didn't detect a flush staining the big man's cheeks.

Cami frowned. "But Mr. Anderson told me I'd be meeting..." She pulled her cell phone from her purse and checked the screen. "One Mr. Spiro Delgado and one Mr. Dalton Simmons."

"And LT told *us* you weren't arriving in Key West until this morning," Doc insisted, clearly mortified that the woman he'd tried—and apparently failed—to shag the night before had turned out to be their attorney.

"I decided to catch an earlier flight and get in one night of R and R." Cami looked like she was biting the inside of her cheek. "Am I to assume that LT and Mr. Anderson are one and the same?"

"Just like Doc is Dalton Simmons and Romeo is Spiro Delgado," Mia clarified quietly. "They all have nicknames."

"Ah." The lawyer nodded. "That would explain it then."

"Oh, for shit's sake." Doc groaned. "I'll just go sauté myself in shame now." He turned and acted like he was going to slink away, but something stopped him. When he swung back, his expression had brightened. "Wait." He lifted a finger. "This is perfect. I have the chance to redeem myself. You know, now that I'm sober."

Cami pulled her sunglasses down the bridge of her nose and let her dark eyes rake over Doc's form. "The problem with that is now *I'm* sober too."

Doc's toothpick hung drunkenly from his slack mouth. He wasn't used to women who didn't fawn over his strapping, long-limbed looks.

"Plus, I don't mix business with pleasure," the lawyer added with a careless shrug. "We'll have to chalk up last night to an *any port in the storm* thing, and act like nothing happened. Because...*nothing happened.*"

Doc winced again. "You don't have to keep rubbing it in."

"Is that what I'm doing?" A smile played over the lawyer's painted lips.

"That's what it feels like," Doc muttered sullenly.

"See? There's where you lost me. I'm a non-carbon-based life-form, remember? I deal in facts, not feelings."

"Well, the *fact* is that I *feel* obliged to prove to you that last night was an aberration. I'm a big believer in not barking unless I plan to bite. So, come on. Give me another chance at the apple."

"Wow." Cami blinked. "Strangely enough, I was able to follow that euphemistic nonsense."

Doc wiggled his eyebrows. "What do you say?"

She sucked on her front tooth and gave him a look that said, *"Not on your life."*

"Ow," Romeo blurted, thoroughly enjoying himself. And not only because Doc had turned his charm away from Mia to focus it on the lady lawyer—although that was a big part of it—but also because there was absolutely nothing in the world more entertaining than watching one of his friends get his ass handed to him by a quick-witted woman.

"What?" Doc glared at him.

"The look she gave you was a metaphorical kick in the balls." He shrugged. "And now my balls ache in sympathy. That's all."

"I'm going to file that under Who Gives a Shit," Doc declared testily before turning back to Cami. "You are a cruel woman not letting me even *attempt* to salvage some of my pride. But I guess I shouldn't be surprised. You know, given your chosen profession."

"I'm not cruel." Cami shook her head. "I'm smart."

"You say tomato, I say cruel."

"Is he always like this?" The lawyer hooked a thumb Doc's way, but she posed the question to Romeo.

"Pretty much." Romeo shrugged.

"How do you stand him?"

"It's a talent very few people seem to possess."

"Hey!" Doc protested. "No ganging up on the guy nursing a hangover. I thought everyone knew about that unspoken rule."

"Pretty sure you have it bass ackwards," Cami countered. "I think the unspoken rule is that everyone is morally *obligated* to gang up on the guy nursing a hangover."

"Are you *really* not going to let me have a do-over?" Doc crossed his arms over his chest.

Any other woman might have thought Doc was taking his teasing too far. But not Cami. The way her mouth twitched told Romeo she was enjoying the drama and banter as much as Doc. And after Romeo had heard the two of them trading awful pickup lines the night before, he couldn't say he was surprised.

"I mean I could let you *try*," she told Doc slowly, as if she were truly weighing the merits of the idea. "But I'd be worried about a repeat of last night. And we all know two wrongs don't make a right. Just look at what your parents created."

Doc stumbled back like she'd punched him.

"Oooh." Mia's lips pursed around a smile. "This is going to be fun."

But not as fun as waking up with you in my arms, Romeo thought. *Not as fun as feeling the weight of your head on my chest or having the smell of your shampoo tunneling up my nose. Not as fun as seeing your little nipples poking through the fabric of your blouse when you didn't know I was looking...*

The memory alone was enough to send his blood racing

south, so he clapped his hands. "Okay, children. Recess is over. Let's load up and get to Wayfarer Island before we run out of ways to make fun of Doc for...uh...suffering his very own mini Cuban missile crisis last night."

"Hey!" Doc objected again. "I want it put on the record that there is nothing *mini* about my missile. Also, what is this? Pick on the Poor Guy Who Suffered a Rare Case of Erectile Misfunction Day?"

"That's a terrible name for a holiday," Mia declared, still looking like she was fighting a grin.

"Agreed," Cami nodded briskly. "It's far too long. Doesn't roll off the tongue. Plus, I don't think *misfunction* is a real word. But even if it *is*, that isn't what happened."

"Isn't it?" All the teasing left Doc's face.

"No." The lawyer pulled off her sunglasses, stuck the end of one earpiece between her lips, and narrowed her eyes. "Don't you remember?"

Doc cringed. "I remember going back to your hotel room. I remember I emptied your minibar of the hobbit-sized Maker's Mark bottles. The next thing I remember is waking up this morning face-first on your floor with one shoe off."

Cami slid her sunglass back onto her face. "You taking off that shoe is how you ended up on the floor. You slipped right off the end of the bed and passed out cold."

"Lord have mercy," Doc groaned. "It's worse than I thought."

"Oh, I don't know." Cami shrugged. "At least you don't snore."

"Damned by faint praise," Doc muttered.

Five minutes later, Cami's rolling suitcase was stored in the cargo hold and Romeo watched as she climbed into the back of the plane. When it was Mia's turn to take the steps, he automatically reached for her hand. The stairs could get slippery on a humid day.

Or at least that's what he told himself.

She glanced down at their joined hands, at his large fingers curled possessively around her much smaller ones. But she didn't miss a beat as she climbed the remaining two steps. And he was left wondering if he was the only one who felt like he'd been hit by a lightning bolt the instant they touched.

Flexing his hand to work out the tension that gripped the muscles after she let go, he frowned when Doc shook his head and said, "Damn, man. You got it bad."

"Me?" he quickly countered. "What about you? I heard you flirting with her, trying to convince her to go back to book one of the Night Angels series."

"So what?" Doc frowned. "You jealous?"

"Hell, no," was his knee-jerk response.

Doc called bullshit by turning his question into a statement. "Dude, you're jealous."

Romeo hated being obvious. He hated more that Doc was right. So he did something he rarely did. He equivocated. "Pfft. When have you ever known me to be jealous?"

"Never. Which is what makes me stop and take notice now."

"I just don't want her hurt," Romeo declared emphatically. "Something tells me she's been hurt enough in life."

Doc cocked his head. "You think I'd hurt her? Why? I *like* Mia."

"So do I! Which is why I'm telling you that you can be a charming sonofabitch even when you're not trying to be. Just make sure she knows exactly where you're coming from and where you're headed, eh?"

"Funny." Doc snorted. "I told her pretty much the same thing about *you* this morning."

Romeo waved a hand through air that was ripe with

the smell of jet fuel and salt water. "Wasted effort. She's not interested in me like that. We're friends."

"Question is," Doc came back immediately, "are *you* interested in *her* like that?"

"Yo." Romeo extended his hand toward Doc. "My name is Romeo Delgado. Have we met? I'm interested in *all* women like that. But she's Miss Commitment and you and I both know I'm Mr. Casual. So, like I said, *friends*."

Doc slapped his hand away. "I'm just saying that for a guy who says he neither has nor wants any particular claim over her, you sure are acting all proprietary and protective."

"I'm trying to look out for her like I do all my friends, *cabron*."

Romeo couldn't be sure, but he thought Doc's eyes narrowed behind his sunglasses. "You realize you only slip into Spanglish when your blood is up, right?"

"So?"

"So I think you should ask yourself why the thought of me flirting with Mia makes you want to snatch me bald-headed."

"Hit you with a brick," Romeo corrected before he could stop himself.

Doc's eyebrows arched over the frames of his sunglasses.

"Can you blame me?" Romeo tossed his hands in the air. "One second you're oozing your Montana mountain man charm all over Mia. The next you're trying to talk our lawyer into giving you another chance for a lap dance. Camilla D' Angelo strikes me as a woman who can smell the one-night stand on you. But Mia? No." He shook his head forcefully. "She's different. If you're not serious about wanting to start something real with her, you should keep your dirty mitts off her and aim your swagger elsewhere. I thought you understood that. I mean, isn't that *exactly* what you were giving *me* shit for when you stopped by her room and found us together?"

"Hell yes, it is." Doc nodded. Then he went mute for a full five seconds. When he finally spoke, Romeo's stomach jumped into his throat like he'd flown through an air pocket and experienced a momentary freefall. "And what if I *was* serious about starting something real with her?"

Romeo hoped the noise around the airport covered up the hoarseness of his voice. "Are you?"

"Maybe." Doc hitched one big shoulder. "I mean, what's not to like? She's smart and surprisingly funny and she's the kind of pretty that sneaks up on you."

Romeo experienced a flash of irritation. "She's pretty. Period. And those eyes of hers are beyond pretty. They're beautiful."

For a long moment, Doc regarded him silently. Then he nodded. "You know what? You're right. She does have beautiful eyes. The kind of eyes a guy could spend a lifetime gazing into."

Before Romeo could sputter a response, Doc pushed past him and opened the copilot's door. A second later, the big man hopped inside the plane, leaving Romeo standing on the tarmac with his mouth hanging open.

What the fuck did I just do? he demanded of the universe.

It wasn't the universe that answered him. It was that small, annoying voice that lived in his head.

You just convinced Tall, Tan, and Tough Guy to get serious about Mia. Just when Romeo thought the voice was finished, it added, *You really are a dumbass.*

His eyes scanned the airport for a spare brick. When none could be found, he made his way around the propeller and opened the pilot-side door.

Climbing into the Otter, he saw Doc was already buckled in with his headset on. But Doc pulled down his sunglasses so Romeo could bear full witness to the wink he added to his cocky, shit-eating grin.

Doc and Mia might be perfect for each other, Romeo thought hotly, *but that won't stop me from kicking the bastard out of the plane over the Straits of Florida.*

CHAPTER 4

11:38 AM...

Mia wasn't crazy about flying.

But it was obvious Camilla D'Angelo *hated* it.

The two women sat across the aisle from each other, behind the bulkhead separating the fuselage from the cockpit. And from the corner of her eye, Mia watched the lawyer's bloodred nails dig into the leather of her seat cushion when the Otter hit a patch of turbulence and bounced, the engine revving and filling the plane with a wall of sound before quickly leveling out.

Even after they flew into calm air, Cami didn't loosen her death grip on the seat, and Mia experienced a spurt of anxiety just looking at the woman.

She knew why *she* wasn't a big fan of air travel. It was the lack of control. The having to trust someone else to get her from point A to point B.

Although, she didn't mind flying when Romeo was the

pilot. He was just so...capable. One of those men who could be dropped naked into the middle of a jungle with nothing but a bundle of twine and a Bowie knife, and in two weeks he'd build a small city complete with indoor plumbing and HVAC.

She was momentarily distracted by the thought of Romeo naked and swinging on a vine through the jungle Tarzan-style before she forced her mind back on track.

What was my point?

Oh, right. That I don't mind flying with Romeo because he can handle anything.

She'd once called him a jack-of-all-trades, but he'd just laughed and said, *"More like a jackoff-of-all-trades."*

Despite his many accomplishments, Romeo was surprisingly self-deprecating.

Leaning over the aisle, she strained her vocal cords above the low hum of the engine. "Don't worry. Romeo is the best pilot you could hope for. One time, he flew us through a thunderstorm so big it was nearly a tropical depression. Landed us in the wave-filled lagoon on Wayfarer Island and motored up to the beach like it was just another sunny Sunday afternoon."

Cami's face was blanched of color, making the rouge she'd swiped across her high cheekbones stand out garishly. Through clenched teeth, she admitted, "My sister died in a plane crash last year. Ever since, I break out in a cold sweat the second the wheels go up."

"I'm so sorry about your sister," Mia said automatically, although she knew from experience that the words never did any justice to the unbearable weight of a loved one's death. "I lost a sibling too. My little brother." Her voice was hoarser than usual because she still had trouble saying the words out loud. "Ten years ago."

Cami pushed her sunglasses onto her head, and Mia saw

the woman's dark eyes were overly bright. "Everyone says the pain fades with time."

Mia snorted. "Everyone lies." When Cami blinked at her, she made a face of horror when she realized what she'd done. "Oh, god! I know that's not what I'm supposed to say!"

Blame it on early trauma or her nature or whatever, but she'd never learned the fine art of casual conversation. Whenever she talked, the truth came tumbling out. Which was undoubtedly why she chose to remain silent so often. That way she could be sure her one terrible truth stayed locked inside.

"No." Cami grabbed the hand Mia had placed on the armrest to stabilize herself while she leaned over the aisle. "Thank you. I'd so much rather hear the truth than platitudes."

Mia felt like she should explain. "The pain is always there. It never fades. But it *does* change from something hard and sharp into something aching and dull. And then you're able to live with it."

Mia lived with her grandmother's death. She lived with her father's death. She struggled every day with her brother's death, however.

But, of course, she reminded herself, *you* should *struggle with that.*

When Cami nodded and tightened her seat belt across her waist, Mia settled back into her own seat. She recognized when someone pulled into themselves to deal with their inner pain. She'd perfected that move herself.

Except ever since coming to live on Wayfarer Island, she'd slowly begun to poke her head out of the hard, protective shell she'd built around herself.

Maybe it was because the men of Deep Six Salvage and the women who loved them had all known the harsher sides of life in one way or another. Maybe it was because they didn't try to hide the traumas that still affected their day-today. Maybe it was because, like her, they'd all been broken somehow, and yet they'd been able to pick up the pieces to find peace and happiness, and that gave her hope for herself.

Hope that one day she might be able to...not forgive herself. But maybe Andy's death would stop being the first thing she thought about when she woke up in the morning, and the last thing she thought about after she closed her eyes at night.

And, oh! How she was going to *miss* everyone on Wayfarer Island once the *Santa Cristina's* treasure was salvaged and it was time for her to move on to the next job. Miss Bran's homemade pasta and his penchant for spouting movie lines. Miss watching Olivia and LT dance on the front porch to the music pouring out of Uncle John's 80's era, battery-fed boombox—Olivia danced with grace; LT danced with what appeared to be a permanently broken leg. Miss Alex's never-ending stream of trivia. Miss practicing Tai Chi with Wolf on the beach in the mornings and fishing with Doc off the end of the pier in the afternoons.

She would miss the way Meat, Mason's fat English bulldog, liked to spend the night on the end of her daybed, because the screened-in porch where she slept caught the breeze coming in off the water. Meat was happiest when he was airing out his junk by lying on his back.

Then there was Lil' Bastard, the colorful rooster who was best friends with Meat. Uncle John who made terrible coffee but grew pretty good weed. And, of course, Romeo.

Yes, she would miss Romeo most of all.

Miss the glint in his eye, the flash of his dimples, and the way he could make her feel safe and calm without saying anything at all.

She hoped beyond hope that Mason and Alex found success in the Spanish Archives and located King Philip's cipher device. But was she being totally selfish to also wish for it to take them a while?

She wanted as much time on Wayfarer Island as she could get. Wanted to spend every second she could with all the people who'd come to mean so much to her. All the people who'd come to feel like family—and yet unlike any family she'd ever known.

A swell of melancholy threatened to overtake her. She considered digging into her purse for her copy of *In Darkness and Dreams*. Lazarus Luxido and all the other characters in Wisteria Manor would surely distract her from the gloomy turn of her thoughts. But she didn't like the idea of reading ahead without Romeo.

He made what was shaping up to be a pretty good book even better because he laughed at the funny parts, widened his eyes at the scary parts, and made playful and insightful comments throughout.

No matter how many novels P.J. Warren wrote in the Night Angels series, Mia knew that book seven would always be her favorite. Because book seven would always be the one she read with the man who looked at her with genuine pleasure in his eyes and made her forget, however momentarily, about the thing that would always set her apart from others.

Staring out the window, she watched the light blink at the tip of the wing and then let her gaze slip to the endless expanse of cerulean waves rippling below. The white hull of a speedboat caught her attention as it kicked thick plumes of water behind it. The Otter wasn't built for high altitude, it didn't have a pressurized cabin, so they flew low enough that she had no trouble counting the four tiny figures in the boat.

They're a long way from shore, she thought absently. Sailboats and yachts plied the open ocean, but speedboats tended to stay closer to land since they were fuel hogs.

No sooner did she have the thought than Doc unbuckled

from the copilot's chair. His tall frame was folded nearly in half as he exited the cockpit, stopping beside her to say, "Grabbing a bottled water from the back." He removed the toothpick from his mouth and included Cami when he asked, "Either of you ladies want one?"

"No thanks." Mia shook her head.

The lawyer lifted a finger. "I'll take one. I think I drank *almost* as much as you did last night. Every cell in my body is shriveled up like a raisin."

Doc opened his mouth to come back with what was sure to be a wisecrack, but he never got the chance. A weird *buzz* sounded throughout the plane and the interior lights flickered. A split second later, a deafening *boom* nearly burst Mia's eardrums, and the Otter barrel-rolled onto its side.

Had she not been strapped in, she would have ended up in the aisle. Because *Doc* wasn't strapped in, he flew across the fuselage and slammed into the bulkhead.

His head bounced off the metal corner with a sickening-sounding *whack*. And when he landed on the floor at Cami's feet, his long limbs were all akimbo.

"Doc!" she shouted, hanging awkwardly from her seat strap. Through Cami's window, aqua waters met her frantic gaze. When she craned her head against gravity to look out her own window, all she saw was blue sky.

Fear threatened to paralyze her as a terrible vibration rattled through the airplane. The shrill cry of alarms nearly drowned out the screaming engine.

She could see Romeo struggling with the throttle and control wheel. She only had a partial view, but enough of him was visible to show the tendons in his tanned forearms stood out in stark contrast against his skin. Sweat rolled down the side of his face, and a hard muscle worked in his jaw.

Whatever he was doing seemed to be working, however. Because slowly—too slowly for Mia's peace of mind—the

Otter pulled itself out of its heavy bank.

"What happened?" Cami cried out to no one in particular as Romeo urged the aircraft to climb higher into the sky, despite the plane having turned into a drunken bird. Its wings rollicked back and forth.

"Feels like a tailstrike!" Romeo called above the *beep, screech,* and *honk* of alarms.

Mia wasn't sure what a *tailstrike* was, but she assumed the name said it all.

Craning her head around to stare into the back of the plane, she fully expected to see mangled metal and a hole the size of a refrigerator where their tail section should've been. She was relieved when all she saw was smoke.

Of course, her relief only lasted a second because... *smoke!*

Just like snakes, no one wanted *smoke* on a plane!

She gripped the armrests so tight her fingers hurt. Her blood seemed frozen in her veins despite the pounding of her heart.

Breathe Romeo was always telling her.

Good advice. But how was she supposed to follow it when she was about to be one in eleven million?

Those were the odds of being in a plane crash. Alexandra Merriweather had shared the statistic with Mia the day Romeo had landed them in the storm and Mia had admitted to Alex she'd been sweating bullets the entire flight.

But just in case I don't *end up being a statistic...*

"I'm unbuckling to check on Doc!" she yelled to Romeo.

"Damnit, Mia!" he shouted. "You—"

"He's hurt!" She cut him off and knelt next to Doc, who hadn't moved a muscle since going down.

She was no doctor, but she'd taken three Wilderness Medicine courses. In her line of work, she was often far from the nearest clinic or hospital. It behooved her to know how to throw a stitch or brace a broken bone.

Propping her back against the bulkhead to steady herself, she pressed two fingers to Doc's carotid. When she felt the steady hammer of his pulse, she let loose with a windy breath of relief. Then she grabbed his right hand and pinched the space between his thumb and forefinger, nearly crying out with happiness when his hand contracted. She did the same with his left hand and got the same results.

No difficulty breathing. No obvious muscle paralysis. I don't think we're dealing with a broken neck. So that leaves...

As gently as she could, she turned Doc's head. Bright red blood slid beneath his ear and stained the collar of his T-shirt.

Probing his skull, she found a goose egg behind his left ear. But thankfully, when she carefully palpated the bones beneath, there was no crackle or flex that would herald a cracked cranium.

"He hit his head!" she yelled in the direction of the cockpit. "I don't think his skull is fractured, but he's out cold!"

"Is there any way to secure him?" Romeo's voice was tight with tension.

That probably scared Mia worse than anything. If Mr. Cool, Calm, and Collected was anxious, they really *were* in trouble.

"We can try!" she called and glanced up to see Cami had once more shoved her sunglasses onto her head. The woman's dark eyes looked nearly black inside the paleness of her face, but her voice was steady when she asked, "How can I help?"

"Let's see if we can drag him into your seat."

The lawyer nodded mutely. And even though her hands shook, she was able to get her seat belt undone in a flash. She knelt on the floor on the other side of Doc's prone body.

Doc wasn't fat by any means. In fact, he had the rangy build most people associated with a mountain man from the wilds of the West. But nearly six and a half feet of big bones, wiry sinew, and lean muscle still weighed a ton.

Mia and the lawyer grunted and strained and heaved and huffed. It was like trying to lift a 220-pound ragdoll. But after a little maneuvering and a lot of cussing on Cami's part, they were finally able to hoist him into Cami's vacated seat.

The lawyer kept him upright with both arms wrapped around his chest while Mia cinched the belt snug across his waist. Once he was strapped in, they gingerly lowered him until his head hung between his knees and his arms dangled down until his big hands lay palm up on the floor.

It was as close to a "brace" position as they could manage with an unconscious man.

Cami was in the process of buckling herself into the seat next to him when Mia heard Romeo put out the first call for help. Her knees turned to Jell-O, and it was a wonder she didn't crumple onto the floor before she made it to her seat.

Mayday made it official. They were screwed.

One in eleven million. Dear god!

"Mayday, mayday!" Romeo's voice was clear and measured, but she could hear the urgency underlying every word. "This is flight number—" He rattled off a series of letters and numbers followed by the type of aircraft. "We have a multi-system failure. I cannot maintain speed, altitude, or heading. Come in, Key West. Do you copy?"

Mia closed her eyes and began counting to ten again. She'd made it to five before she realized no one was talking back to Romeo.

Was the radio part of their multi-system failure?

Six, seven, eight...

"Mayday, Mayday!" Romeo tried again. "If anyone is out there picking me up, this is flight—" He went through the same information as before, but this time he added their current position followed by, "There are four people onboard. We are headed in a south, southeasterly direction. I estimate we have two, maybe three minutes of airtime remaining. We will be ditching."

Mia thought her terror couldn't climb any higher.

Then it did when the engine sputtered and died, and an ominous quiet filled the plane.

CHAPTER 5

11:44 AM...

Romeo had always considered himself a lucky S.O.B.

Despite his less than auspicious start in life, he'd made it as a Frogman—something few who aspired to the role ever achieved. He'd survived more than a handful of missions where he should've found a final resting place inside a body bag. And he had a group of loyal friends and business partners who were closer to him than his own family.

But he feared his luck may have run out.

The Otter was a dead-stick.

To make matters worse, he was pretty sure his tail was either completely gone or so badly damaged, it might as well be gone. Whatever had happened to his beloved plane made keeping the bird in a steady glide impossible.

A cold sweat slicked his skin, reminding him of the night he'd been initiated into the gang and had known he was staring down the barrel of a bad deal. His muscles strained as he worked the flaps, slowing their descent and struggling to keep them nose-up while looking for the best place to put down.

Most people would think that last thing was a no-brainer since there was nothing but open water as far as the eye could see. Just ditch wherever, right? The ocean is the ocean is the ocean, right?

Wrong.

All sea surfaces were not made the same. A trained eye could detect patches where waves broke higher, see whole stretches where the current caused cross-action in the swells, and pick out the deceptive areas that looked like they'd be good for a landing, but were prone, for whatever reason, to the occasional rogue breaker.

He needed the smoothest piece of water he could find because they were coming in hot. Red hot. The chili pepper in his grandmother's homemade salsa hot.

Unfortunately, even if he *did* find a good spot, he might not be able to get them there. He didn't have much directional control. Small adjustments were all he could make.

Luck would play a huge part in this ditching, and he'd just established he'd run out of that exact thing.

Fuck!

He was no stranger to the burn of adrenaline through his veins. For years, he'd ridden that high on a daily basis. But ever since bugging out of the Navy, he'd gotten used to the slower pace of life. Working to regulate his breathing and heart rate didn't come automatically anymore. He had to concentrate on both, reminding his amygdala not to respond instinctively to the fear hormone pumping through his system.

"Is there anything I can do to help?" Mia's husky voice was usually a balm to his brain. Hearing her now, crystal clear since the only other sound to breach the hull of the plane was the harsh rush of the wind outside, only reminded him it wasn't just *his* life he was responsible for.

He had three passengers who were counting on him to make sure they walked away from this with all their favorite parts intact.

And let's be real, all their un*favorite parts too.*

Something foul and nauseating hatched in his stomach and started wriggling around. He regretted the ham and cheese biscuit he'd snagged from the hotel buffet on the way to the airport. The large cup of black coffee wasn't doing him any favors either.

"Stay seated and get ready to brace," he told Mia, trying to keep his tone neutral while wrestling with the controls and eyeing the water that was rising up to meet them way too fast.

Calculating his airspeed, the swell patterns, and the direction of the wind, it didn't register right away that Mia started singing. Soon enough, though, the familiar tune broke through his concentration and, fuckin'-A, did it make him smile.

His Otter was in bad shape. He had no idea where they were or if anyone had heard his call for help. He was about to perform the most harrowing landing of his life. And yet, he was smiling.

Because Mia was singing John Denver's "Leaving on a Jet Plane," the same song he'd hummed weeks earlier in an attempt to relax her when he'd piloted them through one very gnarly thunderstorm.

And yes. The song choice had been intentional. His way of injecting a little levity into a hella tense situation.

Same thing Mia was doing now. *Bless her.*

"You can't be serious." The lawyer's tone was incredulous.

"Sing with me," Mia said. "It helps."

"I can't sing!"

"You *can't* sing, or you *won't* sing?"

"I won't sing unless you want your ears to bleed."

"I think bloody ears are the least of our worries right now."

"True," Cami admitted.

Mia started singing again in that low, throaty voice of hers that was surprisingly on-key given she'd admitted her vocal cords had been damaged. By the time she got to the chorus, the lawyer joined in comically *off*-key.

Truly, he thought, *if tone deaf were a person, her name would be Camilla D'Angelo. Although what she lacks in skill, she more than makes up for with enthusiasm.*

He let their combined voices comfort him, *focus* him. Only when they were fifty feet from the surface of the sea did he stop listening, every ounce of his brainpower fixed on the task at hand.

Trajectory? Good. He'd been able to line the Otter up parallel to the major swells.

Wave height? About two, maybe three feet. *Totally doable.*

Airspeed? Still too fast. *Damnit!*

He gave up trying to regulate his heart and let it clamor against his ribs. A metallic taste coated his tongue, like he'd been sucking on an old penny. From the corner of his eye, he saw what he thought was a white line of sand and the green flash of trees riding in the middle of the sea.

Land? Maybe luck hasn't completely dumped my ass after all!

Or maybe he was simply imagining things, his desperate brain conjuring up a mirage.

He didn't have time to take a second look before... "Brace! Brace! Brace!" he roared as the right pontoon hit the water and immediately bounced them back into the air.

Sweet Mother Mary! This won't be pretty.

"Brace, brace, brace!" he yelled again.

Half a dozen times he was thrown against his restraints before being pressed back into the pilot's seat as the plane bounded from sea to air and back again. *Mia... Mia... Mia...* Her name was an urgent refrain echoing inside his head with every rebound.

He'd danced with death so much, he was no longer moved by the thought of his own demise. But Mia Ennis? She had so much *light* inside her. Sure, she tried to hide it, but he saw it. He saw *her*. And the thought of a world without her in it?

It was too terrible to contemplate.

Then there was Doc—his partner, his friend, his brother-in-arms. He wholeheartedly regretted ever thinking about throwing the bastard out over the Florida Straits. And yeah, he appreciated the irony that they were *all* about to end up in that exact place.

If we live through this, and if Doc truly wants to start something with Mia, I won't stand in the way, he promised... himself? Doc? God? He wasn't sure.

And lastly there was Camilla D'Angelo. She seemed like a decent woman. Surely she was too young, and had far too much left to do in life, to be taken out so soon.

So, we'll make it. It's not our time. It can't be.

Just when he thought they actually *might* make it in one piece, just when they'd slowed enough for him to rake in a shuddering breath, he heard the *crunch* of bending metal and knew one of the pontoons had given its all and could give no more.

Everything that came next happened in slow motion.

With the left pontoon crumpled flat, the tip of the left wing dipped into the ocean. And that was all it took to send them into a cartwheel. At first, all he saw through the windshield was clear, blue water as the nose of the plane plunged into the sea. Then all he saw was sky as what was left of the tail section sank into the drink.

The noise inside the aircraft was incredible. A *groaning, crunching, buckling* of metal. He thought he heard the lawyer scream. He *knew* he heard Mia catch her breath; he was *that* attuned to her. And then...

With one final moan, the Otter came to a teeth-rattling halt. The cacophony of noise was diminished to a few *squeaks* and *thumps* as loose objects settled into place. And a second later...ear-splitting silence.

For a moment, he remained frozen in place. Long enough to feel them climb the gentle rise of a wave and then slowly slide down the back side of the swell. Then, a fresh punch of adrenaline scorched his veins and lit a fire under his ass.

He did a mental inventory of his injuries while unbuckling himself. A hella bruised knee. Otherwise, nada. As Doc would say, he was "fit as a fiddle."

Un-fucking-believable.

Scrambling out of the pilot's chair, he didn't realize he'd opened his mouth until he heard himself bellow, "Mia!"

Her answer was immediate. "I—I'm okay." And her raspy voice had never sounded so sweet.

Clambering out of the cockpit—no easy feat since the aircraft had come to rest on its side and there were no horizontal surfaces to walk on—he nearly choked when the first sight to reach his searching eyes was Mia's pretty face.

She was still strapped into her seat, although she leaned across the one next to her in a fight against gravity. Her hair was a riot of soft waves, proof that she'd been tumbled around like clothes in a dryer. And there was a small scratch on her chin. But apart from that, she seemed unhurt.

A quick scan showed him Doc and the lawyer were in

about the same shape. And despite being a lapsed Catholic, he sent a quick word of thanks heavenward.

At some point during the ditching, Doc had regained consciousness. He blinked in confusion when he asked, "What happened?"

"We crashed," Romeo told him, already on the move because they had minutes, maybe even seconds, before the plane started filling with water.

"Well, why did we go and do that for?" Doc's tone was disgruntled.

Romeo ignored him as he partially ran/partially crawled over the rear seats toward the back of the plane where the inflatable life raft was stored. "Get unbuckled and get ready to leave the aircraft!" he yelled over his shoulder, coughing slightly as a wisp of smoke caught in his throat.

Velcro straps held the deflated watercraft to the wall. Removing those was easy. It was harder hoisting the heavy valise of rubber and coated polyester through the rear exit hatchway once he got it open. The life raft weighed nearly a hundred pounds, and with the Otter on its side, he was basically heaving the deflated raft straight over his head.

After a couple of seconds, and after a *lot* of grunting, he had the life raft resting on the outside of the plane.

He sure as shit didn't want it slipping off and sinking— it was their only chance at survival—so he used one of the straps on the giant duffel to secure the raft to a portion of the locking mechanism on the door.

Determination and a cold sense of desperation had him yelling at his passengers. "This way! Quickly!"

He didn't wait to see if they followed his orders before he began rummaging through the wreckage at the back of the Otter. Twisted metal and the various detritus of a crash met his gaze. But there. There!

He saw what he was looking for and nearly howled

with victory that the case of bottled water appeared intact. No crushed bottles. No missing caps. Just twenty-four glorious containers of pure, life-sustaining H_2O.

Grabbing the plastic covering securing the bottles together, he lifted, expecting the weight of the water to hang heavy on the end of his arm. But the plastic had been torn, and it ripped away from the bottles in one solid sheet.

Shit! On to plan B.

"Here." He thrust two bottles at the lawyer, who was the first to make her way to the back of the plane. "Load up as many as you can."

She blinked at him, not getting why he wanted her to take the water when they'd just crash landed and were about to sink. They had more important shit to deal with, like, you know, *not* drowning.

Then understanding dawned in her eyes.

Her already pale cheeks went chalk white, but she unzipped her oversized purse and held it wide. "Stuff as many as you can inside."

He didn't hesitate, transferring eight bottles into her bag, and handing her two more, which she slid into the pockets of her pants.

"We'll get you up through the exit," he told her. "Once you're outside, stay seated on the body of the plane. You might slide off if you try to stand. Doc, come help me." He motioned with his chin toward his partner, who was last in line. "The ladies are going to need a boost."

Just as he'd feared, the sea had started seeping into the plane. The ocean completely covered the tops of his flip-flops, and he could feel the warm water nipping at his ankles.

She's going under.

He acknowledged the small pang in the center of his chest. His Otter was going under, but she'd held together until the bitter end.

She saved us.

"On my way." Doc slipped past Mia, who stood on the arm of one seat while steadying herself against the headrest of another. When she swallowed, he saw her pulse fluttering in her throat. His gaze jumped to her eyes and...just as he'd thought. Her pupils had gone pinpoint.

"Breathe," he told her as Doc pulled even with him and nodded that he was prepared to hoist the lawyer out of the aircraft.

"I thought I was." Mia blew out a shuddering breath.

"Nope." Romeo shook his head before turning his attention to Cami. "You ready?"

"As I'll ever be," was her shaky response.

She stood on the last row of seats. This allowed her to poke her head and shoulders out of the plane. Romeo and Doc each grabbed a linen-clad leg.

"On three," Romeo called, and started the countdown.

Together, he and Doc tossed Cami through the opening in a flutter of perfume and cream fabric.

"Whoa. Shit!" Doc said as a larger than average wave lifted the aircraft high, its metal skin groaning with the motion.

"Hang on!" Romeo yelled to Cami, bracing himself against the rear bulkhead.

Doc managed to hook an arm around the headrest nearest him, but Mia tumbled over the last row of seats. Doc made a valiant grab for her, but missed, and she landed in Romeo's outstretched arms.

He reeled her in and held her close, feeling her heart beating a rapid tattoo against his chest.

Once again, he was reminded of coming awake that morning. Of her spread atop him. And in that split second between sleep and wakefulness, he'd felt a sense of... He couldn't put a name to it. It was like peace and longing and lust all balled into one. And when she'd rolled off him, he'd wanted so badly to pull her back. To bury his nose in her sweet-smelling hair.

But something had held him back.

The same something that stopped him from burying his nose in her hair now.

She only thought of him as a friend. And even if that wasn't true, even if the longing look he sometimes thought he saw in her eyes was the *real* truth, he wasn't the kind of man to give her what she wanted. And so it was best if he kept his hands—and his nose—to himself.

As soon as the rogue wave moved on and the plane resumed its gentle rise and fall, he cupped her shoulder and gently pressed her away. Every cell in his body cried out with unhappiness, straining toward her like the hand on a compass strains toward due north. But he covered up what he knew was the pained look on his face by asking, "You okay?"

Her delectable mouth pursed into a bow when she briskly nodded. "I'm fine. Thanks for the save."

Any day, every day, he could have told her, but didn't.

Instead, he touched a gentle fingertip to the scratch on her chin—he wasn't sure why, maybe to keep himself from touching those fascinating lips of hers. Then he jerked his gaze away from her lioness eyes because he'd started drowning in them—he was always drowning in them—and called overhead, "Cami! You still with us?"

There was a muffled *thump* as the lawyer adjusted herself on the skin of the plane. A second later, her wide-eyed face appeared in the empty hatchway.

"Holy cannoli." Her shaking voice matched the trembling hand she pressed to her forehead. "What do you guys say to getting out of that plane before another one of those waves rolls by?"

"That's the plan," he told her and pulled the first aid kit

71

off the wall. Handing it up to her, he instructed, "Hold on to this, will you?" Then he turned to Mia. "You ready?"

"God, yes." She climbed the last row of seats until, like the lawyer, she was standing on the headrest closest to the exit. She was shorter than Cami, however. The only part of her that poked out the door was the top of her head.

"Here." He handed her two bottles of water. "Tuck these into your pockets."

She wore the same pair of cotton shorts from the night before. And somehow, despite having slept in them and despite having just been involved in a plane crash, they still looked crisp and clean. She tried stuffing a bottle inside each hip pocket, but the little cotton pouches weren't big enough to hold the containers.

"I have another idea." She opened her purse. It was smaller than Cami's, and what little room she had was mostly taken up by the most recent addition to the Night Angels series.

"Lose the book," he told her and tried not to let the look of disappointment that crossed her face stab him straight in the heart. "P.J. Warren is a baller, no doubt. But water is life."

Wrinkling her nose, Mia went to grab the book but then stopped and snapped her fingers. "Give me a second."

Zipping her purse, she tossed it around her body so it hung at her back. Then she un-tucked her white blouse and Romeo was gifted with a brief glimpse of creamy skin and the most adorable belly button ever created. After tying the tail ends of her shirt together into a tight knot, she wiggled her fingers in a come-hither motion toward the remaining bottles. "Start handing them over."

"Smart," he praised, feeling inordinately proud of her quick thinking as he passed her the plastic containers.

"Comes with the territory." She dropped bottles down her shirt. "Those of us who like to dig in the dirt and the sand are always having to improvise ways to carry around our finds when we forget to bring a specimen bag." She looked a bit like the Michelin Man by the time they were finished, but she'd managed to sock away the remaining bottles of water.

"Same as before." He nodded to Doc, feeling the sea crawling up his shins. Very soon, the bird was going to reach a tipping point and sink like a stone.

"One," Doc said.

"Two," Romeo added and snuck a quick peek at Mia's ass.

So sue him. Didn't matter how bad the situation was, he was still a guy. And Mia had an ass that was made to be ogled.

And honestly? If I'm about to die, I think I deserve one last pleasure.

Together he and Doc said, "Three," and tossed Mia out the hatchway, purse, water bottles, delectable ass and all.

Once she'd situated herself on the outside of the plane, she poked her head back through the exit door. "Two down, two to go," she told them.

Romeo pulled the plastic case that held the flare gun off the wall and handed it up to her without saying a word. He didn't need to. She knew the score.

When he turned to tell Doc he was next, he saw the man's face was ashen. Concern had him glancing up at Mia and telling her, "Slide back. Give Doc some room." He hated to see her disappear from sight, but once she did, he asked quietly, "What is it? Your head?"

Doc jerked his chin once. "No." Then he seemed to reconsider. "Well, that hurts like a sonofabitch, too. But what's really giving me fits is my stupid arm. Think the damn thing's broken."

The tepid water slipped over Romeo's knees but he refused to think about how quickly the plane was filling.

"How bad?"

"Bad enough to piss me off. Not bad enough to make me think we have ourselves a serious problem."

Romeo nodded. "Can you get out on your own?"

"You should go first. I'm the least likely one of us to need a boost."

Romeo shook his head. "You're injured, so you're first."

"Rock, paper, scissors you for it."

"For fuck's sake, Doc! We don't have time for this shit!"

Doc didn't argue. He simply repeated, "Rock, paper, scissors you for it."

"Fine," Romeo grumbled. "But if your stubborn ass loses and you end up drowning, don't blame me. You ready?" He held out his hand and three seconds later his scissors had handily beat Doc's paper.

Even *with* a broken arm, Doc was able to hoist himself through the hatchway in a flash. He was the size of Jolly Green Giant, after all, and once he stood on the backs of the seats, all but his lower half had poked through the opening.

Doc was laid out on the body of the plane when he dropped a hand back inside, wiggling his fingers. "Come on, brother. We saved the best for last."

"Hold that thought." Romeo turned to make his way back toward the cockpit. "And get that life raft inflated while you're at it."

"Are you having a brain-out-of-body experience?" Doc called to him. "You might not *have* a second!"

His only answer as he slogged through the water was to yell over his shoulder, "I secured the life raft to the locking mechanism on the door! Be sure you pull it loose so the Otter doesn't drag everything and everyone down with her once she goes!"

He thought he heard Doc mutter a curse but couldn't be sure. The water inside the plane made a loud *sloshing* sound as it rocked back and forth with the rhythm of the sea.

By the time he'd lurched his way to the pilot's seat, he was waist deep in the drink, the water weighing down his jeans and tugging at his flip-flops until he had to curl his toes to keep them on.

Anyone else might have experienced a grave sense of panic. But the ocean was a SEAL's medium, and Romeo's training had inured him to any fear of it.

Plus, no amount of danger could override his determination to grab the Glock he kept Velcroed beneath his seat. There was something scratching at the back of his brain. Something that told him what happened to his plane hadn't been accidental.

When he bent to search for his sidearm, the sea water met his chin. It smelled of ocean life and jet fuel and that acrid spent firework aroma that always made him think of a battlefield.

The scratching at the back of his brain became a harsh grating.

Who the hell would want to blow us out of the sky?

Before he finished asking the question, he knew the answer.

Any of more than a dozen players.

He and his Deep Six partners had made quite a few enemies during their time with the Navy. In fact, not too long ago they'd been attacked by an Iranian ex-admiral bent on revenge for an op they'd run more than a decade earlier.

Has another ghost from our past come back to haunt us?

"Gotcha!" He located his trusty weapon. After tucking it into the small of his back, he rummaged around for the granola bars he kept in a pouch on the side of his seat—fresh air and open sky always whetted his appetite.

There were only three. Three measly chocolate and

peanut butter granola bars. But three was better than zero.

After stuffing them into his front pockets, he turned to make his way back toward the rear of the aircraft. By the time he was at the exit, he wasn't walking so much as swimming, so he pulled off his flip-flops and stuffed them into his back pockets.

The main body of the plane was almost fully submerged now. Water trickled in through the open hatchway overhead, and he could see the bright orange of the inflated life raft resting atop the inch or less of fuselage that remained above the surface.

"Hurry!" Doc yelled, still bellied out and clinging to the body of the aircraft.

"Get in the damn raft, Doc!" Romeo bellowed. "I'm right behind you!"

Doc muttered something unkind about Romeo's parentage but scrambled into the watercraft all the same.

"The plane's about to go down, Romeo!" he heard Mia scream as he climbed the seats just like the others had. The water coming in through the open hatchway became a waterfall that brutally pummeled his head and shoulders.

Gripping the edges of the exit, he prepared to hoist himself through the opening when the Otter gave one last groan and succumbed to the relentless pull of the ocean's watery arms. The force of the sea rushing into the body of the plane was impossible to fight.

Once again, time slowed to a crawl.

Unlike when the Otter had cartwheeled, however, when there'd been nothing he could do except ride out his fate, now there were steps to take. A very precise set of steps that came to him automatically.

Step one, drink in the last of the air. Two quick exhales and he'd emptied his chest cavity. One long, deep inhale filled his lungs to capacity.

Step two, get real calm and comfortable as the fuselage filled with water and the Otter sank further into the deep. He blinked as the salt water brushed against his eyeballs, making his vision cloudy. But he could see clearly enough to catch the moment the plastic from the case of water bottles got sucked out through the exit. One of the cushions from a seat in the last row followed the plastic from the plane.

Step three, as soon as the cabin equalized, swim up and out of the aircraft. With a hard kick of his legs, and a mighty pull of his arms, he jettisoned himself through the open door.

SEALs spent months—*years*—training their bodies to consume less oxygen than the Average Joe. Which meant when the open ocean welcomed him, he didn't immediately make for clean air.

Instead, he turned and peered down at his beloved plane, letting himself sink right along with her. Letting his blurred eyes rake over her body, searching for any clue that might tell him what had happened to her.

The tail section looked like a banana peel. But the poor Otter was so mangled it was impossible to tell the difference between the damage that'd occurred *before* the crash and the damage that'd occurred *because* of the crash.

For a long moment, he followed the old girl on her final journey into Davy Jones's locker. Paying tribute to her for all the glorious hours of freedom and flight.

You were a good bird, he silently told her, watching more debris float through her exit. *I'll miss you.*

The sea was a curious creature. It didn't cool at a continuous rate. Instead, its temperature dropped at noticeable intervals. It was layered, like one of Bran's lasagnas. And each of those layers was called a thermoclime.

The instant he hit a new thermoclime, when the warm water nearest the surface gave way to an icy coolness that had goose bumps erupting over his skin, he knew it was time to kick toward the light. He realized he'd sunk farther than he'd planned when he saw the sun rippling on the waves far overhead.

Using his arms and legs in tandem, he propelled his body through the water, his ears attuned to the subtle *clicking* and *popping* sounds that could always be heard around the Florida Keys. The sea life was so abundant, the parrotfish, pistol shrimp, and grunts so numerous, that they filled the ocean with their noise until it sounded like swimming through a bowl of Rice Krispies.

He was about halfway to his destination, aiming for a patch of water close to the rectangle of orange drifting overhead, when he saw Doc plunge into the ocean.

The big man was a spectacularly graceful swimmer, his long arms and legs displacing water as easily as a dolphin slicing through the drink. *Usually.* Doc's broken arm interfered with his downward strokes, and it was obvious each movement was agony.

Damnit, Doc!

Kicking harder, Romeo met Doc in the water about twenty feet from the surface. Doc grabbed the collar of his T-shirt to haul him up, but then grimaced and let out a lungful of bubbles when the move caused him additional pain.

Romeo ended up latching onto Doc's elbow and using his legs to catapult them both skyward, his muscles aching with the effort and with the lack of oxygen. By the time the two of them burst into the sun, his lungs were on fire and his eyesight had tunneled.

Raking in a desperate breath, he filled his chest cavity until the rush of O_2 made his head spin. As soon as he could manage a word, he turned to Doc. "What the fuck do you think you're doing?"

"Saving your miserable life, you stupid asshole!" Doc sputtered.

Romeo opened his mouth to come back with something appropriately macho like, *Please, I could've stayed down for another two minutes*—SEALs were nothing if not arrogant pricks, and they were *especially* arrogant about near misses—but he snapped his jaws shut when he heard a soft wail coming from the life raft.

Spinning in the water, he saw Mia sitting on the edge of the watercraft, her hands over her face as her shoulders shook with heartrending sobs.

"Mia?" He scissor-kicked in her direction. His heart, which had been metronome steady while treading water up from the deep, went into overdrive. When a seat cushion popped up in front of him, he shoved it aside, annoyed at anything that blocked his path to the life raft. "What's wrong?" he demanded, spitting out a mouthful of salt water when a wave slapped him in the face. "Are you hurt?"

She lifted her head and he saw her bottomless, golden eyes were filled with tears. Never in their entire acquaintance had he heard her raise her voice, so he was shocked to his core when she yelled at him, "I thought you were dead, you asshole! What were you *doing* staying down there so long?"

Two assholes in the span of ten seconds. I'm really winning hearts and minds today.

"I'm sorry," he swore, realizing he'd scared the shit out of everyone. "I wasn't thinking."

She reached for him when he pulled even with the raft. Even though he didn't need her help, she gave it to him by tucking a hand under each of his arms and yanking.

She was stronger than she looked—*all that diving and digging, I guess*—and he was over the edge in an instant.

"Move back so I don't get you wet," he told her, sitting on the round rubber side of the life raft and swiping the salt water out of his face.

"Screw you," she croaked.

His chin jerked back and he blinked at her in shock. Before he knew what was happening, she was in his lap with her arms wrapped tight around his back.

He could feel the heat of her breath where her face met his neck, smell the sweet nectar of her expensive skin lotion, made stronger because she was warmed by the sun, and appreciate how firm and round her butt was since it was cushioned against his thighs.

He was in heaven. He was in hell. He was...*not* thinking of her as a friend.

CHAPTER 6

11:56 AM...

Never *thought I'd come to the point in my life where I'd need a stronger word than "fuck,"* Camilla D' Angelo thought as she watched Doc tread water toward the life raft.

Then again, she'd never been in a plane crash before.

Now that she had been, she could state with absolute certainty there hadn't been a curse word invented that adequately captured the sheer terror and helplessness one felt when one was falling out of the sky.

Is that what happened to Carlotta before she died? she wondered, shivering despite the relentless sun beating down on the top of her head. *Was my sister terrified? Powerless? Resigned to her fate?*

The authorities had assured Cami the bomb that took out Carlotta's private jet had instantly killed everyone on board.

But what if it hadn't?

What if Cami's sister had been conscious while she tumbled through the air? What if Carlotta had *known* she was living her last seconds? Breathing her last breaths? Feeling her final heartbeats pounding in her chest?

Cami realized she'd been numb with shock since the crash, because thoughts of her sister melted that numbness away. She became aware of her blood roaring through her veins, tasted the saltiness of the sea air filling her lungs, and saw how her limbs shook like the leaves on the trees in the front yard of her childhood home whenever a big nor'easter blew through.

A plane crash. I was just in a plane crash! *Fuck!*

See? Didn't come close to doing the experience justice.

If Doc hadn't thrown a muscled arm over the side of the life raft just then, she might have given into the terror and trauma and burst into tears. Just like poor Mia.

The woman had been a stone-cold rock through everything. The one to tend to Doc after he'd been knocked unconscious. The one to keep singing even after they first hit the ocean going way too fast. The one who'd helped Doc unpack and inflate the life raft with a *pop* and a *hiss* of industrial-smelling rubber. She'd even leaned over and wiped a smudge of something off Cami's face after they'd climbed into the watercraft.

But when the plane sank beneath the surface of the sea, dragging Romeo down with it—and when he hadn't emerged after what felt like twenty years, prompting Doc to curse and plunge into the ocean after him—all of Mia's cool-headed poise had abandoned her.

She'd screamed Romeo's name. Not his nickname either. His *real* name.

"Spiro!"

It'd been the kind of scream to shatter glass. Or shatter eardrums, at the very least.

Cami could still hear it ringing inside her head. And if someone were to ask her to describe the exact sound of horror mixed with heartbreak, she would say it was those two syllables ripped from the back of Mia's raw throat.

"Little help here?" Doc said and Cami was quick to hook her hands under his armpits. The soles of her sandals scrabbled against the side of the raft as she fought for leverage. And when he helped her by giving one mighty kick with his powerful legs, he slipped over the edge of the watercraft like a seal sliding into the ocean.

His big, wet body landed on top of hers, and she let loose with an unladylike *squawk*. Warm ocean water seeped through the material of her suit, and she got a nose full of his scent—a delicious combination of pine trees and fresh mountain air that she clearly remembered from the night before.

Basically, the man smelled like a Glacier National Park commercial come to life, and she would have stolen a moment to enjoy it. You know, taken a little comfort in sucking in the scent of solid land since she'd just been in a *plane crash* and now she was floating in the middle of the ocean. But the weight of his chest was immense, making it impossible to breathe.

Or maybe she was having trouble filling her lungs because his lean hips had settled between her spread legs and his hot, sweet-smelling breath fanned her face.

This was what she'd been after last night. *This right here.*

But she really *didn't* mix business with pleasure. So she ignored her body's instinctive responses to his and tried to wiggle out from under him.

It was like trying to wiggle out from under a city bus.

When he didn't scramble off her immediately, she frowned. Was he the kind of guy to take advantage?

She hadn't thought so last night.

But last night I was all tipsy and in vacation mode and very likely romanticizing him. I mean, honestly, how well do I know the man?

Considering she hadn't even known his real name until an hour ago, the answer was obvious. *Not well at all.*

Opening her mouth to give him a good tongue-lashing, she slammed it shut again when she glanced at his face and found his mouth *not* curved into a smarmy grin, but instead contorted in pain. She tried to project a tough-as-nails persona, but on the inside she was as squishy as a marshmallow.

"Hey." She placed a tentative finger against the side of his jaw. His beard stubble was surprisingly soft, but the muscles that clenched tight beneath her touch were not. "You okay?"

He didn't answer. Simply rolled off her with a long, low grunt, sat up, and touched the back of his head. His fingers came away stained pink, blood mixed with salt water.

"Must've been one hell of a ride," he snorted. "Sorry I missed it."

Jokes? He was making jokes about their *plane crash*?

Well, two can play that game.

Scooting into a seated position with her back against the raft's rubber side, she gave a shrug she hoped came off as nonchalant. "You know what they say. What doesn't kill you gives you a warped sense of humor and post-traumatic stress."

His lips quirked, but just for an instant before his brow furrowed. "Last thing I remember, I was headed to the back of the Otter for some water. How'd I end up strapped into the seat?"

"That would be thanks to me and Mia," she told him.

One dark blond brow winged up his forehead. "I bet that was fun."

"Like a carnival ride and mud wrestling an unconscious gorilla all rolled into one."

He laughed and bobbed his chin. "Well, thank you. Thank you both." He turned to include Mia, who was wrapped tight in Romeo's arms.

No. That wasn't right. It was *Romeo* who was wrapped tight in *Mia's* arms. *Romeo's* arms hung at his sides like he wasn't sure what to do with them.

Cami wondered if it was the crash, the near drowning, or Mia's reaction that had him looking like his world had gone topsy-turvy. But before she had time to reach a conclusion, he shook his head like he was coming out of a trance. Placing one broad-palmed hand flat against Mia's back, he used the other to gently brush a finger down the side of her face.

"It's okay, *cariña*." His deep voice was nothing but a whisper. "I'm okay. We're okay. Just breathe."

Cariña, *is it?*

Cami had wondered if there was something between the flyboy and the marine archeologist. The way Mia had spoken of Romeo's piloting skills had been blatantly admiring, almost reverential. And Cami had *definitely* caught Romeo sneaking a peek at Mia's backside at the airport.

Well, good for you, sis, she thought. Because Spiro "Romeo" Delgado was one *fine* specimen of man. The kind of guy Carlotta would have called an Adonis—all GQ features and granite-hewn body.

Not Cami's taste. She preferred her men a little rough around the edges. And if he was grumpy on top of that?

Be still my heart.

"The Dirty Harry type," Carlotta had teased her. To which she'd always replied, *"So sue me for enjoying a face with a little character. Give me a crooked nose or a chin scar any day of the week and twice on Sunday."*

Speaking of faces with character...

She glanced over at Doc, at the water sheeting off his wild head of hair that hadn't decided what color it wanted to be, and so had become a fascinating mix of twenty different shades of blond and brown. He had a small, flesh-colored mole beside his nose—the male equivalent of a beauty mark. And his full, masculine lips twisted into a disgruntled moue when he pulled out from under his denim-clad butt one of the water bottles Mia had dumped out of her shirt and into the bottom of the raft.

Cami remembered spying him from across the bar the night before, all tall and lean and a little mean-looking with that toothpick sticking out of his mouth. No crooked nose or chin scar. But the crinkles at the corners of his eyes had spoken of a life staring at the horizon. And the stubble on his cheeks had been days old, as if he hadn't bothered to shave because he'd had more important things to do.

High cheekbones. Thick eyebrows. Eyes that were cool and green and reminded her of the ferns that grew in the forests of the Adirondacks where her father had taken her and Carlotta hiking as kids.

All of that had been enough to pique her interest. But it'd been the slightly *broken* expression on his face that'd completely disarmed her.

Before she'd known what she was doing, she'd hopped from her barstool and headed in his direction.

She hadn't been able to explain it then. She couldn't explain it now. She wasn't the type for one-night stands. Yet, that's exactly what she'd known she was getting herself into after he plucked the toothpick from his mouth, let his gaze travel over her body, and asked to buy her a drink.

He'd been a neutron star. She'd been helplessly, hopelessly pulled into his orbit.

"Are you okay?" she asked him again, pointing to his head and then nonchalantly folding the halves of her linen suit jacket over her thin blouse, hoping to hide that it'd turned see-through after getting wet.

"Depends on your definition of okay," he grumbled, digging into the front pocket of his jeans. He pulled out a toothpick that was a little bent, but it went straight into his mouth anyway.

"For real, though, Doc." Romeo kept a strong arm wrapped around Mia's waist when he asked, "How bad is it?"

Cami expected Doc to check his head again, so she was confused when he touched his left arm. There was no mistaking the flicker of suffering in his eyes when his fingers pressed on a certain spot. Her stomach roiled in sympathy.

Or maybe it roiled because the life raft kept rising and falling. Rising and falling. Rising and—

Erp. The dry toast she'd had for breakfast in an attempt to sop up the remaining alcohol in her stomach grew into a giant loaf of bread.

"If I had to guess, and without an X-ray that's all I'm doing," Doc muttered. "I'd say my radius is fractured."

Cami's gaze locked onto his forearm and the tattoo she'd seen the night before. *For RL* was inked into his tan skin in black curly-cue lettering.

They'd been raiding her hotel minibar when she'd asked him what it meant. He'd waved away her question and changed the subject, letting her know without words that their little tryst didn't include a get-to-know-you session.

"The good news is," he continued, "that's not bad as far as breaks go. The bad news is, there's nothing to be done for it except to immobilize it and wait for it to heal. How about everyone else?" He glanced around the raft. "Any aches or pains?"

"No." Mia shook her head. The tears she'd cried had left her eyes red and puffy.

"Miraculously, no," Cami admitted when Doc leveled a look on her. "Although I lost my favorite pair of sunglasses. So that's a pain in my *ass*."

Doc ignored her sarcasm and hitched his chin toward Romeo. "You're favoring that right leg," he said to their pilot.

"Hit my knee on the console during the ditching." Romeo shrugged. "It's nothing."

"I'll be the judge of that." Doc scooted across the bottom of the raft and felt of Romeo's kneecap. Romeo sat stoically through the examination.

Once Doc resumed his spot at the other end of the watercraft, he declared, "It's not broken. Just bruised."

Cami blinked at Doc. "You can tell that just by feeling of it? I thought *Doc* was an honorary handle. Like the one that goes with Pepper or Dre. Like Bugs Bunny's *What's up, Doc?*"

"I'm a medic," Doc said, and she swiveled her chin toward Romeo when she heard him snort loudly.

"Don't let his misplaced humility fool you," Romeo told her. "Doc got his undergraduate from Yale and his medical degree from Johns Hopkins. He was three months away from finishing his residency when he up and joined the Navy. He's a better doctor than half the practicing physicians out there."

Cami eyed Doc askance.

"What?" His scratchy Kiefer Sutherland voice was full of umbrage. "You thought I was just some big, dumb cowboy?"

"You're far too quick with a comeback for me to ever mistake you for missing IQ points," she assured him. "This look of shock on my face"—she pointed to herself—"is me trying to figure out why you would go through so much schooling and however many more years of residency to quit right before you reached the finish line."

Doc shrugged. "Maybe I have a bad habit of not finishing

what I start. Ever consider that?"

The look he sent her transported her back to the night before. To him pressing her against the door of her hotel room and kissing her until her toes curled before pulling away and going to sit on the end of the bed to take off his shoes.

Oh, yes. His deep, slow kiss had certainly made promises he hadn't ended up keeping. But she didn't believe for one second that he was the kind of man generally inclined to leave a task undone.

Whatever had been the catalyst for him getting drunk as a skunk the night before was the same thing that had made him do an about-face in life years earlier. She'd bet her second favorite pair of sunglasses on it.

"I don't believe that for an instant," she told him.

"No?" He stared at her with a lazy self-assurance she knew was meant to throw her off his scent.

Carlotta hadn't dubbed her *The Bloodhound* for nothing. Cami was a dog with a bone when she knew she was right. "No." She shook her head decisively.

"So what *do* you believe?"

She didn't get the chance to respond because Mia's soft voice floated on the warm, salty breeze. "Oh my god! Look!"

They all turned in the direction the marine archeologist pointed, and Cami had to lift her hand to shade her eyes from the sun. "Is that what I think it is?" she whispered breathlessly.

The rise and fall of the life raft made it impossible to get a good look. But it appeared as if a white line of beach came into view one second, when they rode the crest of a wave, and then disappeared from view the next, when they slid down into the watery trough.

There it is. Now it's gone. There it is. Now it's—

Erp. The loaf of bread in her stomach grew soggy and gained ten pounds.

"Land," Romeo confirmed her suspicion.

Cami turned away from the white line of beach when she heard Doc digging into the first aid kit. He located the bottle of pain medication and threw two pills to the back of his throat.

"Whoa." She made a face. "Should you be doing that?"

"Doing what?" He frowned at her.

"Taking pain pills? Don't they thin your blood or something? What if you have a brain bleed from hitting your head?"

"Did you get your medical degree alongside your law degree?"

"No. But I've watched plenty of—"

"Don't tell me. Let me guess. *Grey's Anatomy?*" She could only blink because he'd nailed it. "Lord save me from people who think those shows bear any resemblance to real life." He showed her the bottle of Tylenol. "Acetaminophen is okay. It's things that contain ibuprofen, like Advil, that can increase bleeding."

"Oh." She nodded, satisfied. "I guess you're okay then."

"My medical degree thanks you for your vote of confidence." He smirked and then started rifling through the first aid kit again. After he found a roll of ACE bandage, he slammed shut the lid and turned his attention to Romeo. "What is it?" He hitched his stubbled chin toward the glimmering strip of land. "*Where* is it? You got any idea?"

"Not a clue." Romeo shook his head. "I thought I caught a glimpse of it before we went down. It's not very big. My guess would be it's not much more than a sandbar. Probably doesn't even have a name, eh?"

"Still"—Doc unrolled the bandage—"I like the idea of staying put in one spot rather than drifting around at sea."

"You and me both. Especially since I have no idea if anyone heard my mayday."

Doc's hands stilled. "What do you mean?"

"I think whatever took out the tail section shorted the electrical system and the radio too. Everything went haywire for a bit, and then we lost power altogether."

"Shit."

"My thoughts exactly."

"But surely LT and the others on Wayfarer Island will alert the authorities once we don't arrive," Mia said. Her fare skin was already turning pink from the sun. Cami automatically dug into her purse for her travel-size bottle of SPF 30.

"Even olive-toned girls need protection from UV," Cami's mother had lectured her and Carlotta from a young age. *"And I know everyone wants a tan but get a spray one. The real thing only leads to wrinkles and cancer."*

By the time she and her sister had turned fourteen, they'd been on a strict skincare regimen.

As she sifted through the mound of water bottles in her purse, her hand landed not on the SPF, but on her cell phone.

What are the odds?

She thumbed on the device and sighed heavily when it showed zero bars. "Damn," she muttered. Then she shrugged. "Well, at least we can play Candy Crush until my battery runs out."

The toothpick made a slow journey from one side of Doc's mouth to the other. "Look at you, all Silver Linings Playbook."

"Comes with the territory," she joked. "Haven't you heard? Lawyers are perpetual optimists."

"The only thing I know about lawyers is how to tell them apart from jellyfish." When she cocked her head, he lifted a finger. "One is a boneless, poisonous blob, and the other is a form of sea life."

She rolled her eyes. "We've moved on to the lawyer

jokes, have we? Tell me, is this animosity you have for the legal profession personal or just a general disdain for people who interpret and argue the law?"

Something flickered across his face right before his expression blanked.

Hmm. Curious, indeed.

Dalton "Doc" Simmons was an enigma wrapped in a mystery covered in beard stubble. And there was nothing Cami liked more than putting together a puzzle. Especially a big, tall, golden one.

Except she could tell he'd chosen to treat her question as if it'd been rhetorical, so she dropped the subject and tossed the sunscreen to the marine archeologist. "You're going to want to put that on"—she pointed to her own nose—"before you burn to a crisp."

Mia glanced at the bottle and then offered Cami a smile so big and radiant, Cami found herself blinking stupidly at the woman.

Normally, Mia was sweetly pretty. But the instant she smiled, she became dazzlingly beautiful. Really, Cami almost gasped at the transformation.

"Thank you," Mia said in that strangely quiet voice of hers.

"No." Cami shook her head. "Thank *you*. For cleaning me up after the crash and for keeping me sane *while* we were crashing. Although, I don't think I'll ever be able to listen to John Denver again."

"I thought that was a dream." There was a line between Doc's eyebrows. "'Leaving on a Jet Plane,' was it?"

Since Cami wasn't all that hyped to know he'd heard just how *horrible* her singing voice was, she changed the subject. "Not sure my vote counts. But I third the motion that we head for dry land. Now's probably as good a time as any to tell you all I get seasick."

The look that slid over Doc's face said he thought she was a particular kind of idiot, dumb in ten different ways. "And you took a job representing guys who spend their lives on the ocean?"

"*I* wasn't supposed to be on the ocean. *I* was supposed to be filing paperwork and arguing your case on terra firma." She gave a haughty shake of her head that was ruined because her bun had slipped during the crash, hanging drunkenly off to one side, and the sudden jerk of her chin caused it to smack her in the ear.

She thought he was going to come back at her with something appropriately snarky. Then his lips—those lips she knew were devilishly talented even when he was sky high on giggle juice—curved into a smile. "You've got quite a mouth on you. Anyone ever tell you that?"

"My sister used to say if running off at the mouth counted as exercise, I'd be ninety pounds soaking wet."

"It would be a crying shame if you only weighed ninety pounds," he said lowly. Slowly.

When her belly flipped, she tried blaming it on seasickness.

"And on that note," Romeo intervened. "Let's head for land."

As gently as a man transporting a breakable and priceless treasure, he lifted Mia off his lap and placed her in the bottom of the raft. Then he unhooked the short oars that came strapped to the sides of the watercraft.

"Little help, eh?" He handed one of the oars to Mia, who was suddenly looking rather...aghast? Dismayed? *Or maybe she's still in shock*, Cami told herself.

"Fit it into that oarlock behind you." Romeo pointed to the black ring of plastic on the side of the life raft. When he bent to do the same with the other oar on the opposite side of the watercraft, Cami's eyes landed on the gun tucked into the back waistband of his wet jeans.

"What the hell?" Each of her syllables was clipped. "Why do you need a gun on a life raft?"

She knew the Deep Six Salvage guys were former military men with enough medals between them to sink the Staten Island Ferry. That much had come up during her brief research on them when she was deciding whether to take their case.

But the key word is former, she thought warily. *Why does he have a gun now?*

"Is *that* what you went back to the cockpit to get?" Doc asked Romeo.

"Yeah." Romeo had an oar in each hand, but he dropped one so he could dig in his front pockets. "Well, the Glock and these."

Three smashed granola bars appeared from his jeans. He tossed them into the bottom of the raft where the water bottles, the first aid kit, and the flare gun case already rested. A pair of wet leather flip-flops joined the growing pile of crap.

Romeo's jeans are like a clown car, Cami thought. *What's next?*

Nothing apparently, because he repositioned the oars and began rowing them toward what she hoped would be their salvation.

"Is there something you're not telling me?" Doc asked him.

When silence met Doc's question, Cami realized how eerily quiet the middle of the ocean was. There were no roads, so there was no traffic noise. No trees, so there was no rattle of leaves. No chirp of insects in the grass. No hum of electrical lines strung overhead.

Just wind and water and...nothing.

"I don't think what happened to the Otter was an

accident," Romeo finally said.

Doc stopped in the middle of fashioning himself a makeshift sling. "What makes you say that?"

"It doesn't make sense." Romeo shook his head. "A bird strike can cause damage to a tail section, but not so much that multiple systems fail. I think we were shot out of the sky. That, or someone planted an explosive device I didn't see when I did my inspection."

Fear clawed a path up Cami's throat. Every hair on her head stood on end.

An explosive device. Just like the one that killed Carlotta...

CHAPTER 7

12:04 PM...

*I**t is better to keep your mouth closed and let people think
you are a fool than to open it and remove all doubt."*

For a moment there, Mia had forgotten Mark Twain's
gold rule. She'd opened her mouth—and jumped into
Romeo's arms—and made a complete and total fool of
herself.

Oh! How she wished she could've been cool like Cami,
cracking jokes and passing out sunscreen. But no. She'd
turned into a puddle of snot and tears, proving herself to be
the biggest sniveling ninny on the planet.

The only excuse she had for her behavior was the sheer,
mind-numbing terror she'd felt

while watching the Otter slip beneath the waves with
Romeo still onboard.

It had been as if her soul had left her body and gone
down with him. Growing heavier and heavier as the seconds

ticked by until eventually, just like the plane, her soul had completely disappeared into the deep.

Her mind hadn't been able to comprehend the notion she'd never again see the man who quieted her busy thoughts with little more than a look. The man she could watch for sixty seconds and come up with six hundred things she liked about him. The man who'd entered her life out of nowhere and had come to mean so much to her.

When he'd crashed to the surface, gloriously alive, the harsh pendulum swing from the depths of despair to the heights of happiness had been too much. Her system had overloaded and she'd lost it.

To her utter shame and embarrassment, she'd just...*lost* it.

And in losing it, she'd lost all the ground she'd gained in her efforts to convince him she wasn't after anything from him but friendship.

From the corner of her eye, she watched the flex and bunch of his shoulder muscles as he rowed them toward the glimmering promise of land. She couldn't quite bring herself to look at him full-on just yet. As if her crying jag and the name-calling hadn't been bad enough, she'd gone and compounded her humiliation by clinging to him like a barnacle on the belly of a boat until, finally, he'd had to *physically* remove her from his person.

And the look on his face while doing it?

Sweet heavens, that was worst of all.

It'd been the same look he'd given her the day they flew through the storm. A look that matched his words. *"You're nothing I need, and I'm not anything you should want."*

Chagrin gave her cotton mouth, and she automatically reached for a bottle of water. She was about to twist off a cap when a thought occurred.

"I— Are we already rationing these?" She lifted the

bottle and looked around the raft. Three faces stared back at her blankly. She realized none of them knew the answer to that question, because none of them knew what lay in store.

She'd been right to say those on Wayfarer Island would raise the alarm and get the authorities out searching for them when they didn't arrive back home. But what everyone on the life raft had been thinking, and what no one had said aloud, was that it was a big ocean. *Huge.* And who knew how far off course they'd flown before having to ditch?

It could be days...a week?...longer?...before they were found.

It was Cami who finally spoke up. "I'm thirsty too. I say we crack the caps on a couple of these."

"I agree." Doc dipped his chin. "Let's hydrate." Then he added with a smirk, "Doctor's orders."

Mia twisted off the lid and tried not to gorge herself on the bottle's contents. The water was a balm to her parched throat. And bonus, it cooled her heated cheeks. But after two long draws, she made herself stop and offer what remained to Romeo.

He dropped an oar to take the water. The feel of his callused fingers brushing against hers made her stifle a gasp. She would *swear* electricity arced between them, and she was astounded he couldn't feel it too.

But he didn't so much as flinch. Apparently, the lightning bolts were all one-sided.

Continuing to avoid his gaze, she popped the top on Cami's sunscreen and quickly swiped lotion over her face, neck, and chest.

She would have *loved* to do her arms and legs too, but she didn't want to be greedy.

"Thanks again," she told the lawyer as she handed back the SPF. "You're a life-saver."

"Like I said"—Cami smiled as she tucked the sunscreen

into her purse—"just paying you back for John Denver. That was pretty genius."

"Wish I could take the credit, but that was all Romeo." Mia hooked her thumb over her shoulder at their fearless pilot and current boat motor. "Remember how I told you he flew us through that storm? The part I left out was that he hummed "Leaving on a Jet Plane" the whole time."

"Funny." Cami wrinkled her nose. "And sort of sadistic."

The corners of Mia's mouth tilted up at the memory. "That's what I thought too."

When she felt a tap on her shoulder, she turned to find Romeo holding the water bottle out to her. "You finish it off," he told her.

There was about an inch of liquid left in the bottom, but when she pressed her mouth to the opening, it wasn't the freshness of the water sliding down her throat that occupied her mind. It was knowing her lips were in the exact same place his had been only moments earlier.

It was the closest she would ever come to kissing him.

"You got a little—" He swiped at her nose, and she realized she hadn't rubbed in all the sunscreen.

"Thanks," she whispered, forcing herself to *finally* meet his gaze.

He winked. "What are friends for?"

Oh, god. He was trying to emphasize their friendship— and *only* their friendship.

Heaven help her, she needed to assure him that, despite her tears and her brief stint playing the role of his second skin, she wasn't delusional enough to think anything had changed between them. That his *feelings* had changed.

Opening her mouth to clear the air, she snapped it shut when Doc asked, "So who would want to kill us?" A quick glance in his direction showed he'd fashioned himself a nice-looking sling with the ACE bandage.

"Take your pick." Romeo snorted as he continued to row steadily. "That Syrian general whose compound we firebombed? Family and friends of those Somali pirates we took out off the Horn of Africa during Operation Enduring Freedom? The brother of that AQAP terrorist in Yemen who—"

"Point taken." Doc waved his hand. "We have enemies coming out of our asses."

"I should've done a more thorough inspection," Romeo lamented, a muscle ticking in his jaw. "I think maybe I was distracted at the airport. If I missed something—"

"Stop." Mia lifted her hand. "Stop right there." She pointed at his nose. "The *only* reason we're alive is because of you."

It looked like he wanted to argue, but Doc seconded Mia's take. "She's right. I mean, I was out for the actual ditching. But I know the only reason I'm walking away from it is because of you. Or..." He looked around. "*Floating* away from it, as the case may be."

Once again, Romeo opened his mouth to object, and once again Doc cut him off by turning to Cami and frowning. "What's with you?" he asked her.

The lawyer shook her head and stretched her lips into what might have looked like a smile to someone who was nearly blind. "What do you mean?"

"You're wearing a face like one of those cultural orientation studies," Doc said. When Cami's eyebrow cocked in confusion, he explained, "You know, when researchers try to understand the base emotion that keeps a particular people compliant and in their place in a society. Is it fear, shame, or guilt? Right now, you're projecting all three."

Mia watched the lawyer's throat work over a hard swallow. "I...uh...I guess I should tell you guys that my sister, the one who died in a plane crash last year?" Cami looked at Mia, her face so full of trepidation that Mia automatically gave her a sympathetic smile and nodded for her to continue. "Her plane was taken out by a bomb."

Apprehension rippled up Mia's spine, but it was Doc who spoke. Rather condescendingly, if you asked Mia.

"Wait a second. Let me get this straight. Your sister's plane was bombed out of the sky last year. Our plane was bombed out of the sky twenty minutes ago. And you're just now—"

"We don't *know* it was a bomb that brought us down," Cami interrupted. "Romeo just said he's only speculating."

"I'd trust Romeo's speculations over a lawyer's facts from now until the cows come home."

Cami scowled. "What *is* your problem with lawyers? I mean, really?"

"Apart from them protecting the guilty, charging exorbitant fees, and that a lot of them go on to become two-faced politicians?"

"I'm a *property* lawyer, not a defense attorney," Cami countered, her cheeks going red. "But just so you know, even defense attorneys don't *protect the guilty*, as you say. They argue the *law*. The *law* is there to protect *all* of us from frivolous prosecution. If a prosecutor doesn't have the evidence to convict, then the defendant should go free, and that's just a good judicial system at work." Her words started out sharp and got sharper as she went on. "And I'll have you know I have *zero* aspirations to run for office. Like you, I have a natural aversion to politicians."

"I notice you left out the exorbitant fees," Doc muttered.

"Those are set by my firm!"

"Okay, kids," Romeo interjected. "We have wandered into counterproductive territory here. Let's all be quiet so Cami can explain about her sister." His face softened as he added, "I'm sorry for your loss, by the way."

That was all it took to douse the fire of Cami's indignation. Her shoulders drooped. She massaged her temples. "My father's name is Anthony D'Angelo, otherwise known as Big Tony D. He worked for the Gambino family."

"Ha!" Doc tossed back his head and laughed. But there was no humor in it. "Oh, this is rich." Lowering his chin, he settled a penetrating look on Romeo. "What the hell did LT get us into?"

Mia glanced from Doc to Romeo to Cami. Their knowing expressions meant she was the only one not in the loop. "I...I'm a little lost," she confessed. "Should I recognize those names?"

"The Gambino Crime Family is one of the original Five Families of New York," Cami explained. "Surely you've heard of them."

Mia's brain buzzed with scenes from every mob movie she'd ever seen. "Are we talking *I'm gonna make him an offer he can't refuse* original Five Families? The *funny how? Funny like a clown? Do I amuse you?* original Five Families?"

Romeo snorted. "You've been hanging out with Bran too much."

"No." She shook her head. "It was my grandmother who turned me on to *The Godfather* and *Goodfellas*. Although, *Casino* was her favorite." She wrinkled her nose. "And I always thought it was over-long and tedious. The acting was good, though. You can't fault the actors."

A strange look passed over Romeo's face.

"What?" She tilted her head.

"You're just one surprise after another," he told her.

"Did you think all I cared about was history and artifacts?" She frowned.

He didn't answer, but the look he sent her said he was trying to see inside her head. *Just shoot me now if he can,* she thought.

Since what she was thinking, what she was *always* thinking, was that she wished she could be somebody else. Anybody else. Because maybe if she was somebody else, somebody without an awful, shameful past, somebody who'd been born brave and beautiful, she could be the kind of woman he needed.

The truth was, she agreed with the first part of his statement. She *wasn't* anything he needed—she wasn't anything *anyone* needed. But that second part? The part where he said he wasn't anything she should want?

He was dead wrong about *that*.

She'd never wanted someone so much in her life.

Shifting uncomfortably under his intense gaze, she was glad when Cami cut in with, "The movies don't do the reality of the life justice. And yes." Cami looked directly at Mia. "I'm talking *those* Five Families."

"Dear god." Mia blinked myopically. She was sitting in a life raft with an actual, factual mob princess.

Granny Susan would be thrilled!

Doc was a little more flamboyant with his interjection. "Jesus hopscotching Christ. We hired you to *help* us, not get us killed."

"I don't think the plane going down had anything to do with me," Cami reiterated, and Mia could tell the lawyer was struggling to keep her tone even. "There'd be no reason for someone to try to kill me."

"I've known you less than twenty-four hours, and I can assure you, *that's* debatable."

"Oh!" Cami balled up her fists and Mia thought for sure Doc was going to come away with two black eyes. "I have been nothing but *nice* to you, you insufferable..." Mia could tell Cami was searching for the right word and was a little surprised when the lawyer settled on, "Butthead! I could've had hotel security haul your drunk ass out of my room, but no! I covered you with a blanket and let you sleep it off!"

Doc opened his mouth, but Mia stopped him from saying anything by quietly calling his name. He turned toward her, his brow heavily furrowed. "Are you sure you're feeling okay?" she asked him.

"Hell, no," he grumbled. "I feel like something that came out of a slow cooker. Why?"

She knew what it was to be mercilessly harangued. Her mother had made a sport of exactly that. Which was why she couldn't sit idly by while someone else was dragged over the coals. Even if the person doing the dragging was a man she liked and respected.

Because she liked and respected Doc, she made sure her expression was compassionate even though her words held an intentional bite of sarcasm. "Because your mother may love you but everyone else in this raft thinks you're being a jerk right now. That's not like you."

That brought Doc up short. Romeo too if the bark of laugher he quickly cut off and turned into a cough was anything to go by.

For a full three seconds, Doc blinked at her. Finally, he said, "I think that's the first time I've ever heard you say a cross word to anyone."

"I'm not *cross* with you," she assured him. "I'm just pointing out that you're basically being the human equivalent of a gray sprinkle on a rainbow cupcake, and I wanted to make sure that isn't because you're hurt worse than you're letting on."

"Couldn't have said it better myself," Romeo agreed.

Doc sent Romeo a dirty look before muttering, "I'm hurt. But I'm going to be okay."

"Good." Mia gave him a wide smile. "Then there's no reason why you can't be quiet while Cami finishes telling us why she's sure our plane going down didn't have anything to do with her."

When Doc opened his mouth, Romeo jerked one of the oars out of the oarlock and wielded it like a baseball bat. "The lady did not mince her words, Doc," he warned, having joined Mia in her attempt to use a little humor to turn down the temperature inside the life raft.

"It's not fair that you have the gun *and* the oars." Doc's face was the picture of discontent. But the vehemence had disappeared from his tone. "Come on." He wiggled his fingers. "Hand over the Glock."

"*No hablo ingles, Señor Weaponless*," Romeo countered with a smirk before adding, "But you're more than welcome to come up here and take over rowing."

"I'm wounded." Doc's reply was overly petulant.

"That's a convenient excuse." Romeo snapped the oar back into the round circle of plastic, and then asked Cami, "Did I hear you right? Did you say your father *worked* for the Gambino Crime Family? As in, past tense?"

Cami nodded. "Dad's in prison. He got caught up in an FBI sting involving a check kiting scheme about eighteen months ago. When he was first arrested, someone put a bug in Lorenzo Mannino's ear that Dad was looking to cut a deal with the Feds by informing on the Family. Lorenzo is the current head of the operation." Cami looked at Mia as she imparted this last bit.

"Anyway," she went on, "when my dad was released on bail, Lorenzo had one of his goons plant a bomb on a chartered flight Dad was supposed to take to Philly to meet with one of his lawyers. You know"—she hitched a shoulder, and Mia could tell she was working hard to give them the facts without showing her emotions on the subject—"take out the rat before he had a chance to squeak."

Cami claimed the movies didn't do the life justice, but

listening to her talk reminded Mia of the plot of a Martin Scorsese film.

"The morning of Dad's flight, he came down with a wicked case of the flu. But the plane had already been paid for, so my sister decided to take it to do some shopping. Carlotta loved the Sophie Carlson boutique just off Rittenhouse Square." Cami shook her head as if she'd gotten off track. But Mia suspected it was more because the instant the lawyer said her sister's name, her eyes grew misty.

"To make a long, awful story short," Cami continued despite her voice having gone hoarse, "the bomb meant to take out my dad took out my sister. And turns out, that suited Lorenzo just fine. Twelve hours after the plane went down, a letter arrived at my parents' house telling Mom and Dad they still had one daughter left alive, and if they wanted her...*me*... to stay that way, Dad would do well to keep his mouth shut."

"Which he has," Romeo assumed.

"Which he has," Cami affirmed, looking a little sick at heart. "So like I said, if it *was* a bomb that took out the plane, I don't think *I* was the target. There'd be no reason. My father is keeping up his end of the bargain."

"You don't *think* but you don't *know* for sure," Doc declared.

Cami tossed her hands in the air and the two began to bicker. But Mia stopped listening. Instead, she gathered her courage and turned to Romeo.

Now, while Doc and Cami were distracted with each other, was the perfect time for her to explain her earlier behavior. To apologize for the name-calling and assure him she suffered no misconceptions when it came to what he felt for her or what she could expect from him.

"We're going to be okay," he promised before she could get a word out. "It might take time, but someone *will* find us. You can go ahead and start breathing again."

Of course he'd noticed she was holding her breath.

Although he was wrong about *why* she was doing it.

She nodded. Or at least she meant to. She was too distracted by his mouth, which was curved into a soft smile that made his dimples pop, to know if she actually did it.

"I'm not worried about that," she assured him. "I mean, not *really*. I know no one on Wayfarer Island will sleep until we're found. But Romeo, I should apol—"

"I really wish you'd go back to calling me Spiro," he cut her off, and his words were so unexpected, her chin flew back.

She'd taken to calling him Spiro the night she first learned they shared a love for the Night Angels series. The first night they'd "slept together." But the next day he'd said that thing about her being nothing he needed and him being nothing she should want, and she'd gone back to using his nickname.

Spiro had suddenly felt too...intimate.

"Why?" Her voice was so low she was surprised he heard her.

"I'm not sure." His expression turned contemplative. "I guess because I like it." When she blinked in confusion, he was quick to add, "Like I told you, for the longest time I thought I hated that name. Thought it was a relic from a past I hoped to forget. But when you use it..." He shrugged. "I don't know. It feels like me in a way it hasn't in a hella long time." He made a face. "That probably doesn't make any sense."

"It doesn't have to." Her heart beat harder than when they'd been falling out of the sky. "If it's what you want, I'll do it."

She realized she'd said too much when his gaze laser focused on her face.

"I just mean, we're friends, right?" she was quick to

add. "If you want me to call you Spiro, then I will."

He opened his mouth, but Cami interrupted anything he might have said.

"Look, the truth is we don't know *what* happened. Maybe it was the mob coming after me. Maybe it was somebody who has a beef with you two." The lawyer flipped a finger between Doc and Romeo. "Or..." She let that one word dangle while her gaze alighted on Mia.

"I don't *think* anyone would want to kill me." Mia shook her head, confounded by the mere notion. She'd never stayed anywhere long enough, or gotten close enough to anyone, to make an enemy of them. "I mean, my mother hates my guts and always has. But if she wanted to do me in, she probably would've tried long before now."

"Your mother hates your guts?" Cami blinked as if the concept was foreign, and Mia supposed to most people it was.

She faked tired indifference and waved her hand. "Long story for another time."

"Oh-kay," Cami said slowly, and then she regained her original train of thought. "My point is, the *who* or *what* or *why* of the crash doesn't matter right now. What matters right now is that we focus on what needs to be done to make sure we survive until rescued." She glanced pointedly at Romeo. "And in the name of cooperation and survival, would you like me to take over for you? I'm slightly less proficient at rowing than I am at particle physics, but I'd be happy to give it the old college try."

Mia could see Romeo bite the inside of his cheek to keep from laughing at the lawyer's suggestion. Imagine the High King of Chivalry allowing a lady to do manual labor when he was whole and healthy enough to do it on his own.

For all of Romeo's modern know-how—he was the one everyone turned to when technology failed them—he was sweetly old-school. Mia had no doubt if capes were still in fashion, he'd be the first to remove his and lay it over a mud puddle so passing ladies didn't have to dirty their shoes.

"Thanks for the offer," he told Cami. "But all I need you to do is sit back and relax. I'll have us to the sandbar in half an hour. Forty-five minutes tops."

Cami's expression turned grim. "I was hoping to use the exercise as a distraction from seasickness." She pressed a hand to her stomach. "I think I might hurl, and I don't feel like I know any of you well enough to revisit my breakfast in front of you."

"Go on and blow chunks if it'll make you feel better," Doc told her. "Believe me, we've all seen worse. Besides, you might chum the waters and attract some fish for us to catch. *Now* who's being all Silver Linings Playbook, huh?" He looked inordinately pleased with himself, obviously thinking he'd made up for being a butthole earlier.

"I don't know." Romeo shook his head. "Given our luck today, she might attract a shark instead."

Cami's complexion had been looking a little green. But at mention of the S-word, it turned positively gray. "Are there really sharks around here?"

"Pretty sure there are sharks in every ocean on the planet," Doc said unhelpfully.

"But, like, nurse sharks and reef sharks, right?" Cami insisted. "The cute cuddly ones that I've seen divers petting on the Discovery Channel. No great whites, right?"

When no one answered her, she turned desperate eyes on Mia.

Mia winced when she couldn't give Cami the answer the lawyer so obviously wanted to hear. "Unfortunately, there are great whites around here."

"Fuck." As soon as the word left Cami's lips, she looked mortified. "Sorry. Despite our less-than-ideal circumstances,

I'm still your lawyer. I should conduct myself professionally. If it pleases the court, I would like to retract that fuck."

Mia remembered how intimidated she'd been the first time she'd met the men of Deep Six Salvage. And that'd been a normal day with no drunken shenanigans from the night before, no confused identities, and no plane crashes. All things considered, Cami was keeping it together pretty well.

Since Mia hadn't been able to reassure the poor woman there weren't any man-eating sharks in the vicinity, she thought the least she could do was reassure her that cursing was considered a sport on Wayfarer Island.

"In the parlance of your people," she told Cami, hoping a little humor might put the woman at ease, "consider it stricken from the record. But just so you know, these two"—she wagged a finger between Doc and Romeo—"curse like the sailors they are. And I'm from Chicago where the F-bomb is said more frequently than 'Go Cubs.' Feel free to let 'er rip as much as you like. I can assure you, you won't offend any of us."

"Oh, thank fuck." Cami's shoulders relaxed. "Because I have to admit, a plane crash followed by a row through shark-infested waters certainly qualifies for a fuck-ton of fucks in my fuckin' book."

Doc snorted and praised, "Thatta girl."

Cami made a face before glancing tentatively over the side of the raft at the waves lapping against the rubber. Mia figured the lawyer was picturing the shark from *JAWS* rising out of the deep.

A second later, her hunch was confirmed when Cami said, "Now I know how Chief Brody felt when he said *'We're gonna need a bigger boat.'* Are *all* life rafts this small?"

Mia thought Romeo opened his mouth to answer the lawyer. But a second later, she realized her mistake when he whispered, "Oh, shit."

His face had leeched of color and his dark eyes were fixed on a point over her shoulder. She didn't want to, but she couldn't help craning her head around to see what'd caught his attention.

Her lungs froze in her chest when she saw another rogue wave headed their way.

Only this one was ten times bigger than the one that'd briefly lifted the Otter while they were trying to make their escape.

"Dear god," she breathed, goose bumps erupting up the length of her arms despite the heat of the sun beaming down. It was like her brain was having trouble fathoming the enormity of the rogue wave. And in its efforts to compute, it didn't allow her to rip her gaze away from the malevolent wall of water barreling toward them.

"Any way we can avoid that?" she heard Doc ask.

"Nope," was Romeo's one word reply before he quickly added, "Hurry! Secure everything you can!"

That was all the impetus Mia needed to drag her terrified eyes away from the rogue breaker. She quickly began stuffing water bottles down her shirt. The granola bars made their way inside her blouse too. But when she went to try to find some room for Romeo's flip-flops, he told her, "Forget them." And she watched as he wrenched the oars from the oarlocks and secured them back inside the raft.

Cami had looped the strap of her purse over her head and shoulder and grabbed the flare gun case. Doc had latched onto the first aid kit with his good hand and was in the process of trying to find a way to hold onto it as well as the safety rope lining the inside life raft.

"Here," Cami said. "Let me help."

The lawyer scooted next to Doc. With one hand, she held onto the flare gun case and the safety rope. She used her other hand to reach across Doc's body and latch onto the rope beside him, effectively making herself a human seat belt.

"Come here," Romeo commanded Mia, hitching his chin that she should join him.

She didn't hesitate.

Scooting between his legs, she pressed her back flat against the warm wall of his chest. He snaked one arm around her waist and twisted the other around the safety rope.

She followed suit, grabbing the nylon cord on each side of her and trying not to pass out as her vision tunneled down to a pinpoint of light.

"Breathe, *cariña*." Romeo's breath was warm in her ear. "We'll make it. You just have to hang on."

And just like that, her heart settled from a rapid, erratic flutter to a fast, but steady, beat. It was amazing how he could do that, comfort her and calm her with just a few words.

When she sucked in a breath, her visual field broadened. Although she wasn't so sure that was a good thing, because the only thing to meet her wide eyes was the wave looming above them.

She thought it should roar or moan or *something*. But it was strangely silent as it finally reached them and gently tipped the end of the life raft skyward.

Maybe she was imagining things, but it felt like the air around them suddenly cooled by ten degrees. It was like when the sun moved behind a cloud, except there wasn't a white puff of cumulus in the sky. And she would swear the scent of sea life and salt water grew stronger as the wave bore them higher.

Higher.

Higher still.

From the corner of her eye, she saw the sandbar come into crystal clear focus. But she didn't have time to give it a good look because, suddenly, they rode the crest of the wave. The life raft seemed to teeter-totter for a few seconds. Enough time for Mia to lock eyes with Cami and see the fear in the lawyer's stare that she knew was reflected in her own.

Then they were falling.

That was really the only word for it.

It was like that ride at the state fair that jacked you up high in the sky before letting you freefall into nothing. The only difference was that there was a gradual slowing at the end of the fair ride, and Mia knew the only thing waiting to stop their decent here was the hard, unforgiving surface of the sea.

It felt like it took them an eternity to slip down the back side of the giant wave. But it could only have been a handful of seconds.

Somewhere in the middle, her stomach had floated up into her throat. But when they finally found the trough at the bottom of the wall of water, it thudded back into place.

Her stomach and everything else in the boat.

Seriously, she'd always thought the phrase *teeth-rattling* was figurative. But she literally felt her molars crash together and then jostle around in her gums when the life raft slammed into the ocean.

Cami squealed.

Romeo grunted when Mia's butt inadvertently landed atop his dangly bits.

And Doc cursed as the first aid kit fell from his grip, bounced in the bottom of the raft, and then went sailing overboard.

Mia didn't think.

In fact, she was working on pure instinct when she let go of the safety rope and lunged for the escaped equipment. Two water bottles fell from the top of her shirt when she dove an arm into the drink, barely catching the handle on the first aid kit before it disappeared into the deep.

She wasn't prepared for how heavy it was. She squeaked her alarm as it tried to wrench her over the side of the raft. But a second later, she felt Romeo's big, strong hand catch the waistband of her shorts.

In a flash, she and the first aid kit were dragged back into the watercraft.

It was only after she brushed her hair behind her ear with a shaky hand that she realized what a colossally *stupid* move it'd been to go after the medical supplies.

She expected Romeo to say something to that affect, but he only touched the scratch on her chin, looked deep into her eyes, and asked, "You okay?"

Her voice was a harsh rasp when she nodded. "I think so."

"Good catch," he told her, but she thought she detected a slight tremor in his voice. He wasn't as unmoved by the last twenty seconds as he was trying to pretend.

"You too," she assured him, and watched his Adam's apple travel up the length of his tanned throat.

After blowing out a deep breath, he turned and asked the other two, "You both okay?"

"Define okay," Doc grumbled as Cami carefully let go of the safety rope, dropped the flare gun case, and once again situated herself on the side of the raft. Before Romeo could answer, Doc added, "Let's get to that damned island before another one of those suckers rolls by."

"My thoughts exactly." Romeo dipped his chin, grabbing the oars and resuming his position at the front of the boat.

Mia realized just how shot her nerves truly were when she began emptying her shirt. No matter how hard she tried, she couldn't contain the tremor in her hands.

Cami must have been feeling the same way, because she blew out a deep breath and said, "Okay. I was serious about needing a distraction. Only now I need a distraction from thoughts of enormous, man-killing waves as much as I need a distraction from thoughts of giant, toothy sharks and from the toast that's sitting in the bottom of my stomach like a soggy loaf of...*erp*." Her hand jumped up to cover her mouth.

Mia waited for Cami to hang her head over the side of the boat. But after a second or two, the lawyer lowered her hand and took a deep breath.

"Let's get to know each other," she said. "I'll go first. I was born and raised on Staten Island. My favorite color is green. I enjoy a good Old Fashioned. My mom forced me to take piano lessons when I was a kid even though what I *really* wanted was to become a ventriloquist. My sister broke this tooth"—she tapped one of her front teeth—"when she threw a rock at me in middle school because I told Jimmy Russo she liked him. So now I have a crown. I got my undergrad in political science from NYU and—"

"Aha!" Doc pointed at her nose, and Mia was gratified to hear his voice was a bit scratchier than usual, proof that hers weren't the only nerves that'd come a little unraveled.

They said bad luck came in threes. So far, they'd survived a plane crash and a rogue wave. She didn't even want to *think* what their third trial might look like. And she was glad Cami had offered up a distraction.

"I *knew* it!" Doc added. "You *do* have political aspirations."

"I *did* have them," Cami corrected with a lift of her chin. A chin that was a little wobbly. "And then I volunteered one summer for a councilwoman and realized I'll never have what it takes to make it in politics. I'm not bloodthirsty enough. And that's when I applied to law school."

"I bet your dad was disappointed you switched gears," Doc speculated. "Given what he was involved in, I'm sure he'd have liked nothing better than to have a New York politician in his pocket."

Cami bristled at his assumption. "I wouldn't know if he was disappointed or not. I haven't had anything to do with him since I turned twenty and found out where he got the money for my ballet lessons. And believe me, I have the student loan debt to prove that."

Mia watched Doc's eyebrows arch. Cami's admission obviously surprised him. Although Mia couldn't say *she* was all that shocked. In the little time she'd known the lawyer, she'd gotten the impression Cami had a strict moral and ethical code.

"Anyway," Cami continued, "after law school, I was offered a position at Leeman and Lester in Miami. It was there I began to specialize in property conflicts, especially disputes between individuals and state and federal governments." Without missing a beat, she turned to Doc. "That's me in a nutshell. What about you? What's your story?"

"Not much to tell." Doc's expression went instantly enigmatic. "Grew up in Montana. Won a scholarship to Yale. Then the Navy. And now I'm here."

Cami's mouth flattened. "There you go being all succinct again. I'm having a flashback to this morning's apology letter."

Doc gave a grunt. Which Mia had learned was typical of a man when he didn't have anything else he wanted to say.

Cami sighed, having come to the same conclusion. She turned to Romeo and asked, "And you?"

He lifted one shoulder. "West Coast kid here. Did a stint with the Mexican Mafia in high school until I ran into trouble. Jumped out of the gang and joined the Navy. And like Doc"—he hitched his chin toward the opposite end of the life raft—"now I'm here."

Cami blinked. "I swear, you two are more disappointing than an unsalted pretzel. Is this whole closed-mouthed schtick a holdover from your time in special operations? Like, you're so used to things being top secret that now you don't know how to talk about yourselves?"

When neither man bothered to respond, she sighed again and focused her gaze on Mia. "Come on. Surely *you* can give me some good stuff. Like, why did you decide on marine archeology? Who was your first boyfriend? If there was one thing you could go back and redo, what would it be?"

Mia had the oddest urge to burst forth with nervous laughter. That last question? Talk about a doozy. No *way* was she answering *that*.

"Um." She cleared her throat. "Like I said, I'm from Chicago. My brother and I were mostly raised by my grandmother."

She thought back to what Cami had shared about herself and took her cue from that. "My favorite color is blue. My adult beverage of choice is a gin and tonic. I got my undergraduate degree and my graduate degree from the University of Chicago. I got into marine archeology because my grandmother enrolled me in a diving camp one summer when I was ten, and at the end of the camp we got to dive down on a wreck at the bottom of Lake Michigan. I was immediately hooked. It was just so peaceful and calm under the water. So different from the hustle and bustle of the city."

She squinted her eyes and looked into the middle distance. "My first boyfriend was Patrick Marshal. He kissed me on the bridge over the duck pond in Lincoln Park, and then he broke up with me the next day because he liked Felicity Harper better."

She stopped there, hoping she'd shared enough that Cami would forget about the last question she'd asked.

"See?" Cami glanced back and forth between Doc and Romeo. "Now *that's* how it's done. Also," she added, looking directly at Mia, "Patrick Marshal was an asshat. You're better off without him."

Mia let loose with a covert sigh of relief. Then she grimaced. "You have no idea. Last I heard, he was living in his parents' basement and spending most of his days trolling St. Louis Cardinals fans online."

Cami's expression was commiserating. "See? I knew it. You dodged a bullet and then traded up." She gave Mia a nudge with her elbow and then hitched her chin toward Romeo.

Mia couldn't tell if her heart fluttered or stopped altogether. She felt more alarmed than when they'd been crashing or riding the crest of a monster wave. And how bonkers was *that*? "What do you mean?" she asked carefully.

Cami's eyebrows drew together. "Aren't you two together?"

"*No*," she blurted, completely appalled she'd given the lawyer that impression.

No wonder Romeo was wearing that look when he lifted me off his lap. My behavior was even more blatant than I thought!

"Romeo and I are just friends," she assured the lawyer, wondering how many times in a twenty-four-hour period she'd be forced to repeat that phrase. "And colleagues. And fans of P.J. Warren's Night Angels series. But that's all."

It was pretty thin as far as explanations went, but it was the best she could come up with on the fly.

"Huh." Cami blinked. "Guess I read the room wrong. Sorry about that."

"No worries." Mia tried to sound unbothered.

She turned to Romeo to make light of things. But for the life of her, she forgot what she wanted to say the instant her eyes clashed with his.

She couldn't read his expression, but she would *swear* the air around them vibrated.

Doc, god love him, saved her from further humiliation by asking Cami, "Tell me the truth, Counselor. And don't give me any of that *not mixing business with pleasure* nonsense. Is the reason you won't sleep with me now that we're sober because you find my keen intellect and masculine prowess intimidating?"

"Not mixing business with pleasure isn't nonsense." Cami flattened her mouth at him. "But on top of that, I won't sleep with you now because I know you're arrogant and sarcastic and—"

"Yes?" Doc interrupted. "When do we get to the bad stuff?"

Cami turned an exasperated expression on Romeo while pointing toward Doc. "What is *with* this guy?"

"How much time do you have?" Romeo made a face. "Because that would require a very, *very* long answer."

"Hey!" Doc objected. "Whatever happened to bros before—"

"Don't say it!" Cami pinned Doc with a killing look. "I don't care if you have a head injury. I swear on all that's holy, if you say it, I'm going to slap you so hard, you won't land until next week."

"Sheesh." Doc feigned affront. "I was going to say bros before *broads*. But maybe you prefer dicks before chicks? Pals before gals? I didn't realize you were so sensitive."

"Nice save," Cami scoffed. "And just so you know, the only thing I'm sensitive to is the fact that you're—"

Again, Mia stopped listening and tentatively turned to Romeo.

He rolled his eyes at Doc and Cami, as if to say, *"Can you believe those two?"* Aloud he said, "We're almost there." He motioned with his chin over his shoulder.

She let her eyes slide past him to the gleaming stretch of white sand and the long line of palm trees swaying in the wind. It wasn't much as far as a home away from home went, but it was so much better than drifting with the current in a life raft the size of a sectional sofa.

When she returned her gaze to his face, he gave her another friendly wink, and no matter how hard she looked—and she looked *hard*—she couldn't see any of the wary trepidation that'd been in his eyes earlier.

It worked, she told herself. *He believed what I said to Cami. I didn't ruin everything after all.*

She grabbed hold of that certainty and clung to it with the tenacity of a lamprey on a sturgeon.

CHAPTER 8

12:49 PM...

Fuckin'-A, man," Carter snarled, powering the speedboat to a stop and letting the big engines idle for a moment before killing them. "Where the hell *is* it?"

As quick as the speedboat was, the amphibious aircraft had been quicker.

After the explosives Kenny had wired to the plane only shredded the tail section instead of igniting the fuel tanks and blowing the whole thing from the sky, they'd lost sight of the wounded aircraft when it disappeared over the horizon. The only thing they'd had to follow was the smoke trail. But that had long since disappeared, leaving nothing to look at but undulating ocean waves as far as the eye could see.

"Ya think they didn't crash after all? Think maybe they were able to make it back to Key West?" Robby braced his legs wide on the deck of the speedboat as he lifted a set of high-powered binoculars to his eyes, scanning their surroundings.

The heat of the midday sun was intense as it reflected off the water. All the same, a chill stole up Carter's spine. If Robby was right, if Mia and company had made it back to Key West, then they'd know someone had tried to end them.

I mean, I'm no forensics expert, but I'm pretty sure they'll be able to tell the plane's tail section was obliterated by an explosive.

Which, inevitably, meant there would be questions. Question would lead to the authorities being notified. The authorities being notified would lead to an investigation.

Shit!

The whole point of this plan was so that everyone would think the plane had fallen victim to an unexplained crash. That it'd simply disappeared over the ocean like so many small aircraft did. That all onboard had been lost, never to be seen again.

Carter had spent *weeks* working out the logistics with Robby and Kenny. The three of them had been best friends since the sixth grade. As such, they'd been through a lot of firsts together. First time getting drunk, first time getting high, first time getting laid—Jessica Jones had let them take turns for twenty bucks a pop. It'd just made sense that when Carter needed to kill someone for the first time, he'd gone to Kenny and Robby for help.

Kenny had jumped at the idea. Thanks to the summers he'd spent running around in the woods with his uncle Doyle and his uncle Doyle's militia buddies, Kenny had been preparing for something like this his whole life.

Robby? He'd taken some convincing. Of course, it had helped that there was a payday involved, because Robby had a bit of a gambling problem, and he owed a pretty penny to a loan shark in Kenwood.

Funny how quickly a man puts aside his morals when

he's being threatened with a pair of broken kneecaps.

In the end, they'd all been onboard and, just like always, when the three of them put their heads together, good things happened. Case in point: The Plan.

And it'd been a good plan too, *damnit!* A *great* one. Carter had been sure they'd run through all the contingencies.

But apparently not.

Slapping the steering wheel so he wouldn't slap Kenny, he demanded, "I thought you were sure that blast was going to take them out. What the hell happened?" He nudged the remote-control unit Kenny had used to set off the initial charge on the plane's electrical systems and the subsequent charge next to the fuel tanks.

"Who the hell knows, man?" Kenny huffed. "Maybe one of the blasting caps didn't blow. Or maybe a wire came loose during takeoff. Shit happens."

Robby dropped the binoculars from his face to ask Kenny, "Where'd you say your uncle got that remote detonator again?"

"Beats me. Ya know Doyle." Kenny grinned. Since the man had a pronounced brow ridge, making him look more Neanderthal than Homo sapien, a smile never looked quite right on his face. And given the trouble they were in, Carter wasn't sure how Kenny could even *manage* one. "Thirty years in the Michigan Militia means Doyle's gotta whole lotta shit you wouldn't believe, bought out of the backs of vans and picked up at gun shows. When I went to get this from him"—Kenny toed the remote, which he'd dropped into the bottom of the boat after setting off the explosions—"he told me he and his buddies were trying to do a deal with some Russians for fifty Kalashnikovs."

Robby blinked and shook his head, his wispy blond hair tousled around his face by the breeze. "'Merica. Land of the free to buy weapons of war and home of the brave enough to head out into the woods and play soldier-boy with a bunch of drunk rednecks. Don't you just love her?"

"Hey! That's my uncle you're talking about!" Kenny blustered before chuckling. "But you're right. Doyle is crazy on a cracker."

"Don't you mean a crazy cracker?" Robby winked.

"Ha!" Kenny nodded. "Good one."

"Gentlemen, please." Carter held onto his patience by a thread as he raked a hand through his auburn hair. "Ask yourselves if now is the time for humor."

"Course it is." Kenny shrugged one over-inflated shoulder. He'd gotten his bulk thanks to 'roids and the three hours a day he spent in the gym. "Stop worrying. They may not have exploded in midair like we wanted, but they're down somewhere. They gotta be. You saw how much smoke there was. You saw the fuel pouring out of the bird. You saw how those wings were flapping."

"At the very least," Robby shrugged, "the explosion Kenny set to short out the radio must've worked. We haven't heard them put out a mayday."

At mention of the lack of a mayday call, all three of them glanced at the two radios on the speedboat. One was tuned to Air Traffic Control in Key West. The other was dialed into the Marine Emergency station. Both devices buzzed and hummed with voices, but there was no hint that anyone was in trouble.

"True," Carter muttered. "That's one thing that went right."

"Hey!" Kenny objected. "The only thing that went *wrong* was that the fuel tanks didn't blow. But we're still okay. 'Cause ain't no way they didn't hafta ditch."

Again, a cold chill snuck up Carter's spine. "If they ditched, there could be survivors."

"Which means we gotta find 'em and finish what we

started." Kenny shrugged. "Simple as that."

Simple. Right. As simple as finding a needle in a haystack.

"You have a *plan* for finding them?" Carter demanded.

"They gotta be 'round here somewhere." Kenny had a true South Chicago accent. He was always cutting off consonants and smashing words together. "This was the direction they were headed, and they were having a helluva time staying in the air. They can't be far. I'd bet my right hand on it."

"You sure you don't want to bet your *left* hand?" Robby snickered, his sorry excuse for a mustache twitching. He'd been trying—and failing—to grow the damned thing since they were sixteen. "Your right one's the closest thing you got to a girlfriend."

"Fuck off." Kenny swatted Robby on the ear. Then he winced and scratched his head as he stared at the fourth member of their little murder squad. "Uh. Sorry. I promise my momma taught me not to curse around ladies. It won't happen again."

"Please." Carter's aunt Jane waved a small, manicured hand through the warm ocean air. Carter had never seen her fingernails free of polish. Pink. Always pink. "I've heard far worse from this one." She arched an eyebrow over the frames of her sunglasses at Carter. "And his momma raised him right, too. I can assure you of that."

Carter grimaced. "Except for when she ran off with her boyfriend and left me home alone to fend for myself."

"She was a single mother," Jane insisted. "She *deserved* the occasional escape."

"I was six!" Carter's voice strained above the sound of the waves slapping against the side of the boat.

"Psshh." Jane shook her head. "It taught you independence. You should thank her for that."

It was an old argument. One Carter never won, so he did what he always did and suppressed an aggravated sigh.

Kenny pointed toward the horizon. "That way. Let's keep on keeping on."

"Agreed." Robby nodded and then glanced at Jane, blushing deeply when she pulled down her sunglasses and turned her emerald-green eyes on him. Even at fifty-four years old, and despite the years of substance abuse, Jane Ennis was still one of the most beautiful women Carter had ever seen. "Hang on to your hat, ma'am," Robby told her. He'd lived in Kansas City until he moved to Chicago in middle school, and he'd retained a bit of that Missourian accent. "We're goin' for another ride."

"You make that sound a little naughty." Jane winked. "Don't you know I'm old enough to be your mother, you handsome thing?"

For the hundredth time that morning, Carter wished his aunt had stayed back in the hotel on Key West. Her flirting was enough to turn his stomach—mostly because it reminded him so much of his mother. But Jane had demanded he let her tag along to see the job done.

And she's got the right, he thought, closing his ears to Robby's bumbling response to Jane's honeyed words. *After everything she's been through, after everything Mia has put her through, she's got the fucking* right.

The push of a button had the speedboat's 450 quad motors rumbling to life. But before he could press up on the throttle, Robby shouted, "Wait! There! What's that?"

Carter looked in the direction Robby pointed. Even with his polarized sunglasses, he had to squint against the glare of the sun as it flashed blindingly off the crest of the waves. At first he saw nothing, and he was about to ask Robby what the hell he was talking about. But then...

Without saying a word, he turned the steering wheel

and the idling engines rumbled with suppressed power as he put the boat into gear and piloted them toward the floating object. Kenny was the one to drag the dark blue square out of the ocean once they'd pulled even with it.

"Oops. Sorry!" he said when water sheeted off the item, causing the pain in Carter's ass, otherwise known as his aunt, to yelp and race to the other side of the boat, lest her precious sandals get wet.

"What is it?" Robby peered down at the navy square.

"Looks like the cushion off a seat," Kenny said. He glanced at Carter and lifted an eyebrow above his protruding brow ridge. "Outta the airplane, ya think?"

Carter scanned the surrounding sea, feeling his heart skip when he spied another navy square floating nearby. Next to it bobbed a shiny piece of metal. Letting his gaze widen, he realized there were numerous pieces of trash floating with the current in an ever-widening circle, and the iridescent sheen of spilled fuel made rainbow effects on the waves.

"It's the plane." His voice was hoarse with disbelief and relief. "Or what's left of it."

Robby blinked. "So we're done then? They crashed and died?"

Carter felt a little giddy as he glanced around at the bobbing debris. *Could it really have been this easy?*

CHAPTER 9

12:50 PM...

This entire day deserves a giant middle finger, Dalton
"Doc" Simmons thought unhappily as he helped the
others drag the life raft out of the surf and onto the little
island.

Island. Sh'yeah right. That was like calling a Chihuahua
a dog. Nothing that small and pathetic-looking deserved the
title.

The sandbar stretched *maybe* a quarter of a mile. And
it had some nice palm trees growing in its center that would
provide shade from the relentless sun. But that was all it had
going for it.

No fresh water. No shelter. No birds or animals that
could sustain them should their rescue not happen in the next
day or two.

To recap, in the last twenty-four hours, he had gotten
blackout drunk, had seduced and failed to seal the deal with

a mystery woman who'd turned out to be his lawyer, had nearly died in a plane crash, had busted his head and broken his arm, and now he was stranded on a desert...er...*sandbar* in the middle of the ocean with zero resources.

Definitely a giant middle finger sort of day.

"What now?" Cami dusted off her hands before shading her eyes so she, too, could survey their meager surroundings. "Should we gather sticks to spell out S.O.S. in the sand? Build a tree house? Fashion a fishing net out of palm fronds to maybe catch some—"

"Slow down there, Robinson Crusoe." Doc got dizzy just listening to her making plans. Or maybe that was the head injury. *Hard to tell.* "How about we take a couple minutes to stand here, catch our breath, and appreciate that we're on solid ground and not out in the ocean where we could fall victim to another rogue wave or a man-eating shark. How's that sound?"

"Like a waste of time, quite frankly," she said with a twist of her lips, which, amazingly, were still painted a vibrant red. He wondered what her lipstick was made of. Shellac?

She's got gumption, he admitted against his will. *Gumption and spirit and enough sass to sink a ship.*

Romeo scratched his goatee, humor glinting in his eyes. "I think a tree house might be a little ambitious. How would you feel about a lean-to that protects us from the wind?"

"I mean, a tree house sounds *better*," she insisted. "Less sand. Fewer crabs."

Damnit! Doc *liked* Camilla D'Angelo.

When he forgot about the lawyer thing, he could admit she was the kind of woman he generally enjoyed spending time with. Smart. Funny. Able to keep her wits about her even when the proverbial shit was slamming into the proverbial fan at a hundred miles per hour.

And drop-dead gorgeous.

Although, that last thing was usually a mark in his minus column. He'd always preferred women who were sweetly pretty. Women whose looks added to their overall appeal but didn't define them. Women more like Mia. The Gwyneth Paltrows of the world.

Cami was more of a Kim Kardashian. The kind of beautiful that was like getting hit in the teeth with a tire iron. Face? *Pow!* Body? *Wham!*

Then again, maybe the reason he'd always preferred Gwyneth Paltrow to Kim Kardashian, was that women who looked like Kimmie K. didn't generally go for guys who looked like him. Guys who had uncut hair and untrimmed beard stubble. Guys who couldn't be bothered to match their belts to their boots.

Women who looked like Kimmie K. went for guys who looked like Romeo.

Nope. Scratch that. Rewind. *All* women went for guys who looked like Romeo.

In fact, when Doc had seen Cami crossing the bar, her hips swaying dramatically, those dark eyes of hers the definition of seduction, he'd thought for sure she'd been aiming for Rico Suave himself. He'd nearly snorted his beer through his nose when she'd sidled up to him instead.

And then I went and got so loaded I couldn't show her the good time she was after. It wasn't the most embarrassing moment of his life. But it was damn close. Only slightly edged out by that time during his residency when, in the wee small hours of the morning, he'd tiptoed into the hospital room of a seventy-year-old patient thinking he'd quietly check the man's chart without waking him. Instead, he'd caught the guy with the blanket tossed aside, hospital gown pulled up to his chest, vigorously flogging his log.

Doc had sputtered a mortified, *"Uh. Sorry, sir."*

But the old man had looked nonplussed. *"No worries, son,"* he'd said while casually pulling his gown down to cover himself. *"When ya get to be my age, the flesh is so rarely willin', ya gotta take advantage when it is. No matter where ya are."*

Doc remembered praying for two things then, a full bucket of brain bleach and for the floor tiles to open up and swallow him whole.

"Okay." Romeo bobbed his head, dragging Doc from his reverie. "Let's talk logistics. We need to find the best spot on the island to build the lean-to. It's warm now, but it'll get chilly tonight. We'll use the life raft as a bed. It'll be a tight fit, but we can squeeze in and conserve body heat."

Doc tried to picture it and got stuck on the all-important question of...*who will spoon whom?*

He wasn't very enthusiastic about the idea of Romeo spooning him or him spooning Romeo. He'd been down that road before when they'd gotten cut off from their unit and had spent a night tangled together in a hole they'd dug out of the sand while the desert temperatures plummeted around them.

If memory served, Romeo slept like the dead. And snored.

But the alternative was to sleep boy-girl-boy-girl, and that meant Doc stood a good chance of being snugged up nice and tight next to one Camilla D' Angelo. *That* was a sure-fire recipe for a terrible night's sleep. One plagued by prurient thoughts, an incessant boner, and—

"That will also keep us off the sand and out of those crabs you're concerned about," Romeo added, cutting off Doc's thoughts. "And I don't think we need to spell out S.O.S. because the flare gun will be more effective at signaling any passing boats or low-flying planes. But one of us *should* take a walk around the island to get the lay of the land and see if anything useful might have washed up over the years. I mean, a net made from palm fronds *sounds* badass, but I'm not sure how effective it would be. A tarp or piece of plastic that we could use to catch rainwater if a storm passes would be better." His expression turned contemplative. "I guess we could use the life raft for that but—"

When Cami interrupted, her tone was dubious. "How long do you think we'll be stranded here that we need to catch rainwat—"

"Says the woman who wants to build a tree house," Doc couldn't stop himself from interrupting.

Sheer annoyance fired in Cami's eyes. To *his* annoyance, it caused an answering heat in his blood.

He didn't want to like Camilla D' Angelo. But more than not wanting to like her, he sure as shit didn't want to *want* her.

Not that there hadn't been women since Lily. There'd been more than a few. But they'd been conveniences, an easy way to scratch an itch and drown some sorrows. Not something he craved or needed or desired.

To crave or need or desire a woman felt like a...betrayal.

To crave or need or desire a *lawyer*? That almost felt sinful.

And maybe that's why he'd gotten completely and utterly soused the night before. Maybe he'd recognized the stirrings of true passion and had subconsciously sabotaged himself.

Wouldn't be the first time he'd made a split-second decision that had completely torpedoed everything he thought he was after. Everything he'd been working toward.

"I'm sorry." She dragged him from his musing and harangued him for cutting her off by saying, "Did the middle of my sentence interrupt the beginning of yours?"

So much sass.

"Now, don't get your back up," he attempted to soothe her. "I was just pointing out how silly it is to say we'll be here long enough to need a tree house but not long enough to worry about fresh water."

"First of all"—she narrowed her eyes—"telling an annoyed woman not to get her back up is about as effective as baptizing a cat. Second of all, I don't know why, maybe it's the letdown of the adrenaline, maybe it's the slight headache I have, but I find the sound of your voice particularly grating right now. Do you think it would be at all possible for you to zip it?" She pantomimed zipping closed her own lips.

He didn't answer. Instead he felt the corners of his mouth twitch.

Sooo much sass.

Romeo cleared his throat and got them back on track. "Mia and I will look for the best spot for us to spend the night, get the life raft put in place, and start cutting down fronds to make a lean-to."

The first time Doc had met Romeo was when they'd been assigned to the same SEAL Team. His initial impression of the dude's eager-beaver, gung-ho attitude had been that Romeo was a guy who had a bit of an inferiority complex. Someone who felt he needed to do twice the work to prove himself half as good. But as the years had gone by, Doc had come to realize that Romeo was simply that self-sacrificing. His nature was to serve. Sitting around while there was work to be done never even crossed his mind.

"Doc?" Romeo gave him a searching glance. "I know your head has to be killing you, and your arm probably hurts twice as bad, but would you be willing to walk around the island to see if—"

"Consider it done." Doc lifted his hand, not letting Romeo finish. He was happy to have something to do that would allow him to be alone in his misery.

"I'll go with Doc," Cami said, and Doc barely refrained from groaning. "You shouldn't be alone," she told him firmly. "You have a head injury. What if you pass out, fall face-first into the surf, and drown in an inch of water?" She screwed up her lips. "Although now that I've said that aloud, it doesn't sound like such a bad idea."

"Oh, ha, ha." He faked a laugh. "Not sure why you settled on the law. You'd have made a great stand-up comedian."

She gave a little bow. "I'm here all week." When she realized what she'd said, she grimaced. "Wait. I take it back." She looked around as if trying to placate whatever higher power might be listening. "I really *don't* want to be here all week."

"If you're coming, then come on." He waved his arm, welcoming her to precede him up the beach. The sooner they got started, the sooner they could stop and she would go do something else, *anything* else, but continue to stand next to him and...*tempt* him. "We're burning daylight."

"Gimme a sec." She balanced on one foot and then the other to pull off her wedge sandals. After dropping them into the bottom of the life raft, she shrugged her purse from her shoulder and let it fall beside her discarded shoes. Next went her linen suit jacket. It landed on top of her purse in a flutter. Finally, she bent to roll up the legs of her slacks.

Looking far more fit for the role of castaway, she straightened and blew out a satisfied breath. By contrast, he suddenly *couldn't* breathe, because her blouse was still a little damp and it clung to the round swells of her breasts.

If he looked closely, which you better believe he did, he could *just* make out the shape of her nipples through the cups of her bra. They were a little bigger than half-dollar size, and the centers poked up like pencil erasers.

"That's much better," she declared, unaware that she was *killing him*. She pointed in the direction he'd gestured and asked, "This way?"

"Don't reckon it actually matters," he wheezed. "Seeing as how we'll be doing a circle either way. Lady's choice."

He wasn't sure if she had a reason for choosing the opposite direction from the one he'd suggested, or if she simply did it to be contrary.

Probably the latter, he decided. And why that should make him want to smile, he had no idea. He fashioned a frown onto his face instead and fell into step beside her.

They'd made it maybe twenty yards down the beach when she turned to him and grimaced. "I really stuck my foot in it with Mia and Romeo, huh? Read that situation *way* wrong."

Before he could respond, she lifted an imperious finger. "Although I stand by my initial assumption that she's interested in more than friendship with him. The way she looks at him is like he dropped out of the sky. So which is it? Does she think he's an angel or Superman?"

Doc snorted. "It's probably a little of both. I mean, you've seen the guy, right? I think fallen angel meets superhero pretty much sums him up. All he's missing is the halo and the cape."

"Oh, I've seen him." When she nodded, it caused her fallen bun to smack against the side of her face. Frowning, she pulled out the elastic holding the bun in place, and her long hair unraveled like a rope of black silk until it hung down her back in a wavy curtain.

He had the oddest urge to run his fingers through it. It looked so soft and shiny and cool. He shoved his hand deep inside his wet pocket instead.

"He's beautiful. I'll grant you that." She inclined her head. "But not all women *like* a man who's prettier than they are."

"Not something you ever have to worry about," he

assured her.

The look she shot him was sharp. "Meaning what?"

"Meaning there's not a man on the planet prettier than you are." The words were out of his mouth before he could stop them. And when her jaw slung open and she blinked at him, he wished he could suck them back in.

"Was that..." She shook her head. "Did you just give me a compliment?"

"Why are you acting so surprised? If I remember correctly, I complimented you plenty last night."

"Sure." She nodded. "When you were wearing beer goggles the size of party platters. Today you've given me nothing but grief."

"Not true," he argued. "I told you it'd be a crying shame if you only weighed ninety pounds. That might be the nicest thing I've ever said to anyone."

She snorted. "Boy, do I feel sorry for the women in your life if that's the case. And since we're on the subject, you're right. One minute you're insulting me, and the next you're trying to convince me to sleep with you so you can make up for last night. Your seduction technique is bipolar. Has anyone ever told you that?"

He chuckled and shook his head. "You'd be the first." Then, figuring it was as good a time as any, he added, "And since you brought up last night, I really do feel like a shitheel for the way I acted. My only excuse is..." He stopped and ran a hand through his hair. The wind had dried it into a riot of crunchy tufts around his head. "Well, I guess I don't really have an excuse," he finally finished.

"Sure you do," she countered. "I know a man in mourning when I see one."

He blinked at her. Stunned that she'd so accurately homed in on the crux of the matter.

"You want to talk about it?" she asked softly.

"Lord no. Hard pass." The words were out of his mouth before the thought behind them even had time to fully form. It wasn't his brain that answered, it was his gut. And maybe his heart too.

"That's what I figured." She nodded.

Other women would have pressed him. Half of him expected *Cami* to press him—thirty-eight years of life had taught him many things, but one of those was that the female of the species wasn't satisfied unless everyone was baring their souls. But she kept her lips sealed. And after a few seconds, he realized they were going to stay that way.

For a while, they walked along the beach without speaking, her painted toes disappearing in the sand, his soggy canvas boat shoes leaving large, deep footprints behind. When the silence stretching between them began to feel awkward, he returned them to their original subject.

"As for Romeo and Mia, you're not wrong. Mia's definitely smitten. But take it from someone who's known Romeo for nearly a decade, he's smitten too. He's just better at hiding it because he refuses to admit it to himself."

"I don't understand." The wind whipped a lock of hair across her face. A strand got stuck between her lips, and for a second, he fantasized *he* was that strand, sliding into the warm, wet wonder of her mouth. "If they're both crazy about each other"—she pulled her hair behind her shoulder and he was able to focus again—"what's holding them back?"

"Romeo," he said with a frown. "He thinks Mia is the forever sort, and since he's convinced himself all he wants out of life is to be the town bicycle, he won't start anything with her that might end with her hurt."

"Town bicycle?" Cami frowned. "Oh. I get it. Everyone gets to ride." She shook her head. "Really? He doesn't strike me as a lifetime bachelor."

"I'm not convinced he is." Or maybe it was more

accurate to say Doc had started having his doubts about Romeo's Hugh Hefner plan the moment one Miss Mia Ennis entered the picture.

When Cami glanced over at him, he shrugged and immediately regretted the move when it caused his already throbbing arm to grow teeth and start snapping and snarling like a rabid dog.

He must've groaned or winced or something, because her expression immediately melted into one of concern. "I have some prescription pain meds back in my purse that you're welcome to use as long as they're the kind that won't make you stroke out or hemorrhage or whatever." When he lifted an eyebrow, she wagged her finger. "And *no*. I'm not a script junkie, so you can wipe that look right off your face. I only use the pills once a month when I have terrible menstrual cramps."

The easy way she spoke about such personal information—truly, he was beginning to think Cami lacked any sort of filter—made it tough to keep his expression impassive. He must not have been totally successful, because she rolled her eyes.

"Please. You're a doctor. I'm sure you've dealt with far worse than period pain over the years."

"Sure." He inclined his chin. "Although I read an article recently that said the pain some women experience is like that of a heart attack. And *that* was a real eye-opener. I had no idea."

"I've never had a heart attack, so I wouldn't know." She grimaced. "But I can assure you, once a month, for about thirty-six hours straight, if I don't have the pain meds, I want to crawl in a hole and die."

He winced. "That's gotta suck."

Her expression was one of resignation. "It's life. And the key to happiness is to roll with the punches."

"Is that the key to happiness? And here I thought it was staying away from assholes at all costs."

"Impossible," she scoffed. "There are too many of them to avoid altogether."

"Especially in your line of work, I reckon."

She narrowed her eyes. "You really *do* hate lawyers, don't you?"

He slid her a quick glance before admitting, "I used to think so. Now I'm not so sure."

"Oh, be still my heart." She pressed a hand to her chest. He had to force his eyes away from her ample cleavage. "Two compliments in the span of ten minutes. Careful, you might just turn a woman's head."

Camilla D'Angelo's smile was so wide and full of teeth that it made him wonder if it made her jaw hurt. And damned if he didn't find himself grinning in return.

That is until her smile had him thinking about her mouth.

And her mouth had him thinking about her tongue.

And her tongue had him thinking about the kiss they'd shared the night before.

He'd been completely toasted by that point, so the recollection was fuzzy. But he seemed to recall the eager way she'd gripped his shoulders. The feel of her luscious breasts pressed against his chest. And the glittering invitation in her eyes as she'd stared up at him.

The moment his mouth had touched hers? He would swear he'd felt something deep inside him lock into place.

No, he silently insisted now. *You were drunk and imagining things, hearing an echo from the past.*

He ignored the small, quiet voice inside his head that called him a liar. He ignored it because the last time he'd felt that sensation, as if one of his missing puzzle pieces had snapped into its rightful spot, he'd ended up falling ass over teakettle in love.

And lord knows, I'll never do that *again.*

CHAPTER 10

12:54 PM...

What's that?"

Carter glanced away from surveying the flotsam that remained from the crash of the amphibious plane. As much as the thought of seeing a dead body turned his stomach, he was really hoping to spot one. You know, to make sure everyone aboard the aircraft really *had* died. "What's what?" he asked Robby.

"*That.*" Robby pointed toward the horizon.

Once again, it took Carter a few seconds to see anything beyond the glare of the sun atop the waves. But when he finally spotted what Robby gestured toward, an immediate sense of foreboding crackled at the back of his brain.

"Where are the binoculars?" He spun in a circle, his eyes pinging desperately around the speedboat.

No, no, no. Please don't make this harder than it has to be.

"Here." Robby pulled the binoculars from around his neck and passed them to Carter, who wasted no time pushing his sunglasses to the top of his head and lifting the magnified lenses to his eyes. It took him a couple tries to adjust the magnification, but the instant he did, he let loose with a low, vicious curse.

"What?" Kenny questioned. "What d'ya see?"

"Survivors," Carter snarled. "They fucking made it."

He stabbed a finger in the direction of the island—which was little more than a glimmer of white and a wash of green to the naked eye.

"All of 'em?" Kenny asked, looking annoyingly unperturbed by this shitastic turn of events. The fucker was supposed to have blown them out of the damned sky, not knocked out their tail section, leaving them enough plane left so they could ditch and *survive*.

Kenny had *assured* him he knew just where to plant the explosives *"And if I fuck it up, which I won't, they'll still crash and die."*

So much for that *theory*, Carter thought now, trying to smother the anger that burned through his veins. "I don't know," he admitted carefully. "I didn't count heads. See for yourself." He passed the binoculars to Kenny.

With a nonchalance that made Carter want to scream, Kenny lifted the magnified lenses to his face. After a moment, Kenny muttered, "I only count two people on the beach and neither one is your cousin. I think— No. There she is in the trees." Lowering the binoculars, he nodded. "Yup. They all survived. Damn."

Damn didn't quite cover it. Which was why Carter let loose with, "Goddamnit. God*damn*it!" as he stalked toward the helm, prepared to fire the engines.

"Wait a minute." Kenny frowned. "What's the plan?"

"We have to go over there and kill them. *Duh.*"

"Did you forget that they're Navy SEALs?" Robby squeaked.

They'd considered and discarded about a hundred different ways of offing Carter's cousin. But they'd finally settled on driving down to Key West, waiting for Mia to make a trip there from Wayfarer Island, and then turning her plane into a firebomb on her return flight, because that had been the only plan that didn't include them potentially having to come face-to-face with a bunch of Navy SEALs.

But this is different, he thought.

He voiced that exact sentiment aloud. "No, I haven't forgotten. But this isn't Wayfarer Island or Key West we're talking about. They don't have access to their weapons here. They don't have anywhere to run and hide. We can take them all out from a distance with Kenny's gun." He motioned with his chin toward the matte black weapon lying on the console.

"Hang on." Kenny patted the air, his heavy brow wrinkled. "Let's think about this. I thought your whole thing was you wanna leave behind no trace. Blowing four people to smithereens will leave behind a fuck-ton of traces."

"Our *whole thing*, as you call it"—Jane sniffed—"is to kill them. Period. End of story."

There was a cold gleam in her eyes that Carter recognized. It had made its first appearance on a stormy night eight weeks ago when he'd gone to tell her he wanted to quit. That she didn't pay him enough to continue to put up with her bullshit.

She'd been on a three-month bender at that point. He'd bailed her out of jail once for jumping the curb in her Mercedes and taking out a fire hydrant. She'd seduced and then dumped his boss after begging Carter to introduce them, which had made the man fire Carter from the first job he'd had in years that he actually liked. And for two weeks straight, she'd failed to pay him his stipend, forcing him to go to the lawyer who controlled her trust to beg for back pay.

That'd been the last straw. He *hated* having to crawl on his knees with his hand out to her snooty attorney. The man looked at him like he was something stuck to the bottom of a shoe. It was humiliating.

"I already texted Mia to let her know I'm quitting," Carter had said to his aunt. *"I told her if you need something, you're going to have to get it from her. I'm out."*

Jane's eyes had narrowed. *"What did she say?"*

"That she understood. But that, given your history, she feels like she needs to keep up the boundaries she's set. Which means I guess you're on your own."

That's when it'd gleamed to life in his aunt's eyes…that cold, calculating look.

"I could pay you a lot more if she was dead," Jane had said. *"If you help me kill her, I'll give you twenty-five percent of the money Richard left behind."*

Carter had been shocked to his core by her suggestion. He'd known there was no love lost between Mia and Jane. But a mother murdering her own daughter? It was unfathomable. Horrific.

He'd said exactly that to her. Which was when she'd told him what *really* happened to Andy. About how Mia had gotten into Jane's pain pills and, *"stuffed her face full of them before feeding the rest to Andy like candy."*

According to Jane, the housekeeper had found them in enough time to rush them to the hospital to have their stomachs pumped. Mia had survived the incident without any permanent side effects. Little Andy hadn't been so lucky.

Apparently, the overdose had fried his brain. And from the onset of puberty, he'd lived with terrible mental illness.

Carter might have been able to forgive Mia for the pill incident. After all, she'd only been a little thing. What he *couldn't* forgive was what she had ultimately done to her baby brother.

When Jane told Carter about the vicious letter from Mia that Jane found beside Andy's body, Carter had instantly understood how Jane could so callously speak of ending her daughter's life.

"She was sick and tired of him, and she made sure he knew it," Jane had said with tears standing in her eyes. *"Because Andy idolized her, he decided ending his own life was the only way to make her happy."*

Mia acted all sweet and quiet and gentle. But in truth, she was a selfish, murderous bitch.

That's all it'd taken to have Carter agreeing to Jane's plan. He figured he was helping take a vicious criminal off the streets. Sending a stone-cold killer where she belonged.

To hell.

If he and his friends happened to make a little pocket change in the process? All the better. And when his conscience tried to remind him that the three people *with* Mia didn't deserve to die, he simply ignored it.

"Who cares about evidence left behind on an island in the middle of nowhere?" Jane added with a huff, pulling Carter from his thoughts. "Who's even going to see it?"

"Someone will eventually," Kenny stated with certainty. "There might not be a call to start a search for 'em yet, but there will be soon. And dollars to doughnuts, someone's gonna stumble onto the island. If they find a crime scene, they'll open an investigation. And again, that's the last thing we want, right?"

Even though the radios had continued to broadcast nothing but business as usual, Carter knew Kenny was right. Sooner or later the plane would be reported missing, and the search would begin.

He ran a hand through his hair. "I say we motor up to the island, shoot them, and load up their bodies. We'll get rid of any blood left behind, cover up any tracks we leave in the sand, and make sure the island looks like no one ever set foot on it. We can weigh the bodies down and dump them overboard at intervals between here and Key West. Let the ocean do what the ocean does best. Eat, eat, eat."

"But we only have the one gun," Robby pointed out. "And there are four of them."

"Four people against a twelve round clip?" Kenny scoffed. "I'll take those odds any day."

"So what?" Robby shook his head. "You plan to jump out of the boat and start sprayin' bullets?"

Kenny grinned. "You got a better idea?"

Robby blinked and looked at Carter for guidance.

Sighing heavily, Carter admitted, "It's our best option at this point."

"But won't Mia recognize you?" Robby asked, and then pointed at Jane. "And *her*. Won't she be suspicious about what you're doin' all the way out here when you're supposed to be in Chicago?"

"Once we get closer, you'll pilot the boat," Carter told Robby. "Aunt Jane and I will hide around the back of the pilothouse until it's done."

"All right." Kenny rubbed his hands together like a cartoon villain.

Robby—looking unconvinced by Carter's newest plan, but not having a better idea—took the binoculars and made his way to the bow of the boat.

Carter had restarted the engines when Robby turned toward him, alarm in his eyes. "What now?" Carter cut the engines, feeling his patience fraying another inch.

"Look!" Robby moved across the decking so he could shove the binoculars into Carter's hands.

"What am I looking for?" Apprehension lifted the hairs on the back of Carter's neck at the same time he lifted the magnified lenses to his eyes.

"The trees," Robby said. "The guy *in* the trees. Check out what he has tucked into the back of his jeans."

Carter scanned the little island until the man Robby was talking about came into focus. The dude had on a sky-blue T-shirt and jeans. And when he bent to pick up a palm frond, Carter saw what was causing Robby to have a conniption.

"He's packing." Those two words were little more than a growl as Carter handed the binoculars to Kenny. "That motherfucking is *packing*."

CHAPTER 11

1:34 PM...

Romeo wished he could take back asking Mia to call him by his given name.

He wasn't sure why he'd done that. He hadn't even realized he'd *wanted* to. But something about the moment had made him blurt out the request.

Maybe because they'd just survived a plane crash. Or maybe because she'd been so scared for him that it'd made him feel cherished and special in a way he never had before.

Regardless of why, he'd asked her to call him Spiro, and now she was all wigged out.

It was like when she first arrived on Wayfarer Island. She wasn't just quiet. She was giving *Silent Bob* a run for the money in the mute department.

She'd listened while he explained how they were looking for a place in the center of the island—preferably a small depression—where they could put the life raft and then build a windbreak with palm leaf mats. She'd nodded once they *found* that place and he started pulling down palm fronds. And she'd watched his hands with interest while he showed her how to peel off the individual fronds, remove the middle stick, and then lay the remaining leaflets out flat before beginning to weave.

She'd even hummed her interest when he'd told her, "I learned to make these when I was on leave in Thailand. An old woman on a beach in Phuket taught me."

But she hadn't made another sound since. And now the silence had stretched so far between them, he couldn't figure out how to bridge the gap.

Once again, the irony of the situation wasn't lost on him.

The first time he'd spent the night with her and awakened to her new-found tenderness toward him, he'd presumed—*wrongly*—that she thought he was open to more than friendship. When he'd made it clear he wasn't, she'd been quick to inform him that one, even though everyone was entitled to their wrong assumptions, *his* wrong assumptions made him an ass. And two, just because she was sweet and caring toward him didn't mean she expected romance in return.

Now here he'd asked her to call him Spiro, and damned if he didn't get the impression *she* was the one worried *he* wanted more.

The real kicker? She wasn't wrong.

He *did* want more.

He wanted to *know* her. Know all the reasons she broke out one of her rare smiles. Hear all her dry jokes. Learn what it would take to make her sigh with happiness. Understand all her flaws and hear all about her mistakes the same way he wanted to understand all her strengths and hear all about her victories.

He'd never experienced anything like it. This craving

to *know* another human being on every level. And if he'd been someone else, anyone else, he'd have jumped at the opportunity for more.

He wasn't someone else, though. He was *him* and—

He was stopped from further reflection when he glanced over and found her lips curved into a wistful smile.

He'd always thought of her as slightly ethereal. But the expression on her face now was so soft and gentle, he almost leaned forward to brush a finger over her cheek. Just to make sure she was real and not a figment of his imagination.

"What are you smiling about?" he asked, glad to have something to break the silence.

She didn't lift her eyes from the work her hands were doing, which meant he had to lean forward to catch her quiet words.

"I don't know exactly." She shook her head. Then, she reconsidered. "No. That's not true. I'm smiling because I'm happy to be alive. I'm happy *you're* alive. I'm happy to have two working hands so I can help you build our shelter. It's the little things at times like these, right?"

When she laughed softly, he swore he heard the sound with something other than his ears. Something that beat heavily inside his chest.

"We humans are miracles," she added, glancing up at him.

Like always, the instant their eyes met, he started drowning. Sinking further and further into her amber-colored gaze until he was deeper than he'd been when he'd followed the Otter on her final journey.

In so deep he could barely think.

In so deep he definitely couldn't breathe.

Which was why his voice came out sounding like he'd been snacking on the sand instead of sitting in it when he asked, "What do you mean?"

"I mean we walk around every day knowing everyone and everything we care about can be snatched away in the blink of an eye." She snapped her fingers, and he was momentarily distracted by how delicate her hands were. So small and thin and feminine-looking.

Everything about her called to the man in him, the protector in him. Until he wanted to spend his days hulking over her, snapping and snarling at anyone who ventured too close. Keeping her safe from the big, bad world.

She didn't need him to do that, though. The more he got to know her, the more he understood that she was living proof mighty things could come in small packages. That sometimes what seemed as breakable as glass could be as strong as a diamond.

"We walk around knowing our time is finite and that the people we love will one day cease to exist," she continued. "And still we find ways to smile. To experience joy. I just..." She shook her head in wonder. "When I stop to think about it, it seems miraculous. Don't you think?"

"I guess so."

As soon as the words were out of his mouth, he wanted to pull them back in. They sounded so *lame* compared to her heartfelt speech. His only excuse was that he couldn't think around the longing that grew deep inside him. A longing he couldn't pinpoint exactly.

All he knew was that it had her name on it.

And then, in the next instant, that longing morphed into thoughts about how Alex and Mason were on their way to Spain to find the cipher. Thoughts about how once he and his partners located the *Santa Cristina's* treasure, Mia would move on.

Her leaving had always been a given. From the moment he'd met her, he'd known she wouldn't be a permanent fixture in his life. But her heading out to her next job had been some nebulous thing way out in the future. Now it felt... imminent. Inevitable.

He wasn't ready.

Wasn't ready to let her go. Wasn't ready to give up the way she made him feel. Wasn't ready for the memory of her to be the brightest light in a life that would seem dull and dreary by comparison.

A frown pulled at the corners of his mouth, and he knew he'd been quiet for too long when she cleared her throat. "I, um... I want to clear the air between us."

Oh, no. Here it comes. It's her *turn to try to let* me *down gently. To tell* me *that all we can ever have is a friendship.*

"I owe you an apology."

He wHe He blinked in surprise. "You do? For what?"

"For calling you an asshole."

When a laugh burst out of him, he supposed he'd proved her right. Humans *could find* delight in the strangest of places and at the oddest of times.

"I stayed down too long and scared the hell out of everyone." He waved away her concern. "It *was* an asshole move. You had every right to bust my balls."

"Still"—she shook her head—"we're friends. Which means I shouldn't call you nasty names."

"My partners are my *best* friends, and at least one of them calls me a bastard or a dickhead or a sonofabitch on the daily," he assured her.

"But that's said in *fun*," she countered. "Not in—" She frowned.

"Anger?" he supplied helpfully. "Exasperation?"

"No." Her voice dropped a decibel. "Sheer, unadulterated terror."

His steely heart, the one he'd meticulously forged so many years ago, melted. Just a little. Or maybe a lot. Because he'd never known such compassion.

He'd certainly never experienced the like from his mother. After his father had died, Renata Delgado had spent all her time exchanging one gangster for the next. Her only ambition had been to be the latest conquest of the homeboy most likely to climb the ranks of the organization. And it hadn't mattered if the men she'd invited into their home had slapped Romeo across the face for talking back or kicked him across the room for shits and giggles, because that was the life. And his mother loved the life.

She was a barrio babe to her very core.

Then there'd been Romeo's older brother, Alejandro. He *certainly* hadn't been the touchy-feely sort. In fact, Alejandro had made it his mission in life to "toughen up" Romeo by beating him bloody on the regular. And then, once Romeo came of age, Alejandro had exchanged the beatings for lessons in gang politics, hoping the two of them would one day rise to the top of the Mexican Mafia power structure.

"With my brains and brawn keeping the homeboys in line, and your pretty mug keeping the homegirls horny and willing, you and I could rule the roost, hermanito,*"* Alejandro had dreamed aloud.

Needless to say, Romeo's enlistment into the Navy and eventual admission into the SEAL Teams had been a *huge* disappointment to his family. Even all these years later, they still made that clear anytime he called his mother in L.A. or his brother in Pelican Bay.

But Mia? Mia with her silent mouth and expressive eyes. Mia with her avid mind and elusive smile. Mia with her dry wit and love of paranormal romance. *She* had always treated him with tenderness and sympathy and kindness. And she made him feel like...

Well, she made him *feel*. Full stop.

Some of what he was thinking must've shown on his face, because her brow pinched. "Don't you know how much

I've come to cherish our friendship? I feel like you make me a better me."

He blinked in surprise. He'd always felt like *she* made *him* the best version of himself, but he'd never dreamed she could feel the same.

She mistook his surprise for something else, though, because she was quick to add, "No. Stop looking at me like that. I'm not stupid enough to think that just because I care about you and prefer a world with you in it that there's room for anything more. I know you don't like me like *that*."

For real though, he felt like he was a WWII pilot flying a heavy bomber through a field of flak. *Boom!* She hit him with one shocking announcement and before he had time to recover... *Boom!* There went another.

He blinked so quickly, his vision took on a strobe effect. "*What?*" he demanded.

She sighed and went back to weaving fronds. "I know I'm not your type. So you can stop worrying every time we fall asleep together, or I say something nice to you, or I cry when I think you've drowned yourself that I've gone and..." She screwed up her mouth. "*Set my cap for you*, as my grandmother would say."

All he could do was continue to blink.

Concern flashed across her face. "Did you get sand in your eye?"

"Wh-why..." He had to clear his throat and try again. "Why would you think you're not my type?"

"Oh, come on," she scoffed. "It's no secret you've made a sport of seducing beautiful women. And we both know I don't qualify."

He hadn't made a *sport* of it. He'd just been playing the role he thought he'd been born to.

But that was beside the point.

"You don't think you're beautiful?"

Her lips flattened into a straight line. "No." When he opened his mouth to argue, she pointed at him again. "And before you go being your charming self and lavishing me with compliments, please know I'm not a biscuit. There's no need to butter me up. Facts are facts and, despite what our politicians would have us believe, there's no such thing as *alternative* ones."

"Umm. Exactly which facts are you referring to?" he asked carefully.

"Well..." She started ticking off a list on her fingers. "The fact that my nose is too short. My chin is too sharp. My mouth is too small. My hair isn't straight and it isn't curly, which means it's the mess that happens in-between. And I barely have any boobs to speak of. I know what I am, and I know what I'm not. And it's okay that you don't like me like *that*. I feel honored just to call you a friend."

For a couple of seconds, he stared at her in disbelief. Then he ran a hand through his hair. And when *that* didn't give him enough time to gather his thoughts, he took a moment to smooth his goatee.

Finally, he managed, "Okay. There's a lot to unpack here. But let's start with who gave you that."

Her eyebrows pulled together. "Gave me *what*?"

"That laundry list of things you think are wrong with you."

"Um. Society? Social media? Fashion magazines? Take your pick." The look on her face was a blatant *well, duh*.

"Nah." He shook his head. "When a pretty woman doesn't believe she's pretty, it's because someone has told her so. Who told you so?"

Her mouth slung open, that mouth that she thought was too small but that he thought was absolute perfection. Then she snapped it shut and glanced down at the half-finished palm mat. She played with the edge of a leaflet with one hand while fiddling with one of her diamond stud earrings with the other—the latter a sure sign she was agitated.

"I suppose that would be my mother," she quietly admitted.

"Your *mother*?" he asked in disbelief.

She nodded and he had never hated someone he'd never met, but he felt an instant animosity toward the woman who'd supplied Mia with half her chromosomes.

"You mean the drunk." As soon as those four words left his mouth, he heard how crude they sounded together, especially when accompanied by his skunk eye. He backtracked. "Sorry. That was rude. Addiction is a soul-crushing sickness and I shouldn't—"

"Believe me," she interrupted. "There's no need to apologize. I doubt you could say anything about Mom that I haven't thought myself."

I don't know about that, he thought bitterly. He had some pretty choice words for the woman, a few of which he figured Mia had never even heard before.

But, of course, he kept them to himself. Talk of family was a tricky business, with vague and moving lines that an outsider had to tread carefully or risk crossing one.

"Have you ever met someone who, no matter how much they have, they always want more?" Her question was rhetorical, so he remained quiet. "That's my mom," she said with a downward jerk of her chin. "She always thinks the grass is greener on the other side. But then once she *gets* to the other side, she kills the grass."

She winced. "I shouldn't be talking about her this way. It's unkind and ungenerous of me."

He sighed and scrubbed a hand over his face to give himself time to swallow the words perched on the tip of his tongue. Words like, *Screw that witch for what she did to her own daughter* or *Sounds to me like she doesn't deserve your kindness or generosity.*

Instead, he said, "Look, I get it. When it's family, we try hella hard to give them the benefit of the doubt. But sometimes the people who share our blood are rotten at their core. And it's okay to admit that."

He finally had. Because there'd only been so many excuses he could make for his mother and his brother, so many times he could tell himself they were simply a product of their environment, before he'd had to admit they'd made their choices. And their choices had been bad ones. And enough bad choices eventually made a bad person.

Mia sighed and stopped messing with her earring. Now both of her delicate hands fiddled with the edge of the mat.

A mat that was looking better than his.

She'd picked up the technique as if she'd been born to it. And maybe it was all the years she'd been pulling priceless artifacts out of the seabed that made her so good with her hands or—

An unbidden vision of *exactly* what he'd like her to use her talented little hands for suddenly popped into his head. It was so carnal and erotic, he was surprised he didn't spontaneously combust.

Not that spontaneous combustion would be all bad, he thought. *At least the others would be able to keep warm tonight beside my smoldering corpse.*

"I've always wondered which came first?" she pondered aloud, and he gave himself an imaginary slap across the face while silently berating himself to get his head out of the gutter. She was baring her soul and he was fantasying about a handy.

She's right. I am such *an asshole!*

"Did the addiction make her hateful and unhappy?" She cocked her head. "Or was she hateful and unhappy and turned to the pills and the booze to make herself feel better?"

"It's a classic chicken/egg scenario." He hoped she didn't hear how hoarse his voice had become. "But the real question is, does it even matter? Whichever one came first doesn't change the fact that she was a terrible mother to you."

"I used to think it mattered." She made a face. "I used to think if it was the addiction making her so mean, then she could be loving and supportive if she could just get sober." One rounded shoulder moved up and down inside her blouse and he had the oddest urge to pull her collar aside and press his lips to that graceful curve of bone and muscle. "But she's been in and out of rehabs my whole life, and it never seemed to matter if she was drunk or sober. She's always been...her. I've given up hope she'll ever be the mother I want or need."

"Or deserve," he was quick to add.

Her gaze shot to his face at the same time her hand shot to her ear to twist on her earring. He saw something dark and heavy move behind her eyes. "I don't know about that part," she whispered.

He turned his head slightly. "You don't think you deserved a loving and supportive mother?"

"Do any of us truly *deserve* anything? Isn't thinking we *deserve* things just entitlement in disguise?"

"No," he declared staunchly. "Bad people *deserve* to suffer the consequences of their bad choices and actions just like good people *deserve* good things to happen to them."

"That's the rub, though, isn't it? How much bad does someone have to do before they're a bad person? And is it possible one or two awful acts can obliterate a lifetime of good deeds?"

"Are you talking about something in particular?" He raised his eyebrows in question.

Her smile was tight when she shook her head. "Just getting philosophical, I guess."

He got the impression there was more to it than that, but

he feared she'd clam up if he kept at her. He said carefully, "There's no one right answer to your question. It all comes down to circumstances and how good or bad certain acts or deeds are. Also, how *many* bad acts or deeds there are. Like, if a person can learn from their mistakes and never make them again, then there's room for redemption. But if they just keep doing the same bad shit over and over again? No." He shook his head. "I think it's safe to label them as a lost cause."

She sighed. "Like I said, the no one right answer is the rub."

He desperately wanted to ask her what she meant. But again, he felt like he was treading precariously close to an invisible line. He asked instead, "Is your mother's addiction what made your dad move you and your brother out of the family home?"

That dark, heavy thing crawling behind her eyes grew darker and heavier still.

Shit.

By trying to avoid stepping over one line, he'd inadvertently jumped over another.

Before he could apologize and tell her she didn't need to answer if she didn't want to, she surprised him by nodding. "Yes. He never came out and said it, but I know he blamed her, at least partially, for what happened to me and Andy."

"What happened to you and Andy?"

Her eyes flew wide. It was obvious she'd accidently revealed something she wasn't ready to reveal. And even though he was *dying* to know what she was talking about, because, you know, he wanted to know *everything* about her. Especially this, since he got the distinct impression *this* was what lay behind the sadness he often saw in her eyes and the silences she so frequently fell into.

But she wasn't ready. That, too, was obvious.

He made sure his smile was as gentle as his voice when he told her, "It's okay. Maybe someday you'll trust me enough to tell me." When she opened her mouth, he lifted his hand and stopped her from making an excuse by asking, "Why didn't your dad just divorce your mom and keep you kids? That seems like the better plan to me."

She pursed her mouth into a sad little moue. "My father was a man who felt his responsibilities keenly. He thought staying with Mom was the noble thing to do. Plus, I think he truly loved her. Although, if you ask me, he mistook lust for love. My mother was a stunningly beautiful woman. Still *is*, in fact, despite the booze and the pills."

She hitched a shoulder. "Dad always said that his mother was the best. That me and Andy would have all the love we needed in Granny Susan's house. And he was right." She stared beseechingly at him, willing him to understand. "Dad tried to do the best by each of us. And he died thinking he'd failed *all* of us. I hate that."

Another corner of Romeo's steely heart melted. Because here was sweet, kind Mia feeling sorry for the father who, in his opinion, had forsaken her in so many ways.

Since he couldn't reassure her that he agreed with what her dad had done, he decided his best course of action was to rectify some of the damage her *mother* had done.

"Okay, let's set the record straight, eh?"

At her perplexed look, he started in on her list. Just as she'd done, he ticked off the items on his fingers. "Your nose isn't too short. It's adorable. A little button nose that Hollywood starlets pay thousands of dollars to have plastic surgeons recreate. Your chin isn't too sharp. It—"

"Stop." She rolled her eyes. "I told you I don't need compliments. I was—"

"Hush, woman." He leveled a quelling look on her. "Now, where was I?" He scratched his goatee. "Oh, right.

Your chin. It's charming and sweet and just a little bit stubborn-looking. Which I'd say suits you to a tee. Your mouth *is* small," he added. When her gaze dropped to her lap, he was quick to continue, "Small and so plush and this delicate peachy-pink color that reminds me of a rosebud. You have the kind of mouth that belongs in a Renaissance painting."

She rolled her eyes again and glanced past the trees to the waves lapping hungrily against the sand.

"What?" he demanded. "What are you thinking?"

"I'm thinking—" She stopped and turned back to him. Her frown became a rueful semi-smile. "I guess I'm thinking I'm having a hard time processing so much bullshit at once."

He could tell she expected him to laugh. When he didn't, she tried to turn away again.

He didn't let her.

Catching her perfect chin in the palm of his hand, he forced her to hold his gaze. "Now see? Normally, I'd let you get away with that."

"Get away with what?"

"Using self-deprecating humor to change the subject. But not today. Today I'm making you listen when I tell you that your hair is beautiful. It's soft and shiny and frames your face perfectly."

When she shook her head ever so slightly, the delicate skin of her jaw rubbed against the hard calluses on his palm. Just that easily, a warmth settled in the bottom of his stomach. It was followed by a tingling sensation at the base of his spine.

Desire.

He knew it well.

And yet he was beginning to think he'd only flirted with it, skimmed along the very edges of it, before Mia came along.

"Don't shake your head at me, woman. I know what I'm talking about. Now, about your boobs..." he added quietly, wondering if she could hear how the stirring of his passion had lowered his voice.

"Oh, god." She squeezed her eyes shut. "Please don't."

"That's fine," he told her. "You don't have to look at me for this part. But I want you to hear me, Mia. Your breasts are perfect. Your frame is too small for anything more than what you've got. And besides, all a man needs is a mouthful. And you have two perfect scoops of ice cream that look like they'd melt in a man's mouth."

She groaned her embarrassment, but he wasn't finished.

"And all of that is before we get to your eyes." He still held her chin, so he felt her pulse beat a rapid tattoo against the pads of his fingers when her lids fluttered open.

He pointed to her eyes. "Yeah, those. Hands down, you have the most beautiful eyes I've ever seen. Lioness eyes is how I think of them."

He couldn't keep staring into her eyes without losing himself in them, so he focused on her lips. And that was a *big* mistake. Because he was suddenly having trouble remembering why he wasn't kissing her.

Why *am I not kissing her?*

Oh, right. She comes with all the strings attached and I'm Mr. Footloose and Fancy-free.

"Then there's your smile..." He rubbed his thumb over her pouty bottom lip and watched her mouth fall open so she could drag in a surprised breath. "You don't bring it out very often, but when you do, it's so radiant, it lights up a room."

"Spiro..." His name was a whisper on the wind, but it hit his ears like a siren's call. His blood went from a soft simmer to a rapid boil. Behind his button-fly, his cock went from semi-hard to granite.

"It's taking every ounce of self-control I have not

to press you back into the sand, climb on top of you, and show you just how wrong you are when you say you're not beautiful. When you claim I don't like you like *that*."

She jerked her chin from his hand. "You're just saying that because you feel sorry for me. Because—"

Foolish woman. "Does this look like pity to you?" He reached down to wrap his hand around the throbbing column of his erection.

When her eyes locked onto his hardness, her pupils dilated until they nearly eclipsed the gold around them. "I—" She bit her lip and started messing with her earring again. "I don't get it."

He let go of his cock. "What don't you get?"

"You *want* me?"

He lifted one eyebrow and pointed to his flag flying at full staff. "*Cariña*, isn't that obvious?"

"No." She shook her head firmly, looking so adorably ferocious that he had the strangest urge to boop her on her button nose. And then, you know, *fuck* her. "Because if you wanted me, if you *really* wanted me, you wouldn't have said what you did."

His eyebrows pinched together. "What did I say?"

"That I'm nothing you need and you aren't anything I should want."

He waved a blithe hand through the salt-tinged air. He would swear the sun dappling down through the trees overhead heated her flesh until he could smell the subtle scent of her lotion. A smell that always reminded him of money and class and sweet, soft Mia. "I stand by that statement."

"I—" She stopped and glared at him, looking like she suddenly wanted to reposition his nose onto his forehead. "Are you being intentionally obtuse or are you trying to make me so confused I tear my hair out?"

"We've already established that I really *like* your hair,

so I'd say—"

"Spiro!" She threw her hands in the air, her cheeks flaming with irritation.

As much as he fought to keep the satisfied smile off his face, he couldn't help himself. His name on her lips was everything. "Yes, Mia?" he asked innocently.

"Don't bat your lashes at me." She pointed at him, and he was careful to stop blinking at all. "And put away your dimples while you're at it," she grumbled, and he sucked in his cheeks.

He knew he must look ridiculous. But he could tell she was mollified because she gave a quick, satisfied dip of her chin.

"Now explain yourself," she demanded. "Explain how you can claim to want me, but also think I'm nothing you need and you're not anything I should want."

"That's easy. I want you because you're sweet and smart and sneakily funny. But mostly because you're sexy as hell." When she opened her mouth to argue, he shoved a finger over her lips. Her hot breath bathed his skin and his cock lurched behind his fly as if it thought to replace his finger with itself.

The imagery *that* brought to mind made him ache so badly, his eyes nearly crossed.

He had to clear his throat to continue. "If I take my finger away, do you swear to be quiet and let me finish?"

Indecision made her hesitate. For a woman who chose to remain quiet so often, she sure seemed to have a hard time keeping her mouth shut when she had something to say.

Eventually she nodded.

"Okay," he said. "Let's try this again. I want you because you're amazing and sexy as hell. But your phone battery lasts longer than my relationships. Which is why I'm not anything you should want. And I've made a lot of mistakes in my life, but I don't want *you* to be one of them. I like you, Mia. More than that, I care about you and respect you as a person and a friend. If I hurt you, that would be a scar I carried forever. Which is why you're not anything I need."

Proud of himself for how eloquently he'd framed his explanation, he couldn't help adding, "See? Simple."

He expected her to say something along the lines of *Oh! Yeah. That makes total sense.* So he was a little perplexed when she just continued to blink at him.

Eventually, she tucked a strand of hair behind her ear and said slowly, "Let me see if I have this right. You want me. But you won't act on it because you're bad at relationships and—"

"Not bad at them," he cut in. "I just don't *do* them."

She rubbed her temple. He wasn't sure if that was a step up or a step down from fiddling with her earrings. "Okay. So you want me, but you won't act on it because you don't do relationships. And because you don't do relationships, you think I'll get hurt. Have I got the gist of it?"

He nodded. "Told you it's simple."

Her snort was delightfully unladylike. But there was nothing delightful about her next words. "Wow. Too bad you can't count jumping to conclusions as exercise. If you could, you'd be able to skip a week's worth of workouts."

The look he shot her said he heard her sarcasm. "And what's that supposed to mean?"

"It means you assume I *want* a relationship."

His chin yanked back so hard he was surprised it didn't hit his chest. "Don't you?"

"No!"

He didn't realize his mouth had slung open until a gnat buzzed by. Slamming his jaws shut, he shook his head and stared at her in disbelief.

Despite her current vagabond lifestyle, she'd always

struck him as the type of woman who'd settle down someday. Probably with a history professor who wore tweed and drank fine Scotch and golfed on the weekends. They'd live in Chicago, have two kids—a boy and a girl—and raise them in one of those old three-flats the city was known for.

She'd still go on excavations, of course. And in the summers, Mr. Tweed and the two rugrats would join her in faraway lands where they would eat exotic foods and learn a little of the local languages.

He'd seen it all so clearly in his mind's eye.

How could I have been so wrong?

Then it occurred to him...

Maybe I'm not wrong. Maybe when she says she doesn't want a relationship, she doesn't mean ever. *She just means with* me.

The thought shouldn't bother him. It *shouldn't*; he'd just admitted he didn't do relationships. So why did he suddenly feel like someone had stabbed him in the heart with a fixed blade KA-BAR?

Yet again, she proved when it came to assuming things he really *did* make an ass out of himself, because she added, "Not every woman dreams of the wedding and the husband and the house in town with two point three kids running around. You get that, right? You get that it's not 1950?"

"Alex says the new statistic is actually one point nine kids."

"Hear that?" She cupped her hand around her ear. "It's me not caring because that's not my point."

Had he really thought discovering her salty wit and dry sense of humor was more exciting than unearthing long lost treasure?

I take it back, he thought irritably.

Aloud, he said, "Anyone ever told you that sarcasm is the lowest form of wit?"

"Oh!" The look on her face said that, along with relocating his nose to his forehead, she was also seriously considering rearranging a few of his teeth. The front ones in particular. "Go back to weaving your stupid mat. I don't have the patience to pretend like I like you right now."

He waved away her statement for the lie it was. "You like me. You said so yourself. No backsies."

He knew he'd hit the mark when she had to suck in her cheeks to keep from smiling. After a couple of seconds, she couldn't help it and chuckled. The sound was like bubbles of happiness that burst in the air.

But she didn't say anything more, simply returned her attention to the frond weaving. And he was left to follow her lead, his head still spinning that he'd been so wrong about her. Then, a thought occurred. "So no traditional Ozzie and Harriet life for you, but don't you ever want to go back to Chicago?"

"God, no. Why would you think that?" She looked genuinely perplexed.

"It's home, isn't it? And every Chicagoan I've ever met thinks it's the greatest place on Earth. They're all *No ketchup on my dawg* and *Da Bears* and *Yo, ya wanna grab some deep dish?*"

She rolled in her lips. "Was that...supposed to be a Chicago accent?"

He grimaced. "No good?"

"You sounded more like The Count from *Sesame Street*."

"There goes my career as a voice actor."

And holy shit. There it was. That mega-watt smile that had him gaping at... Just. How. Fucking. *Gorgeous*. She was.

"Don't get me wrong." Her lips relaxed back into a closed-mouth grin. Good thing, too. It meant he could stop blinking stupidly and, you know, breathe again. "Chicago is a great town. But it's not home." Her closed-mouth grin slid into a frown. "I'm not sure I've ever really felt like I *had* a home. Not the traditional kind, at least. Home was never four walls and a roof for me. Home was my granny Susan's two loving arms and big, squishy heart. When she passed, any sense I had of *belonging* went with her. And then when Andy and Dad both died, there was nothing keeping me in Chicago."

Her expression darkened and he got the impression that, once again, they were pressing too close to another one of those invisible lines. She proved it when she quickly turned the conversational tables on him. "What about you? Are you going back to L.A. after you find the treasure?"

"That's the plan." He nodded. "Not because it feels like home, though. More because it's where I think I can do the most good. I want to start an outreach program for kids like me. Kids born into the life who would love for someone to offer them a way out."

She blinked. Her expression was...he couldn't say for sure...maybe *stunned*? "You want to start a charity that focuses on children in trouble?"

He didn't know if he should be offended by her surprise or not. "Yeah. Why does that shock you?"

"It doesn't." She shook her head. "In fact, knowing you like I do, it makes perfect sense. *Of course* you want to use your portion of the treasure to help others. You're you."

"Don't give me more credit than I deserve," he told her. "I'm doing it because I need to try to make up for the harm I did while I was there."

Now it was *his* turn to stop himself from talking since he teetered on the edge of admitting something he'd never admitted to anyone. Then, he thought, *fuck it. If anyone can understand it's Mia. Mia with her limitless kindness and compassion.*

"You know how I told you I was supposed to kill a guy to complete my initiation into the gang?" He couldn't bring himself to look at her even though he could feel her gaze on him. Instead, he focused on weaving one leaflet in and out of the line of leaflets.

"But you didn't do it." Her voice reached out to him so sweetly. "You shot him in the leg instead."

He nodded and then had to swallow the lump in his throat in order to get out this next part. "But what I didn't tell you was that I didn't have very good aim back then. What I hoped would be a glancing shot ended up shattering the dude's femur and ripping through the artery in his thigh. He had to have the leg amputated. And he was this really good surfer. Everyone thought he had the chops to go pro."

Overhead, the wind teased the trees and made their tops *click-clack* against each other. His voice barely lifted above the sound when he added, "I ended that dream for him."

Anytime he thought of what he'd done, he got queasy. Saying the words out loud, especially to someone as kind and good as Mia, made him want to puke up blood.

"Have you ever tried to find out what happened to him?" she asked. "What's become of him since?"

"Sure." He nodded. "I hunted him down on social media a half dozen years ago and apologized. Asked him if there was anything I could do to make it up to him." He grimaced. "But how can you make up for taking a man's leg and totally fucking up the future he'd fantasized about since his dad put him on a surfboard when he was five years old?"

Mia didn't answer. Instead, she asked a question of her own. "What did he say?" Romeo screwed shut his eyes, remembering how he'd cried like a baby after reading the guy's message on Facebook.

"He told me he exchanged one dream for another. Said he lived in Pasadena with the love of his life, who he met in the hospital, and that they have three little girls together. Then he told me that it sounded like I was doing some good in the world, and that if I really wanted to make it up to him, I should keep on doing good."

He glanced out at the waves, at the sun turning their crests to quicksilver. "For a long time, I thought that meant staying in the Navy, fighting and maybe dying for my country. But then I made that deathbed promise to Rusty."

His gaze slid to the tattoo on the inside of his forearm. He'd rubbed his finger over the curly-cue letters so many times, he didn't even realize when he was doing it anymore.

Rusty, you sonofabitch. You saved us all. I hope you're giving hell to all the angels in heaven, my brother.

"And you had to change your plans about how you could keep doing good in the world. Hence, the outreach program." Her voice sounded huskier than usual. "So that maybe some of the kids from your old neighborhood won't have to suffer under the weight of regrets like yours."

"Yeah." He dipped his chin. Then he looked up to give her a rueful smile. "So when you asked if one bad deed could obliterate a lifetime of good, I guess my answer is...*I sure as shit hope not.* I plan to work really hard to make sure the scales are tipped in my favor by the time I shuffle off my mortal coil."

"Ugh." She frowned at him playfully. "Just when I think I can't like you any more than I already do, you go and say stuff like that."

As difficult as it'd been for him to admit to the thing he was most ashamed of, that's how easy it was for her to make him feel better about it. One sweet word out of her mouth, combined with the glow of affection in her eyes, and he felt a small sense of absolution.

"Yeah, yeah." He rolled his eyes. "You like me. But you don't like me like *that*."

She stared at him for a good five second count. Then, "Who told you that?"

His heart screeched to a stop so hard, he wouldn't have been surprised to see skid marks across his chest. "You did that day we flew through the storm. You said all you felt for me was friendship, and for me to assume anything else made me a, quote, *supercilious ass*."

"Well, what was I supposed to say?" Exasperation raised her voice an octave. "I wasn't going to sit there with a dejected expression on my face while you told me you didn't want me."

"That's *not* what I said!" He realized he'd raised *his* voice when it echoed out over the beach. Modulating his tone, he added, "Nothing could be further from the truth. I *do* want you. I have since the first moment you set foot on Wayfarer Island."

"Well that's the way I took what you said." She waved a hand through the air. "And so yes, I called you a supercilious ass and told you all I wanted was friendship. Can you blame me for trying to save just a *little* bit of my pride?"

"But that's not true?" Something was wrong with his lungs. They'd stopped working. "You *do* want me?"

"Duh." She rolled her eyes as if she'd never heard a more idiotic question.

At first, her answer didn't sink in. Then it did, and... *Boom! Boom! BOOM!* It was like the field of flak had gone ape-shit. His heart raced but no blood got to his head. His lungs worked like bellows but no air filled his chest. Adrenaline fired through his system, lighting up every nerve, every synapse until...

A sudden sense of calm settled over him. A sense of... *inevitability*.

Mia Ennis wants *me. She wants* me.

All his reservations and reasons for holding himself

back from her were... Well, they'd gone the way of the dodo bird since she wasn't looking for a relationship. Since all she was after was something quick and dirty and fun, and he knew just the man for *that*.

"You realize you're too good for me, right?" He turned his head and watched her through narrowed eyes.

"Pah-lease." She snorted. "If anyone is too good for anyone, *you* are too good for *me*."

"How do you figure? You're educated. You're classy. You come from money and—"

"Let me stop you right there." She raised her hand. "Coming from money doesn't make a person good or bad. As for being classy, what does that even mean? That I like expensive skincare products? Have you *seen* my complexion?" She pointed to her face. "I'll be as wrinkled as a prune by the time I'm forty if I don't take care of myself. And having an education doesn't make a person smart. Some of the dumbest people I know have degrees. On the other hand, one of the smartest men I've ever met, *you*, didn't even graduate high school and had to sit for his GED."

"You..." Everything inside him got really quiet, and really, *really* still. "You think I'm smart?"

He'd never had a woman call him smart before.

Sexy, handsome, hung... *Those* were the things women said about him.

"Are you kidding?" She laughed. "Spiro..." Once again, his name on her lips had tiny, effervescent bubbles of pleasure sparkling through his veins. "You're a Navy SEAL, a pilot, a treasure-hunter, the founder of a soon-to-be charity. You can fix anything with moving parts. There isn't a piece of software out there that you can't troubleshoot. And your guacamole is five times better than Bran's and *he's* the chef. You might be the most accomplished man I've ever met. There isn't a single subject you can't talk on. I mean, you might not be an expert on everything, but you know something about most things. And if that's not smart, I don't know what is."

When he continued to stare at her in disbelief, she cocked her head. "You really don't see it, do you? You're still stuck in the past, stuck thinking you're that gangbanger from West L.A. But you left that guy behind a long time ago. Now you're...everything. Everything a man should be, brilliant and strong, honest and loyal, brave and thoughtful. *Those* are the reasons I want you. Well, and because I look at you and feel like smiling for no apparent reason, or maybe you're the only reason I need."

Then she did it again.

She gifted him with one of her radiant smiles.

And he believed her. Or, at the very least, he believed that *she* believed what she'd said because she didn't possess the acting chops to fake that level of sincerity.

She wanted him, but not for his face or his body. She wanted him for *him*, for the person he'd been working so hard to become since leaving Los Angeles.

The last little bit of steel encasing his heart melted away. And in its place was a throbbing, red-hot ball of lust mixed with tenderness and passion and an emotion he couldn't quite put his finger on.

Mia Ennis wants *me. She wants* me.

This time, when those two sentences rang through his head, they held a whole new level of meaning.

"What about Doc?" The words burst out of him like they'd been shot from a cannon.She frowned. "What about him?"

"I thought maybe you two—"

"Seriously?" she interrupted. "You thought me and Doc?" When he nodded, she snorted and shook her head. "No way. I mean, I *like* Doc. I think he's a good guy when he isn't all butthurt about lawyers. But we're friends. Just friends."

"That's what you said about us." He couldn't help reminding her.

"Well, with him, I *mean* it," she declared staunchly.

And there it was, the last reason why he couldn't have her had been swept away.

His gaze must've gone predatory, because her eyes widened. "Spiro, what—"

Before she had a chance to say anything more, his lips were on hers. He didn't remember closing the distance between them. He didn't remember shooting a hand around the back of her head to pull her forward. And he didn't remember closing his eyes and puckering up.

But he'd done all three, working on pure instinct.

When he swept his tongue over the seam of her lips, his first thought was...*soft*. His second thought was...*warm*. He didn't have time for a third thought because the sound of footfalls crunching through the sand had Mia pulling back.

"Woohoo!" Doc's deep voice reached them a couple seconds before the man himself did. "Once you see what I found"—Doc huffed to a stop in the sand behind Cami, who'd been the first to arrive on the scene—"you're going to want to kiss me."

"I highly doubt that," Romeo muttered, silently calling Doc every dirty name he knew in English *and* Spanish for having the shittiest timing on the planet.

His thoughts must've shown on his face, because Doc blinked and glanced from Romeo to Mia and back to Romeo. The toothpick in Doc's mouth tilted up slightly, right along with Doc's eyebrows. "Are we interrupting something?"

"Oh, yeah." Cami nodded vigorously. "We definitely are."

"What did you find?" Mia prompted and Romeo saw her cheeks flaming redder than usual. He nearly pounced on her when she lifted a hand to her mouth as if to hold in the heat of his brief—all too fucking *brief*—kiss.

The lawyer's hands were behind her back, but a rod tip poked up behind her head. Which meant her dramatic flourish when she revealed the fishing rod was a little anticlimactic. "Ta-da!" she said. And then she frowned at Doc. "And just so we're all clear, *I* found the fishing rod."

Doc looked instantly indignant. And then he proved that a medical degree didn't stop him from reverting to his former ten-year-old self. "Liar, liar, pants on fire!"

"I *did* find it," Cami insisted. "I'm the one who dug it out of the sand. All you did was point and say, *What's that?*"

Doc blinked. "So what, exactly, would be your definition of the word *find*?"

"I think the generally accepted definition, which is *to lay hands on*."

"I beg to differ that's the generally accepted definition. I think the generally accepted definition is *to catch sight of*."

Cami fisted a hand on her hip. "Are you really going to argue semantics with a woman whose understanding of words is an integral part of her job?"

"Pfft." Doc waved a hand. "Being a lawyer doesn't automatically make you a word wizard. But it *does* make you a—"

"Okay!" Romeo clapped his hands. For real, though, if this was what the two of them considered foreplay, he'd hate to see what the ultimate act might look like. He envisioned a lot of jockeying for the superior position combined with loudly voiced instructions on the "correct" way to do things. "The *real* question"—he jerked his chin toward the rod and reel; it took everything he had to turn his mind from Mia and her soft, warm lips—"is does it work?"

"It *does*!" Cami hooted. She demonstrated that the line around the spool unwound when she pulled on it, and then rewound once she worked the reel. "But that's not even the best part. The best part is...drum roll, please." When no one made the drum roll noise, she sighed. "You guys are no fun." Turning to Doc, she made a come-hither motion with her fingertips. "Go on then. Show them."

From out of the folds of his sling, Doc withdrew a silver lure meant to look like a baitfish. It had a touch of rust in places, just like the reel, but its two treble hooks looked remarkably intact and sturdy.

"It's a minnow crank bait," Doc said unnecessarily since Romeo had done more than his fair share of fishing while living on Wayfarer Island. Although maybe it was necessary for the ladies' edification. "And the rod and reel and this here lure are good news for two reasons. The first one being it means fishermen come to this island. Hopefully they *frequent* it. And the second one being we now have a way to catch fish that doesn't involve making nets out of palm fronds."

"Hey!" Cami whacked Doc on his good shoulder. "I still think that was a good idea. I mean, if they can make place mats"—she gestured with her chin toward Romeo's creation—"then surely *nets* wouldn't be too difficult."

"They aren't place mats," Romeo was quick to insist. "Or at least they *won't* be once we make five or six more of them and attach them all together. They'll be a tarp."

"Why would someone leave a perfectly good rod and reel on a sandbar in the middle of nowhere?" The thing about Mia being so closed-mouthed was that when she finally spoke, everyone stopped talking and listened.

"I reckon whoever was using it hooked into something big," Doc said. "Probably had the thing ripped out of their hands. Then, whatever was on the other end of the line spit out the hook. The current eventually pushed the entire rig back onto the beach."

"I don't care *why* it's here," Cami stated emphatically. "I never look a gift horse in the mouth. This rod and reel are the first good thing to happen to us all day. Well..." She smiled cattily. "The first good thing to happen to *me*, anyway. The first good thing to happen to *you* guys was getting to know me."

"Please." Doc rolled his eyes. "You might be the reason we're all in this mess."

"This old argument again?" Cami huffed. "It's far more likely *you're* the reason we're all in this mess and—"

Romeo sighed and shoved to a stand, having had enough of Tweedle Drinks Too Much and Tweedle Can't Stop Rising to the Bait. Wiggling his fingers toward the rod in Cami's hand and the lure in Doc's, he said, "I guess I better get to fishing. Cami?" The lady lawyer looked at him expectantly. "Mia will teach you how to weave palm fronds. Doc?" His partner looked at him *less* expectantly. "How about you stay out of the way and try not to pick any more fights?"

"Me?" Doc blinked innocently. "Pick fights? Never."

Romeo made a face before gesturing again toward the fishing equipment. Cami handed over the rod and reel no problem. Doc, who'd always been bad at following orders— for fuck's sake, the man barely took suggestions—was less cooperative.

"Would it kill you to say please?" There was a familiar gleam in Doc's eyes.

"What did I *just* say about picking fights?" Romeo demanded.

"Fine." Doc passed him the lure. "I'm just pointing out that there are nicer ways for you to ask for things. No need to be a demanding asshole."

Romeo turned to Mia. "See? I *told* you my friends call me nasty names on the reg."

In typical Mia fashion, she was back to smiling with her mouth closed.

Then, because he couldn't help himself, and because he was dying to get a reaction out of her, he added, "And later on, I'd like for us to revisit that last thing we were...uh... *discussing* before these two bozos interrupted us."

"Hey!" Cami harrumphed. "I take exception to being lumped into the bozo category with—"

He stopped listening because Mia's eyes had grown to the size of gun range targets, and her cheeks flamed so hot he was surprised her hair didn't catch on fire. The way she licked her lips told him everything he needed to know.

She was glad he'd kissed her—even though, as far as his kisses went, it hadn't come close to counting as his best work—and she was looking forward to more.

Despite the loss of the Otter, despite them being stranded on a desert island, and despite the ever-present prospect that someone might have tried to kill them, there was a definite skip to his step as he made his way out to the beach to catch them some dinner.

CHAPTER 12

3:44 PM...

So..." Cami said leadingly.

Mia looked over at the lawyer in question, but she got distracted from asking *So what?* by Cami's contribution to their shelter.

She thought she'd been precise in her instructions on how to keep the weave tight. But she must've left out a step or something, because Cami's loose, lumpy creation didn't look anything like the mats she and Romeo had made. In fact, Cami's attempt at a mat looked more like a lopsided net.

It crossed Mia's mind that if Romeo's rod and reel didn't work, they just might be able to put Cami's palm frond net theory to the test.

When Cami saw the direction of her gaze, she sighed. "I probably should've warned you the reason I decided to make a living using my mouth is that when it comes to using my hands, I'm all thumbs."

Mia rolled in her lips to contain a laugh. "Hence the desire to become a ventriloquist instead of taking piano lessons."

"Exactly." Cami nodded. "I figured out what my strengths were *very* early in life. Unfortunately, it took my mother a little longer to catch on. She made me continue with piano for four years until my teacher finally told her I could take lessons for the next *forty* years and still not progress much past 'Chopsticks.'"

"Nothing wrong with a good rendition of 'Chopsticks,'" Mia assured her.

Cami snorted and started pulling apart the leaflets.

"Starting over?" Mia asked.

"Third time's the charm, right?"

Mia considered saying, "*Not according to your piano teacher*," but she didn't know Cami well enough to whip out her more sarcastic side. Instead, she refocused on her own mat.

Well, that wasn't entirely true. She only *partially* focused on the palm fronds on the ground in front of her because Romeo was standing shin-deep in the surf as he cast his line into the waves, and the bunch and flex of his finely honed muscles would've been a sight to behold even had he still been wearing his T-shirt.

But he wasn't.

Gulp!

He'd pulled off the baby-blue cotton tee and tucked it into the back pocket of his jeans, so it hung down his backside. Which meant she couldn't see the high, tight, curve of his denim-clad butt. But the unencumbered view of his naked back *more* than made up for it.

The heavy muscles on either side of his spine created a deep valley between them. His wide shoulders narrowed down to his lean hips. And his tan skin gleamed with sweat and the glint of the sun as it beamed down on him like it couldn't stop itself from worshipping at the altar of his manly form.

Letting her eyes drift for the hundredth time from the top of his dark head to the bulge of his muscled calves, visible because he'd rolled the bottoms of his jeans up to his knees, she nearly whimpered.

Or maybe there was no *nearly* about it since Cami glanced at her sharply. "Oh, yeah. Now I remember where I was headed before I got sidetracked by my less than mediocre weaving skills. So..." The lawyer wiggled her eyebrows. "I wasn't wrong to assume there's something brewing between you and O Romeo, Romeo, where for art thou Romeo. I *knew* my romance radar couldn't be that far out of whack. So how'd he do it?"

Mia ignored the heat in her cheeks and asked, "Do what?"

"Kiss you. I saw you two all lip-locked when I came around the corner." She leaned in and lowered her voice. "Was it sudden? Like, did he swoop in and ravish your mouth? Or was it slow? Did he brush aside your hair, cup your cheek, and never break eye contact?" She sat back and gave a dramatic shiver. "Oh, both ways are delicious. I can't decide which is my favorite."

Mia was only half paying attention at that point because she was still coming to terms with two very mind-blowing revelations. The first one? Romeo *did* like her like that. The rather, ahem, impressive-looking bulge in his pants had spoken for itself.

She got all flushed and flustered just thinking about *that*. So she decided not to think about it, and instead focus on the second revelation.

Since Romeo liked her like that, and since she'd assured him she wasn't hunting up a happily-ever-after, he was anxious to act on the fact that he liked her like that.

Oh, my god. Did the world tilt? No? That was just every bone in my body turning into jelly?

She realized she'd been quiet for too long when Cami sighed. "Please tell me you aren't one of those principled people who thinks it's vulgar to kiss and tell. Because I'm stuck on an island with no cell service, no internet, and no TV. The only entertainment I have is the drama between you and Romeo."

Mia grabbed onto the opening Cami had inadvertently given her like a drowning woman grabbing onto a life raft. Really, how was she supposed to talk about her and Romeo when she was still trying to come to terms with the idea that there *was* a her and Romeo?

"Seems to me like you and Doc do plenty to cause drama and entertain each other," she countered.

"Nice." Cami nodded. "But you forget who you're dealing with. I practice misdirection and redirection for a living. We're not talking about me and Doc. We're talking about you and Romeo."

"Damn." It was Mia's turn to sigh. "You're good."

"Thank you." Cami inclined her head. "Now, kiss and tell."

"There's nothing to tell," Mia insisted. "It barely lasted a second. I'm not even sure it should count as a kiss."

"You have a little bullshit right here." Cami pointed to her own mouth, and Mia decided the next time she wanted to let her sarcastic flag fly, she wasn't going to hesitate. "That counted as a kiss, and you know it."

Cami was right, of course.

Spiro "Romeo" Delgado, the sexiest, most wonderful man Mia had ever met, had kissed her lips and she would swear she'd felt it in her toes.

And in all the places in between.

"Which is why you keep glancing at him and making that little squeaking sound in the back of your throat," Cami added.

"Ugh." Mia's shoulders drooped in defeat. "I was hoping that was only in my head."

"Afraid not." Cami made a face. "But hey, I get it. I mean, he sort of looks like a beached lion out there. All tawny-skin and masculinely brutish as he prowls through the surf, hunting up our dinner." She stopped and grinned. "Oh, I like that. Maybe I should give up this whole lawyering gig and write novels. The really dreamy, really steamy kind."

Cami comparing Romeo to a lion had Romeo's words spinning through Mia's head. *"Hands down, you have the most beautiful eyes I've ever seen. Lioness eyes is how I think of them."*

But as hot and raw as his words had been, they hadn't compared to the look on his face. Never in Mia's life had a man looked at her like it was taking every ounce of willpower he possessed not to grab her and rip off all her clothes.

She wasn't really the clothes-ripping type. Or, at least, she never had been before Romeo.

"So what's the next step for you two?"

She was relieved when Cami interrupted her thoughts. Much more time remembering the look on Romeo's face and she might melt into a puddle. And then who would finish their palm frond tarp?

Certainly not Cami.

"What do you mean?" she asked, determinedly going back to work.

"I mean, it's obvious there's going to be some wild monkey sex happening. But after? Are you thinking an engagement ring followed by a beach wedding?" Cami snapped her fingers. "I know this *great* wedding planner in Miami who specializes in beach ceremonies. I'll give you his number when we get back to civilization and—"

"No." Mia shook her head. "It's not like that."

Cami's wide grin turned into a frown. "What's it like then?"

That was the million-dollar question, wasn't it?

Mia had spent so long assuming there was no chance of having anything more than a friendship with Romeo that she'd never stopped to think what having more than friendship with him might look like.

Would it be a one-night stand? Would they become lovers for...however long she continued to work with Deep Six Salvage? Would it be something in-between? A few rolls in the sand until they'd scratched their itch?

Although, she couldn't imagine *any* amount of scratching that would soothe the itch Romeo had built inside her. He was sexual poison ivy. Sexual chicken pox. Sexual folliculitis?

She wrinkled her nose, realizing she'd driven that particular analogy about as far it should go.

Right. So the question had been *what is it like then*? And her answer was, "I don't know. I just know there won't be any engagement rings or beach weddings."

Cami nodded. "You're a modern woman. No engagement ring because the entire diamond industry is a scam. DeBeers is a monopoly. They hold, like, what? Eighty-five percent of all the rough diamonds in the world, but they only let a few of the little suckers trickle out at a time to create the illusion of scarcity and rarity so that they can keep the prices abnormally high?"

Mia stared. She decided then and there if Cami hadn't become a lawyer, she'd have made an excellent radio talk show host. The woman never seemed to run out of words.

"But you could still do an engagement ring," Cami added firmly. "Just do a nontraditional one. Like a sapphire.

You said blue is your favorite color, right? Or...what's your birthstone?"

"Topaz, but—"

"Topaz?" Cami cut her off. "That's perfect. The exact color of your eyes!"

Lioness eyes... Again, Romeo's words echoed through Mia's head.

"Now, if you're not into beach weddings," Cami continued, "I'm sure Enrique could—"

"Let me rephrase." Mia was once again forced to interrupt the flow of words streaming from Cami's mouth like Lake Michigan streamed into the Chicago River when the lock was opened. "There won't be an engagement ring or a beach wedding because there won't be an engagement or a wedding. Ever. Period. End of sentence."

For a full five seconds, Cami stared at her. Finally, she ventured, "For...who? You or him?"

"Neither one of us is interested in taking any sort of plunge that doesn't end with us finding sunken treasure." Mia grinned at her own wit.

"Oh-kay." Cami nodded even though she looked a little bewildered. "You're both lone wolves, content to hunt the hills alone. I get it. I mean, I *wish* I got it. If I got it, life would probably be a lot less complicated."

The lawyer made a dramatic gesture. "Alas, behind this ball-busting lady lawyer facade beats the heart of an old-fashioned romantic. I want the ring and the wedding and the house and the kids. I want holidays and family." Her eyes took on a faraway look when she continued. "Then, you know, that peaceful fade into retirement, matching front porch rockers, grandkids running through the sprinkler system on hot summer days. The more storybook and clichéd, the better." She laughed. "Hard to fathom, right? A career-minded broad like me wanting to get all domestic?"

"No." Mia shook her head. "I think lots of people, most maybe, fantasize about the sort of life you're describing. Getting to have it all, the career, the family, the accomplishments both professional and personal."

Cami shrugged. "But it requires finding the right man, and so far he's proved elusive."

Glad for the distraction from her own thoughts, Mia asked, "What are you looking for?"

"What every hetero woman is looking for, I guess." Cami flicked her fingers casually. "I want a man who's loyal, devoted, emotionally available, intellectually curious, and handsome without knowing it. A man's who's quick with a smile, but with a bit of an edge to keep things interesting."

She bobbed her eyebrows and kept going. "A man who'll luxuriate in a bubble bath with me, but who'll also share the household and child-rearing duties, because Momma gotta bring home the bacon, too. And fair is fair."

She tapped her lips before adding, "A man who has some miles under his tires, but who's retained enough of his inner child to be open to new ideas. A man who's honest, who values integrity, who's independent because being wanted is sexy but being *needed* becomes burdensome over time. A man who respects himself enough not to take shit from anyone, but who isn't so hard that he can't bend without breaking. You know, basically I want Prince Charming so long as Prince Charming believes in a post-patriarchal society. And throw in a little bit of sex god while you're at it."

Blinking, Cami shook her head. "It suddenly occurs to me why I haven't met my Mr. Right. It's very possible he doesn't exist."

Before Mia could respond, Cami employed a little of that redirection she seemed so proud of. "But let's go back to you. Or, more specifically, you and Romeo." The lawyer gave her a friendly nudge. "If there's not going to be any first comes love, then comes marriage, then comes Romeo pushing a baby carriage, that leaves the wild monkey sex."

Blowing out a shaky breath, Mia admitted slowly, "For a...while now, I thought I'd jump at the chance for exactly that."

"But?" Cami prompted.

"But..." She struggled to untangle her jumbled up thoughts. "But what if sex ruins the friendship we've built?"

She *cherished* Romeo's friendship. It was unlike anything she'd ever experienced before. It was...easy. Comfortable. She felt like she'd known him forever, and yet she knew there were a million things she'd yet to learn about him.

Things she *wanted* to learn about him.

Things she thought she could spend *years* figuring out.

"What if..." She hesitated and had to swallow the discomfort that tried to strangle her. "What if he ends up being disappointed in me?" When she saw Cami's eyebrows draw together, she was quick to explain. "I mean, I'm not a virgin or anything. But I'm sure my body count is nowhere *near* his, and what if I don't have enough experience to—"

"Nope." Cami interrupted her by raising one red tipped finger. "Sex isn't rocket science. It's not like there are unfathomable mysteries that you've yet to comprehend. Sex is sex. Are there things Romeo has tried that you haven't? Probably. But that doesn't mean you don't know how to do it and do it *well*."

Mia thought back to the last man she'd slept with. He'd been a fellow marine archeologist helping her on a sunken city site off the coast of Greece. If the number of times he'd come knocking at the door of her trailer after a hard day's diving was anything to go by, Cami was right. Mia *did* know how to do it and do it well.

That, or Mia and Dr. Adam Chasson had *both* been too

inexperienced to know when sex sucked.

"In my experience," Cami continued, "the only thing that disappoints a man sexually is when the person he's with isn't having a good time." She slid Mia a sly glance. "Something tells me Romeo will make sure you're having a good time. And if he doesn't"—she narrowed her eyes—"I trust you'll tell him what needs to be done. Because I've noticed you're one to hold your tongue, but take it from me, the last place you should remain mum is in the bedroom."

Mia felt one corner of her mouth twitch. "If only I had your way with words."

"Oh, that part is easy." Cami waved a hand. "You just have to immerse yourself in sarcasm and bullshit until you're fluent."

Mia's lip-twitch turned into a full-on chuckle.

"But back to your first concern," Cami pressed ahead with barely a pause. "When it comes to the friendship part, I think the answer is simple. Your friendship will morph into friends with benefits. My sister swears by the arrangement."

Cami caught what she'd said and all the color drained from her cheeks. "Or...she *swore* by it. Damn." Her eyes reflected her inner pain when she looked at Mia. "How long until I remember to talk about her in the past tense?"

Empathy made Mia's heart squeeze tight.

She remembered all too well the agony of slamming into the realization that people she loved were part of her past and would never again be part of her present. Those early days when she'd wake up and, for a couple of minutes, forget that Andy or her grandmother or her father was gone, and then... *pow!*...get hit once again with the reality of their loss.

Those days had been *agonizing*.

Yet, there were times now that she *missed* that phase of mourning. Because while it was horrendous to be forced to face the finality of death time after time, sometimes that was better than the constant ache once the knowledge truly set in.

"It's different for everyone," she said quietly. "When you have the time to prepare, like I did with my grandmother when she was diagnosed with lung cancer, I used the past tense pretty quickly after she was gone. For my father, who died of a sudden heart attack, it took me a lot longer to get there."

Cami cocked her head. "And what about with your brother?"

Mia had to close her eyes when the backs of her eyeballs began to burn. Even after ten years, talk of Andy's death still pushed her inexplicably close to tears. "A few months, I think. My little brother was never mentally healthy, so..."

She trailed off when she realized what she'd said wasn't true, strictly speaking.

Andy had been such a happy baby. Such a funny, full-of-life toddler. But he'd never been the same after they came home from the hospital.

And that was Mia's greatest failure. Which had led to her unbearable shame. Which had culminated in her ultimate sin.

"I fell somewhere in the middle of being prepared and being caught by surprise with Andy," she finally added, her voice so rough she barely recognized it.

"I'm so sorry." Cami placed a hand on top of hers.

"Yeah." Mia sighed. "Me too. For you, I mean. For your loss. Everyone talks about how terrible it is to lose a parent or a child, but no one ever talks about how hard it is to lose a sibling."

"It really drives home that old saying: *life's too short*," Cami agreed. "Which brings us full circle in this conversation. Life's too short for us to be constantly worrying about the consequences when amazing opportunities present themselves. Plus, don't we owe it to those who were taken too soon to live life to its fullest?"

Before Mia could answer her question, Cami pushed on. "So what if sex changes your friendship with Romeo? There's no guarantee your friendship won't change anyway. I mean, friends come and go. If you and Romeo do this, at least you'll have the memory of it to hold onto when you're all alone and the nights turn cold."

Mia desperately wanted to buy what Cami was selling. The lawyer made it sound so simple and reasonable. Well, that and Mia may have undersold herself when she told Cami that for a while now she'd jump at the chance for some wild monkey sex with Romeo. It was more like she'd take a flying leap over a cliff with no safety net waiting at the bottom.

And maybe that was a good analogy. Because as fun as the fall would be, the landing might hurt like hell. And yet, even so, she couldn't deny that she was—

Cami interrupted her thoughts. "You're going to do it, aren't you?"

"You make a compelling argument," Mia admitted.

"Thank you." Cami inclined her head. "I like to think so." Then, her eyes narrowed. "But..."

"But what?" Mia frowned.

"That's what I'm asking *you*. I can see there's a but rolling around inside your head." Cami pointed to a spot between Mia's eyes.

"If you're this much of a bulldog in regular life," Mia said, "what are you like in the courtroom?"

"Pretty much the same," Cami conceded with a chuckle. "I just use a lot more *your honors* and *if it pleases the courts.* So...what's the but?"

Mia bit her lip. "But what if, despite everything we've talked about, this still ends up being a really bad idea and one or both of us gets hurt?"

Cami waved away her concern. "Bad ideas make for

great stories. And as for getting hurt? Take it from Garth Brooks, it's way worse to miss the dance than it is to miss the pain."

Mia snorted. "Never figured you for a country music fan."

"I'm not. But I make an exception for Garth."

Am I really going to do this? Mia asked herself. *Am I really going to take Spiro "Romeo" Delgado as a lover?*

Heaven help her, she was. Because Cami and Garth were right. Life was too short and Mia didn't want to miss the dance.

Plus, now she could view leaving Wayfarer Island as a good thing. Her leaving would create a hard stop for their affair, and it felt good knowing from the beginning how it would end.

It made her feel more in control.

CHAPTER 13

4:14 PM...

At least one of us will be getting laid soon, Cami thought as she stole a look at Mia and found the marine archeologist wearing a secretive little smile.

Of course, the last thing *Cami* was doing was smiling when she returned her attention to her palm leaf mat.

Mia had managed to make three of the big, green suckers in the time it'd taken Cami to make one. Not *even* one. Because she was half finished, and her weave looked no tighter on her third attempt than it had on her first.

Glancing at Mia's hands, she diligently watched the process for the umpteenth time. And yet when she tried to recreate it? It was all Hashtag Nailed It.

Mia's mat looked like it belonged under a dinner plate at a fancy island resort. Cami's mat looked like...well, not a mat. Maybe a basket? Or...a hammock for a family of Central Park squirrels?

Her sorry attempt at weaving reminded her of the time Carlotta had tried to teach her to French braid. They'd ended up having to cut three inches off Carlotta's hair because Cami had so thoroughly tied it in knots. And then Cami had let Carlotta cut three inches off *her* hair out of solidarity.

Their mother had been furious to find their raven locks lying in a pile on the bathroom floor. But they'd thought their new bangs looked kind of cute. And who cared if the left side of Cami's hair was shorter than the right, or that there was a huge hunk missing from the back of Carlotta's head?

The memory of that day, all the whispers and giggles while she and her sister took turns wielding the scissors, renewed the ache that lived in the center of her chest. She sent a silent sentiment into the abyss. *Oh, how I miss you, my sweet sister.*

Letting her head fall back, she closed her eyes and concentrated on the warmth of the wind as it slid over her skin. On the sound it made when it rattled through the palm trees overhead. On the smells it brought with it...salt water, hot sand, and sun.

"What did you give him anyway?" Mia's voice interrupted her momentary mediation.

Cami dropped her chin. "Give who what?"

"Doc." Mia pointed over her shoulder toward the life raft. Its garish, orange hue stood out in stark contrast to the creamy color of the sand and the caramel color of the tree trunks.

The only way to know Doc inhabited the watercraft was to see the two *huge* bare feet propped on the round rubber side, or to hear the deep, resonate snores that wafted up from within.

Cami giggled. "I gave him one of my period pills." When Mia lifted an eyebrow, Cami raised a hand. "Hey, he looked on the bottle and said he'd be fine to take it. And who was I to second-guess him?"

"Should we"—Mia wrinkled her nose—"go see if he's okay?"

"He sounds fine to me." Cami smirked. "In fact, he sounds better than fine. He sounds like he'll be out for the next couple of hours. And if those pills affect him like they affect me, he'll wake up with a serious craving for red wine and potato chips dipped in chocolate syrup."

Mia laughed. "Is that a thing?"

"It is at my house," Cami assured with all due seriousness.

Mia pressed a hand to her stomach when it let out a loud growl. "Oh, god. We must stop talking about food. I'm starving. Have you seen Romeo catch anything? He's been at it for a while now."

Cami's own stomach balled into a fist at the thought of food. Or rather, at the thought of *no* food. "No." She grimaced. "Not so much as a minnow."

"I'm suddenly understanding how the Donner Party felt," Mia muttered.

Cami scooted a few inches away. "If talking about food has you turning all Hannibal Lecter, then by all means, let's change the subject. Between me, Doc, or Romeo, no doubt I'm the tenderest and the tastiest." She tapped her lips in thought. "What sort of chitchat are you up for? We could list the weirdest places we've ever done it. Or we could rate the worst dates we've ever been on. Or we could admit the three most embarrassing moments of our lives so far. Any of those topics strike your fancy?"

Carlotta had loved to play this game on dateless Friday nights while wearing comfy pajamas and stuffing their faces full of junk food and wine.

Mia slid her a sly glance. "How about we go back to you and Doc? You never did answer my question."

"What question was that?" Cami tried acting nonchalant.

Doc was... Hmm. She wasn't sure *what* he was. All she knew was that one minute she wanted to punch him in the nuts, and the next minute she wanted to pounce on him and kiss him all over his insanely appealing face.

"I guess it wasn't so much a question as it was an observation," Mia admitted. "You two can't seem to make up your minds whether to like each other or loathe each other."

"Why do those things have to be mutually exclusive?" Cami knew her smile was wry. "It's true. He irks me, and it's hard for me not to answer every question he asks with a middle finger when he starts in on the lawyer stuff. But he's also smart-alecky and a little bit brooding. And I swear that combination is like honey to a bee for me. I keep coming back for—"

She stopped talking and frowned over at Mia. It was obvious by the marine archeologist's posture and the direction of her gaze, she'd stopped listening. Cami quickly turned her attention to the vast, rolling ocean, but whatever had caught Mia's attention alluded her own eyes.

"What do you see?" She felt the hairs on her arms lift with a sense of expectation.

Mia's voice was even quieter than usual. Cami had to strain to hear her over Doc's snores. "I...I'm not sure. I thought maybe...there for a second it looked like...a boat?"

When Mia pointed, Cami followed the direction of her finger. At first she saw nothing but blue on blue on blue. But then...

"Holy shit!" She was on her feet in an instant.

"Do you see it?" Mia stood beside her.

"I think so. I think I see..." She trailed off, because she couldn't be certain her eyes weren't deceiving her. Or that her brain wasn't conjuring up a mirage of what she so desperately wanted to see.

She would swear she caught a glimpse of a white hull. But it was so far away, and it disappeared so quickly behind a wave that—

No! A flash, like sunlight glinting off glass, blazed across the distance and she was convinced. There was a *boat* out there!

We're saved! she silently cheered. Aloud, she wheezed, "Flare gun!"

The sand did its best to slow her steps when she bolted toward the life raft. Mia wasn't any quicker, falling into step behind her and only catching up once Cami skidded to a stop next to the rubber watercraft.

"Doc!" Cami yelled, grabbing his big, solid shoulder to give it a shake. He was using the flare gun case as a pillow. "Wake up!"

He didn't flinch. There's wasn't even a lull in his snoring.

"Doc!" she yelled, louder this time. And when that didn't work, she tried, "Dalton!"

"Mmm," he muttered and smacked his lips.

"Screw this," she grumbled. Time was of the essence. The boat was already so far out. And who was to say it wasn't getting farther away with each passing second?

Reaching beneath Doc's head, she grabbed the handle on the flare gun case and gave it a yank. Instead of pulling it out from under him, however, she only managed to jostle him enough so he rolled onto her arm. Given her precarious position, cantilevered over the side of the life raft, that was all it took to completely unbalance her.

A loud yelp shot out of her as she tumbled on top of him, bumping her forehead on his scruffy chin.

That was enough to wake him. He blinked open his eyes and frowned at her when she pushed up on one hand and used the other to rub her forehead. In a voice that was rough from sleep, he said, "You're giving me whiplash, woman. One minute you're telling me you don't mix business with pleasure, and the next I wake up to you molesting my unconscious body. Make up your mind. Are we doing this or not?"

He slapped one of her body parts that no man on the face of the planet had ever slapped outside the bedroom...or without her throwing a drink in his face.

Since she didn't *have* a drink, she simply sputtered and wished she'd said something articulate and cutting. But her brain had gone offline the moment his hand met her ass, because it repositioned her just enough so she felt the hard column of flesh that pressed into her lower belly.

And yes. She knew it didn't mean anything. He was a man. He'd been asleep. Erections caused by slumber were a simple fact of biology.

Still...*wowza*.

In the next instant, her faculties returned—*thank goodness*. And with them came her acerbic tongue.

"Everyone is entitled to be a prick once in a while, but you are seriously abusing the privilege today." She pushed away from his chest and the broken arm she knew she had to be crushing. Although why she should care after the way he was behaving was anyone's guess. "And let me assure you, I was taught to think before I act. So if I smack the shit out of you for touching my ass without permission, understand I thought about it and came to the conclusion that it was the only appropriate choice left to me."

He blinked and glanced to the side. When he saw his hand palming her butt, he seemed genuinely shocked.

Was it possible he'd still been half asleep when he grabbed her and mumbled that nonsense? He was definitely still half-baked. She could tell by the size of his pupils.

Good ol' period pills. Works every time.

"What the hell's going on?" he demanded, removing his hand like her butt cheek might light his fingers on fire.

"What's going on is that you're lying on the flare gun, and we need it because there's a boat!"

He scowled. "And you thought the best way to get it was to crawl on top of me and—"

"I didn't crawl on top of you, you idiot! You rolled onto my arm when I tried to grab the case, which made me *fall* on top of you!"

"Likely story." He harrumphed.

"Oh!" She wanted to smack him. She really, *really* wanted to smack him.

She might have done exactly that had Mia not stopped her by saying quietly and succinctly, "People. Focus. Gun case."

"Right." Cami reached behind Doc and whipped out the case. His head landed on the bottom of the watercraft with a *thud*.

"Hey!" he complained. "Head injury, remember?"

"Serves you right for grabbing my ass, you big pervert," she sniffed peevishly while scrambling over the round rubber side of the raft. She would *swear* the skin over her lower stomach tingled where it'd been pressed against his hardness.

"You can't blame a man for what he does when he's high on pain meds and half asleep!" he protested to her back because she was already running for the beach with Mia hot on her heels.

Again, the sand did her no favors in her effort to cover ground. By the time they splashed into the surf next to Romeo, she was completely out of breath.

"What the—" Romeo flinched at their sudden arrival. Then his eyes traveled down to the flare gun case in her hands and he automatically lifted his gaze skyward.

"No," she said, or rather *wheezed*. She really needed

to renew her gym membership. A thirty second run through the sand shouldn't make her feel like there was an elephant sitting on her chest. "It's not..." *Pant, pant.* "A plane..." *Pant, pant.* "It's a..."

"It's a boat!" Mia finished for her, pointing in the direction they'd seen the watercraft. Romeo lifted a hand to shade his eyes. "Where? I don't see it?"

Neither did Cami.

Damnit! It probably sailed away while Doc was—

"There!" Mia pointed, and Cami followed the archeologist's finger until—*oh thank goodness!* There it was, the flash of the white hull and the glint of sunlight reflecting off glass.

"I do too." Romeo nodded quickly. "Here. Trade me."

He thrust his rod into Cami's hands at the same time he snatched the flare gun case from her. He had Mia hold the case while he flipped the latches and grabbed the flare gun from its foam cutout. His movements were so quick they were nearly a blur as he armed the thing with a cartridge and pointed it in the direction of the sky above the boat.

Cami winced, expecting a loud *boom*. When he pulled the trigger, the flare gun made more of a *cracking* sound, followed by a *squee* as the flare flew out over the water.

She watched their bright, sparkly cry for help arc across the blue sky and had the urge to laugh with glee. *We're saved!*

"They saw it, didn't they?" she said once the flare flamed out.

"Give them a second," Romeo murmured.

When one second stretched into two which stretched into ten, Cami couldn't stop herself from looking at him expectantly. Her heart sank when he cursed and ran a hand through his hair.

She turned her gaze to the open water and searched for the glimmer of the white hull or the flash of sunlight on glass.

No matter how hard she strained her eyes, all she saw was wave after wave after wave.

"They didn't see it." Her voice was almost as quiet as Mia's. Louder, she added, "Quick! Use another flare!"

"No." Romeo shook his head. "If they were too far out to see the first one, then they're definitely too far out now to see a second one. And we only have one flare left. We should save it for when a plane or boat comes closer, eh?"

Her shoulders drooped. "I guess that's that then."

"No." Mia spoke up. "That's not that then, because..." She grabbed Romeo's wrist so she could see the face of his big diver's watch. "We're officially more than four hours late for our arrival on Wayfarer Island. Surely LT and the others have raised the alarm by now. Surely the search is underway." She looked at Romeo. "Don't you think?"

He smoothed his goatee. "Not necessarily. I've been late before because of weather or a mechanical issue or because I just got held up picking up supplies or whatever."

When he saw Mia's expression fall, he was quick to add, "But LT is definitely getting worried by now. My guess is he'll be putting in a sat phone call to air traffic control soon. And when they tell him our plane left on time, he'll do more than raise the alarm. He'll have everyone and their dog out looking for us."

"I suppose that's something," Cami sighed, hanging onto the reassurance she saw in his face as hard as she hung on to the memory of her sister. Then she saw something else flicker in his eyes, and once again she heard herself asking, "But?"

He looked uncomfortable. "But this time of year, we've only got about three more hours of daylight. I don't know how much looking the search crews will do after it gets dark."

Before Cami could respond, Doc sauntered up on the beach behind them and said in his deep, scratchy voice, "I take it the flare didn't work?"

It was on the tip of Cami's tongue to blurt, *Thanks to you!* If he hadn't delayed her from getting to the case, maybe the boat would've been close enough to see their signal for help. She swallowed the words, however, because holding up the weight of her disappointment meant she didn't have the energy for another verbal battle.

"They were too far out," Romeo told Doc. "They didn't see it."

"Oh good." Doc nodded. "I'm starting to love this place. Thinking about moving here permanently."

Cami rolled her eyes, in no mood for humor. But then she yelped when the rod was nearly jerked from her hands. "Guys!" she shouted. "I think I got one!"

"Huh." Romeo scratched his goatee. "Guess I've been doing it all wrong. I was fishing when I should've been letting my lure bob in the surf."

"Well, what are you waiting for?" This from Doc. "Reel it in."

Cami grabbed the little handle on the reel and started cranking. But the action was harder than they made it look on TV, and she remembered that thing Doc said about the original owner of the rod and reel. *"Whoever was using it hooked into something big."* And *then* she remembered what Mia had said about great whites being in the area.

Suddenly, all she could picture was the shark from *JAWS* hooked onto the end of the line, seconds away from dragging her into the sea and biting her in half.

"Take it!" She yelled at no one in particular. "Somebody take it!"

Romeo looked momentarily startled by her outburst, but he was quick to shove the flare gun into Mia's hands and grab the rod and reel from Cami. She breathed a sigh of relief as soon as she was no longer attached to what, in her mind, *had* to be a mammoth shark, and waded quickly through the surf onto the safety of the beach.

"Aren't you about as useful as a rubber beak on a woodpecker?" Doc observed after coming to stand next to her.

She scowled at him. "You know what? I'm starting to envy people who have never met you."

He chuckled. "Oh, come on." He nudged her. "You thought you hooked into *JAWS*, right?"

She hated being so transparent. Transparent and ridiculous, because *of course* she hadn't hooked a great white.

"Wrong." She shook her head. "I've just never fished before. I didn't want to be the reason we starved to death."

He snorted. "You reckon that explanation would work on your home planet of Horseshitia?"

See? She fought a grin. *Smart-alecky. Soooo smart-alecky.*

She glanced over to see if, indeed, he was broody too. But she got distracted by the way the late afternoon sun glinted in his green eyes. And for some reason, she was suddenly reminded of the fun they'd had the night before, all the flirting and teasing and joking.

Despite wanting to kill him at various times that day, she could still admit...

It really is too bad I don't mix business with pleasure.

CHAPTER 14

4:28 PM...

Shit!" Robby paced the length of the boat after Carter motored them farther away from the little island. "They *saw* us."

"No, dude," Kenny grumbled. "They probably saw *you* and the sun glinting off the lenses of the field glasses."

Kenny turned the word *probably* into *prolly*. But what really got Carter's goat was the use of the phrase *field glasses*.

Kenny used military lingo because he fancied himself a soldier even though the U.S. Army had rejected his application twice. The first time because Kenny had a juvenile felony conviction for selling meth. And the second time because Kenny had such bad credit that it affected his potential security clearance.

Truly, Kenny Smith was a piece of work. But he was *Carter's* piece of work, especially when it came to their current situation, and so Carter bit back the sarcastic comment sitting on the tip of his tongue.

"I told ya to put those fuckers away," Kenny continued chewing Robby's ass. "But once ya got a look at that black-haired dude, ya haven't been able to keep your eyes off him."

Carter rolled his eyes. Kenny thought the biggest insult was to question another guy's sexuality. Truly, the man still lived like it was 1995.

"So what if they saw us?" Carter said to mollify Robby and shut Kenny up. "It's not like we're going to respond to the flare and go get them. At least not yet."

After they'd determined the one bastard was armed, they'd decided their best bet was to wait until after dark, sail as close to the island as they dared so that the engine noise didn't reach the shore, and then jump in and swim the rest of the way. They would sneak up on the unsuspecting group under cover of night and wait for Mia to separate herself on a walk or on the way to take a pee break. Once she was alone, Kenny would slit her throat. After that, the plan would remain the same. Cover up any blood evidence, swim her body out to the speedboat, and then weigh down her corpse and dispose of it on their way back to Key West.

If Carter was being honest, he liked this option better than any they'd come up with yet. As much as he'd convinced himself those flying with her were simply collateral damage—and hell, the U.S. government used that excuse plenty—he'd never really been able to wrap his mind around offing three innocents.

"Yeah," Robby insisted, dragging him from his thoughts. "But now they know we're here."

"They know we *were* here," Carter corrected. "If we can't see them, they can't see us. They'll assume we missed the flare and moved on."

"I still think we're wasting time," Jane said with a huff, adjusting her hat when a gust of wind tried to tug it off her head. "We have a gun. They have a gun. But we have the advantage because we have the element of surprise. They're never going to think a boat motoring up to the island is filled with people looking to kill them. They'll think they're being rescued. Kenny can take out the one who's armed first. After that, killing the others will be like shooting fish in a barrel."

Kenny lifted an eyebrow. "I *do* like shooting fish in a barrel."

"No way." Robby shook his head. "It's too risky. What if you don't kill the gunman? What if you only wound him and he has time to draw his weapon? I didn't sign up for getting shot."

"Robby's right," Carter agreed. "Plus, this way we don't have to kill anyone but Mia. The one we're really after."

"But if we leave the others alive, don't you think they'll wonder what happened to her?" Jane pressed. "Don't you think they'll wonder how and why she vanished off an island in the middle of nowhere?"

Carter shrugged. "They might *wonder*. But there won't be any way for them to figure it out. We'll make sure of that."

"And the plane?" Jane persisted. "If we leave them alive, they might want an investigation into what happened to it. Ever think of that?"

Carter *had* thought of that. "It's too deep to dive out here. What? You think they're going to convince the Key West police department to spend cash on a submersible to come out here and take video of the wreckage?"

Jane crossed her arms and frowned—Carter ignored that his two best friends stared at her cleavage—but she didn't offer up another excuse.

"Good." He dipped his chin. "Then we're all agreed?"

None of them had time to answer him before the radio tuned to the Marine Emergency channel came to life. The voice sounding over the airwaves was low and a little tinny, but otherwise as clear as a bell. "Be advised all ships sailing in Hawks Channel or the Straits of Florida. An amphibious aircraft, body color blue and white, has been reported missing in the area. Four people on board. If anyone has seen the aircraft or signs of the aircraft, please report in. Over."

Carter felt his stomach drop down and try to exit his ass. "Shit. They're starting the search."

"Not yet," Kenny assured him. "They'll wait to see if anyone has spotted the aircraft before calling in the Coast Guard."

"But how long will they wait?" Robby demanded.

"Not sure." Kenny shrugged and glanced up at the sun. "But we only got a coupla hours until sunset. Chances are nobody's gonna stumble across the sandbar before dark. We can still stick with the plan. Or we could do as the lovely Jane suggests"—he winked at Carter's aunt who preened like a teenager—"and hit 'em now. Take 'em all out." He looked expectantly at Carter. "What's it gonna be?"

"Let's stick with the after dark plan," Carter decided with a firm dip of his chin. When he heard his aunt snort, he curled his hands into fists and added, "We'll keep listening to the radios, and if we think they're getting close to searching this area, we'll go with Aunt Jane's plan, move in early, and end them all."

He looked around the boat at the three faces staring back at him. Robby looked relieved. Kenny looked indifferent since, either way, he would get to off someone. But Jane? Well, she looked impatient. And maybe a little pissed.

"Don't worry. We'll get it done," he assured her. "One way or another, you'll have your justice. And we'll all get our money."

CHAPTER 15

6:15 PM...

thought that would be a crap-ton of disgusting, but it was actually pretty good." Cami wiped the back of her hand over her mouth and sighed contentedly.

Romeo smiled briefly at the lawyer. But it was like Mia was a magnet and his eyeballs were metal. Because before he knew it, he'd turned back to watch her pop the last morsel of fish from her improvised palm leaf plate into her mouth. She delicately sucked on her fingertips, and when her pink tongue flicked out to lick her lips, he barely refrained from groaning out loud.

Sweet Mother Mary...

He had a hard-on fat enough to choke a mule. And since fully half of the people sitting around the fire would no doubt like nothing better than to *not* bear witness to the party in his pants, he distracted himself by wrapping the leftover portion of fish into a palm frond.

The meat wouldn't keep for long. But it would still be good in the morning for breakfast. And as the sun sank farther into the west, he thought it was a sure bet they'd still be on the sandbar come the dawn.

"What kind of fish did you say that was?" Cami asked him over the orange and yellow dance of the flames from the fire they'd built to cook the fish.

"Snook," he told her.

The long silvery fish with the big, black stripes down its sides had given him quite a fight. By the time he'd pulled it onto the shore, he'd been covered in sweat and his forearms had burned with fatigue.

Doc, never one to let a guy catch his breath, had immediately clapped him on the shoulder and declared, "Get a fire burning and let's eat!"

Since Romeo had worked up quite an appetite battling the beast, he'd shaken off his weariness, wiped a hand over his brow, and gotten busy doing exactly as Doc suggested.

The matches out of the first aid kit had come in handy for lighting the pile of driftwood the others had gathered from the beach. *Thank you, Mia, for your fast thinking back on the life raft.* And the makeshift spit he'd created had worked pretty damn good at barbecuing the fish, even if he did say so himself.

The snook had been big and meaty, so it'd taken a while for it to fully cook over the open flame. And by the time it'd been done through, the outer parts had turned a little dry. But thankfully, the packages of Italian dressing Cami had produced from her purse had spiced up even the most overdone portions.

Truly, the lawyer's leather carryall was like a swap meet; it seemed to have a little bit of everything.

"Snook?" She wrinkled her nose now. "Sounds like the imaginary woodland creature country kids get city kids to spend all night hunting."

Doc chuckled. "That's *snipe*. And by the expression on your face, you're speaking from experience."

"I have a couple of bratty cousins who live in Upstate New York," she admitted. "One summer when my sister and I were visiting, they took us into the woods with gunny sacks and had us sit under an old oak tree half the night, waiting for a snipe to run into the bags. We finally figured out we'd been had at about two o'clock in the morning."

Doc laughed again. "You city kids *were* fun to tease."

"I take it you sent someone on a snipe hunt in your misspent youth?" She arched an imperious eyebrow.

"Sure." Doc nodded. "Every year when the Boy Scout troop from Billings would come camp on my neighbor's ranch, me and the local boys would take them out snipe hunting."

"Little savages," Cami declared hotly. Then she returned them to the original subject. "But back to the fish. While I can't say I approve of the name, I do approve of the flavor. Light, white, and with just the right amount of firmness. And with the Italian dressing?" She lifted a hand to give a chef's kiss.

"So why *do* you keep packages of dressing in your purse anyway?" Doc asked, peering carefully into the bag under discussion as if he thought a leprechaun or a unicorn might jump out of it next.

Cami sighed. "The place I eat lunch gives me two packets of the stuff for my chef's salad. But since I gain five pounds just *looking* at oil, I only allow myself one. What?" She frowned at Doc. "What's that look for?"

"Oh, sorry." He glanced around. "Did I accidently roll my eyes out loud?" When Cami curled her hands into fists, he was quick to add, "I only meant that you'd look good with a little extra. So indulge in the two dressings." He did a pretty good impression of Donna from *Parks and Recreation* when he added, "Treat yo'self!"

"Says the man who can probably eat five thousand calories a day and still lose weight." Cami's eyes roved uncharitably over Doc's lean form.

"Good lord, woman. I was trying to give you a compliment."

"Were you? Sorry. I guess it's a touchy subject. And not because I'm that vain, but because high blood pressure and diabetes run in my family, so maintaining a healthy weight is not just an ideal, it's a must. And I'm *so* jealous of anyone who doesn't have to worry about every bite they put in their mouths. Plus, if I'm being honest, I'm still a little peeved at you for ruining our chances of an early rescue."

That was the second time since sitting down to dinner that Cami had accused Doc of being the reason they were all still stranded. Romeo wasn't surprised when Doc said, "I reckon it's time you embraced your inner Elsa and just...*let it go*."

Cami's lips twitched. "Did you just admit to watching *Frozen*?"

"I did." Doc's expression was unflappable. "Disney is badass, and any man who claims otherwise is insecure in his masculinity."

"You know what? You are absolutely right," Cami agreed with a forceful nod. "Which movie is your favorite?"

"*Toy Story*, hands down. The combo of Woody and Buzz Lightyear is pure comedy gold."

"Mmm. That *is* a good one. Although"—she lifted a finger—"it was produced by Pixar and only *released* by Disney. Not that that matters, but, you know, precision in all things and—" She pointed her finger at Doc. "No! No more lawyer jokes. I'm lawyer joked out for the day." When Doc obediently closed his mouth, she nodded her satisfaction and added, "My favorites are *The Little Mermaid* and *Aladdin*." Her smile turned dreamy. "I love a good star-crossed lovers trope."

Romeo saw something odd pass over Doc's face at that. And he was intrigued when Doc didn't come back with a smart-ass response and instead turned quickly to Mia to ask, "And what about you? Got a favorite Disney movie?"

The gentle breeze had turned cooler with the lowering of the sun. It caught a lock of Mia's hair, brushing it across her face. Romeo had to tuck his hands under his legs to keep from smoothing it behind her ear.

When she did the deed for him, she made the move look so sweet and innocent and unconsciously sexy, he nearly groaned again.

"If we can count Pixar movies, then mine is *WALL-E*," she admitted quietly. "I adore that little robot."

Romeo had been red hot for her all evening long. No, that wasn't right. He'd been red hot for her since the first moment he saw her. It was just that *now* he knew he could *act* on all that red hotness. But her admission burned something new inside him. Something decidedly *north* of what'd been burning previously. Something that lived a little left of center of his sternum.

He didn't need a degree in psychology to draw a correlation between her chosen life and a movie about the last robot on Earth. A lonely, sensitive creature that marveled at things left behind by a society long since gone.

"I always thought that movie was sad," Cami murmured. "But brilliant too. There's hardly any dialogue and yet you find yourself entranced by the story." Before anyone could respond, she eyed Romeo. "How about you?"

"*Beauty and the Beast*," he confessed without having to give it a second thought. "I like the idea of a woman falling for a man because of who he is on the inside instead of how he looks on the outside."

He immediately realized he'd revealed too much when everyone got quiet. Opening his mouth to make a joke to distract them from their speculations, he was relieved when Doc saved him the effort by asking Cami, "Why not tell the salad place to keep the second packet of dressing?"

"Because I'm paying the same price whether I get one or two, and I'm cheap. Did you not hear what I said about student loans? Anyway"—she waved a hand—"I save the second packets for times like these. You'd be surprised how often dressing comes in handy."

"Stranded on desert islands a lot, are you?" A teasing smile lifted one corner of Doc's mouth.

Romeo tuned out whatever Cami said in response and once again focused his hungry gaze on Mia.

Ever since he'd realized there was nothing keeping them apart, ever since that kiss, he hadn't been able to think of anything besides getting her alone so they could do it again. Do it *right*.

Do it long.

And slow.

And deep.

If he thought she'd been an earworm before, that was nothing compared to what he suffered now.

Look up single-minded in the dictionary, he thought, *and a picture of my horny mug will be right there next to the definition.*

Emphasis on horny.

"You want to go for a walk?" he asked her quietly.

Not quietly enough, apparently. Cami glanced across the flickering flames and said, "Wait. Do you think we could split one of the granola bars for dessert? My hangover is demanding sugar. And now that we know we can catch fish, do we still have to be so stingy with the rations?"

When Romeo agreed to her request, she squealed and tore into a granola bar wrapper like a kid tearing into Christmas presents. She was careful to hand out four perfectly equal pieces, hardly more than a bite each. But before any of them could savor their portions, she held hers aloft. "What should we toast to? Surviving a plane crash? Riding a rogue wave? Catching a snipe?"

"Snook," Doc corrected.

"Whatever." She shook her head. "Or to the health of those who are, hopefully, out searching for us at this very moment?"

Doc lifted his piece of granola bar in the air. "Here's to fair winds and following seas for all of our would-be rescuers."

"Cheers." The four of them "clinked" their granola bites together and then shoved the morsels into their mouths.

Mia had a sweet tooth and Romeo watched—of course he watched; he couldn't *stop* watching—as she closed her eyes and savored the chocolate and peanut butter-flavored granola as if it was the best thing she'd ever had in her mouth.

Until I give her something better, he thought wickedly.

When she opened her eyes and caught him staring, some of what he was thinking must've been written across his face. She blushed and quickly returned her gaze to the spark of the fire. The flames reflected in her eyes and made them look impossibly gold, like two ancient coins hauled up from the deep.

"I've always wondered what that means." Cami cut into his thoughts. "Following seas? Following what, exactly?"

"I thought you claimed to be a wordsmith?" Doc arched an eyebrow.

Cami sighed heavily. "Is it possible for you to answer a question without being deliberately provocative?"

"Sure." Doc shrugged. "But where would be the fun

in that?"

"Oh," Cami groused. "I can tell you're spoiling for another argument, but I'm too full and content to give you one. Or to give a shit about anything, really. Although..." She lifted a finger and grinned at her own wit. "I could probably scrounge up a rat's ass if I was forced to."

Doc said something that Romeo didn't catch because he purposefully tuned out everything and everyone that wasn't Mia.

"Hey." He reached over and rubbed a tiny speck of chocolate from the corner of her imminently kissable mouth. Without thinking, he placed the sweet sliver on his tongue and didn't even attempt to hide his hungry growl when her eyes followed the chocolate between his lips. "Come walk with me. We'll find a good spot to watch the sunset." He hitched his chin toward the life raft. "And maybe you can read to me a little before the light is completely gone, eh?"

The Night Angels series was one of his favorites. And he dearly *loved* to hear Mia read aloud. But if he was being honest, he had an ulterior motive. They were nearly to a sex scene.

He'd been waiting *weeks* to hear her read aloud one of P.J. Warren's sex scenes, because the author wrote wonderfully explicit ones. And Mia had a phone sex operator voice that was sure to turn the prose into pure porn for the ears.

Plus, you know, maybe a sex scene will lead to sex, which will lead to hotter sex, which will lead to dirtier sex.

See? Single-minded. Single. Fucking. Minded.

Emphasis on the fucking.

Mia didn't say anything. Her answer was to push to a stand so she could retrieve the novel, and Romeo barely contained his grumble of satisfaction.

His eyes glued themselves to the sway of her hips and her perfect heart-shaped butt as she made her way to the watercraft. And when she bent over the side of the life raft? There was no way he could stop the growl of hot-blooded hunger. It came up from the very depths of his being.

"Yo, Casanova," Doc called to him. "What the hell are you doing?"

Slinging wood like a damned lumberjack, he thought. Aloud he said, "What do you mean?"

Doc's mouth flattened into a straight line. "You *know* what I mean. What the hell are you doing with Mia? Before, you did a pretty good job of hiding that you'd like to eat her whole. But the last couple of hours you've been staring at her like she's a bottomless bowl of Bran's pasta and you've been wandering in the desert for the past three years."

Shit. After the way Doc had been coming on to their lawyer, and after Mia had assured him that she and Doc were only friends, Romeo had forgotten Doc's words back at the airport. Maybe *conveniently* forgotten?

Now they came screaming back to him.

"What if I was *serious about starting something real with her?"*

Rubbing a hand through his hair, he winced. "You were just winding me up back at the airport, eh? You weren't serious about starting something with—"

"Of course I wasn't serious," Doc scoffed, and Romeo let loose with a windy breath of relief. "But the fact remains, you haven't suddenly become someone you're not, right? And neither has she?"

"Don't worry," he assured Doc, unable to stop the grin that stretched his mouth wide now that there really, *really* wasn't anything standing between him and the woman he craved more than his next breath. "I was wrong about her. She's not looking for forever. She's like me. So it's all good."

Doc leveled a look on him. "Famous last words."

Before Romeo could answer, Mia returned and he forgot

what he'd even wanted to say. One look at her pretty face, at the way she tentatively bit her lip and offered him a small, secretive smile, melted every single one of his brain cells.

"Fine," he heard Doc mumble. "Go on and be a couple of fools. But leave the gun."

That was enough to drag Romeo's gaze from Mia's mouth and get the ol' synapses firing. "What?" He frowned at Doc. "Why?"

"Because we still don't know if someone is out to kill us. And something tells me you're going to be distracted from guard duty."

"Actually," he said, "the more I've thought about it, the more I'm convinced that if it *was* an explosion that took out the Otter's tail section, it was likely planted back at the airport. Some sort of timed device or altitude trigger or something. Whoever tried to off us—"

"If, in fact, someone *did* try to off us," Cami interrupted, ever the lawyer. "We still don't know that for sure."

"Point taken." He canted his head. "*If* someone tried to off us, then the *alleged* assassins"—he looked to Cami and she gave him a thumbs-up—"probably assume their plan worked. LT has no doubt alerted the authorities. I bet our disappearance is all over the local news. If there was a bomb, whoever planted it is probably back on dry land congratulating themselves on a job well done. I'd say we're safe out here."

"Yeah." Doc nodded. "Makes sense. Still, you better leave me the gun. Because you're not going to need it, and I just might."

Romeo cocked his head. "For what?"

"To shoot our lawyer if she keeps using her sharp tongue to take strips out of my hide. Obviously."

"Oh, ha, ha." Cami slapped Doc's uninjured shoulder.

Before the two of them could dissolve into another

round of flirting ill-disguised as insults, Romeo pulled the Glock from the back of his jeans and passed it to Doc without another word of protest. Arguing with Doc was always good for chucks and yucks, but the *real* fun was to be found elsewhere.

Elsewhere being anywhere that included Mia. Alone with him. And preferably naked.

Pushing to a stand, he offered her his arm. "Shall we?"

Her only response was a quick exhalation. And the moment her little fingers curled around his bicep, he felt two things in equal measure.

One was lust. A deep, all-encompassing, all-consuming *hunger*. And the other was pride that someone like her, someone so good and kind and smart and sexy, would want *him*.

He noticed the sand had turned cool beneath his bare feet as he led her toward the western tip of the island. For a long time, he stayed as silent as she did. Listening to the waves *hiss* against the shoreline. Enjoying the gentle warmth of the evening breeze as it teased across his skin. Sneaking glances at her pretty profile and fantasizing about running his finger from the slope of her smooth forehead down to her button nose and ending under her stubborn little chin.

Eventually, though, he couldn't stand her silence any longer. "You're being awfully quiet this evening." He realized what he'd said, and rephrased. "I mean, quieter than usual. What's on your mind?"

She tentatively met his searching gaze. For a moment, he thought she wouldn't answer. Then, she did. And *when* she did, the simple truth of her words, and the way she said them without ego or artifice, hit him like a grenade from a rocket launcher. "The answer to that question is the same as it's been for the last couple of months. *You.* You're what's on my mind. It's always you."

"My god, Mia." His voice sounded like it'd been raked over rocks on the way out of his mouth. "You have no idea—"

He stopped there, because he wasn't sure what he even wanted to say. That she had no idea what she did to him? That she had no idea how she made him feel? That she had no idea that it was taking the last bit of his willpower not to pull her to him so he could taste the mouth those sweet words came out of?

She placed a gentle hand in the center of his chest, and his heart thudded up to meet her touch. "Are we about to become lovers?" Her expression seemed pensive.

When the wind whipped some of her hair across her face, he did something he'd been longing to do since the day they met. He brushed the wavy lock behind the delicate shell of her ear, letting the strands slip slowly through his fingertips.

Softer than I imagined, he thought. *Silkier too.*

Would the rest of her end up being softer and silkier than his fantasies? If so, it was going to take all his manful focus and discipline not to skip the foreplay, strip her naked, and plow into her tight little body like the animal she reduced him to.

Never in his life had a woman made him feel so...*primal.*

"I want that," he admitted in a voice so low it was barely more than a growl. "Is that what you want?"

His heart tripped over itself when something that looked very much like indecision moved behind her eyes.

"Yes," she finally answered, and he realized his shoulders had tensed, because they suddenly relaxed. "But..." She frowned. "Can you promise, no matter what, we'll stay friends? I don't think I could stand it if—"

He silenced her by placing a finger over her lips. He'd have rather used his mouth for the job, but once he started kissing her, he wouldn't be able to stop. And right then she needed his words, not his tongue.

Hot damn, the things I'm going to do to her with my tongue...

"I will never stop being your friend, *cariña*," he swore to her.

She looked relieved. But it only lasted a second before her brow beetled again.

He used her troubled expression as an excuse to run his finger over her forehead, down her pert nose, and beneath her stubborn chin. There, he stopped, tilting her face up so that she was forced to hold his gaze. "What is it?" he asked quietly. "Tell me."

"I haven't..." She rolled in her lips when the words seemed to get stuck in the back of her throat. After a second, she tried again. "I haven't had as many lovers as you have. I might not be what—"

He didn't let her finish. He didn't need to. "Mia, my sweet, sexy woman, believe me when I say that's nothing you have to worry about."

She nodded. But he could tell she was still nervous.

Who could blame her? Doc had accused him of staring at her like he'd like to eat her whole. What small, delicate creature *wouldn't* be nervous when she found herself caught in the sights of a much bigger, much hungrier predator?

But he wasn't going to eat Mia in one giant gulp. Fuck, no. Mia wasn't a fast-food french fry. She was a seven-course meal from a Michelin-starred restaurant.

He was going to eat her slowly, lick by lick. Suck by suck. And bite by delicious bite.

But first...

"Breathe, *cariña*." He tucked another unruly strand of hair behind her ear because he couldn't get enough of touching her. "We aren't going to start now."

Not that he didn't *want* to. He'd have liked it if they never *stopped* after that first kiss. But she was all up in her head, and that's the last place he wanted her. When he made his move, and he *would* make his move, he wanted her totally in her body.

He wanted her in her body so she could fully appreciate all the marvelously obscene things he planned to do to it. To *her*.

"Let's sit down." He gestured to a small log that had washed up on the beach. It was bare of bark and made smooth by its time at sea. "Will you read to me?"

When she nodded, he led her to the driftwood. After sinking down beside her, he let out a contented sigh when she unzipped her purse, took out the book, and began to read.

Her husky voice drifted in the salty evening air, sounding like pure seduction. And the blush on her cheeks was a soft, delicate pink that matched the sunset-tinged clouds.

It was an odd feeling to know that, despite the loss of his plane, despite their precarious predicament, he'd never been happier than he was right then. Sitting next to her. His thigh touching her thigh. The waning light bathing them both. And the anticipation of what was to come humming softly in the air around them.

And what happens after? the voice in the back of his head asked.

He wished the sonofabitch had a face so he could plant his fist in it. The voice had never cared about *after* before, so why the hell was it talking about *after* now?

After doesn't matter, he assured the voice *and* himself. *After we'll be friends, just like I promised. And in the meantime...*

She would be his. And that would be enough.

He would make sure it was enough.

CHAPTER 16

6:39 PM...

L azarus leaned in and whispered, 'The night is ours,' and his words were warm on Ursula's skin. She shuddered at the passion that made her blood run hotter than the full moon. Then Lazarus, her sworn enemy, the man who had promised to see her dead, kissed her. And the night itself became a dark seduction," Mia read aloud.

Her voice choked on the last two words and she dared not turn the page. The rest of the chapter was sure to be all about the vampire, Lazarus Luxido, seducing the werewolf princess, Ursula Lobo. And like Ursula, Mia's blood was already on fire. If she read any further, she might get so worked up that she jumped on Romeo with all the panache of a horny fifteen-year-old copping her first feel.

That would definitely prove he was wrong when he told me that my lack of lots of lovers was nothing I need to worry about.

After closing the book, she carefully slid it back into her purse. Tentatively, she met Romeo's stare, expecting him to tease her about stopping before finishing the chapter. She was caught off guard when all he said was, "We might see the green flash tonight."

"Who?" She blinked, unable to focus on his words when her eyes were busy diving headlong into his melting chocolate gaze.

His chuckle was low, indulgent. "Not who. *What.*" He pointed toward the sun as it touched down on the rippling waves at the horizon.

She'd always thought he had the sexiest hands. So large and wide-palmed. Long, knobby-knuckled fingers. Nail beds that were slightly rounded with ends bluntly cut.

They weren't beautiful like the rest of him. They were far too rough for that.

Working hands. Worn and scarred. Strong and capable.

But just like the rest of him, they screamed *man.* She wondered, not for the first time, how easily they could make her feel like a woman.

Ridiculously easily, she decided.

All it would take was one touch of his callused fingertips against her hungry mouth, one graze of his broad palms across her eager flesh, one pass of his thumb over the aching tips of her—

"It's a rare phenomenon that sometimes happens at sunrise and sunset when the conditions are just right," he went on, unaware that her mind was headed down a one-lane path toward the Bone Zone.

Damn you, P.J. Warren!

The woman's books would make a priest have impure thoughts.

Or maybe Mia was being unfair to Ms. Warren. Maybe the blame for Mia's musings rested solely on Romeo's shoulders. His big, wide, fantastically muscled—

"The air needs to be clear, like it is now," he continued, and she forced herself to concentrate on the words coming out of his mouth instead of the way his lips formed around them. Lips that looked so firm and kissable and— *Argh!* "And you have to have an uninterrupted view of the horizon, like we do now."

He dropped his hand and grabbed hers, interlocking their fingers. His palm was warm and dry. Her hand felt impossibly small inside his.

What other parts of me will feel impossibly small when compared to him?

"Watch," he finished softly. "It'll be quick if it happens at all. Just a flash of green when the top of the sun sinks below the water."

She held her breath in anticipation as the molten globe slipped lower and lower. Lower and lower. Lower and then...

It happened. A strobe of bright, nearly neon green flamed on the horizon.

She stared hard, not believing her eyes. Before she could blink, it was gone.

"I saw it!" she whispered excitedly.

"Mmm," he nodded. "It happens more down here than it does other places. I've seen it a handful of times since moving to Wayfarer."

"Amazing," she breathed. She'd always thought that narrow-lit time at dusk and dawn was enchanted. A magical space between two worlds. But after seeing the green flash, she was convinced the twilight hour was truly bewitched.

Or maybe I read too much paranormal romance, she thought with a silent chuckle.

"Why have I never heard of it?" she asked.

"Probably because you've never been around Alex at sunset. If you had, she would've filled your ears full of all the reasons why it occurs."

"Well, then, I'm glad I missed seeing it with her, and happy I got to see it with you. I don't care about the science behind it. All I care about is that it was...*wonderful*," she finished lamely because she was too embarrassed to say *fantastical* or *magical* or *romantic*.

Although, it was all those things. Especially that last thing.

In fact, she couldn't recall a *more* romantic moment.

Yes, they had been in a plane crash. Yes, they were stranded on a desert island that looked like it might wash away in the next hurricane. And yes, they had no idea who wanted to kill them or even *if* someone wanted to kill them. Not to mention, they didn't have the first clue when they would be rescued.

But the setting sun had set the sky on fire in vibrant shades of red, gold, and orange until it seemed like a graffiti artist with a bold hand had painted the world to the west. Romeo was by her side, her hand held so possessively inside his. And very soon now, he would possess other parts of her. *All* the parts of her.

The thought was delicious.

It was also a little crazy-making.

"We aren't going to start now," he'd said before leading her to the log.

What did he mean? When *would* they start? Was he waiting for her to say something to let him know she was ready?

Dear god, was she ready. She'd *been* ready since day one on Wayfarer Island.

Or...was he waiting for *her* to make the first move?

Gah! I'm so bad at this!

She'd held many titles in her first three decades of life—daughter, sister, student, archeologist—but seductress

223

had never been one of them. All her lovers... Ha! *All*. As if there'd been a multitude. She could count them on one hand and still have a finger left over. Anyway, *all* of them had been the ones to approach her. To kiss her. To start undressing her.

Not that she was *opposed* to being the instigator. She was as modern minded as the next gal. You know, equality of the sexes and all that razzmatazz. But she was clueless when it came to knowing how to start—

"The wheels are spinning so fast up there, I think I see smoke coming out of your ears." He tapped her temple.

"That obvious?" She made a face.

"You want to tell me about it?" When she hesitated, he added, "Or talk to me about anything? I swear you could be listing the scientific names of molds and every word out of your mouth would still sound hot."

When she cocked her head, he was quick to add, "I know you don't like it when I talk about your voice. And I promise I'll never mention it again after this. But, Mia, it is *so* unbelievably sexy. This soft, rusty-sounding bedroom voice. You have no idea how many times I've fantasized about making love to you and hearing you whisper in my ear."

She nearly fell off the log at the thought of Romeo imagining them together. Maybe...*touching* himself while imagining them together?

Much to her astonishment, and she had absolutely *no* idea where her courage came from, she heard herself ask, "What do I say in your fantasies?"

One dark eyebrow winged up his forehead. She'd surprised him as much as she'd surprised herself. But he quickly recovered.

No. He more than recovered. He saw her subtle flirtation and raised her all the way to dirty talk. "My name." He gave her a wicked, knowing sort of smile that instantly had an ache forming at the junction of her legs. "You say my name, my *real* name, as I make you come."

She wasn't holding her breath anymore. God, no. It whooshed out of her on a long, shivery sigh.

Oh, how she wanted exactly that. Wanted *him*. Wanted all the things his smile promised.

But she still didn't know where to begin. And if she kept looking at the desire in his eyes, desire he made no attempt to hide, she really *would* pull the fifteen-year-old-girl move— hop into his lap, smash their mouths together, and shove her hand down his pants so she could wrap her fingers around the hungry column of flesh he'd been sporting in his jeans all evening.

Another thing he's made no attempt to hide.

Blame it on her lack of experience when it came to the art of seduction. Blame it on her nervousness because, come on, this was *Romeo* sitting beside her. Romeo with his perfect face and his perfect body and his oodles of lovers. But suddenly she heard herself admitting, "You know how I told you my voice sounds this way because my vocal cords were injured when I was little?"

When a line appeared between his eyebrows, she silently chided herself. *Shut up, Mia! What are you doing?*

She was ruining a perfectly lovely, perfectly romantic, perfectly *sexy* moment. And why? *Why?*

She didn't know. All she knew was she couldn't stop herself. "It's because I was intubated for three days when I was seven years old. I got into my mother's pain pills and overdosed. The tube they used on me in the hospital was too big or something because—"

"Sweet Mother Mary," he cursed, and she saw a muscle working in his jaw.

Gone was the hungry look in his eye. It'd been replaced by a lethal gleam. Gone were the soothing circles his thumb had been rubbing on the back of her hand. Now his fingers were tight around hers. And gone was that lovely, anticipatory *hum* of excitement. It'd been replaced by a hard, sharp sort of tension that crackled like a downed electrical line.

It's official. Moment ruined. Way to go, Mia, you dumbass!

"That woman should be jailed for her incompetence as a parent," he finished on a vehement snarl that had a vein popping out in his forehead.

Mia turned to look at the horizon. The sky had faded from vibrant graffiti art into a pastel palette of pinks and purples and blues.

I could keep my mouth shut, she contemplated as a sickening sensation swirled in her gut. *I could let him think all the blame rests solely on Mom's shoulders.*

As quickly as she had the thought, she discarded it. She couldn't tell him *everything*, of course. But she could tell him what had started her down the path to hell, and maybe that would be enough.

Enough to what? The question rang inside her head as clear as the bells at the Holy Name Cathedral in downtown Chicago.

Enough to satisfy this need I have to share more of myself with him than I've ever shared with anyone.

Enough to make this thing we're about to do feel like more than a simple fling.

Enough to...release some of the weight that comes with carrying around so much unspoken guilt.

"Save some of that disdain and contempt for me. I'm not completely innocent," she whispered.

She could feel he'd cocked his head even though she wasn't looking at him. Even though she *couldn't* look at him when she admitted this next part.

"I wasn't the only one I hurt with those pills." Her voice

was little more than a breath of wind. "I gave some to my baby brother too." That sick sensation swirling in her gut became a whirlpool of nausea. "It nearly killed him. *I* nearly killed him."

A long moment passed without Romeo saying anything. So long, in fact, she peeked over at him, not surprised to find his eyes glued to her face. They narrowed slightly when he asked, "Why?"

She chuffed out a humorless laugh. "That *is* the question, isn't it? My dad always assumed I did because I thought they were candy."

"Why would you have thought that?"

"Because that's what my mother told me they were."

"Your mother." He spat the two words as if they were poison.

She wasn't sure why, but it caused a memory to bloom to life inside her head...

Momma sat at her vanity in a short, shiny robe that Mia desperately wanted to touch. But she didn't dare. The last time she'd tried, her mother had slapped her hand away, hard, saying, "Keep your sticky fingers off me! You'll ruin it!"

Instead, Mia moved out of reach of the robe's temptation and crawled onto her parents' big bed. Lying on her belly, she propped her chin in her hand and watched her mother use a fluffy-looking ball on her nose.

"What's that, Momma?" She knew her mother liked to talk about the things she did while sitting at her special makeup desk.

"It's powder," her mother said. "It keeps my nose from being shiny."

"Your nose isn't shiny," Mia offered obediently. "Your nose is beautiful."

Momma smiled at her in the mirror and Mia felt a little

flutter in her stomach. She'd done well. She'd said the right thing.

So often she didn't *say the right thing, and then Momma would yank her up by the wrist and throw her out of the room before slamming the door in her face.*

Feeling a little more confident, she ventured, "Will you do lipstick next?"

"Mmm." Her mother nodded. "Which color should I choose?"

"Pink!" Mia crowed immediately, knowing her mother's favorite color was pink.

"Perfect choice." Momma pulled a tube of lipstick from the row of lipsticks lined up atop the vanity.

When her mother swiped the color over her lips and then smacked them together, Mia knew just what to say. "Now your lips are beautiful too."

Momma's eyebrows pinched together, and Mia felt an answering pinch in her chest. "Now they're beautiful? They weren't beautiful before?" Her mother's voice had taken on a tone that Mia knew all too well. The pinch in her chest became more of a twisting sensation. Like someone had grabbed her heart and was trying to wring it out like a wet washcloth.

She swallowed, not knowing what to say to make things right.

"You're always beautiful, Momma," she tried, and then felt like she could breathe again, like her heart could beat again, when her mother's brow cleared.

She stayed quiet while Momma clipped on earrings and messed with one particular lock of shiny, auburn hair that didn't seem to want to stay in place. When it finally did, and her mother dipped her chin in satisfaction, Mia asked her, "Where are you going tonight?"

"To a fundraiser with your father." Momma leaned into

the mirror and brushed a lip gloss wand over her lips until they were slick.

"A fun-raiser?" Mia perked up. She liked fun. She wasn't sure how she was supposed to raise it, but she'd sure like to try. "Can I come?"

"It's not for children," Momma said, and Mia's bare feet, which had been kicking in the air behind her, fell onto the mattress in dejection. Her mother never went anyplace that was for children. "But your nanny is taking you and your brother to see a movie," Momma added. "You'll like that."

Mia sighed. She liked her new nanny. The brown-haired woman was nice and she was teaching Mia some French words. But Mia had liked her old nanny better. Her old nanny had had silvery-blond hair like Rapunzel. Her old nanny had baked cookies and sometimes she'd let Mia lick the batter bowl.

But Mia had learned not to become too attached to any of the people who worked in the Ennis household. The housekeepers and nannies never lasted long. Inevitably, Momma would get mad at them for something and, by the next morning, their bags would be packed and Mia would never see them again.

Mia's eyes drifted over to the emerald-green dress hanging from a hanger over the top of her mother's closet door. It had a filmy skirt that reminded Mia of fairy wings and a sequined bodice that looked like a mermaid tail.

She couldn't wait until she was big enough to wear a dress like that.

Of course, she'd never be as beautiful as her mother. No one was ever as beautiful as her mother.

"What's that, Momma?" she asked when her mother twisted off the white cap on an orange bottle, shook out something round, and placed it on her tongue.

Her mother's gaze was sharp as she stared at Mia in the mirror. But then Momma smiled and said in a sugary sweet voice, "That's Momma's candy."

"It's *her* fault what happened to you and your little brother," Romeo snarled as Mia finished with the reverie.

"No." She shook her head. "I *knew* the pills weren't candy. Not really."

A line formed between Romeo's eyebrows. "Why did you eat them then? Why did you give them to your brother?"

"That's the thing." She swallowed and shook her head. "I don't know. I don't remember doing it. I don't remember anything about that night after coming home from watching *A Bug's Life*."

She'd racked her brain for the last twenty-four years trying to recall what had happened that night, trying to remember why she'd done what she'd done. But, just like always, there was nothing.

Or...not nothing. It was more like a gray mist clouded her mind whenever she tried to peer too deeply.

"Maybe I did it because I was acting out?" She frowned. "Because I was tired of being ignored by my parents? Or maybe the answer is simple. Maybe I did because I was a kid, and kids are idiots who eat paste and stuff LEGOs in their ears."

"Wait a minute." He raised his hand. "If you don't remember the night it happened, how do you know *you* were the one to feed the pills to your brother? Maybe *he* fed them to *you*."

"No." She shook her head. "The housekeeper found me and Andy in *my* room. The pill bottle was on *my* nightstand. I even had a couple of tablets still in my hand. It was me."

She chanced a tentative look into his face. She expected to see at least a small measure of censure. But instead, all she saw was compassion.

Of *course* he only felt compassion. He was Romeo. The tenderest, most warmhearted man she'd ever known.

"That must've been a terrible weight to bear as a child," he whispered.

It *had* been. But it was nothing compared to the burden of shame and regret that'd come after. To the load of blame and self-loathing she'd been carrying around since her twenty-first birthday.

She couldn't tell him about *that*, though. So she did what came most natural to her. She lapsed into silence.

And wished she had a time machine.

If she had a time machine, she would fire it up and take them back to when they'd been staring at each other with longing in their eyes. Back to when he was telling her about his fantasies. Back to when the very air between them throbbed with unquenched desire.

Regrettably, she was no H.G. Wells. The only thing she could do was point to a glimmer of starlight in the rapidly darkening sky and say, "First star of the night. Make a wish."

She could tell he wanted to say more about her mother. But he took pity on her and turned to look at the twinkling star.

After a moment, he closed his eyes to make his wish and she noticed, not for the first time, how impossibly long his eyelashes were. So sooty and thick. When he blinked open his eyes, she was gratified to see some of the heat had returned to his gaze.

With deliberate gentleness, he caught her chin between his thumb and forefinger. Leaning in close, he whispered, "I wished for *you*." His breath puffed against her lips and smelled like peanut butter and chocolate. "I wished for all of you. Starting now."

Just like Cami had described, he didn't break eye contact as he slowly closed the distance between them. Before his mouth could touch hers, however, she scolded, "You're not supposed to tell your wish. Then it won't come true."

He turned his head slightly, a teasing twinkle in his eye. "It won't?"

"Oh, who am I kidding?" She grabbed the collar of his T-shirt to keep him close. Glad *he* had made the first move, since she'd proved herself incapable of that very thing. "Of *course* it'll come true. You have me. I'm yours for..." She swallowed the word that was perched on the tip of her tongue. A word that sounded a lot like *forever*. "For as long as you want me."

His answer was a rumble of anticipation that rolled up from the depths of his chest.

Then he kissed her.

After weeks of secret yearning and unrequited passion, she half expected him to ravish her mouth. To savage it. For his kiss to be this marauding entry that lacked finesse and was all about animal aggression.

Which would've been fine. In fact, two seconds ago, she might've said that was exactly the kind of kiss she preferred.

But the Mia from two seconds ago was a damn fool, because this kiss? Oh, this kiss was *so* much better than fine. It was so much better than animal aggression.

This kiss was all about temptation. Titillation.

A gentle press of his warm lips against hers. A tiny flick of his hot tongue at the seam of her mouth. An achingly tender seduction that made her feel precious. Priceless. Like she was the greatest treasure he'd ever known.

Gripping his shoulders because she wasn't sure she could stay on the log on her own, she opened her mouth to his sweet ministrations.

That seemed to be all the consent he needed.

His tongue swept past her teeth, licking languidly. His lips nibbled and sucked, mapping the contours of her mouth, leaving no corner unexplored or unloved.

His big, warm hands came up to frame her face, tilting her head this way and that, but never breaking the rhythm of his tongue as it stroked and played and *learned* her.

Seriously, she'd never experienced a more devastatingly *thorough* kiss in her life. And when she groaned her pleasure? Because she just couldn't help herself? It was like she flipped a switch inside him.

His devastatingly thorough, achingly tender kiss became ravenous. *Now* he was all animal aggression and primal need. All hungry, searching lips and hot, probing tongue. All fiery passion and mindless desire. With one arm around her back, he pulled her to him until her nipples brushed against the heated wall of his chest.

She heard herself whimper.

It was a whimper of desire. A whimper of need. A whimper of longing for him to keep kissing her. To never stop kissing her. Because his kiss alone was better than any sex she'd ever had, except...

She ached. She ached so badly. And his kiss alone wasn't going to assuage that ache.

She wasn't sure how he knew she needed more, but somehow he did.

Murmuring something against her lips, something she couldn't understand because it was in Spanish, he hooked a hand behind her knee. Before she knew it, he'd lifted her onto him until she straddled his lap.

One large hand tunneled through her hair, holding her head so he could continue to savage her mouth. His other hand splayed warm across her back, keeping her pressed tight against him.

He was huge and powerful. A hot, immovable mountain of muscle. She felt herself going soft and submissive in response. If she could've melted into his skin, she would have.

"I want you, Mia." His voice was thick with urgency as he breathed the words against her lips. "I need you." The hand at her back slid down to her hip. His grip was a little rough as he rocked her pelvis against the merciless hardness of his throbbing erection. "Can you feel how much I need you?"

This is what real lust feels like, she thought a little giddily. Before, she'd only grazed the surface of passion. Only dipped her toe into the pool of desire. Only skirted along the edges of physical hunger.

She knew that was true because never, *never* had she felt this way with any of her previous lovers. Never had her entire body tingled with arousal, with awareness of her partner as a man, with the need to be *one* with him in every way.

This is what the poets write about, the crooners sing about, the artists try to capture in their work. This is raw and rough and basic and lewd. But it's also luscious and delicious and decadent and it feels so...right.

Her eyes flew wide when she realized the sensations bombarding her might be more than carnal pleasures.

They might be—

Oh god! Is that what it feels like to fall in love?

No, she assured herself in the next breath. *I want him. And when you add* wanting *him on top of liking him and respecting him and feeling safe around him, it's easy to mistake all of that for love.*

Even though they were inside her own head, the words still rang false.

Okay, so what if she *was* falling in love?

It didn't change who she was.

It didn't change who *he* was.

It didn't change...anything.

If it was love, she would love him. And then, when the

234

time came, she would leave him. If it was love, he'd be with her always, like a fingerprint on her heart.

And that would be enough.

It would have to be enough.

CHAPTER 17

6:59 PM...

The feel of Mia's body clinging so tightly to his own was a tender kind of torture.

Romeo could sense the sultry heat of her sex even through both sets of clothes. And the way she rubbed herself against him? The way she rode the hard ridge of flesh that pulsed hungrily inside his jeans?

That wasn't a tender kind of torture. That was pure torture. Period.

It was taking everything he had not to pop the buttons on his fly, take out his raging cock, and plunge into her until he was seated to the hilt in all her tight, slick heat.

His need for her was immense. Bigger than he'd ever known. Deeper than he'd ever dreamed. Hotter than even his wildest fantasies.

Every time he kissed her, her lips grew sweeter, greedier, more irresistible. And he thought he might go on kissing her forever. Except...

As talented as her mouth was, he was impatient to explore the rest of her. To see if her neck tasted as sweet as it smelled. To see if the skin over her shoulders felt as soft against his lips as it looked. To press his tongue against her pulse point and feel if her heart raced as quickly as his did.

Releasing her lips with a desperate moan, he left a trail of hot, open-mouthed kisses down the length of her neck. She tasted even *sweeter* than she smelled. She tasted like sunshine and some head spinning combination of flowers and fresh fruit and *woman*.

Her unique flavor on his tongue was enough to have the fire inside him growing hotter. But when he clamped his lips around her pulse point and she gasped his name? "Spiro!" Well, *that* was a bucket of kerosene tossed onto the flames.

His responding growl was low and possessive-sounding. The animal she brought out in him had risen to the surface, and the beast wasn't satisfied with simply claiming her mouth or her stubborn little jaw or her sweet-tasting neck. The beast wanted *all* of her.

Every. Single. Inch.

And he wanted it fast and hard and dirty. He wanted it raw and rough and so very raunchy that even *Romeo* was shocked by its vehemence. By the desperately explicit images that bloomed to life inside his head.

He had to reassure the animal that all of that would come later. Fuckin'-A, it would. But this first time? This first time, he wanted slow and tender and...most importantly... thorough.

Oh, so thorough.

But in order to make sure *he* was the one in charge and not the beast, he needed to slow things down. *Way* down. Because he could tell by the urgency of Mia's hips moving over him, by the erotic sound that came from the back of her throat—a sound that was part moan, part groan, and all sexy seduction—that she was hell-bent on rubbing herself to completion.

And about to take me with her.

Truly, his cock *ached* with the need for release, and he was so hard he could feel himself stretching his skin to its limits. His balls had pulled up high and tight against his body in preparation for orgasm.

Pulling back from her oh-so-delicious neck, he cupped her face with both hands. "Mia... Slow down, *cariña*. There's no rush."

She lifted her lids and he saw her golden eyes were silvered by the starlight. The desire shining in them, combined with the soft temptation of her passion-swollen lips, was everything he'd ever dreamed of.

And more.

"Come for a swim with me," he coaxed. "I've watched you in the water at the dive site so many times. And each time I've wished you were naked. Wished I could see the sunlight glowing on your skin. Wished I could watch the waves lap hungrily at this part of you..." He flexed his hips in demonstration, rubbing his hardness against her. "Wished I could watch your nipples pucker the moment your breasts touched the surface."

Plus, he needed a dip to cool his ardor. He was seconds away from tossing all his long-held plans for a slow, thorough seduction right out the window and, instead, doing what the animal inside him wanted.

She caught her bottom lip between her teeth, grinning a seductress's grin. "The sun sank a while ago. I don't think it's possible for it to glow on my skin."

"Starlight works just as well," he assured her. "Better even."

He saw the hesitation in her eyes. Saw how the thought

of stripping naked in front of him made her nervous.

Thanks to her damned mother, who'd filled her head with perceived flaws, she truly had no idea just how abso-fucking-lutely *gorgeous* she was.

He planned to remedy that. To show her what he saw when he looked at her.

Pure perfection.

"I'll go first." He quickly whipped his shirt over his head before she could think to argue.

It was one-hundred percent agony lifting her off his lap and setting her aside on the log, but he managed it so he could stand. And if she'd had any doubts just how *badly* he wanted her, she didn't after that. Because his jeans rode low on his hips and the head of his cock poked above his waistband.

Her breath hitched. Her eyes flew wide. He could see her pulse hammering in her throat.

"Mmm." He nodded. "See what you do to me, *cariña*?"

He cupped his erection quickly, just one subtle stroke to ease a bit of the pain, before moving his hands to the buttons on his fly. With a flick of his fingers they were undone. A second later, his jockey shorts and jeans lay in a puddle at his feet.

He stood before her then. Breaths coming quick and shallow. His fully erect cock bobbing with each of his heartbeats.

The woman, *bless her*, didn't even *attempt* to hold his gaze. Hell no. She stared straight at his dick, and he would swear he could feel the heat of her gaze bathing over his most sensitive flesh like a hot, wet tongue.

His cock bucked, begging for her touch. When she lifted a hand to do exactly that, he could only groan and say, "Not yet. If you touch me now, I might not have the strength to take this slow."

Her lioness eyes were lit with a pure, killer instinct when

she looked up at him. "And why would that be a bad thing?"

"It's not a bad thing." He grabbed her hand to pull her to a stand. "In fact, I hope to show you what a *good* thing fast and furious sex can be. But that's for another time. This time, this first time..."

He slowly undid the top button on her blouse. Her pulse beat in the hollow of her throat, and when the button popped free of its hole and his fingers gently grazed the upper slope of one breast, it went from a quick tattoo to a rapid flutter.

"This first time, I want to touch and taste, rub and lick every inch of you. I want to learn what will make you moan, what will make you writhe with pleasure beneath me, what will send you careening over the edge."

"My god." The two syllables sawed out of her. She blinked in surprise when she glanced down and saw he'd undone the rest of her buttons while he'd distracted her with his words.

Her bra was white and lacy, as delicate and feminine looking as the woman who wore it. The cups lifted her breasts like an offering, and he didn't hesitate to accept.

Following the edge of one scalloped cup with his fingertip, he watched, satisfied, as the nipple beneath pinched tight against the lace.

Responsive, the beast in him growled.

Pulling her to him, he hissed when his naked cock pressed against the fabric of her shorts and the warm skin on her lower belly. Slipping her blouse over her shoulders, he tossed it atop his jeans. And while his arm was behind her back, he took advantage and unsnapped the clasp of her bra. She gasped when the two sides sprung free in an instant.

Her breath was hot against his chin as she stared up at him. "You're good at that."

"I'm good at a lot of things," he assured her as he bent to reclaim her kiss-swollen lips. "Let me show you."

Distracting her with his teeth and tongue, he peeled away her bra, flinging it toward the growing pile of clothes. When her tightly bunched nipples grazed the hair on his chest, she groaned and he drank down the sound, took it into himself so that it was imprinted upon the very fabric of his being.

So that it would remain part of him. Always.

For long moments, despite the urge to step back and let his hungry eyes roam over the treasures he'd just uncovered, he did nothing more than revel in her devilishly talented mouth.

Not that that was a hardship. Truly, Mia was a natural when it came to kissing.

Her lips were soft and plush, her tongue was eager and searching. She nibbled and sucked and followed his every move instinctively. Then, to his surprise, she went up on tiptoe, framed his face with her hands, and took over the lead from him.

He wasn't sure who made which noise. But one of them moaned and the other grumbled when she dipped her tongue into his mouth. Setting up a slow, languid rhythm that he knew would translate to other pleasurable activities.

He imagined his cock entering her body in rhythm to her tongue. Deep, slick strokes that shoved the head of his dick high and tight against her cervix. Slow, luxurious thrusts that made his balls slap her ass as her tight little body welcomed his entry.

He couldn't stand it a second longer.

He needed her naked. He needed to have nothing separating them but the sweat that slicked their skin.

"I'm going to finish undressing you now," he whispered against her lips.

When she nodded, his fingers made fast work of the snap on her shorts. The zipper went even quicker. Two seconds later, her shorts along with her panties lay in a mound of material at her feet.

He lifted her away from her clothes, and then pulled her tight against him until they touched everywhere. Breast to chest. Thigh to thigh. But most importantly, *skin to skin*.

It was the most amazing, most fantastically carnal thing ever. Where he was hard and hot, she was soft and warm. And she fitted against him so perfectly. It was almost like she'd been made for this. Made for tucking in tight against him.

Made for *him*.

The temptation of her skin was too much. When he ran his hands over her shoulders, down her sides, grazing the sides of her breasts along the way and feeling goose bumps rise to the surface everywhere his fingertips touched, he realized his imagination hadn't done her justice.

She was so much softer.

So much silkier.

So, *so* much sexier than he'd ever imagined.

"Your hands feel so good on me," she gasped into his mouth. "Don't stop touching me."

"Never," he promised, palming her ass at the same time he kissed his way to her ear.

Hot damn! He'd fantasized about her round, firm backside. Despite having a petite frame, the woman had an ass like no other. Looking at it turned him on so much.

But feeling it? That was even better.

It was round and firm, and overflowed his hands, making him so damn *lustful* that he found himself grinding his erection into the lower curve of her warm belly even as he laved and sucked her earlobe, stopping briefly to dip his tongue into the tiny hollow.

"That feels so good. *You* feel so good," she whispered, hooking her heel behind his leg to better align their bodies.

Her aim was spot-fucking-on.

Suddenly, his throbbing shaft rested between her delicate folds.

His hips flexed of their own accord, dragging the head of his dick across her swollen clitoris. They *both* hissed at the jolt of red-hot pleasure.

It would be so easy, he thought as his breaths strangled in his chest. *One thrust and I could be inside her.*

But no. *No!*

He had a plan, damnit! A fantasy that, for months, he'd been reliving over and over inside his head. A dream to make their first time together perfect. Or, if it couldn't be perfect, make it so good that fifty years in the future, she'd look back on this moment and think, *That was the best I ever had.* He *was the best I ever had.*

"Mia." His voice was so hoarse he barely recognized it as his own. "I want to look at you. Please, let me look at you."

She whimpered. "Just...keep doing what you're doing. Don't ruin it."

Her words were arrows straight to his heart. Since she'd already melted the steel he'd encased around the organ, they easily pierced it.

If he ever met Jane Ennis, it would take every ounce of restraint he possessed not to strangle the woman.

"Oh, *cariña*." He pressed his lips tight against her imminently kissable ear. "Looking at you won't ruin anything. Looking at you will only make it better."

Before she could protest, he stepped from the circle of her arms.

"Just as I thought." His words came out a low grumble since his vocal cords were raw with lust. "You're beautiful." When she tried to drop her chin, he caught it with his finger and forced her to hold his gaze. "And I'm going to prove it to you. I'm going to wipe the disbelief from your expression. Starting now."

Before she could protest, he ran a reverent finger over her clavicle. "Your skin is flawless." He leaned down to drop a kiss on the delicate bone. "So creamy and smooth and sweet smelling. And your breasts?" He cupped one small, round globe in his hand, plumping it. "So soft and pretty and topped with the most fascinating little nipples. I thought they would be a delicate pink. But they're a dusty-rose color. And..." He passed his thumb over the crest, watching it furl into a tight bud. She sucked in a ragged. "They're so responsive."

"I want your mouth on me," she whispered. "Please. I need to feel your mouth on me."

Apparently, the one place Mia *wasn't* reticent was the bedroom. And that suited Romeo just fine. Better than fine. He liked a woman who knew what she wanted and didn't hesitate to ask for it.

"I'm going to put my mouth all over you," he vowed, delicately tracing the little tattoo inked beneath her left breast.

Mia had always worn wetsuits or one-pieces, so this was the first time he was seeing it. It was sweet, two honeybees, and he knew it must mean something. But he was too desperate to fill his mouth with her flesh and couldn't be bothered to fill it with words to ask her about her ink's significance.

Wrapping an arm around her back, he pressed her over it so that he could suck her nipple into his mouth. She became a supplicant in his embrace, going boneless, her head falling back as she tunneled her fingers through his hair.

He used his tongue to press the tip of her breast to the roof of his mouth. Then he flicked it back and forth and listened, gratified, as she mewled her ecstasy.

For long minutes, he enumerated the glory of her individual parts. The tiny turn of her waist. The perfect oval of her belly button that he'd been sporadically fantasizing about ever since sneaking a peek at it while inside the plane. The delicious flare of her hips. The long, smooth expanse of her thighs.

He touched every body part he praised, either a gentle brush of his fingertips or a firm grip that told her how hungry she made him. He rubbed his goatee over every part of her too, because she seemed to like that, like the rasp of his whiskers across her sensitive skin. And you can be certain he *kissed* every part. Laved it with his tongue. Sucked it between his lips. Nipped it with his teeth.

By the time he was left with the part of her he'd been longing to taste since the first time he saw her sitting primly on her little daybed on the screened porch back on Wayfarer, he was so gluttonous for her, he barely refrained from tossing her onto the sand and burying his head between her thighs.

No finesse.

No subtlety.

Just a raw, ravenous *feasting* on her most intimate flesh.

Instead, he knelt in front of her and whispered, "And this part of you?" He softly rubbed his thumb through the tiny triangle of auburn hair at the top of her plump sex. "It's so perfect. Swollen and wet and everything a man dreams of when he dreams of a woman who wants him."

Pressing his thumb against the throbbing nub, he looked up into her golden eyes, expecting to see the pleasure he gave her. But what he saw reflected there was himself.

Himself the way *she* saw him.

Someone strong and capable and worthy. Someone she wanted. Someone she...trusted.

And that was the sexiest thing of all.

"Please keep touching me," she begged, her legs quivering as he used his thumb to rub slow circles against the bundle of nerves made solely for a woman's bliss. "Put your fingers inside me. I ache so much."

"Mmm." He hooked a hand behind her knee so he could drape one smooth, lovely leg over his shoulder. "That would be my pleasure."

He was glad he was still looking up at her face, because he saw her catch her bottom lip between her teeth and give him a sexy little smile. "No. I'm hoping it'll be *my* pleasure."

"Cheeky minx," he said in English. He followed that up with something far more salacious in Spanish.

When he gently probed her opening, he found the slick heat of her. And for the first time all night, he didn't go slow. He didn't need to.

He'd already tormented and teased her into readiness. Now, what she needed was release. A quick, hard orgasm to take the edge off and allow her to luxuriate in all that was still to come.

Sliding one finger inside her, he wasn't surprised to find her tight. To feel her muscles clamp down against his intrusion. But when she hissed, "God, yes," and let her head fall back, he knew he'd made the correct choice in getting right to it.

And speaking of getting right to it.

He pushed a second finger beside the first. It wasn't easy. She was a small woman and he had big hands. But once both fingers were inside her, he leaned forward to press his mouth over her sex.

The taste of her was salty and sweet. The smell of her was willing, wanton woman. Setting up a rhythm with his fingers that he reproduced with the flick of his tongue, he cataloged her every response. Each thrust of her hips was clue. Each catch of her breath was lesson. And very soon he learned what she liked. What would send her over the edge.

"God, yes." Her fingers gripped his hair so tight she made the strands pinch. But the pain was even more of an inducement. It told him she was no longer in her head. She was completely inside her body, and all she was doing was feeling.

Feeling his fingers stroking into her hot, wet sheathe. Feeling his tongue swirling and rubbing and stabbing at her sex until she was riding his face.

With his free hand, he stroked himself. He couldn't help it. He had to lessen a little of his own ache even as he worked to build the ache inside her.

When he felt her inner muscles quiver, he changed the motion of his fingers. Instead of a steady stroke, he wiggled them forward, finding the rough patch of flesh behind her pubic bone that was sure to send her careening over the edge.

"I need you to—" The words caught in her throat when he softly bit the inside of her thigh.

His words were muffled against her skin, when he told her, "I know exactly what you need."

Then he gave it to her by clamping his mouth over her clit and flicking hard and fast with his tongue until she caught her breath at the same time her body caught his fingers, clamping down so hard that his knuckles rubbed together.

"Spiro!" She screamed his name as her womanhood pulsed.

He let go of his raging dick then. He had to. With his name ringing in his ears, with the feel of her body shuddering around his fingers, with the taste of her orgasm bathing his tongue and filling his nose with the scent of spent woman, he was seconds away from shooting all over the sand.

Instead, he used his free hand to grip her hip, to hold her steady as her release rippled through her in ever shrinking circles until, finally, she gave one final shudder and...

Her knee gave out.

"I got you." He caught her before she could hit the sand, cradling her against his chest and staring down into her pretty face.

Her cheeks were red from ecstasy. Her pulse fluttered in her throat so rapidly he was reminded of a hummingbird's wings.

Hooking an arm behind her knees, he stood and waded into the ocean.

"Spiro," she panted. "Put me down. I'm too heavy. Your bruised knee—"

"Hush, woman," he told her. "All I'm feeling right now is pleasure."

The water was cool without being cold. It was a welcome reprieve when it lapped at his balls and slipped over his heated shaft.

"Wow." She shook her head as if words failed her. "That was..." She shook her head again.

"Yeah." He knew the smile he wore was more than a little wicked. "And we're only getting started. Just you wait."

CHAPTER 18

7:19 PM...

Mia welcomed the embrace of the ocean when Romeo released her legs and lowered her until her bare toes touched the sandy bottom.

The water slithered over her heated, still-throbbing sex. The waves lapped at the undersides of her breasts, occasionally leaping up to tickle her nipples. And Romeo's flesh against hers was a hot counterpoint to the coolness of the liquid.

God, what just happened to me? she wondered dazedly.

But, of course, she knew the answer.

Romeo had happened to her.

Everywhere he'd touched had made her writhe with bliss. Everywhere he'd rubbed that wonderfully erotic goatee had made her beg for more. Everywhere he'd kissed had made her moan and arch into his mouth.

She wasn't sure if it'd taken him seconds or minutes to

send her flying over the edge. All she knew was that the need for release had grown until her whole body had become a snarl of raw, hungry nerve-endings.

And her orgasm?

It'd been earth-shattering. Seriously, she'd felt the ground shift beneath her. Which was why she'd fallen into his waiting arms.

When she lifted her eyes now, she discovered his gaze fixed on her breasts. There was no mistaking the hunger of his expression.

She couldn't fathom it, but when he looked at her, he didn't see where she was lacking.

All he saw was beauty.

And, miraculously, with him all she *felt* was beautiful.

Beautiful and a little bit wicked.

"Your turn." She reached down to grab the long, hard erection that brushed her hip.

Even though she'd gotten a good look at it when he stripped in front of her—so straight and thick, with a nice, broad head. And even though she'd felt it throbbing against her belly when she was pressed tight against him. *Nothing* had prepared her for the feel of him in her hands.

He was as hard as a rock. As big around as her wrist. And so hot he nearly burned the palm of her hand.

"Mia..." Her name on his lips was the most perfect sound she'd ever heard as she rubbed her fingertips over his shaft, from the base to the tip, mapping every vein along the way.

She was surprised, and more than a little delighted, when his whole body quivered. That she could make a big, strong man like him—a man with so much experience in this area—tremble was incredibly empowering.

I am woman; hear me roar!

But then he grabbed her wrist to stop her play. "If you

keep that up..."

He seemed to lose his voice when she wrapped her fingers around him to give him a good, long stroke. She finished his sentence for him. "What? I'll make you come?" She'd never been a coquette before, but she felt decidedly coquettish now. "Good." She went up on tiptoe to nibble on his lower lip. "I want to make you come. I want to feel your cock pulse in my h—"

He didn't let her finish. Slamming his mouth over the top of hers, he pulled her to him so tightly that she was left with no recourse but to release him. It was either that, or risk giving him an injury.

Her growl of frustration grew into a whimper of lust when he wrapped her legs around his waist. Now his erection split her folds, pulsing hungrily against her clit. She decided it was a fair tradeoff.

Their hands were everywhere they could reach, cataloging every expanse of skin, every jut of bone, every line of muscle. Their mouths were open and greedy, trying to satisfy a hunger that seemed insatiable.

She realized Romeo liked to have his pulse point sucked on when she did exactly that and felt the answering throb of his dick. He moaned when she flicked her tongue over his skin, sucking in his smell—salt water and wind and those twin scents of warm cedar and oiled leather that would always remind her of him.

All the while the sea danced around them, sliding its cool, watery fingers over flesh that was hot with passion. Lapping greedily at body parts that were swollen and sensitive to the tiniest touch.

"I wanted to go slow this first time," he growled, his hands on her hips, rubbing her up and down his length until her toes curled and she thought she'd go crazy for wanting him *inside* her. "But I don't think I can—"

She removed her mouth from his delicious neck so that she could frame his face. The words *make love to me* were on the very edge of her tongue. But if this *was* love she was feeling, she knew it was all one-sided.

Instead she said, "Fuck me, Spiro. Please. I want to feel you inside me. I *need* to feel you—"

That's all she managed before he cursed long and low and stalked out of the water.

She thought to let go of him; she knew she must be heavy. But when she started to unhook her ankles from behind his back, he smacked her ass and hissed, "Stay right where you are."

A fresh rush of wetness ran between her legs. "My, my." She pursed her lips. "Aren't you the bossy one?"

She knew the wind was cool as it blew over her wet skin, but he was so hot around her, a human blast furnace, that she didn't register a chill. He stopped briefly on the beach, grabbing something from the pocket of his jeans, before walking them into the trees.

Carefully, he lowered her to the ground. She expected to feel sand beneath her back, so she was surprised when all she felt was a cool, smoothness instead. Looking around, she realized she was lying on a palm leaf pallet.

"Is this what you were doing when you left while the fish was cooking?" She lifted an eyebrow.

He'd gotten the fish cleaned and put on the spit, but then he'd asked her to watch it. *"I need to take care of something,"* he'd said, and she'd assumed he'd gone to wash up.

Now she knew he'd had other things in mind. Decidedly *naughty* things.

"You were that sure this was going to happen?" she teased as he stood over her, looking like a bronze god in the starlight dappling down through the palm trees overhead.

"I was that *hopeful* this was going to happen," he

corrected. Then he shook his head and added, "My god, Mia. You're gorgeous. I want you so much." As if to prove his point, his hand shot down to his shaft.

Her head lolled back against the fronds. *This is madness*, she thought as she watched his grip tighten over his dick. *A fever dream too carnal and decadent to be real.*

Yet, it *was* real.

And it was already better than she'd ever imagined.

And we haven't even gotten to the really good stuff, she thought a little giddily.

Catching her bottom lip between her teeth, she drifted one finger over her collar bone, across the slope of her breast, and let it come to rest on her nipple.

His eyes watched the journey of her finger with a predator's interest. And when she whispered, "Come take me," his nostrils flared.

Slowly, he lowered himself onto the palm leaf pallet even though she could tell it was costing him. Even though she could tell he wanted to mount her and go at her with everything he had. And then he was kissing her and touching her with an urgency that had her instantly burning.

This is what I was born for, she thought as he moved down her body, his lips burning a trail of open-mouthed kisses from her shoulder to her sternum and over to her breast. *This one perfect, passionate, pleasure-packed moment with the first man I've ever truly trusted. With the only man I've ever...*

Loved.

There it was.

The truth she could no longer deny.

She *was* in love with Spiro "Romeo" Delgado.

Tears pricked the backs of her eyelids. They weren't tears of sadness or heartache. They were tears of joy.

Even though it wouldn't be everything most people dreamed of when they dreamed of falling in love, it was so much more than she'd ever thought she'd have.

This one perfect moment with this one perfect man.

"Please." She pulled his mouth to hers. "I can't wait anymore. I need you too much to wait anymore."

He whispered something in Spanish that sounded deliciously dirty before he rolled away. The cool night air rushed in to fill the spot he'd vacated, and she shivered as goose bumps raised her skin. When he turned back, she saw he had a condom in hand—the thing he'd grabbed out of his jeans, obviously.

"I love a man who's prepared," she teased. Then, she realized she'd used the L-word. Not wanting to ruin the moment, she quickly added, "Let me," and took the condom from him.

Tearing off the wrapper and positioning the round ring of latex over his flushed, swollen head was something she did in the blink of an eye. But rolling the rubber onto him? Oh, she did that slowly. Letting her fingers linger, watching her hands play, listening to his breath catch.

Spiro.

The man who made her feel beautiful. The man who made her feel cherished. The man who made her feel... worthy.

Even though she wasn't.

"Mia..." Her name was a reverent sound on his tongue. "I can't wait either."

He moved over her then, settling his weight until their bodies touched everywhere. She could feel her heartbeat between her legs. Or maybe that was *his* heartbeat.

Or perhaps it's the two of our hearts beating together.

And *that* imagery made her smile.

"There it is," he whispered hoarsely. "That beautiful smile that melts me."

He was smiling too. But his was a slow, seductive grin

that promised unspeakable pleasures.

Before she could say anything, he reached between them and positioned himself at her entrance. She hadn't realized she'd caught her breath until he instructed, "Breathe, *cariña.*"

She was in the middle of a shuddering sigh when he pressed into her. Just an inch. But even that stretched her, invaded her, filled her full at the same time it promised to give her so much more.

He dropped a kiss onto her lips. "You okay?"

She couldn't speak. Every nerve ending rang like a klaxon. All she could do was nod, grip his hips, and urge him forward.

He didn't hesitate. But neither did he rush. He slowly, inexorably continued to shove into her. And with each new inch, it felt like too much. Too much pleasure. Too much ecstasy.

Yet it wasn't enough. Because he hadn't fully claimed *all* of her. There were still inches to go and...

With a low grunt, he seated himself fully.

She gasped as his plump head rammed into her cervix, as her walls strained to accommodate him, as her clitoris buzzed at the feel of his pelvis smashed tight against hers.

She thought it couldn't get any better.

And then it did.

Because he started to move.

Just a gentle retreat that dragged his shaft along her screaming nerve endings, followed by a slow, forceful advance that touched places inside her she didn't know she had. Retreat and advance. Retreat and advance. His hot, hard manhood stroking through her wet, welcoming womanhood.

"You're so deep inside me," she whispered against his lips. "I've never—"

She couldn't finish her sentence when he lengthened

his strokes. What had been decadent delight became pure pleasure.

She was no longer Mia. She was Sex. A being whose entire existence was centered around the place between her legs. The place where they were tethered so tightly. The place he teased. The place he tormented.

Hooking her heels behind his pistoning butt, she met him stroke for stroke. Her sheath melting around him when he pressed into her and clinging desperately to him when he retreated.

He must've felt she was close. That, or the mindless sounds coming from the back of her throat told him as much. Because he ripped his mouth away from hers and whispered hotly in her ear, "Say my name, *cariña*. Say my name when you come."

That was all it took.

She was like an underwater volcano, everything inside her was molten hot, glowing and roiling, and his words were the catalyst for her eruption. Her body pulsed and sucked and milked his as her orgasm rolled through her, hot and violent.

And his name was an eruption all its own.

"Spiro!"

CHAPTER 19

7:52 PM...

Romeo exploded.

That was really the only word to describe it. *Found his release* was far too tepid a phrase. *Orgasmed* was way too pedestrian a word. And *came* was hella succinct for what he experienced.

It was a peak that could pass for a neutron bomb. A violent detonation that rolled through his body in heated waves, searing his nerve endings along the way.

And hearing his name on her lips as she found *her* release? It was *so* much better than he ever imagined. So much more carnal and erotic. But also so much more... *intimate*. As if, with his body thrusting heavily inside hers and his name filling her mouth, they were one in a way he'd never experienced before.

For one golden moment, they'd become a single being made of pure bliss.

His brain had gone *boom* right along with his body. Which was why it was a long time after the last cannonade of release thundered through him before he realized he was crushing her. Her ragged exhalations finally pierced through his bombed-out mind, and he pressed up on his elbows so he could take some of his weight off her—and so he could stare down at the woman who'd just given him the best sex of his life.

She blinked open those amazing lioness eyes. Her voice was huskier than usual when she asked, "Is it always like this for you?"

Is she kidding?

Unlike her, he hadn't recovered enough to speak. All he could do was shake his head.

"Oh, good." She lethargically lifted a hand to pat his sweat-slick shoulder. "Me either."

Her statement sounded flippant, and he couldn't help wondering if that was to cover up how moved she was by the experience. Because if she was even *half* as affected as he was, the topography of her whole world had changed.

There was life *before* they'd become lovers. And now there was life after.

And life after is so, so, so much better.

Once his fine motor skills were restored, he gently rolled to the side, hissing the instant their spent bodies disengaged. He was quick to dispose of the used condom, and just as quick to pull her onto him, positioning her exactly as she'd been that morning when the last vestiges of sleep slipped from his brain.

Difference between then and now? Now he didn't ignore the impulse to bury his nose in her hair. Except it wasn't only her shampoo he smelled. It was her shampoo mixed with warm sunshine mixed with well-loved woman.

My *woman*, he thought. And the little voice in his head

was quick to remind him, *For now.*

"Mmm." She snuggled closer and twirled her fingers through the crinkly black hairs that grew between his pecs. Then she stilled. "You think we should be doing this?"

"Doing what?"

"Cuddling. Are friends with benefits allowed to cuddle?"

He stared up at the stars playing peek-a-boo between the fronds of the palm trees. "Is that what we are? Friends with benefits?"

"I'd like to think so."

Even though he couldn't see her face, he knew the expression she wore just by the timbre of her voice. She was smiling. Not the mega-watter that made him go dumb and blind, but the small, closed-mouth smile that made her look like she was keeping a secret.

He frowned in response.

Friends with benefits. It sounded so...shallow.

"I don't know if friends with benefits are supposed to cuddle." He hoped his sudden discomfiture wasn't revealed in his voice. "I've never had any friends with benefits."

She pushed up on her elbow. Her brow furrowed as she stared down at him. "I was under the impression *all* you had were friends with benefits." The starlight caught in the strands of her hair, turning it to rose gold.

"Nope." He shook his head. "I've only ever had the benefits. No friends."

He thought she might be put off by the thought of his liaisons having been so hollow and meaningless. He was a little surprised when she chuckled. "Forget the nickname Romeo. Romeo only ever loved one woman. You should've been nicknamed Casanova." Before he could respond, she cocked her head and continued, "Is that why you don't want to get married or commit? Because why settle for one woman when you can have any woman you want? *Every* woman you want?"

Her question touched on a topic he hadn't thought about in years. Or...okay, that wasn't true. He hadn't thought about it in years, and then she showed up and, suddenly, he'd started being hard-pressed to think of anything else.

Started wishing things were different.

Started wishing *he* was different.

His eyes unfocused as his mind drifted back to a phone conversation he'd had with his mother three years after joining the Navy. He'd called to tell her he'd completed his flight training, and that he was officially a certified pilot—something he'd done in what little downtime his active service afforded him. But instead of being excited for him, instead of being proud of him, his mother had only sounded disappointed.

"Does this mean you won't be coming home to help Alejandro? You're hooked on all this armed forces stuff, eh? Gonna join the Air Force next?"

The OtterBox case on Romeo's cell phone crackled a warning when he tightened his grip. "No. I'm not joining the Air Force. I just thought it would be fun to learn to fly. And Alejandro doesn't need my help." His words were clipped. "Sounds like he's doing fine on his own."

His mother had been all too happy to inform him that his older brother was now third in command and still clawing his way up the food chain in the Mexican Mafia. Romeo got sick to his stomach thinking about the awful things Alejandro must've done to rise so high so fast.

"Whether Alejandro needs you or not," his mother persisted, "you should still come home after your contract is up. You only have one more year and then you can put all this relaje *bullshit behind you and jump back in."*

"I'm not a turncoat, Mamá.*" He used the English version of her Spanish slang. "I don't* want *the life. I want*

to make a career in the Navy, have the house with the white picket fence, and maybe find a girl who grew up in the 'burbs to love me. Be normal."

His mother made a tching sound. "You're handsome enough to turn any head you want. But what happens when your good looks wear off, eh? What happens when these suburban putas realize under all that pretty packaging, you're just another piece of Chicano trash?"

His mother hadn't known it at the time, but her words had reminded him of what his high school girlfriend, Gina Lopez, had said the day he told her he was taking the deal the judge offered him.

He'd assumed Gina would wait for him to finish his stint in the Navy. After all, it'd been her idea for him to rob the corner store, which had led to him getting nabbed by the five-oh, which had led to him going before Judge Biltmore, which had led the judge to giving him a choice between being tried as an adult or agreeing to do his time in the military.

But Gina had simply stared at him incredulously before throwing back her head and laughing.

"Wait for you? Why would I do that?" she asked.

"Because..." Romeo blinked his confusion. "That's what people who love each other do, isn't it?"

The look of utter derision that came over her face haunted him. "I don't love you. I'm with you because you're hot, you know how to bone, and because I thought you were going places in La eMe." She used the nickname for the Mexican Mafia. "But behind that handsome face is nothing but a scared little boy. You were too afraid to kill that surfer so you could join Alejandro on his way to the top. And now you're too cowardly to face your sentence like a true homeboy should. Oh, novio, don't you get it? All the girls want you. But love you? No." She shook her head. "Love is for men, not for boys."

And if Romeo had needed *further* proof of the truth behind his mother's and Gina's words, he'd gotten it from Rachel Murphy, the woman he'd dated for six months before being accepted into the SEAL program.

He'd known he wouldn't be able to see much of Rachel while he went through the training, and he'd been reassuring her that he wasn't breaking up with her. In fact, he'd been telling her he'd very much like to see where their relationship was headed when she cocked her head and frowned at him.

"What do you mean 'where it's headed'?" she asked. "It isn't headed anywhere. You're too pretty for forever, cookie." She pointed at him. "What woman wants to be with a man who's constantly having ass thrown in his face?" She shook her head. "It's too much temptation for you, and too much worry for whatever woman might think to try to tie you down. Take it from me, you should use what god gave you and sow those wild oats until you run out of wild oats to sow."

That had been the last time he'd considered the idea of anything long term. The last time he'd fought against what had become glaringly obvious to him...

Women thought he was good for one thing and one thing only.

He realized he'd been quiet for too long when Mia frowned. "I didn't realize that would be a tender topic."

"It's not," he said quickly. Too quickly. He'd spoken without thinking. *After* thinking, he realized his words were a lie.

It *was* a tender topic. Even after all these years.

To make up for the untruth, he gave her a fast, slightly watered-down version of the conversations that'd led him to a lifetime of bachelorhood. "You hear the same thing enough times from enough people, and you run out of ways to deny the truth."

In typical Mia fashion, she didn't say anything for

a while. When she finally *did* answer, also in typical Mia fashion, her words were carefully chosen. "You might well be the most beautiful man I've ever met. But all those women were idiots. The way you look is the least interesting, and certainly the least note-worthy, thing about you."

"Are you saying we'd still be here now"—he waved a hand to indicate their pretzeled bodies—"if I had a peg leg, an eye patch, and face scar like Tony Montana?"

He saw her bite the inside of her cheek. "First of all, *Scarface*? Another of my grandmother's favorites. She always said Montana was one of Hollywood's greatest villains. Second of all, a peg leg and an eye patch? Hells yeah. I love me a good pirate. *Argh.*" She winked and then her expression grew somber.

"But in all seriousness"—her voice dropped an octave—"I'm not here with you now because you're all twisted steel and sex appeal. I'm here with you now because you're funny and smart and kind. Because you're honest and loyal and dependable. Because you make me feel safe and happy and... calm. Because of what's here." She touched his temple. "And what's here." She pressed her fingers against his chest, and he wondered if she could feel how his heart went all skippity-doo-dah.

"You really believe that, don't you?" His voice was barely a whisper.

"I don't *believe* it. Belief is reserved for things that aren't irrefutable facts." She placed her hand against his cheek, and he instinctively nuzzled his whiskers into her palm. "Your mother told you behind your pretty face is nothing but trash? She's wrong. Behind your pretty face are all the amazing things you've done and all the horrendous things you've overcome. Your high school girlfriend told you women love men and not boys? Well, I can safely say that you are *all* man. And I mean that in the best possible way. No toxic masculinity here. You use your strength and male privilege for good, not evil."

He thought about throwing her own words back at her. *I'm not a biscuit, so there's no need to butter me up.*

Except it was obvious she wasn't trying to flatter him. She believed every word coming out of her mouth, and that left him speechless.

"And that woman you dated before you became a SEAL? The one who told you you're too good-looking, and any woman you choose would be constantly worried about you straying? That says more about *her* insecurities than it does about you. I have no doubt if you ever decide to make a vow to some woman, you'll never break it, come hell or high water."

If he thought making love to Mia had changed things for him, that was nothing compared to the transformations happening inside him with each new word out of her mouth.

It wasn't simply the topography of his world that was changed now. Oh, no. He was living in a *new* world. A world where a woman didn't care about what he'd been born as, and instead appreciated all he'd become. A world where he wasn't relegated to the role others had made for him, because the path he'd forged was all his own. A world where Romeo didn't exist, because there was only Spiro.

Mia's Spiro.

Those two words whispered through his head, and they were as crystalline and clear as the sky at 60,000 feet.

He *was* hers.

Little by little, inch by inch, with every sweet smile or sneakily funny remark or tender touch, she'd wiggled her way into his heart until she'd stolen the whole damn thing.

I love her.

The realization didn't hit him like a lightning bolt from the blue. It was more like her words gave him the courage to finally admit something that had been lurking around in the far reaches of his mind for quite some time.

"Thank you." His voice sounded strained. "You have no idea how much that means to me."

She smiled. "I'd say you're welcome, but that implies I was giving you compliments, and I was just giving you the truth."

Before he could respond, she gave him a quick—far too quick—peck on the lips and snuggled back onto his chest. Her warm cheek was cushioned against his pectoral muscle so that her ear was positioned directly over his heart.

Or I guess it's her heart.

And that was more than a little terrifying because... "Why don't *you* want a happily-ever-after?"

She stiffened slightly and remained quiet for a while. Then, "It's not that I don't *want* one. Who doesn't *want* one? It's more that I wouldn't have the first clue how to make a long-term relationship work. It's not like I was *modeled* a happy, healthy marriage. Plus—"

She cut herself off, and he got the impression that, once again, she'd nearly admitted something she wasn't ready to admit. Except this time, he couldn't let it go. He *had* to know. "Plus *what?*"

"Plus...my job keeps me on the road for good chunks of time. Relationships are tough enough without throwing in a few thousand miles of distance. Or so I've been told," she finished, and he blew out a covert breath.

She wasn't opposed to commitment because of some soul-deep aversion to monogamy, or because she didn't believe in romantic love, or because she couldn't see herself being happy unless she was footloose and fancy free.

Which meant there was hope.

Hope for what? the voice asked.

Hope that I can change her mind about forever like she

just changed mine.

But that would come later. For now...

"Will you tell me more about Andy?" he asked carefully.

He heard her swallow. And when she spoke, her voice was thick with emotion. "Andy was wonderful. The sweetest, gentlest boy I've ever known. He had a beautiful singing voice. He was an excellent storyteller. And he *loved* to read, mostly science fiction. But he wasn't the same after we got back from the hospital. I mean, he *seemed* okay for a while. Maybe a little quieter, but all the doctors said was that was to be expected. Then, right around the time he hit puberty, the anxiety and depression manifested themselves. And along with them came thoughts of suicide and bouts of self-harm."

"And you think that was brought on by the overdose when he was three?"

"None of the doctors said so, but Mom always insisted the brush with death irreparably altered Andy's brain chemistry."

Again, Romeo had the distinct urge to wrap his hands around her mother's neck and squeeze. "And because you thought you were responsible for his brush with death, you also felt responsible for his mental illness."

"I don't *think* I was responsible for his brush with death. I *was* responsible for it," she insisted.

"Mia—"

"No." Her soft cheek brushed against his chest when she shook her head. "I'm not going to argue the point. You asked about Andy, and I'm telling you."

There were a million things he could say about who was responsible for what, but Mia could be amazingly stubborn when she chose to be. And because she *was* so very stubborn, and also because she was so principled and scrupulous and accountable to the point of performing emotional hara-kiri, he knew anything he might say would fall on deaf ears.

Instead, he told her, "Please, go on."

"Andy was in and out of institutions from the age of twelve. At around seventeen, he seemed to be getting better. I remember how happy Granny Susan was to have him home. And then Granny Susan died, and Andy had to go live with Mom and Dad."

When she shivered, he pulled her snug against his side. He didn't think it was the cool ocean breeze that made goose bumps pop out over her skin.

"He finally succeeded in taking his own life six months later," she finished, her voice so quiet he had to strain to hear her.

Rolling her onto her back, he held himself above her. Her golden eyes were bright with unshed tears, and the pain in them was so sharp he would swear he could feel it cutting into his soul.

Brushing her hair back from her face, he said the only thing he could. "I'm so sorry." And yet the words didn't do justice to *how* sorry he was. How much he wished he could take away all her heartache and hurt and replace it with only love and laughter.

Her eyes dropped to his chin. "Which reminds me of something I've been meaning to ask you," she said on a whisper.

He couldn't imagine what her brother's death had to do with him, but still he urged, "Shoot."

Her eyes caught and held his. "Would you let me make a donation to your outreach program once you get it started?"

Caught off guard, his initial instinct was to decline her offer. The idea of accepting money from her, even for something as noble as his charity, didn't set right.

She must have seen the hesitancy in his eyes, because she quickly explained how her father, after having set up a trust for her mother, had left the bulk of his estate to her.

How she'd vowed from the beginning to donate the money to troubled youths in honor of her little brother. And how Romeo's outreach program struck her as the *perfect* cause since he would be the one running it and she knew he'd make sure the money was put to good use.

"How much are we talking?" he asked, although, he knew he'd end up saying yes to her offer no matter what. He could see how much it meant to her.

"Five million dollars."

It was a good thing his mouth was empty. If he'd been eating, he would've spit out his food in one of those dramatic Hollywood holy-shit moves. "Sweet Mother Mary!"

"I know that sounds like a lot, but—"

"It doesn't *sound* like a lot. It *is* a lot. Don't you want to keep some of it for yourself? What if you fall on hard times or...or..." He shook his head helplessly. *Five million dollars! Who gives that away?* But he knew the answer. *Mia. Mia gives that away.* "I don't know. Decide to quit your job and write the next Great American Novel?"

"Like I said, Andy was the storyteller. And I don't *want* the money." When he frowned at the shadow that moved through her eyes again, she was quick to add, "I want *you* to have it. Will you take it?"

Five million dollars! Holy fuck!

She mistook his continued hesitation for rejection and pleaded, "Please, Spiro. I *want* you to have it."

"Mia..." A knot had formed in his throat. He had to swallow it down before he could continue. "Of course I'll take it, if that's what you want. I'll do *anything* you want." And he realized he'd never spoken truer words in his life. "On one condition."

A little line formed between her eyebrows. "What's that?"

"You let me name the program after him."

For a long time, she said nothing. And he thought maybe she was somehow offended by his request. But then her chin trembled, her lips puckered, and she hiccupped on a sob.

"Oh, Spiro." She dragged him into a hug. Her warm breath tickled his ear. "Why are you so wonderful?"

"Me?" He pressed up to find tears had left shiny streaks down her temples. He used his thumbs to brush away the wetness. "You're the one who wants to give away your entire inheritance to charity." When she only sniffed and blinked as more tears filled her eyes, he asked softly, "Did Andy have a nickname?"

Her brow pinched. "Why?"

"Because sometimes nicknames are more meaningful."

Shaking her head in wonder, she whispered, "You really can read minds. I swear." Before he could ask what she meant by that, she continued. "His nickname was BeeBee. I kept mangling *baby brother* when he was born, and those two words got shortened to the first letter in each, which eventually became BeeBee."

"That explains this." He drifted his fingers over the tattoo on her rib cage.

She nodded. "That way I always have a reminder of him close to my heart."

"That's it, then." He dipped his chin. "It'll be the BeeBee Foundation, and the logo will be two bumblebees. Which"—he smiled—"is kind of perfect. You've heard it said bumblebees shouldn't be able to fly, right? That their wing to body mass ratio is all off? And yet they fly anyway because they *believe* they can? That's the program I want to build. I want to take kids who have all the odds stacked against them, and I want to make them believe they can fly."

In fact...it was *so* perfect he couldn't help but feel like there were larger forces at work. Like maybe Mia coming to Wayfarer Island had been serendipity. Like them becoming lovers had been inevitable. Like him *falling* for her had been...fate.

He realized he was smiling when she pressed a cool fingertip into one of his dimples. "Thank you," she whispered. "Your charity will be a more beautiful tribute to Andy than I could ever have imagined."

"No. Thank *you*," he countered. "Because if Alex and Mason don't find the cipher device, now I'll still be able to open the program."

"Alex and Mason are going to find the cipher device," she insisted staunchly. "I can feel it."

"You know what? Me too." For the first time since they'd begun to search for the treasure, he honestly believed they were close to locating it.

Of course, once they *did*—and after it was hauled up according to Mia's exacting standards—she would be off to her next job, and *that* had a sense of urgency expanding in his chest. "Mia, I..."

He drifted off because...What? What did he want to say?

Oh, right. He wanted to tell her that he loved her, that he was *in* love with her. He wanted to ask her to take a chance on him even though neither one of them had any idea what it took to make things work. He wanted...her.

Just her.

All that was her.

Always.

Maybe *she* was the mind reader, because she cleared her throat and patted his shoulder, indicating he should roll off her. When he did, she sat up and glanced at the black waves that turned silver when they broke against the beach. "It's too early to go to sleep. What do you say to more P.J. Warren?"

He didn't give a fuzzy fuck about Lazarus Luxido at the moment, but he could tell she wasn't ready to hear all the things he wanted to say to her. Not yet.

Glancing at the moon riding low in the sky, he murmured, "It's too dark, isn't it?"

"I can use the light on my cell phone until the battery runs out."

Before he could throw any more wrenches in the works, she stood and made her way to the beach and her purse. The stars bathed her gloriously naked body in their light until her pale skin looked pearlescent.

She's so fucking beautiful, he thought, his passions stirring at the sight of her.

But the warmth in his blood chilled when that horrible voice that lived inside his head whispered, *What happens if you can't make her fall in love with you?*

It was too awful to contemplate. But he supposed the answer was simple.

He would whisper her name on dark, lonely nights as he stared at the stars and remembered that, once upon a time, he'd known what it was to hold the woman of his heart inside the circle of his arms.

CHAPTER 20

8:15 PM...

Carter was running on adrenaline.

It made him irritable.

Well, that, and the fact that their plan had changed *yet again* thanks to Robby spying the dark-haired dude passing off the weapon to the light-haired dude, and Mia and the dark-haired dude separating themselves from the other two in the group to go have a little slam-bam-thank-you-ma'am on the beach.

Even though Kenny had been looking forward to getting blood on his hands, he'd insisted he should cover the guy who was armed should things go sideways. Which made sense; use a gun to cover a gun. And Kenny didn't trust Robby or Carter with the pistol since neither one of them had any experience wielding a sidearm. Which had left the job of using the knife on Mia up to Robby and Carter. Except, Robby had balked. No, not balked. He'd flat-out *refused*.

And so it was up to Carter to do the dirty work.

To take out Mia. To shuffle her off her mortal coil. To do her in.

Jesus. Even the euphemisms sound awful.

"Remember what she did," Jane said to him, her harsh whisper competing with the sounds of the waves slapping against the sides of the boat. Starlight was usually flattering, but it only made Jane's features stand out in severe relief. "Remember what she is. She *deserves* this."

Carter couldn't do anything more than nod. His gorge had risen, and he feared if he opened his mouth, he might hurl.

He tried blaming his rancid stomach on the two monster waves they'd battled while waiting for the sun to set. *What is* with *this section of ocean, anyway?* he wondered. It was like it was a sentient being bent on mayhem. But he knew the real reason it felt like his gut was rolling in sick circles was because he didn't have the stomach for murder. At least not the face-to-face kind.

Either some of what he was thinking showed on his face, or Kenny just knew him well enough to know the thoughts spinning wildly through his head. "Do her from behind," Kenny instructed. "Grab her forehead and slit her throat from ear to ear. She won't have time to scream. She won't have time to fight. And you won't hafta watch the life drain from her eyes. You got this."

Carter swallowed and nodded again.

He wished they could hold off. Maybe if they held off, Mia and the dark-haired dude would finish up and rejoin the group. Then Carter and Robby and Kenny could go back to the plan where they waited for her separate for a pee break, and Kenny could do the deed. But the hunt for the missing plane was all over the emergency channels. And the Coast Guard was closing in.

They had to make their move. Now.

While Kenny and Robby watched the two by the fire—Kenny covering the man who was armed and Robby keeping a weather eye out for Carter's signal—Carter would sneak up on his cousin and wait to get her alone. After he was finished using the knife on her, he would wrap her body in the lifejacket he was bringing with him and float her out to the boat. Then he'd flash his cell phone, just once, to let Robby and Kenny know it was safe to sneak off the island and swim back to the boat.

Easy, right?

Except not *nearly* as easy as simply blowing up the plane.

Damn Kenny! he thought for the hundredth time that day.

"Everybody ready?" Kenny asked, prepared to slip off the side of the boat and start swimming toward the island in the near distance. The fire burning in little sandbar's center made it shine like a beacon in the vast blackness of the nighttime sea.

No, I'm not ready. Not by half, Carter thought a little desperately. But he nodded his head all the same.

"Huzzah!" Kenny whispered before sliding into the ocean. For a big man, he was remarkable stealthy.

Robby made the tiniest splash as he followed Kenny into the drink. Swiping his wet hair out of his face, he turned and looked expectantly up at Carter.

If you want something done right, you better do it yourself, Carter coached himself before slipping off the side of the boat and gasping at the coolness of the water that embraced him. Goose bumps peppered his flesh and raised the hair at the nape of his neck.

"Here." Jane handed down to him Kenny's huge Bowie knife. Moonlight glinted off its evil silver blade. "Good luck."

For just a moment, looking up at his aunt, he thought about calling the whole thing off. They could rethink this whole thing and regroup. Find *another* opportunity to kill Mia.

Jane must've read the hesitation in his eyes, because her gaze went razor-sharp. "We've come too far to turn back now. Finish it."

CHAPTER 21

8:34 PM...

Doc shifted uncomfortably.

The meds Cami shared with him had worn off long ago, so he could feel every heartbeat in the bump on his head and in the bones of his fractured arm. Also, it was impossible to forget that somewhere close by Romeo and Mia were wrapped in each other's arms. Which only made him acutely aware that the sexiest woman he'd ever met was sitting a foot away from him. And *that* meant he'd been sporting semi-wood the whole time, and now his balls ached right along with his injured limb and noggin.

Glancing over at the cause of his latest malady, he found her staring into the fire. The orange flames reflected in her dark eyes which, when combined with her ruby lips and raven hair, made her look a little witchy, reminding him of that old Eagles tune.

She held me spellbound, indeed, he thought. And then

he followed that up with, *What the hell, nothing ventured, nothing gained.*

She'd shot him down a dozen times, but maybe thirteen was his lucky number.

He leaned close enough to make her uncomfortable. And even though she would never admit it, close enough to make her a little excited too, because there was no denying the heat in her eyes when she turned to him and demanded, "What?"

"I'm just thinking that once you get past the part where we're stranded in the middle of nowhere, this little island is actually pretty...and kind of romantic. It seems a crying shame to let Romeo and Mia have all the fun." He lifted one eyebrow in invitation. "Come on. I won't be as good as I usually am without the use of both arms, but I can still promise you a night you'll never forget."

Her delectable mouth puckered with feigned distaste. "You need to chuck that idea straight into the fuck it bucket and move on."

"Damn, woman, you are seriously giving me frostbite." He faked a pout.

She snickered and pretended to be holding something in her hand. "This is my cup of care." She peered down at her hand. "Oh, look! It's empty."

He felt laughter rumbling around in his chest, but he didn't give into it. Instead, he pinned her with a narrow-eyed look. "Am I *really* supposed to buy that nonsense about you not mixing business with pleasure? I'm supposed to buy that you've never kissed the IT guy at the company Christmas party or gone out for drinks that turned into drunken shenanigans with a colleague?""No purchase required," she stated flatly. "I'm telling you, business and pleasure are oil and water. No mixing. None."

He frowned. "That's really unfortunate for you."

"How so?"

"Because I've heard it said that everyone who plays it safe always dies wondering."

Her glance was shrewd. "Wow. Profound. You're like Yoda. You know, if Yoda was completely full of shit."

He couldn't hold back his laughter any longer. It tumbled out of him. An instant later, he sobered.

He wasn't a superstitious man. And he was far too scientifically minded to believe in such things as a sixth sense. But growing up in the wilderness of Montana, and then spending a decade running missions for the government, had honed his instincts and taught him to never second-guess that scratchy feeling at the back of his head that told him he was lined up in someone's crosshairs.

His hand slowly sought the grip on the Glock stuffed into the back of his jeans. Looking away from the fire, he allowed his eyes to adjust to the darkness. When he turned back, he peered over Cami's left shoulder, and immediately noticed two things.

One, Cami was smiling that huge smile with all those blindingly white teeth. And two, a large, dark shadow moved beside a palm tree about thirty yards behind her.

Adrenaline scorched through Doc's veins, burning away all the pain that'd dogged him. He lifted the Glock in an instant. From the corner of his eye, he saw Cami's eyes fly wide. "I take it back!" she yelled. "You're not like Yoda at—"

That's all he heard before he yelled, "Come out where I can see you with your hands up!" When the shadow hesitated, he added, "Do it now, or I swear on all that's holy I'll pull my trigger and drop you dead!"

Slowly, the shadow edged away from the tree. Even though he couldn't make out the man's features, he had no trouble identifying the object held at the end of the bastard's arm.

The barrel of a pistol was like a black hole; it absorbed all light.

"Drop your weapon!" Doc roared, his vision tunneling until all he saw was the weapon and the arm attached to it. But the shadow ignored his command and took a menacing step forward. Deadly intent had a smell, like sulfur, and Doc would swear he smelled it drifting on the wind.

When the shadow's arm moved slightly, in preparation of firing and absorbing the kickback, Doc didn't hesitate. He pulled his trigger.

In such close confines, the *boom* of the Glock was deafening. But even though he barely registered it, from the corner of his eye, he saw Cami instinctively cover her ears.

It was from the corner of his eye, because he dared not take his eye off his target. A target he'd managed to hit. Center mass. Kill shot.

He'd learned long ago that when it came to gunplay, there was no such thing as a shot across the bow.

Unfortunately, the man's brain didn't register that his body was already dead. As the shadow fell sideways, he managed to squeeze off a shot.

"Down!" Doc launched himself atop Cami and pressed her hard into the sand as he felt the hot puff of displayed air that accompanied the bullet as it flew by his shoulder.

Half of him registered the warmth of Cami's breath against his cheek, the softness of her breasts cushioning his chest, and the heat of her womanhood because her spread thighs cradled his hips. But the other half of him was completely focused on pushing to his feet, aiming at the second shadow that disengaged from the palm tree closest to the downed gunman, and yelling, "Stop right there unless you want to end up like your friend!"

The second shadow skidded to a halt, lifting his hands

high into the air. "Don't shoot!" A panicked voice cut through the darkness. "I surrender!"

Doc's heart thudded heavily in his chest. It'd been a minute since he'd found himself on the receiving end of a narrowly missed bullet.

He had to admit, he didn't miss the sensation.

Not to steal a line from Roger Murtaugh, he thought, *but I am getting too old for this shit.*

Behind him, he heard Cami push to her feet. He thought about telling her to stay put. But then he realized he had no idea if these two jackholes had brought buddies with them.

In which case, it'd be better for him not to have to divide his attention between them and Cami. "Stick close to me," he told her from the side of his mouth. "I mean, like white on rice."

She didn't hesitate, hooking a finger through his belt loop and plastering herself against his back until her breasts bracketed his spine.

"Keep up with me," he commanded as he took a step away from the glow of the fire and toward the man who continued to stand with his hands in the air. "Match every move I make."

They were maybe ten yards from the man by the time he could make out the guy's features. Wispy blond hair. Small, dark eyes that reminded him of something that scurried around on the ground. And the most pathetic excuse for a mustache Doc had seen on any guy older than fifteen.

Also, the dude was soaking wet. Water dripped from his hair and the hems of his board shorts.

They swam here?

As soon as the question drifted through his mind, he knew the answer. *No. They have a boat nearby. They dropped anchor and swam to the sandbar so their engine noise wouldn't alert us to their arrival.*

Which meant their malevolent intentions had been planned. Which meant this wasn't simply a wrong place/ wrong time situation. Like, this little sandbar wasn't the meeting place of drug dealers and their mules, and Doc and crew hadn't simply stumbled into a situation that didn't have anything to do with them.

This had *everything* to do with them.

Which meant Romeo had been right. They hadn't experienced some sort of bizarre, but natural, mid-flight catastrophe. These motherfuckers were surely the same ones who'd tried to blow them out of the damned sky.

"How many of you are here?" he demanded.

Mustache Man's Adam's apple traveled up the length of his throat. "C-can you please point that thing somewhere else?"

Doc was aiming the Glock between the man's beady eyes. But he nodded and said, "Sure thing," before pointing the pistol at the man's crotch. The guy's cheeks paled in the moonlight. "Now," Doc growled menacingly, "I'm going to ask you one more time, and then I'm going to blow your dick off. How many of you are there?"

"Th-three," the guy wheezed, then glanced down at the hulking mass of a human carcass. "N-now, just two, I guess. Oh, my god!" His face scrunched up, making him look even more rat-like. "You killed Kenny!"

Doc peered down at the dead man with gritty resolve, having long ago lost his ability to feel sorry for any fucker who tried to end his life.

"I was nearly killed by a guy named *Kenny*," he muttered. "Jesus hopscotching Christ, just when I thought my night couldn't get any worse, I find myself in the middle of a *South Park* episode."

Mustache Man blinked at him uncomprehendingly. And okay, so gallows humor was obviously lost on those who hadn't spent years dodging bullets and living on the edge.

"Who the fuck are you?" he demanded of the man. "And why the hell are you trying to kill us?"

Before Mustache Man could answer, Romeo's deep voice boomed through the night. "Stop!" The command was followed by the sound of splashing, and that was immediately followed by the sound of a struggle, by the *thuds* of landed punches, by the grunts of pain when bone met bone.

Doc couldn't see what was happening on the beach. A stand of palm trees obscured his line of sight. So he ripped his gaze away from the tune of hand-to-hand combat—after all, Romeo was the most skilled fighter he'd ever known, having mastered Krav Maga and jiujitsu—and narrowed his gaze on Mustache Man.

"Did you shoot down our plane?" he asked Mustache Man, taking a step toward the body, determined to grab the gun that was lying on the ground beside the dead man's splayed hand. The dude had fallen sideways but had rolled face-first into the sand. Which was a blessing since it meant his lifeless eyes and the blood seeping from his body were both concealed.

"Y-yes." Mustache Man swallowed again. This time, the journey of his Adam's apple made a *clicking* sound in his throat.

"Why?" Doc took another step toward the dropped weapon.

The sound of crunching footsteps, accompanied by a flurry of profanity, stopped Mustache Man from answering. From around the stand of palm trees, Romeo and a third man appeared. Romeo had the guy's hands wrenched up high and tight behind his back as he frog-marched him closer to the group gathered around the body.

The new arrival was as wet as Mustache Man, his long auburn hair dripping water onto his skinny shoulders. Blood ran from his nose over his chin. His left eye was cherry red, even in the starlight, and it was obvious he was going to have one hell of a shiner come the dawn. There was a murderous twist to his lips as he continued to snarl obscenities over his shoulder.

Romeo ignored him as he asked Doc, "Have you asked how many they have with them?"

Doc nodded. "This one"—he hitched his chin toward Mustache Man—"says there's only three."

"This one told me the same thing," Romeo said. Then he yelled over his shoulder, "Mia! I think it's safe to come out!"

From somewhere farther down the island, Mia's soft, husky voice sounded. "On my way!"

Romeo stepped slightly to the side, and that's when three things became glaringly clear. The first was that ol' Auburn Hair hadn't managed to land a single punch. Romeo's face was as handsome and unmarred as ever. The second was that Auburn Hair had come to shore equipped with a big-ass blade, which Romeo held in one hand. And the third was that Romeo was as naked as the day he was born.

Cami, who was still plastered to Doc's back, choked. Then she whispered, "Whoever said clothes make the man was dead wrong."

Doc had the sudden urge to shift his aim from Mustache Man's genitals to Romeo's.

CHAPTER 22

8:42 PM...

Mia darted out from behind the palm tree she'd been hiding behind and raced toward the beach to grab her discarded clothes. She dressed at the speed of light and then snagged Romeo's jockey shorts and jeans before jogging toward the glow of the fire in the distance.

Adrenaline pumped through her system, making her vision go pinpoint.

No. It's not the adrenaline making my eyesight wonky, she realized. *I haven't drawn a full breath since we heard the gunshot.*

After she'd retrieved *In Darkness and Dreams* from her purse, she'd read the sex scene aloud to Romeo. Only, it hadn't turned out to be a sex scene. At least not in the traditional horizontal hula sense. Instead, P.J. Warren had written that Ursula Lobo had seduced the obscenely sexy Lazarus Luxido by giving him a slow, intensely erotic blow job.

After Mia finished reading, she'd snapped the book closed and turned to Romeo with what she'd hoped was a seductive grin. *"Let's see if that's as hot in real life as it is on the page,"* she'd told him.

For the record, it had been *hotter*.

If she lived to be a hundred years old, she would always remember the way Romeo had arched beneath her, his hands tangled in her hair, her name a harsh whisper torn from the back of his throat as he exploded into her mouth.

"God bless P.J. Warren," he'd said once he stopped breathing like he'd been stuck under water for too long. *"And god bless Mia Ennis,"* he'd added before flipping her onto her back.

He'd kissed her until the flames of passion had once more become a conflagration, and then he'd nibbled his way across her jaw, back to her ear, and down to her neck. By the time he'd gotten to her collarbone, she'd been begging him to kiss her nipples. And his hot lips had just closed over one greedy peak when she'd told him, *"P.J. Warren didn't write about this."*

"Sure she did," he'd said, briefly blowing across her nipple and watching it furl tight. *"In book three."*

Mia had groaned, remembering the sex scene in book three where the alpha werewolf spent an hour going down on his fated mate, making her climax so many times that she passed out from the pleasure.

She had been all set to let Romeo give the scene his best shot when the unmistakable *boom* of gunfire ripped through the stillness of the night, and he'd torn himself out of her arms so quickly, she'd been left holding nothing but the empty airspace his big, warm body had occupied.

"Wha—" she'd started to ask, pushing up on her elbows. He'd cut her off by hissing, *"Stay here! Stay down!"* And

then he'd taken off through the trees and darted down the beach, his long, strong legs making fast work of the distance despite his bare feet sinking into the sand.

When a shadow disengaged from the tree line, making a mad dash for the water, Romeo had immediately changed directions, cutting the mystery man off and tackling him into the surf. It'd been too dark for Mia to make out much, but she'd seen the glint of moonlight as it reflected off the long blade the intruder wielded.

Her heart had immediately jumped into her throat. But she shouldn't have worried. Romeo, with moves that reminded her of something out of a kung fu movie, easily disarmed the man and then proceeded to beat on him for a bit before marching him up the beach toward the glow of the fire.

But even after she'd lost sight of the men when they disappeared into the trees, she hadn't moved. Romeo had told her stay down and stay put. And that's exactly what she'd done because she wasn't an idiot, or one of those ridiculous damsels in distress who disregarded the advice of someone trained in dealing with danger because she thought her meager skill set might be of some use when, in fact, she just created a distraction.

She'd nearly cried out when she'd heard him call her name.

And even though her heart still raced a mile a minute, she felt like she had her fear under control when she walked up behind him. Of course, seeing him standing so tall, his beautiful naked back dripping seawater but otherwise unmarred despite the wicked looking knife that could've done so much damage, probably went a long way in tamping down her terror.

The man he'd battled with stood in front of him. Or rather, was being *held* in front of him. Romeo had the guy's arms wrenched up behind his back so high his shoulder blades poked painfully against the cotton of his T-shirt.

She couldn't see the man's face, partly because she didn't have the right angle, but mostly because she got distracted by the behemoth face-planted in the sand. She could tell the overgrown guy was dead by his utter stillness.

By contrast, the skinny blond man standing next to him twitched like he'd stepped in an anthill. Of course, the fact that Doc was aiming at the dude's balls might have something to do with his nerves.

"I, uh, brought your clothes," Mia told Romeo, taking a step closer so he could see her out of his peripheral vision.

Two things happened then. The first was that Cami said, "Oh, come on, Mia. The only men in my life right now are Ben and Jerry and their amazing gift to the world known as Chunky Monkey, so this is a rare treat. Don't ruin my fun." The second was that Mia saw the profile of the man Romeo held captive.

Her kneecaps turned to immediate dust, and it was a wonder she didn't crumble onto the sand. She knew her expression was a mixture of confusion and dismay when she whispered, "Carter?"

"You know him?" Doc asked at the same time Romeo said incredulously, "This is your cousin?"

She didn't answer either of them. Instead she took a step back when Carter turned and his green eyes bored into hers.

Her mind raced with a million questions, but the biggest one was...*why? Why is he here? Why is he looking at me with a hatred so hot it burns the very air around us?*

She voiced her first question aloud, and he smiled. The expression looked sinister thanks to the blood staining his teeth.

"I would think that's obvious." He shook his head and let out a laugh that sounded hard and brittle.

Understanding dawned, and traitorous tears pricked behind her eyes. "It was you? *You* brought down the plane? *You* tried to kill us?"

"For the record," he said, "I was only after *you*. Everyone else was collateral damage."

She stumbled back another step, shaking her head uncomprehendingly. Again, that one question rang inside her mind. "*Why?*" she demanded again. "I don't understand."

"Don't you?" His upper lip curled, once again revealing his blood-stained teeth. "Or have you pretended to have the moral high ground for so long that you actually believe you belong up there?"

"Careful how you talk to her." Romeo jerked Carter's hands higher behind his back, forcing Carter up on tiptoe lest Romeo pop his shoulders out of joint.

"Carter, I seriously don't understand what you—" That's all she managed, because the twitchy guy let out a cry of desperation and lunged for the pistol lying next to the dead man.

Everything that came next happened in slow motion.

The blond man fumbled with the weapon at the same time Doc yelled, "Stop or I'll shoot!" Carter wrenched out of Romeo's startled grasp. Cami screamed bloody murder. And Mia found herself staring down the barrel of a big, black handgun as the blond dude tried swinging the gun around to aim at Doc.

If it'd had time, her heart would have jumped out of her throat. But all it managed was to skip a beat before two deafening—nearly simultaneous—*booms* cleaved the night in half.

She saw the flash at the end of the twitchy guy's weapon and expected to feel the agony of a bullet tearing through her flesh a split second later. But instead, all she felt was horror when Romeo leapt in front of her.

He jerked when the round plowed into him, and then he hit the ground at her feet, groaning.

"*No!*" she heard someone scream. Dropping to her knees beside him, she realized that someone was her.

Grabbing his shoulder, she tried turning him over to see where he'd been hit, but stopped what she was doing when she heard Cami yell, "Quick! He's getting away!"

From the corner of her eye, she saw Carter kicking up great clouds of sand as he raced for the beach.

"Damnit! *Damnit!*" Doc cursed, obviously wanting to give chase but knowing Romeo needed him.

He dropped to his knees beside Mia and helped her roll Romeo onto his back.

She breathed a sigh of relief when she saw him blink quickly, when she saw the large vein in his neck pulse thickly.

He's alive! Thank god, he's alive!

Her inner celebration was fleeting, however, because the next things she noticed were that his lips were colorless, and his usually bright eyes were clouded with pain.

"Spiro..." His name was a plea and a prayer rolled into one. She jerked her gaze down his body, searching for his gunshot wound.

When she found the bullet hole, high up on the right side of his chest, she nearly retched her dinner into the sand.

Somehow, she managed to keep the snook down and instinctively pressed her hand over the bullet hole—*they always say to apply pressure, right?* Then she glanced up at Cami, who was staring in horror at the blond man.

Doc's slug had caught the gunman right between his eyes. He'd fallen lifeless on top of his companion, but most of his gray matter was glistening on the sand behind him.

Under normal circumstances, Mia would've been gaping in terror and revulsion too. But she barely spared the dead men a glance before whispering desperately, "Cami!

Quick! The first aid kit!"

Cami blinked as if she was coming out of a trance. Then she nodded and ran toward the life raft.

"Doc?" Mia's urgent eyes sought out the one man who could tell her how bad Romeo's injury was.

"For shit's sake, Romeo." Doc quickly unwrapped his ACE bandage sling. Mia had to strain to hear him above the sound of her heart thundering in her ears. Fear didn't just have a taste, like sucking on an old penny; it had a sound too. "Why do you always have to play the part of the hero, huh?"

Romeo shook his head, unable to answer. He was sucking in air, but it sounded like he was drowning. His big chest worked in a terrible rhythm, the center sinking in.

"That's right." Doc tossed aside the bandage and flexed his fingers. "And now you've gone and given yourself a damned pneumothorax."

Mia didn't know what a pneumothorax was, but it didn't sound good. "How can I help?" Her voice was thin. When she realized Doc hadn't heard her, she determinedly cleared her throat and repeated her question.

"The bullet either pierced or nicked his lung," Doc explained. "Which has allowed the air to seep out. And now it's trapped between his lung and the wall of his chest, causing his lung to collapse." Doc patted Romeo on the shoulder. "But don't worry, brother. I got you. I'll just have to stab you in the chest, okay?"

Some people might enjoy Doc's deadpan bedside manner. Mia wasn't one of them.

The last thing she wanted from Doc was jokes. What she wanted from him was a *miracle*, for him to snap his fingers or wave a magic wand and make Romeo whole again. Or for him to turn back time so she could stop Romeo before he could take the bullet aimed at her.

"You foolish, wonderful man," she whispered to Romeo,

barely noticing the hot tears that streaked down her face as she kept her hands over his wound, trying with all her might to stem the flow of his blood from his body. "That bullet had my name on it. Why did you step in front of it?"

All Romeo could do was shake his head.

"I know." Her words caught on a sob as she felt more of his warm blood seeping between her fingers. "Like Doc said, you're a hero. You can't help it."

She wanted to curse god or fate or the universe or whoever was in charge for being so stupid and cruel. The idea of Romeo dying to save her was so unfathomable, it had to be a mistake. Romeo was so good, so pure of heart, and she was...*her*.

Even though she didn't believe in such things, she was desperate enough to plead with whatever higher power might happen to be listening.

Please! If you have to take someone, take me! Don't take him! Don't—

She wasn't able to finish her prayer before Cami skidded to a stop next to them, handing Doc the first aid kit and asking, "What can I do?"

"Keep your mouth shut," Doc said as he threw open the lid to the kit. "I need to concentrate. And I can't do that with you being all quick and quippy."

Mia saw Cami open her mouth to argue. Then Cami realized anything she might say would prove Doc's point. She snapped her mouth shut again.

"Iodine," Doc grumbled, digging around in the kit. "Where the fuck is the iodine?"

Cami pointed to a brown bottle tucked into the corner and Doc grabbed it.

"Okay, find me a scalpel while you're at it," he told her as he continued to root around in the kit. When Cami found that, too, he grumbled, "I suppose tubing would be too much to ask for?"

He and Cami both spent a handful of seconds scrounging through the medical equipment while Mia's own lungs refused to work out of solidarity with Romeo's.

Hurry, hurry, hurry! she thought hysterically, biting her tongue to keep from saying the words aloud.

"Damnit!" Doc glanced around him. "I need something long and hollow. Like...a reed or a straw or—"

"How about a pen?" Cami asked. "I have a cheap plastic one in my purse. If you pull out the ink well and the top and bottom, it's basically just a tube."

"Perfect." Doc nodded. "Grab it. Quick."

Cami jumped up to scramble back to the life raft at the same time Doc squirted the iodine over his hands. He splashed a healthy portion over the right side of Romeo's chest.

"Should I take my hands away from the wound?" Mia rasped, trying to keep the fear and horror she felt out of her expression. She needed to look calm and composed because she could feel Romeo watching her, and she wasn't sure if he was using her face as a gauge to see how bad things truly were, or if he was using her face as a focal point to keep himself from panicking because he was suffocating.

Either way, she couldn't give into the hysteria bubbling inside her.

"No," Doc said. "I'm going to be cutting into his second intercostal space, which is below the bullet wound. So just keep applying pressure."

Mia hadn't the first clue what an intercostal space was, and quite frankly she didn't give a hot damn. The only thing she cared about was Romeo's life and following Doc's orders to a T. If he'd told her to stand on her head while crossing her eyes and singing the national anthem, she'd have done that too.

"Here!" Cami thrust the clear plastic barrel of a pen at Doc with one hand. In her other hand, she carried the flare gun case.

As Doc doused the hollow pen barrel, inside and out, with the iodine, he said to Cami, "In case you were thinking we could use the flare gun to cauterize his wound, I hate to tell you—"

"The flare isn't for Romeo," Cami cut him off. "I grabbed it to signal the boat. But then I thought, what if the boat is *their* boat?" She hitched a thumb toward the two dead men.

"What boat?" Doc demanded as he walked his fingers along Romeo's ribs.

Romeo continued to clutch for breath, and Mia held his gaze, telling him with her eyes, *You got this. Just hang on and let Doc do his work.* Of course, silently she was still urging Doc to *hurry, hurry, hurry!*

"*That* boat." Cami pointed.

Mia didn't bother looking over her shoulder. Instead, she continued to hold Romeo's gaze, willing some of her strength to flow into him. But Doc briefly glanced in the direction Cami pointed.

"That's not their boat. That's a Coast Guard Cutter," he told her. "Use the flare." Mia had a moment to feel relief. *We're saved!* But it was all-too-brief, because in the next breath, Doc said to Romeo, "Try not to move. This is going to hurt like hell."

Obviously Doc thought Romeo didn't have time to wait for the Cutter and the medical bay that was on board. And *that* told Mia *exactly* how dire Romeo's situation was.

Once again, she sent a plea out into the abyss. *Please! If you have to take someone, take me!*

Romeo gave a nod to tell Doc he was ready, and Mia gritted her teeth when Doc shoved the scalpel between

Romeo's ribs. Romeo's jaw clenched, his eyes screwed shut, his bare heels beat slightly against the sand. But other than that, he remained perfectly still.

She'd always known he was tough. But she'd had no idea just *how* tough until that very moment.

The man had been shot in the chest, and now Doc had stabbed him, shoved a finger inside the stab wound to hold it open, and was in the process of pushing the empty pen barrel between his ribs. Yet somehow, he kept himself from writhing and howling.

Two things happened simultaneously, then. A loud *hiss* of air rushed through the open end of the plastic tube and Cami pulled the trigger on the flare gun.

Mia barely spared the flare a glance as it arced across the star-spangled sky before' once again pinning her gaze to Romeo's face. His eyes were open again, and he was no longer gasping for breath. Panting a little, sure. But it was obvious Doc's ministrations had worked. He was breathing.

He's breathing! Which meant Mia should probably breathe too.

She raked in a lungful of air, feeling the rush of oxygen go straight to her head. "Spiro?"

"I-I'm okay," he said hoarsely.

She thought, *Yes, you can breathe. But you've still been shot, and you're still bleeding!* The proof continued to ooze between her fingers. With every drop he lost, she felt like a drop of her soul went with it.

She'd survived heartache plenty of times with the loss of her grandmother, and then her brother, and finally her father. But she wasn't sure she could survive Romeo's loss. Or, more precisely, she wasn't sure she'd *want* to survive it.

What would be the point of living in a world without him in it?

"Thanks, Doc," he wheezed.

Doc had lifted a wrist to wipe the sweat from his brow, but Romeo's words seemed all the impetus he needed to return to work. He dug back into the first aid kit at the same time he said, "You can thank me by stopping bleeding."

"I second that," Mia whispered harshly.

"I'll do my best." Romeo tried for a smile but didn't quite manage it. His lips twisted into a grimace of pain and Mia's heart twisted right along with them.

Ripping open a package of gauze pads and a self-adhesive bandage, Doc nodded to Mia. "Go ahead and move your hands," he instructed.

She hesitated briefly because her muscles refused to obey her brain. It was like her body couldn't help but continue to do the one thing it knew to do to try to help keep Romeo alive. Eventually, however, she was able to overcome her temporary paralysis and slowly pulled her hands away from Romeo's chest.

She wasn't sure what she was expecting to see. Blood squirting, maybe? She felt slightly reassured when the bullet wound merely oozed deep red droplets.

As Doc covered the hole with the gauze and went about securing the dressing in place with a bandage, she scooted around to Romeo's opposite side so she could frame his face. Her bloody fingers left handprints on his cheeks, but she didn't think he cared. *She* certainly didn't.

"What can I do?" She searched his agony-soaked eyes, wishing she could trade places with him.

"I could go for one of your kisses right about now," he wheezed. "You know, as a distraction."

She swallowed the sob that threatened in the back of her throat and bent to press a trembling kiss to his lips. And then, because she was already there, she pressed another one to the corner of his eye. And then another one to his brow bone.

She couldn't *stop* kissing him. With her lips on him, she

could feel the warmth of his skin, feel the heat of his breath as he slowly exhaled. *Assure* herself that he was alive.

"Wait!" Carter's voice sounded from somewhere out in the water. She lifted her chin and peered through the trees, spotting him some distance offshore. He was a darker shadow bobbing in the vast darkness of the ocean. "Stop! Don't leave me!"

She realized the roar of engines she heard weren't coming from the Cutter, but were, in fact, coming from a speedboat that'd been anchored about a hundred yards from the sandbar. She could just make out the white jets of water kicked up by its engines as it sped away.

Who is driving the boat? she wondered.

Of course, in the next second, when Romeo lifted a hand to smooth a lock of hair behind her ear, she forgot about everything but him.

"Breathe, *cariña*," he whispered.

"Me? *You* breathe. Just keep on breathing."

And then she kissed him again, because she needed to occupy her mouth. Otherwise, the words sitting on the tip of her tongue might just slide out.

I love you, Spiro. I am so madly in love with you.

CHAPTER 23

9:51 PM...

The floor in the hallway outside the medical bay on the Coast Guard Cutter was rock hard beneath Mia's butt. The ship was built to slice through the seas, and yet it still buoyed up and down. Given Mia's underwear was full of sand and, as a result, her butts cheeks were chafed like she'd taken a pumice stone to them, any slight tilt to the left or to the right when combined with the uncompromising flooring material increased her discomfort tenfold.

She kept shifting to find a more comfortable position. But there seemed to be no such thing.

What I could really use, she thought, *is a trip to the head to shake out my underwear.*

But she refused to budge from her spot on the floor until she knew what was happening with Romeo.

Doc and the onboard Coast Guard doctor had disappeared into the ship's small exam room half an hour earlier. When she'd tried to follow them in, Doc had said, *"Look. It's close quarters in here as it is. I promise to come get you once we're sure he's stable or if he takes a turn for the worse."*

Since she wasn't a medical professional who could help with Romeo's care, and because she wasn't sure it was her *place* to butt in—what was she to Romeo, after all? Not a wife. Not even a girlfriend—she'd been left to stare longingly at him as he was transferred onto an exam table before Doc softly closed the door in her face.

She tried to comfort herself now with how strong Romeo's grip had been when he'd held her hand while being carried off the island and placed into the rigid-hulled inflatable boat the Coast Guard had used to get them from the sandbar to the anchored Cutter. She told herself, *he was breathing, and his bleeding had slowed. Both excellent signs.*

But despite her internal, one-woman pep rally, she wouldn't breathe easy until Doc came out and told her Romeo really *was* out of danger. Until she could see him with her own eyes. Until she could touch him and feel the warmth of his skin, place her head on his chest and hear the steady beat of his heart.

"I know I've only known him a few hours," Cami said, and Mia was reminded the lawyer had joined her in her hallway vigil despite one of the Coast Guard crew members offering Cami a room to rest in. "But in those few hours, I've seen just how strong he is. He's going to pull through this. He's going to be okay."

In the span of a day, Mia had come to greatly admire Camilla D'Angelo. The woman wasn't only smart and funny and equipped with a purse that was packed with just about everything under the sun. She was also kind and generous and was proving to be incredibly supportive.

And she was nearly killed because of me. They all *were.*

Guilt had been a rabid dog, eating at Mia ever since

she realized Carter was behind the explosion on the Otter. It finally broke through her reserve.

"I'm so sorry, Cami." She fought to hold back the tears that clogged her throat. "So unbelievably sorry."

"For what?" Cami's black eyebrows drew together.

"For nearly getting you killed. For nearly getting *all* of you killed. For Doc's broken arm. For Romeo's destroyed plane. For your lost sunglasses." The words tumbled out of her mouth so quickly, she wasn't sure Cami followed her.

Then she remembered she was talking to the High Queen of Rapid Banter. "What are *you* apologizing for? It's not your fault. The blame rests solely on your cousin's shoulders." Cami's expression turned curious. "Why *does* he want you dead anyway?"

Mia sighed heavily. She never would've thought Carter capable of murder. Petty theft? Sure. Some selling of illegal substances? Absolutely. But *murder*?

Returning her gaze to the door directly across from her, she willed it to open for what felt like the millionth time. But like it'd been doing for the last thirty minutes, it remained stubbornly shut. Which meant she didn't have an excuse for not answering Cami's question.

Just to be clear, it wasn't that she didn't *want* to answer the question. It was more like it was all so awful and senseless and...it felt so sleazy that she was *ashamed* to answer the question. Her family, her own *blood* had done this to her. To *them*.

Taking a deep breath, she quickly explained about her mother's addiction and about how that addiction had led to Mia's father leaving Mia most of his money. She touched briefly on how she and her mother had been estranged for most of Mia's life and how Carter had been filling the role of her mother's caregiver—for a price, of course—since Mia's father had died. And she finished with, "So maybe he thought if I was out of the picture for good, Mom would get the money? And then *he* would get a piece of it? It's the only thing I can figure."

"Which explains his crack about you and the moral high ground." Cami's upper lip curled with distaste. "No doubt he's convinced himself that he *deserves* the money since he's been shouldering the burden of your mother's care."

"It's all so embarrassing and...and..." Mia stuttered as she fought to find the right word. She finally landed on, "And *sordid* to think that you and Doc and Romeo got pulled into this. I'm *mortified* that my *family* brought us all here."

"Take it from me." Cami's voice was flat. "That's nothing to be mortified about. We don't get to choose who we're born to."

When Mia glanced over at the lawyer, she saw the woman wore a weary look of comradery. It occurred to her that Cami, maybe better than anyone, understood what it was to be ashamed of the people she was supposed to be the most proud of.

"Whoever said *blood is thicker than water* obviously had no experience with toxic family members," Mia observed quietly.

"It was Matthew who said it. The biblical Matthew," Cami told her. "Or rather, who *wrote* it. But he's been misquoted for centuries."

"Really?" Mia was happy for any momentary distraction from her fear for Romeo and her guilt over what her cousin and his companions had done.

"The scripture actually reads: *The blood of the covenant is thicker than the water of the womb*," Cami explained. "Matthew was talking about oaths, the *blood* oaths people entered into back then, and how those bonds were stronger and more important than the bonds of family. Today, most scholars read the verse and take it to mean that the promises

300

we make to people, the vows we pledge to friends or lovers or whoever, are stronger than the bonds we share with the people we were born to."

"I don't know about you," Mia murmured, once again thinking of everyone living and working on Wayfarer Island, of how they'd been more of a family to her than anyone had been since her grandmother and brother died. "But I like that version much better."

Cami didn't have time to respond before the door to the medical bay opened. *Finally.* Mia was on her feet in a flash, feeling sand shower from the bottoms of her shorts.

"How is he?" Her usually quiet voice was loud enough to echo down the hallway.

She hadn't given Doc time to step over the threshold before asking her question. And when he waited to answer until he did, and until the ship's doctor joined him, she was hard pressed not to throttle him.

Of course, her *true* murderous tendencies came out when he closed the door before she could go up on tiptoe and get a peek at Romeo.

Damnit!

"He'll live," Doc assured her, and her breath of relief was so huge that it deflated her like a popped balloon. The anxious tears she'd managed to keep at bay suddenly flooded her eyes. "He'll need surgery to remove the bullet," Doc added. "But we've got the bleeding stopped for now, and he's breathing fine on his own."

"Breathing fine thanks to your battlefield thoracostomy," the Coast Guard doctor said—he'd told Mia his name before disappearing into the medical bay, but she'd forgotten it because her entire focus had been on Romeo.

"Can I see Romeo?" Mia asked, desperate to get a glimpse. Just one tiny peek to reassure herself that what Doc said was true.

"He's been given some pretty heavy painkillers to get him through the ride to the hospital," Doc told her. "He's out cold."

"I don't care. I'm fine to stand beside him while we—" That's all she managed before an official-looking woman in the navy-blue Coast Guard uniform called her name, "Miss Ennis?"

"Y-yes?" Mia asked hesitantly when the woman stopped in front of her.

"My name is Captain Rachel Mallory." The captain extended her hand, and Mia automatically shook it. "I thought you'd like to know we have your cousin in custody and secured in a room we've set up as a temporary brig."

"Okay." Mia nodded. "Thank you letting me know."

"How did you find us so quickly?" Doc asked the captain. "When our mayday didn't go through, we reckoned we'd be stranded on that little sandbar for days, or at least until the morning."

"Your partner…uh…Mr. Anderson, is it? He must have friends in high places. Because every Coast Guard ship from here to Miami is out hunting for you guys. And we were given strict orders to work through the night. My ship was tasked with patrolling this section of the search grid, and one of my deckhands saw your fire burning."

"Lucky," Doc said.

"Thorough," the captain countered before once again focusing on Mia. "Like I said, we have your cousin in custody, but we don't have his accomplice, whoever was piloting the speedboat. We could've given chase, but I deemed it was more important that we get back to Key West so Mr. Delgado can receive the medical treatment he needs."

"Yes." Mia nodded vehemently. "Thank you. I completely agree and appreciate you taking the time to tell me."

The captain smiled faintly. "I wish this was simply a courtesy visit, but the crewman I have guarding your cousin tells me he's asking to speak with you."

The thought of seeing Carter again after what he'd tried to do to her and the rest of them, after what his cohort had managed to do to Romeo, made her gorge rise.

"Pardon my French, ma'am," Doc said. "But you can tell your crewman to tell that bastard to go fuck himself. He doesn't deserve to breathe the same air as decent folks."

"It's okay," Mia reassured Doc, loving him for his concern. "Honestly, I want to see him. I have questions."

Questions like, *why* had he done what he'd done? She'd told Cami she assumed it was about the money, but she couldn't be sure until she heard it from the horse's mouth. Questions like, *who* had been driving the getaway boat? Because an unthinkable possibility had popped into her head, and it'd been eating at her almost as much as the guilt.

"You might not like the answers," Doc cautioned.

"I likely won't," she agreed. "But I have to know all the same."

She'd spent most of her adult life running away from the truth about her family, about her past, about herself. It was time she asked the hard questions head-on and stopped being afraid of the answers.

"I'll come with you."

"No." She placed a hand on Doc's arm, the one that *wasn't* wrapped in shiny white bandages and secured in a brand-spanking new sling. "He's more likely to talk if it's just me. Besides, I'll feel better knowing you're here looking after Romeo."

Doc didn't attempt to hide his worry for her. Even so, he nodded and promised, "I won't leave his side."

After giving his arm a grateful squeeze, she asked, "Can I see him? Just a quick peek? I won't even go into the room.

I'll just—"

Doc didn't let her finish before opening the door to the exam room. He stepped aside so she had an unencumbered view of the narrow bed.

Romeo was under a sheet. Even though he was pale, he wasn't *deathly* pale, which was a relief. The sheet fluttered with his deep, steady breaths, and she could see the big vein in his neck pulsing rhythmically.

She closed her eyes and thought about what her granny Susan would say at a time like this. *That makes me feel better than a hallelujah.*

Funny, she'd only ever known her grandmother as a Chicagoan. And it wasn't until she'd gotten older that she realized all her grandmother's favorite sayings were a product of her having been born and raised in Nowhere, Alabama.

With her heart feeling tons lighter, Mia turned and nodded to the captain that she was ready. The uniformed officer acted as her escort and Mia was happy for the guidance because she quickly became lost in the ship's rabbit's warren of hallways.

Eventually they turned a corner near the back of the vessel—Mia knew they were near the stern because the engine noise was louder than it'd been in the hallway outside the medical bay—and she saw a crew member standing at attention beside a metal door.

The man too young to buy cigarettes much less be in the Coast Guard. But she could tell he took his job *very* seriously by the way he snapped the captain a fast, stiff salute.

"Seaman Jones will stay at his post outside this door," Captain Mallory said to Mia. "Don't hesitate to yell if you need him."

Mia nodded her thanks. After the captain disappeared around the corner, and after Mia had offered Seaman Jones a wobbly smile, she grabbed the door handle. Then the ship listed sideways.

No, she realized, *that's not the ship. That's me.*

Taking a deep breath, she slowly counted to ten.

Seaman Jones mistook her hesitation for fear and was quick to reassure her, "He's handcuffed to a table that's bolted to the floor. He won't be able to reach you as long as you stay away from him."

She managed another smile of thanks, which felt no less wobbly than the first one. Stepping into the room, she softly closed the door behind her.

Just as Seaman Jones had said, Carter was handcuffed to a table in the center of the narrow space. He sat in a metal folding chair. Its twin had been placed on the opposite side of the table.

Slowly making her way toward the empty seat, she noted how the overhead light cast the entire room in a harsh white glow that made Carter's skin look particularly pale. His freckles stood out in contrast. His dark eyebrows were slanted at a menacing angle. And his injured eye and busted nose had both begun to swell.

Has he always looked this mean? she wondered. *Or do I just think he looks mean because he blew the plane I was flying in out of the sky?*

"Is he alive?" he asked without preamble once she was situated in the chair opposite him. "The guy Robby shot?"

It was beyond strange to be sitting across from someone who'd tried to kill her, especially when that someone shared her blood and had known her since the day she was born.

She was glad her horror didn't manifest itself in her voice when she said, "Why are you asking? It's not like you care. You were planning to kill all of us anyway."

His tone was one of ill-disguised impatience. "I'm asking because *attempted* murder is better than murder in the first. Florida still has the death penalty, you know."

"Is that seriously all you wanted to talk to me about?" She knew her expression was incredulous. "Whether or not Romeo is alive?"

"Drop the innocent act, Mia." His green eyes—so much like her mother's—became nasty slits. "I know exactly who and *what* you are."

"And *what* am I?" she asked, despite the sinking feeling that whatever he said next would likely crush her already bruised and broken spirit into a million tiny pieces.

"A murderer." A vein throbbed in his forehead when he snarled the word. "You might not have been the one to hand Andy the razor blade. But you may as well have been. Your mom told me all about the note."

She flinched at the harsh truth in his words. A truth that'd slowly been killing her for over a decade. Except... "What note?"

Her mind flashed back to the morning after she turned twenty-one, to her parents' condo and her father telling her Andy had finally succeeded in killing himself...

Her mother's knees were pulled up to her chest as she rocked at the end of the sofa. Her mascara ran down her face in black rivers. There was such accusation in her eyes when she stared at Mia.

"I don't understand!" Mia wailed. She thought she'd known heartbreak when Granny Susan died, but nothing had prepared her for the pain of losing her little brother. Losing him and knowing she was ultimately the one to blame. "When I spoke to him on the phone last night, he sounded okay. He said he was desperate to tell me something. But he didn't sound like—I didn't think he—" She shook her head and said again, "I don't understand! Why now?" Through her tears she stared hard at her parents. "Did he leave a note explaining?"

Her mother glanced briefly into the corner where their

newest housekeeper stood wringing her hands. When Jane turned back to Mia, her eyes were as dry as a bone and as cold as ice. "There was no note."

"The note you wrote to Andy the night of your twenty-first birthday." Carter dragged her from the memory. His stare was openly hostile. "The one telling him he'd been a burden on your family for long enough and that he should finish what he'd started more than a dozen times before."

His words were so horrific, she physically recoiled.

Her voice shook when she demanded, "How could you ever think I'd do something like that? I *loved* Andy. He was my responsibility, not just because he was my baby brother, but because it was my fault he suffered so much. I would *never* hurt him." She thought back about what *had* happened the night of her twenty-first birthday, and added quickly, "Not intentionally. Not like you say. And if I could trade places with him right now, I would."

Carter's left eye twitched as he stared at her, looking like he was trying to determine the truth in her words. "Why would your mother lie to me about something like that?"

"I have no idea," she answered honestly.

They both lapsed into silence then, the only sounds in the room were the rhythmic *thrum* of the Cutter's big engines and the subtle *hiss* of the waves rushing by the hull. Then, to her dismay, Carter threw back his head and laughed.

It wasn't a sound of joy or amusement. It was a sound of defeat.

When he dropped his chin, his expression looked ravaged.

"I know why." He choked on a sob as tears filled his eyes. "It was so I'd do her dirty work for her. That bitch did me dirty just like she'd done to every man in her life. I don't know why I thought I'd be any different. All I know is Robby and Kenny are *dead* because of her."

Mia watched as his shoulders shook, watched as snot and blood bubbled from his ruined nose. Despite everything, she felt a pinch of sympathy for him. She knew all too well how easily Jane's beauty and charm could pull the wool over a man's eyes. Heck, she'd grown up watching her father fall victim time and time again.

Of course, whatever sympathy she felt for Carter was eclipsed by the rising foreboding inside her. "She knew you'd try to kill me?" She shoved her hands beneath her legs because she didn't want him to see how badly they were shaking. "For the money?"

Carter either didn't hear her or didn't care to answer her, because he said through his tears, "What happened to them? Do you know?"

"Who?"

"Kenny and Robby," Carter clarified. "Did the Coast Guard gather up their bodies? Or did they leave them to rot on that sandbar?"

"I don't know," she answered truthfully. "I didn't see what happened to them."

Carter looked down at the table. His shoulders shook again as another round of grief rolled through him.

Mia knew what it was to be broken. She recognized the condition in others. And for a long time, she sat in silence and watched her cousin cry. Cry for his friends, no doubt. But also cry for himself and for the predicament he found himself in.

When his sobs were reduced to shaky sighs, she asked the question that'd been gnawing at her ever since she'd seen the white water kicked up by the speedboat as it zoomed away from the sandbar.

"Carter?" He glanced up at her, the whites of his eyes laced with blood vessels. "Was Mom the one piloting the getaway boat?"

His nostrils flared as a new batch of tears streamed down his face. "Who else?"

It was a good thing Mia was sitting down, because the agony caused by Carter's admission would've driven her to her knees otherwise. Scalding hot tears burned the back of her throat, making it impossible to speak. But, really, what was there to say anyway?

What did someone say when they found out their own mother had tried to kill them?

CHAPTER 24

Four days later...

When Mia wafted into Romeo's hospital room like a summer breeze, he forgot about his injury and sat up in bed.

The pain in his chest was manageable—if he didn't move. When he *moved*, it felt like he'd been stabbed by a hot sword that'd been dipped in rubbing alcohol.

He did his best to hide his momentary misery. But Mia had attuned herself to any subtle variation in his expression.

She made a *tsking* sound before setting aside the paper cups she carried. Bustling over to his bed, she thoroughly and efficiently fluffed the pillow behind his back and then situated the one behind his head so he was properly supported.

"What have I told you about pushing it?" she demanded. Her perfect mouth was pursed into a disapproving bow, and he had an overwhelming urge to kiss it.

Why fight the urge? he thought, the pain meds making

him a little giddy.

Since he couldn't jump out of bed and ravage her like he wanted to, he grabbed her hand and pulled her down until her head was level with his. "Kiss me," he demanded, still coming to terms with the idea that he could make that kind of request of her.

She narrowed her eyes. "You're just trying to distract me from scolding you."

"Not true," he assured her. "I'm trying to distract myself from the pain in my chest."

She turned her head and glared at him from the corners of her eyes. "That's playing dirty, and you know it."

He grinned, making sure his dimples winked in the florescent lighting.

When she sighed and pressed a quick and rather unsatisfactory smack on his lips, he grumbled, "A coffee run followed by a perfunctory peck on the mouth? What is this? Have we been married for twenty years or did the magic suddenly disappear while I was out of it?"

"I think I need to talk to your doctors about upping your pain meds," she grumbled, but the corners of her plush, pink lips quivered around a smile. "You are *far* too vigorous for a man who was shot in the chest just four days ago. You're going to hurt yourself."

"Kiss me, woman," he growled, and then watched her catch her bottom lip between her teeth. "A *real* kiss. Something to make my toes curl."

The flirtatious twinkle in her eyes had him cursing his confinement. What he wouldn't *give* to be able to strip her naked and spend a day or two re-exploring all that glorious feminine terrain he'd claimed on that nameless sandbar.

She cut a quick glance toward the door. When she saw there were no medical professionals lurking nearby, she grabbed his face and laid one on him. Truly, the woman kissed him like she had after she'd read the blow job scene in *In Darkness and Dreams*.

The memory of what she'd done to him *after* reading that scene and *after* kissing the holy hell out of him had his blood running hot. He hated to do it, but he had to rip his lips away from hers. "Sweet Mother Mary, we have to stop. They haven't removed my catheter yet."

"You asked for it." Her smile was self-satisfied as she grabbed the paper cups she'd set aside. She handed him one of the cups before popping the top on her coffee and blowing across the steaming liquid.

Fitting his mouth over the hole in his coffee's lid, he took a grateful swig. He'd been craving java ever since he'd awoken from surgery—everyone on Wayfarer Island pretty much lived on the rocket fuel LT brewed. But the hot liquid that hit his tongue was too thick to be jitter juice.

"What is this?" He made a face of disgust.

"Hot chocolate. Your surgeon said studies have shown caffeine may be bad for wound healing. You're off the sauce for a while, my friend."

"Just when I thought this torture chamber couldn't get any worse," he groaned.

"Oh, cry me a river. Plane crash? No problem. Shot in the chest? Piece of cake. But no coffee? *Wah!*"

He fought a grin but ultimately lost the battle. His lips stretched wide as he stared at her.

In the few days he'd been in hospital, Mia had blossomed. She wasn't just talking more, she was smiling more and laughing more.

And definitely busting my balls more, he thought contentedly.

Her transformation was particularly amazing given the personal *hell* she was living through. Her cousin was in jail on charges of attempted murder and felony murder, the latter because his two buddies had died during the commission of a crime he'd planned. And her mother...her own *mother*...had tried to kill her and was still on the lam.

But instead of caving in on herself, she'd been his ray of sunshine.

All the members of Deep Six Salvage had shuffled through his hospital room to pay their respects or to call him a big baby for lounging around in bed when there was work to be done—he would expect no less from his found family. But they had come and gone. It was Mia who'd refused to budge from his side. Who'd made it clear to the nursing staff that *visiting hours* didn't apply to her.

That gave him hope she would say yes to the idea he planned to propose.

And speaking of ideas…

"Wait a minute." He lifted a finger. "Doesn't hot chocolate contain caffeine?"

"The smallest amount." She pursed her lips. "Not nearly as much as coffee, so don't think you've got me over a barrel, mister. No coffee. End of story."

He crossed his arms in mock discontent. *Big mistake!* The move had another flash of momentary torment shooting through him. Mia was at his side again in an instant, making sure his IV line remained uncrimped, smoothing the blanket over his legs, and generally being a diminutive, adorable, strawberry-blonde Florence Nightingale.

"I'm so sorry you're hurting," she apologized for what felt like the thousandth time. "I'm so sorry I got you into this mess."

And for the thousandth time, he assured her no apologies were necessary. "It could've just as easily been someone from my past or one of Cami's father's mob associates who tried to kill us. It's *better* it was your mother and your cousin."

"How do you figure that?" Her button nose wrinkled.

"They're not hardened criminals. They botched the job and we're all still alive thanks to their incompetence."

Her expression remained clouded. "I still can't help feeling responsible."

"Of course you do." He sighed. "Because you're you."

"What's that supposed to mean?" She crossed her arms over her chest, which made her look completely...edible.

But it wasn't his stomach that growled. It was the animal she brought out in him.

As much as Romeo would've loved to give the beast free reign, he had to talk it down with a, *"Down, boy."* But he followed that up with a promise, *"As soon as I'm recovered, I'll let you have your way with her."*

"It means some people deal with trauma and tragedy by getting angry and bitter. Others simply go numb," he told her. "*You* on the other hand? You automatically feel guilty, feel responsible. But *believe* me when I tell you the only ones responsible for what happened are either dead, in jail, or running for their lives." He knew it was a touchy subject, but since he'd brought it up, he figured he might as well finish it out. "Unless...have they found her?"

On the way to pick up the coffees...er...one coffee and one *hot chocolate—the horror!*— Mia had told him she planned to call Detective Dixon to get an update on how the search for her mother was going.

"No." She shook her head. "They found the speedboat in a mangrove stand on Sugarloaf Key. But there are no signs of Mom." She screwed up her mouth. "Which, I'm looking at as a blessing. At least with Dixon busy searching for her, he's given me and Doc and Cami a break. I swear he's taken our statements a dozen times since the sandbar."

"The guy is a bulldog, no doubt." Romeo nodded. He hadn't given his statement to Dixon a *dozen* times. But he'd done it three times and counting. And that low number was probably only due to Dixon taking pity on him because of his weakened state. "He just wants to make sure to dot all his Is and cross all his Ts so some slimy defense lawyer doesn't get your mom or your cousin off on a technicality."

"Slimy defense lawyer?" One corner of Mia's mouth quirked. "You've been hanging around Doc too long." She waved a hand and changed the subject. "But enough about Mom and Carter. Let's talk about some good news, shall we?"

"You mean how P.J. Warren has given us not one but *two* amazing sex scenes in this edition?" His grin was purposefully salacious as he thought back to the evening before when Mia had read to him from *In Darkness and Dreams*. "Do we dare read on and hope for three?"

Before she could answer, he added, "Which reminds me, did you do like I asked and hit up Nurse Andre about when they'll take out my catheter and whether or not it's okay for a guy in my condition to get a blow job?"

Mia's mouth flattened into a straight line. "You know I didn't. And I swear if *you* ask him, I'll never show my face in this hospital again."

"Spoilsport," he complained.

"Pervert," she came back.

"You say that like it's a bad thing."

"Spiro!" She huffed her frustration. "Stop flirting with me. I'm *trying* to give you some amazing news!"

He faked affront even though he *loved* hearing his name on her lips. He never tired of it. "How amazing can it be if it's not about blow jobs?"

She tossed her hands in the air. "You are *such* a guy."

His grin was slow and lazy. "And yet you wouldn't have me any other way."

"Hmm." She narrowed her eyes. "I'm not so sure about that." And then, because she knew he wouldn't give her an opening unless she took it, she plowed ahead with, "LT used the sat phone to call my cell while I was making the coffee run."

"Coffee and *hot chocolate* run," he corrected. "You cruel and callous woman."

"And guess what?" She blazed ahead as if he hadn't spoken. "Alex and Mason found the cipher device! It still exists!" Her mouth screwed itself into a moue. "Well, they didn't actually find it. But they found out who has it. It's in the private collection of some wealthy Portuguese antiquities dealer. They've reached out to the man to try to get in to see it, and they're waiting to hear back." She clapped her hands. "Can you believe it?"

All he could do was shake his head. A hurricane of emotions swirled through him then. On the one hand, he was beyond happy. This was everything he and his partners had been working toward for so long. But on the other hand, being one step closer to finding the treasure meant that Mia was one step closer to leaving.

But does it have to be that way? he asked himself a little desperately.

Himself answered back with, *No way to know until you ask.*

Except it wasn't a question that jumped out of his mouth. It was a statement.

"I love you."

He wasn't sure who was more surprised by his outburst, him or her.

Her. Definitely her, he decided a second later when her face blanched and the pulse beating in her throat went thready.

Fuck. So much for living up to your nickname. Romeo was romantic. That was just...clumsy.

"Breathe, Mia," he instructed quietly and watched her

suck in a ragged breath. He opened his mouth to add, he wasn't sure what, but she beat him to the punch.

"I love you too."

He blinked, not quite believing his ears.

His *heart* believed them. And it couldn't decide whether it wanted to burst with joy or fly out of his mouth on wings of happiness. Maybe both. Fly out of his mouth and then explode like a confetti cannon, leaving little paper hearts raining down around them.

He had to make sure the pain meds weren't making him hallucinate. "You do?" he asked cautiously.

"Of course I do. You're the most amazing man I've ever met. The most amazing *person* I've ever met." She shrugged. "How could I *not* love you?"

With every word out of her mouth, his elation grew. In fact, it was so big by the time she finished speaking that he would swear it took up all the space inside him, swelling in his chest and his throat. Which was why his voice was breathy when he said, "Okay, then. Let's throw out our plans to stay forever single. Let's see if two people who don't have any idea how to make a relationship work can actually go the distance. Let's give this...give *us*...a chance. Let's be each other's ride-or-die. What do you say?"

As far as speeches went, it wasn't great. *Let's be each other's ride-or-die? Really? That was the best I could come up with?*

When she lowered her head, seemingly unable to meet his eyes, his soaring heart sunk like an anchor.

She whispered something he couldn't hear. His voice was louder than he would have liked when he asked, "What? What did you say?"

She lifted her head, and he saw her eyes were filled with tears. "I can't, Spiro. I wish I could. I wish I was a different person." She hiccupped on a sob as a tear spilled over her bottom lid and raced down a cheek he knew from experience was warm and satiny soft. "I wish I was someone who was... worthy of you."

"What are you *talking* about?" His agitation was evident in his voice. "You *are* worthy of me. You're the only person who's ever looked at me and seen *me*. You're everything I've ever wanted but didn't think I could have. Mia—"

"But I'm *not* worthy of you!" she wailed. "I'm not who you think I am!"

His mind flew back to the conversation they'd had about marriage, to his feeling that there was more to the story, more to her reasons for not wanting a happily-ever-after, than just not thinking she'd be any good at it because she'd never been shown the way.

"Then who are you?" he asked quietly. "What aren't you telling me?"

The tip of her nose was pink when she shook her head. "I can't." Her thin shoulders quaked, and he motioned for her to come closer.

"Of course you can. You can tell me anything."

His frustration and his panic increased when she shook her head again and, instead of coming closer, she actually took a step back. A step away from him.

His heart lurched in his chest in a bid to follow her.

"But I *can't*," she insisted. "Because I want you to always look at me the way you're looking at me right now. Please, Spiro..." For the first time, he experienced no joy when he heard his name on her lips. "I want...I want to live in a world where you're out there somewhere thinking of me as someone who's good. Someone who could be worthy of you."

He shook his head helplessly. "What are you talking about? You don't think you're good?"

She didn't answer him. Instead she said, "But it would

kill me if you ever saw me the way I see myself. The way I am."

"Mia, I—"

"Time to check your vitals and do another breathing test," the big, male nurse who'd worked the day shifts boomed as he sauntered into the room. His gaze pinged between Romeo and Mia, and he was quick to add, "Or I could come back in fifteen minutes."

"Yes," Romeo blurted at the same time Mia said, "No. Please, do what you have to do to make sure he gets better."

Andre looked unsure as he watched Mia walk stiffly to the door. Romeo didn't need a mirror to know *he* looked panicked.

Maybe it was arrogant, but he'd never wanted a thing so much only to have it beyond his reach. Not that he could remember wanting anything or anyone as much as he wanted Mia. But the things he *had* truly gone after? He'd always gotten.

Maybe I've lived a charmed life after all.

"Mia, don't go," he said hoarsely, feeling like if she walked out the door, he might never see her again.

She stopped at the threshold, and he felt a moment's relief. It was fleeting, because the next words out of her mouth sounded like goodbye. "Thank you, Spiro. Thank you for loving me. It's the greatest honor of my life. But you deserve someone so much better than me."

And then she was gone.

CHAPTER 25

Five days later...

Doc walked into Romeo's hospital room and smiled when he saw Romeo sitting on the edge of the bed, dressed not in an indecent hospital gown, but in jeans and a T-shirt. Doc was also pleased to note Romeo's color was back and the beard he'd grown while recuperating was gone.

In fact, the bastard looked healthy enough to run a marathon. And the only way anyone would know he'd been shot in the chest a week and a half earlier was the outline of the bandaging showing through the thin cotton of his shirt.

Thank you, germ gods, for sparing my friend.

Doc had been worried about Romeo developing an infection ever since he'd had to open the guy up on the sandbar. Not that Doc wasn't used to battlefield triage. He'd done it plenty of times during his eight years in the Navy. But plenty of those times his patient had gone on to need high doses of antibiotics, because a nonsterile environment was heaven to microscopic bugs that liked nothing better than to wreak havoc on the human body.

Thankfully, Romeo had turned out to be one of the lucky few who'd experienced no complications and whose healthy body had allowed him to heal at an astonishing rate. After he finished slipping into a pair of leather flip-flops, he lifted his head and gave Doc a desperate look. "Please tell me it's time to go."

Doc chewed thoughtfully on his toothpick. "What? You're tired of getting sponge-bathed by pretty nurses already?"

"More like I'm tired of having foreign objects shoved into my body by savages claiming to *do no harm*," Romeo grumbled. "Plus, my nurse's name is Andre. He looks like he could bench-press me. And his bedside manner seems to have gotten stuck in heckle mode. Which means *none* of my sponge bath stories will end up in Penthouse Forum."

Doc bit the inside of his cheek. He'd met Andre.

Clearing his throat, he informed Romeo, "Well, then, sing my praises because I am the bearer of good news. We're just waiting on your discharge paperwork to clear, and then we're out of here. I booked us a flight with Larry at Seaplane Charters. He's ready to go wheels up as soon as you are."

"Aw, man. Larry?" Romeo frowned. "He smells like pot roast and flies barefoot."

Doc shrugged. "Beggars can't be choosers. Larry was the only one available today. As for the barefoot thing, his plane, his rules. Isn't that what you always told me? Oh, and speaking of planes..."

Doc pulled an envelope from his back pocket. "Mia said these insurance forms for your claim on the Otter are all filled out. All you have to do is sign them and mail them."

Romeo's gaze turned razor sharp. "You saw Mia today?"

Doc crossed his arms. For the first four days following

321

Romeo's surgery, Mia hadn't budged from his side. And she'd waved away anyone on the Deep Six crew when they'd offered to take a shift at the hospital. Then, five days ago, she'd called in reinforcements, claiming she had things to do and couldn't be stuck keeping an eye on the nurses and doctors to make sure Romeo received the tender, loving care he deserved.

Doc had called bullshit then; he called bullshit now.

Something happened between them. Something that's made her rabbit and kept Romeo in a piss poor mood for the last five days.

"Yeah," he nodded, eyeing his partner closely. "We're staying at the same hotel. I stopped by her room before coming here. Why?"

"How'd she look?"

"Same as always. Crisp and clean and pretty." He cocked his head, considering his answer. "Maybe a little tired. Like she hasn't gotten much sleep. Funny thing is, she asked me the same thing about you."

A muscle started ticking in Romeo's jaw. "What did you tell her?"

"That you're a terrible patient, pissy and impatient, but that you'll probably be back to fighting form any day now." When Romeo only nodded, Doc decided the time had come to get some answers. "Are you going to tell me what the hell happened?" He sucked on his teeth and turned his head to pin Romeo with a look from the corners of his eyes. "Or, more specifically, what did you do?"

Romeo could pull off affront better than most people. It was the dimples. They created creases in his cheeks when he let his mouth hang open. "Me? Why do you assume *I* did something?"

"Because you're a guy. And life has taught me that when shit goes bad, it's usually our fault." He shrugged. "Blame it on the testosterone. It's a terrible hormone. Makes us act without thinking."

Romeo had stood from the bed when Doc informed him all they were waiting on was for his discharge paperwork to clear. Now he slumped back down on the edge of the mattress, wincing slightly when the move caused him pain.

Pain is good though, Doc thought with satisfaction. *Pain means life.*

"I fell in love with her is what I did," Romeo whispered with a doleful shake of his head.

Doc lifted a brow, hating to find out that he'd been right when he worried Romeo and Mia would end up hurting each other. Not because they were a bad match. Quite the opposite. He thought they were a damn near *perfect* match. But they'd both spent most of their adult lives pushing people away, keeping their relationships surface-level.

And old habits are hard to break.

"I take it from your hang-dog expression that you told her and she..." He stopped and started again. "And she didn't return the sentiment?"

Although, if she didn't, she was lying, he thought. *Because I've seen the way she looks at Romeo. It's the same way Olivia looks at LT. The same way Alex looks at Mason. The same way Lily looked at me.*

Lily...

Nearly nine years had passed since his wife's death, and yet anytime he said her name, even inside the confines of his own mind, he felt a terrible pressure in his chest. As if *he* had been the one to take a 9mm slug to the lung.

"Nope." Romeo shook his head. "That's the thing. She *does* feel the same way."

Doc blinked. "Then I don't understand."

The tick in Romeo's jaw was apparently contagious. Another one popped up beneath his left eye. "That makes two of us. In one breath, she told me she loved me. And then in the next breath, she said she's not worthy of me." His frown deepened. "Or maybe she said she's not worthy of my love? I was pretty high on pain meds, so the details are a little sketchy. And when I tried to ask her what she meant by that, she ghosted out of here so fast I'm surprised she didn't leave skid marks on the hallway tile."

Doc pulled on his ear, not envying Romeo his current predicament. He'd never met a woman who could be convinced to talk when she'd made up her mind to do the exact opposite. And Mia Ennis? She was closed-mouthed on a *good* day.

"What are you going to do?" he asked cautiously and watched Romeo's stare go mutinous.

"For the first five minutes, I cried my heart out, thinking if she didn't want me, then I wouldn't force the issue. That I'd let her become nothing more than a faded memory in my heart. A sepia-toned picture in my head. A lesson in unrealized potential."

"And after those first five minutes?" Doc prodded.

"I decided to say *fuck it* to bowing out gracefully. If she doesn't want to give this thing between us a chance, she's going to have to tell me why. Or I swear on all that's holy, I'll dog her every step to the ends of the earth."

Romeo shoved to his feet, looking forbidding with his legs spread and his hands fisted on his hips. Even though Romeo was generally affable and good-natured, the man had a stubborn streak a country mile wide. Once he set his sights on something... Watch out.

"But don't worry," Romeo added. "I won't confront her at the airport. I'll wait until I can get her alone on Wayfarer."

Doc realized Romeo assumed Mia would be flying home with them. He hated to be the one to break the news, but... "Mia's in Miami."

Romeo blinked as if Doc had suddenly started speaking Swahili. "Miami? What the hell is she doing in Miami?" Then he paled. "She didn't quit on us, did she?"

"No," Doc was quick to reassure him. "The police there found and arrested her mother. Mia and Detective Dixon caught a flight to the mainland about an hour ago. They're going to question Jane Ennis first thing tomorrow morning. Although"—Doc made a face—"I think Mia's questions might be a little different than the detective's." He cursed and shook his head. "Her own mother." He felt ill thinking of it. "Can you believe it?"

Romeo had gone from looking panicked to looking pissed. "You let her go face that monster *alone*?"

The vehemence in Romeo's voice blew Doc back a step. "No. I just said Dixon was with her."

Romeo ran a hand through his hair and started pacing. "That man is as cuddly as a rock. She's going to need comfort. Support. A friendly shoulder to cry on. Sweet Mother Mary, why didn't anyone *tell* me?"

Before Doc could answer, a booming voice said from behind him, "Time for you to go, my dude!"

Startled, Doc spun only to find Romeo's nurse pushing a wheelchair through the doorway. The man had shoulders like a linebacker, but he could move like a freakin' ninja. "We really need to get you a bell," Doc grumbled.

Andre ignored him. "And good riddance, I say," he told Romeo. "Because I am *so* sick of hearing your name in the break room." He donned a falsetto voice. "Ooooh, that Mr. Delgado is so funny. Ooooh, that Mr. Delgado is so sweet. Ooooh, that Mr. Delgado is so dreamy." He harrumphed. "I used to be the cock of the walk. Then *you* showed up, and it's been nothing but blows to my ego ever since."

Romeo's shrug was insouciant. "Hey, man. Don't hate me 'cause you ain't me."

Andre snorted. "See? Was that supposed to be funny?"

Chuckling, Romeo pointed to the wheelchair. "I proved I can shave on my own. I proved I can shower on my own. And much to my dismay, I proved I can shit on my own, so is that thing really necessary?" His expression suddenly sobered. "Wait. Was the whole proving I can shit on my own your way of paying me back for stealing your mojo? If so, mission accomplished."

Andre laughed. "Okay," he admitted. "So maybe you're a *little* funny. And even though I'd have loved to be the inspiration behind taking you down a notch, proving you can poop before being discharged is hospital policy." He patted the wheelchair's seat. "Just like being wheeled to the front door. So come on. The sooner I get you out of here, the sooner I can go back to being the most handsome guy in the place."

Doc knew Romeo would've liked to protest further, but his desire to leave the hospital outweighed his desire to walk out on his own two feet. They were halfway down the hall when Doc remembered he hadn't told Romeo the most important news yet.

"Alex and Mason finally got in to see the owner of the cipher device," he said. "They decoded the symbols and they're catching the next flight out. They should be home around noon tomorrow."

Romeo blinked up at him in surprise. "Did they say what the decoded message said?"

Doc shook his head. "They want us all to be together when they tell us."

For the first time in a long time, possibly since the day his wife had died, Doc felt a frisson of excitement about the future. As if maybe they really *might* find the treasure, and then there might be a chance for him to find a little...maybe not happiness...but contentment.

Closing his eyes, he could see the ranch he'd fallen in love with as a little boy. The rolling hills dotted with cows. The old log house built in the valley. So much open space and clean air and...solitude.

He frowned and blinked open his eyes. That last part had lost a little of its original appeal and he didn't dare delve too deeply into why.

"Fuckin'-A," Romeo breathed. "It's actually going to happen, isn't it? We're going to find it."

Doc chuckled. "I'll see your fuckin'-A and raise you a hot damn."

They lapsed into silence while Nurse Andre pushed Romeo through the automatic glass doors at the front of the hospital. The cab Doc had called to take them to the airport was idling by the curb.

After Romeo stood from the wheelchair, the nurse wasted no time whipping around and heading back inside. He'd just pushed through the automatic doors when he called to Romeo over his shoulder. "N'Sync said it best, *bye, bye, bye.*"

Romeo snorted. "Don't act like you won't miss me!"

In answer, Andre shot him the bird without ever turning back to give him one last look.

Laughing softly, Doc held the taxi's back door wide for Romeo. But instead of sliding inside, Romeo placed a hand on top of the open door. "Let's go to Miami. I want to be there for Mia when she talks to her mother tomorrow."

"That is a bad idea for two very good reasons," Doc told him firmly. "One, from the sound of the way you and Mia left things, you showing up would probably cause her *more* emotional distress instead of less. And two, you really shouldn't be making that trip. I know you think you're superhuman, but you need to go home, rest, and recuperate. Mia will be back on Wayfarer tomorrow."

If looks could kill, Doc would've been six feet under. "I hate it when you're all reasonable and rational," Romeo grumbled.

"I know. Clearheaded practicality is my cross to bear."

"You could come with me. *Cami lives there.*" Romeo offered this up like a prize, and for some reason, thoughts of the sexy lawyer, thoughts of flying to Miami and surprising her, caused Doc's nuts to suck back up into his body.

"And that right there is the *third* reason why it's a terrible idea to go there."

CHAPTER 26

Later that evening...

Cami nodded to the bartender when she saw Mia push through the front door with its painted lager sign. Even though the bar was just around the corner from her office, it was too divey for most of her coworkers. Which meant she didn't have to worry about any of them stumbling in and trying to talk shop.

That suited her just fine since she'd done nothing but work her ass off since hearing that Alexandra Merriweather and Mason McCarthy had pinpointed the cipher device—and she had the crick in her neck, the pain in her lower back, and the eyestrain to prove it. She'd read every brief and ruling and argument she could get her hands on regarding maritime salvage laws in preparation for when Mason and Alex were allowed in to view the device and *hopefully* decode the message left in the captain's journal.

But besides the bar being a reprieve from the probing

questions of curious colleagues, it also reminded her of all the holes in the walls she'd grown up with on Staten Island. And even though she hadn't been a New Yorker in more than six years, she still found herself seeking out places that gave her a taste of home. The sense of the familiar. Especially when she was feeling out of sorts.

And I've been feeling out of sorts ever since coming back from Key West.

For the first couple of days, she'd blamed her general malaise on the fallout from everything she'd experienced. Plane crash, near drowning, seeing two men shot dead... *That's more than enough to make anyone suffer a little anxiety and depression.* But as the days had worn on, she'd began to think her down-in-the-dumps attitude might be due to something else.

Of course, she refused to delve too deeply into what the *something else* might be because she was fairly certain she didn't want to know the answer.

When the marine archeologist looked around the dimly lit space, Cami waved and shouted, "Mia!" over the hard-driving sounds of Greta Van Fleet pounding out of the jukebox.

Mia smiled and began weaving her way through the wobbly tables and rickety chairs toward the bar. Compared to the men and women fresh off work and still wearing their dark suits, Mia looked bright and pretty in a flowing white skirt and a yellow, short-sleeved sweater. Like a delicate bud of jasmine among a field of dark, thorny holly bushes.

A gin and tonic arrived in front of her as soon as she grabbed the barstool beside Cami—Cami remembered Mia saying it was her favorite—and she offered Cami a word of thanks before immediately sticking the cocktail straw between her lips and giving the drink a long pull.

"Careful," Cami cautioned. "I had Eric pour the booze

in that drink in direct proportion to my gratitude to you for calling me up and giving me an excuse to cut out of work early. Proceed with caution."

Mia made a grateful sounding *ahhh* before setting the cocktail down on the polished mahogany bar top and wincing. "Sorry. I should've started with, 'Hey Cami. Good to see you again. Thanks for meeting me for a drink.' But after the day I've had, I was in sore need of a little liquid fortitude."

Cami lifted an eyebrow and took a small sip of her old-fashioned. "Care to elaborate?"

Mia made a face. "Well, for starters, the police found my mom. *Finally.* That's why I'm here. Detective Dixon and I flew in so we'd be on hand as soon as the county jail opens tomorrow. He's champing at the bit to interview her. But he's promised I can go see her first."

Cami glanced behind Mia toward the front doors. "Dixon? You didn't bring him with you, did you?"

If Cami was a bulldog when it came to examining and cross-examining people, then Dixon was a *junkyard* bulldog. Passing the bar exam was less stressful than sitting through his endless quizzing and questioning and re-quizzing and re-questioning.

"No." Mia shook her head. "He's having dinner with friends. He used to work here in Miami. Narcotics, I think."

Cami's shoulders relaxed. Of course, one look at Mia's pinched face had her tensing again out of sheer sympathy. "What are you going to say to your mom?" she asked tentatively, trying and failing to imagine what the woman must be going through.

For all of Cami's bad blood with her father, she couldn't conceive of a world where he would try to kill her. For heaven's sake, he'd turned down the deal the Feds offered him, a deal that would have significantly shortened his prison sentence, just to keep her *safe*.

Mia's upper lip curled. "It's less what I'm going to say to her, and more what I'm going to ask her."

Cami cupped her chin in her hand. "What are you going to ask her?"

She half expected Mia to say something along the lines of *How could you?* Or maybe *Why would you ever consider such a thing?* So she was surprised when Mia said, "I'm going to ask her if my little brother left a note the night he died. She always said he didn't. But I remembered something recently, or it's more like a conversation I had with Carter sparked a memory, and it's made me wonder if she lied."

The lawyer in Cami meant she couldn't help but ask the important question. "What if he *did* leave a note? What will that change?"

Mia popped one narrow shoulder up and down. "Probably nothing. Dead is dead, right?" Her frown deepened. "But I can't shake the feeling that if Mom lied about it..." Mia trailed off just as a light bulb went on in Cami's head.

"Then there was something in the note she didn't want people to see," she finished for Mia.

"Exactly," Mia nodded.

Cami felt sick to her stomach at the next thought. And she knew the only way to get rid of the nausea was to voice the thought aloud. "Are you thinking since she was willing to kill you that she might have had something to do with your kid brother's death?"

Mia's lips thinned into a straight line. "It's crossed my mind. Which is why I want to look her in the eye when I ask her about the note. I'll know if she's hiding something."

Since Cami didn't know *what* to say in response to that, she said nothing at all. Instead, she took another sip of her old-fashioned and let her eyes drift around the bar.

The place was packed with mostly the white-collar sort since the bar was planted squarely in the central business district—although, there were a few groups of guys sitting around in work boots and coveralls. A man in an expensive-looking pinstriped suit smiled when her gaze landed on him. He lifted a finger to his forehead in a little salute.

She quickly continued her perusal of the place. Not wanting to give the guy the idea that she was interested when she wasn't.

Not that his chin dimple and brown eyes and Superman hair weren't nice to look at. But she couldn't help making the comparison between what she felt when she spotted him, a fizzle of indifference, to the electricity that'd sizzled through her system the night she'd looked across the bar and laid eyes on Doc.

Dalton "Doc" Simmons, she thought with a twist of her lips. *How he manages to be the most amazing and most awful man I've ever met, I'll never know.*

"Oh!" Mia interrupted her thoughts. "I have news. Alex and Mason *finally* got in to view the cipher device this morning. They cracked the code and know where the treasure is."

Never in Cami's life had she thought she'd be part of a treasure hunt. But she could say without a shadow of a doubt that it was just as thrilling and exciting as *The Goonies* had made it look.

"Where is it?" Her question came out in hushed tones.

Mia shook her head. "They're not saying. They're going to tell us when we're all together. They caught the red-eye out of Madrid tonight." She swiped her phone screen and checked the time. "Or they *will* catch it tonight. You'd think as much as I travel, I'd be good with the time differences, but they always confuse me. Anyway"—she waved an impatient hand—"I'm booked on the same flights tomorrow as they are. Miami to Key West and Key West to Wayfarer."

Cami dug into her purse and pulled her phone from the

zippered side pocket. "Give me your flight information," she told Mia.

"Why?" Mia blinked.

"Because as Deep Six Salvage's lawyer, I need to know where the treasure is. Whether or not the crew can claim all of it or some of it or none of it once it's salvaged depends on its location."

Mia grimaced. But as an archeologist, she probably knew quite a bit about who got to claim what when it came to antiquities. "It'd be a crying shame if they didn't get to keep at least *some* of the loot after all the time and effort and money they've put into the hunt," she muttered, sliding her phone next to Cami so Cami could read the flight information still shining on the screen.

Five minutes later, Cami had herself booked on the flights. Thumbing off her cell, she blew out a breath and proclaimed, "Technology. You got to love it."

"You know"—Mia scrunched up her face—"I used to think the same thing. But after living on Wayfarer Island, I've come to appreciate life unplugged. I sleep better. I read more. I feel like there's more time in the day. I don't know." She shrugged. "Once I leave, I may start implementing a no electronics policy once a week."

Cami noticed how a look of utter sadness came over Mia's face when she said *once I leave*. And Cami used it as an opening to ask the question she'd been dying to ask ever since Mia sat down.

After all, she didn't have her *own* romantic fairy tale to moon over, so the next best thing was to moon over someone else's.

"How *are* things between you and Romeo?"

Mia's expression became unreadable. "He's fine. Good. He was released from the hospital this afternoon. I'm sure he's back on Wayfarer by now."

Cami cocked her head. "That's great to hear, but it's not what I asked. Did something happen after I left? Last time I saw you, you were floating on cloud nine, and now my mere mention of his name has made the skin around your eyes pinch."

Mia's sigh was so wounded and weary sounding, it nearly broke Cami's heart. "He told me he loves me," she admitted quietly.

"That bastard," Cami declared with mock vehemence. When Mia didn't respond, she dropped the banter and asked, "And the problem with that is you don't love him back?"

"No." Mia fiddled with the diamond stud in her ear. "I love him back. I might love him more than I've ever loved anyone. But he wants a *relationship*. He wants to give this thing between us a shot. He wants to try for forever."

"That *bastard*," Cami swore again. Then, "Oh, wait. *Why* is that a bad thing?"

"Because, even on his worst day, he's ten times the person I am." There was a hitch in Mia's raspy voice. "He deserves so much more than me."

"Nope." Cami lifted her hand. "Let me stop you right there. I know I don't know you well, but I've seen you at your worst. And I can safely say that you are brave and generous and kind. Romeo would be lucky to have you."

"No." Mia shook her head sorrowfully. "There are things about me that you don't know."

Cami felt her eyebrows knit together. "So tell me."

Mia shook her head again and Cami sighed because she recognized an uncooperative witness when she was looking at one. Before she could think of what to say next, the bartender came by with two drinks. "Courtesy of the gentleman at the end of the bar," he said.

The good manners Cami's mother had instilled in her made her give Chin Dimple a smile of thanks. But she was careful to keep it from edging into a smile of invitation. After turning her attention back to the newly arrived drinks, she sighed. "Do you think we should tell him he's fishing with the wrong bait? Why do men always think we want cosmopolitans?"

"Blame it on *Sex and the City*." Mia nursed her gin and tonic as she eyed with distaste the red cocktail sitting on the bar in front of her.

"Annndddd speaking of complicated love lives, those ladies wrote the book." Cami threw a commiserating arm around Mia's shoulders. "Why does it have to be this way, huh? Why does life have to be like a box of chocolates where we never know what we're going to get? Why can't it be like a bowl of cherries? All sweet-tasting and packed full of pleasure?"

"I wish I knew," Mia whispered, and Cami thought for sure she caught Mia blinking away tears.

She felt a world of sympathy for Mia's plight—even though she didn't understand it—but her sympathy was overshadowed by the edginess that rippled up her spine at the thought of seeing Doc again.

She would never admit this to anyone, but she'd *missed* him since returning to Miami. And she couldn't help thinking that's what had kept her in such a funk the last few days.

Because I don't know why *I've missed him*, she thought irritably. *Anytime I'm with him, I feel like I'm dodging emotional machine gun fire...*

CHAPTER 27

The next morning...

Visiting someone in jail was exactly like they showed in the movies.

Mia had been careful to don jeans and a demure top because when she'd asked Detective Dixon about the visiting procedures, he'd told her she wouldn't be admitted if she wore "revealing clothing." She'd given her ID to a very dour-looking woman behind bulletproof glass. And then she'd stood chewing her lips while one uniformed officer waved a metal detector over the entire length of her, and another allowed his very determined canine sidekick to sniff her in places she'd have rather not be sniffed.

But now, *finally*, she and Dixon had their visitors' badges pinned to their shirts as they followed a guard down a long hall made of concrete blocks and painted a rather depressing industrial gray. Mia felt a momentary sense of panic when the guard stopped beside a door painted the same navy blue as all the other doors they'd passed and said, "The inmate is already inside."

How am I supposed to do this? How am I supposed to face my own mother after she tried to kill me?

But then a wave of determination washed over her. And with it, came a sense of calm.

She's the prisoner; I'm not. She's not the one in control; I am.

For the first time in her life, when it came to her mother, Mia held the upper hand.

Dixon's suit was rumpled as if he hadn't bothered to iron it after unpacking it from his bag, and there was a suspicious stain on his tie that she thought was probably maple syrup. But what his disheveled appearance hid was a rapier-sharp mind and a kind heart. The latter was there in his eyes when he turned to her and asked gently, "Are you sure you're up for this?"

She nodded. "I need to look her in the eye one last time and know her for the villain she is."

Dixon grimaced. "I'll be right out here with the guard when you're finished."

"Thank you." She offered him a tentative smile and placed her hand on the door handle. She didn't count to ten; she didn't need to. But she listened when Romeo's voice echoed through her head, telling her to *breathe*.

After raking in a steadying lungful of oxygen, she stepped into the interrogation room. Like the makeshift brig on the Coast Guard Cutter, the space was bare of everything except for a table and two chairs. The only difference was that *this* room boasted a camera tacked into the corner. It's piercing red eye blinked in seeming concentration.

Her first thought when she let her eyes land on her mother, dressed in an orange jumpsuit, her face free of makeup and her hair piled atop her head in a messy bun, was...*she looks old.* Her second thought was...*And not nearly as intimidating as I remember.*

Grabbing the empty seat, she found that for the first time in her life, she didn't have trouble meeting her mother's eyes. In fact, she stared into them, letting the seconds and the silence drag out. Feeling...not much of anything, actually. Which reminded her of something she'd read somewhere.

The opposite of love isn't hate. The opposite of love is indifference.

It felt good to be indifferent. For years she'd held out hope that her mother would love her. And then when she'd finally accepted that would never happen, she'd still held out hope that her mother would get better, get sober, find happiness and contentment.

Now she knew her continuing to hope for anything for her mother was like watering a dead flower and expecting it to grow. Jane Ennis would never be anything other than what she was. And now that Mia had finally accepted that, there was...peace.

Peace enough that she didn't rise to the bait when her mother's upper lip curled. "Well?" Jane demanded. "Is that all you wanted from this visit? To sit across from me with that smug, superior expression on your face?" Her mother had always had the unique ability to make her tone sound hot and cold at the same time.

"No," Mia replied calmly. "I came to ask you a question."

Jane darted a quick glance at the camera in the corner. "You must mistake me for an idiot if you think I'll say anything to incriminate myself."

"I don't give a flying fuck about anything that's happened the last couple of weeks," Mia said, and her mother's chin jerked back. Mia had never cursed in front of her parents, always thinking it was disrespectful. But Jane no longer deserved her respect.

In fact, she thought, *she never did.*

"I want to talk about what happened ten years ago," she added evenly.

Jane tried to purse her lips, but the collagen she'd had injected into them ruined the affect. "I don't know what there is to say about that that hasn't already been said."

"Tell me about the letter."

Something skittered across her mother's eyes then. Something that reminded Mia of a bloodsucking insect that only came out at night. "I don't know what you're talking about.""Yes, you do," she countered. "You told Carter that I wrote a letter to Andy, encouraging him to end his life. But we both know that's not true. Although, talking to Carter made me remember something. A look that passed between you and your housekeeper. What was her name?" Mia snapped her fingers. "Oh, right. Luda Petrov."

"I don't know what you're talking about," Jane insisted again, but Mia detected the slightest quiver in her mother's voice. "There was no look and there was no letter."

Mia sat back in the chair, crossing her arms. "I googled Luda last night. She's still in the Chicago area. Still cleaning houses. I bet if I called her up, she'd tell me what I want to know. And I bet she'd be only too happy to—"

"*Fine*," Jane spat. "Yes, there was a letter. But I burned it because it was nothing but the ravings of a mad man and I was *embarrassed* for our family, for *Andy*."

Hearing her mother talk about her brother so callously replaced all the indifference Mia felt with the urge to reach into her mother's mouth and rip her spine out through her lying throat. "Andy was mentally ill," she said through gritted teeth. "He wasn't crazy. You'd know that if you'd ever bothered to attend *any* of the family therapy sessions."

"Pfft." Jane tried to wave a hand, only to have the gesture cut short because she was handcuffed.

Maybe it was petty and vindictive, but Mia felt a sense of satisfaction when she heard the metal cuffs rattle against the steel bar bolted to the table.

"No *sane* person kills themselves," her mother insisted.

Mia was immune to Jane's attempts to obfuscate. "Who was the letter to? What did it say?"

"It was to you," Jane admitted easily, and Mia experienced a pang. Of *course* Andy had written his final words to her. She'd always been his shoulder to cry on, the one to lend an ear or give advice, the one who'd always loved him unconditionally. "But I don't remember what it said," Jane was quick to add.

"Sure you do," Mia argued. "You just said it was filled with the ravings of a—"

"The *details*, Mia," Jane snarled. "I don't remember the *details*."

Mia dragged a slow breath in through her nose. "Do you supposed Luda would remember the details?"

Hatred.

That's what Mia saw in her mother's eyes then.

Pure, unadulterated hatred.

Through a jaw that looked like it wanted to snap shut around each word, her mother gritted, "You *know* what it said. You've alluded to that fact twice now."

Confusion had Mia's brow furrowing. "What are you talking about?"

"Don't play dumb and coy with me, Daughter," Jane hissed. "You forget I'm your mother. I carried you in my belly for nine months. I know you better than anyone."

Mia could've said Jane didn't know her all. She could've said Jane was a "mother" in title only. Instead she demanded, "When have I alluded to knowing what was in Andy's letter?"

"At Gene and Georgetti's you said you weren't the only

341

one responsible for what happened to Andy. You said *I* had a role in things. And then you texted Carter that, given our history, you needed to keep up the boundaries you set with me."

A cold foreboding scratched up Mia's spine until goose bumps peppered her flesh. "What did Andy's letter say, Mother?" she demanded through gritted teeth.

Jane narrowed her eyes. It was obvious she was trying to determine if Mia was playing some sort of mind game, or if Mia really *didn't* know what the hell Jane was talking about.

Jane waved a hand and said flippantly, "He said he was sorry for ending his life on your birthday, but that he really believed the best gift he could give you was to relieve you of the burden he'd been to you his whole life."

Hot, sharp tears stabbed at the backs of Mia's eyes.

Poor, sweet Andy. She felt his loss as keenly as if it'd happened ten minutes earlier instead of ten years earlier. *How could you have ever believed yourself anything other than a blessing? You were my baby brother. I loved every last piece of you.*

"He said he'd been working with a new psychiatrist who'd helped him gain some clarity through..." Jane frowned as if she was trying to remember. Then her face cleared. "I think he used the term *regression*. Anyway, this supposed clarity made him realize he'd failed to end his life so many times before because, even though he didn't want to go on living, he didn't truly feel like he could leave this world until he'd convinced you that you weren't responsible for what happened to him."

Mia knew her mother was telling the truth because Andy had said almost those exact words to her dozens of times. "What else?" she demanded.

"Nothing else." Jane blinked innocently. "That's all I

can remember."

"Bullshit," Mia hissed and watched her mother's chin jerk back. "I can tell you're lying. Now either you finish telling me what was in Andy's letter, or I'll call up Luda. You know if I get the information from her, you'll have lost the opportunity to put your particular spin on it."

Jane's pupils dilated. It was obvious she was hiding something. But like any true narcissist, she latched onto the bait of telling the tale in her own words. "He rambled on about how his newest therapist had helped him see the truth. How she'd helped him remember the night you both ended up in the hospital." Her mother hesitated then, and Mia thought for sure she saw a spark of fear flash in Jane's eyes.

"And?" she demanded.

"And he said it wasn't you who gave him the pills."

Mia frowned. "Then who was it?"

But as soon as the question tumbled from her mouth, a disjointed memory flickered through her head like one of those old reel-to-reel movies on the fritz.

Her mother putting Andy in bed beside Mia, still wearing the green cocktail dress she'd worn to the fun-raiser.

Her mother coaxing her to drink a glass of water that tasted bitter and felt gritty on her tongue.

Her mother whispering, "Shhh. Go back to sleep."

Mia jerked out of the muddled recollection with a start. Her voice was barely a whisper when she said, "*You.*" Her hand jumped to her chest as if it thought to keep her pounding heart from beating through her rib cage. "*You* tried to kill us. I *remember*."

After all these years, the mist cleared and she finally, *finally* remembered.

Jane could've won an Oscar for her performance then. She widened her eyes in shock, gasped sharply, and said, "I did *no* such thing!"

343

But Mia knew she had. "*Why?*" she demanded, staring at her mother's hair and wondering how it was that Jane managed to cover her horns. Breathing through her mouth because she thought for sure the smell of sulfur must be wafting through the air.

Her own mother hadn't just tried to kill her once, she'd tried to kill her *twice*! The second time obviously because she'd thought Mia had remembered about the *first* time. Just like poor Andy.

Mia had always known Jane was selfish and cruel, but it was so much more than that. The woman who'd birthed her was actually *evil*.

"I'm admitting nothing." Jane darted another quick glance toward the blinking camera light.

"Did Dad suspect?" Mia asked hoarsely. "Is that why he sent us to live with Granny Susan?"

Jane sniffed and licked her lips, which made the smile she sent Mia look greasy. "He sent you to live with your grandmother because I was always the most important thing to him. He knew I didn't care for motherhood."

Mia could only shake her head in wonder and horror. She didn't believe her mother for an instant. Her father may not have *known* that Jane had been the one behind the overdose, but Mia felt sure he'd had his suspicions.

Jane being Jane, however, had twisted the narrative inside her own head to make it seem like he'd done it out of his overwhelming adoration of her. It was truly astounding.

And truly demoralizing. Because it meant justice would never be served. Jane would never be able to see herself for the villain she was, for the *monster* she was.

But it's enough that she'll spend the rest of her life rotting in jail, Mia decided. *Because at least there she won't be able to ruin anyone's life but her own.*

"Goodbye, Mother." She pushed up from the chair.

She had her hand on the door handle when Jane called to her back, "That's it? You don't want to—"

"Yes." Mia cut her off as she gave her mother one final glance. "That's it."

As she stepped into the hall, she realized that truly *was* it. She hadn't just closed the door on her mother, she'd closed the door on her past life. On all the regret and shame that'd plagued her since she was seven years, on all the guilt and self-contempt that'd haunted her ever since her twenty-first birthday.

Squaring her shoulders, she lifted her chin and thought... *I didn't overdose my baby brother. I wasn't the one to blame for his illness. I'm not responsible for what happened the night I turned twenty-one.*

I'm not the murderer.

I'm not the monster.

I never have been.

It's always been Mom.

People talked about feeling like a weight had been lifted. That didn't do justice to the sensation of being relieved of a lifetime of self-loathing. Mia wouldn't have been surprised to find herself floating up toward the ceiling like Charlie and Grandpa after gulping down the fizzy lifting drink in *Charlie and the Chocolate Factory.*

But, miraculously, her feet stayed on the ground. Which was good. Because that allowed her to turn and smile at Dixon. It felt astonishingly good to tell him, "She's all yours."

As she watched the police officer enter the room she'd just exited, Cami's words from the night before came back to her.

"What will it change?"

Well, it turned out that finding out what Andy had wanted to tell her, what he'd written to her the last night of his life, changed...*everything.*

CHAPTER 28

Noon...

Romeo stood on Wayfarer Island's crescent moon-shaped beach with the rest of the Deep Six crew. As always, the water was crystalline. The breeze was cool. And the sun was warm.

Paradise.

Except he was too keyed up to appreciate its decadence.

Any minute now Mia will land, and I still haven't figured out what I'm going to say to her. How I'm going to say it.

Which was a problem since he got the distinct impression their conversation was going to be the most important one of his life.

"Take a deep breath, brother." Doc clapped a hand on his shoulder. "And then go drag Meat out of the surf before he eats any more waterweeds."

Romeo frowned over at his partner. "It's your turn."

"Rock, paper, scissors you for it."

But before they could see which one of them had the dubious job of coaxing Mason's fat English bulldog out of the water, Olivia squealed, "Meat! Damnit! Stay out of the waterweeds! You're just going to yack them up later!"

"Oh, good." The toothpick in Doc's mouth tilted up when he smiled. "Problem solved."

Romeo watched as LT's long-legged wife ran to the edge of the water, where Meatloaf—aka *Meat*—snuffled through the surf, looking for aquatic delicacies. Li'l Bastard, the Welsummer rooster who'd been a stowaway from a supply run to Key West, pecked at the sand next to Meat, going after the tiny crabs that dared to poke their telescoping eyes out to see what all the hubbub was about.

Everyone else on the beach chuckled when Meat gave Olivia his best juke move, starting one way before quickly changing directions, causing Olivia to curse his name and run after him. But Romeo didn't join in their humor. He couldn't.

He was too anxious to laugh. And his anxiety only notched up when the noise of a plane engine suddenly sounded above the *hiss* and *shush* of the surf.

Shielding his eyes from the sun, he watched as Larry lined up the nose of his amphibious aircraft perpendicular to the beach. Romeo's jaw clenched. Not because Larry was coming into the lagoon too high and too hot. Or not *just* because of that. But because it was time.

Time to talk to Mia. And I still don't have a clue what to say.

Despite the bad angle, Larry landed the aircraft without incident and motored the plane onto the beach. The *roar* of the engine was replaced by the soft *clatter* of the wind through the palm trees when he cut the power.

Larry hopped out of the pilot-side door, barefoot as usual and dressed in his standard-issue uniform of stained tank top and cutoff jean shorts. He waved to the gathered group, and then quickly opened the door to the cabin. When a pair of smooth legs appeared on the plane's top step, Romeo did as Doc suggested and took a deep breath.

Of course, it rattled out of him on a windy sigh when the smooth legs turned out to be connected to their lawyer and not Mia.

Beside him, Doc cursed. "What the hell is she doing here? I just got over my last case of hives."

"You sure those weren't goose bumps?" Romeo returned Doc's gesture by clapping a hand on the guy's shoulder. Doc knocked his hand away and Romeo faked a wince. "Ow. Careful. Injured man here, remember?"

"Please," Doc scoffed. "You and I both know the only pain you're in right now is directly in my ass."

Even though Romeo wouldn't have thought himself capable of a chuckle two minutes ago, that was enough to have one rumbling out of him. Of course, he sobered right up when another pair of bare legs appeared on the plane's top step. But the new gams didn't belong to Mia either.

Alex exited the plane ahead of Mason, and Romeo noted how both of them had the wired, wild-eyed look of people who'd just spent the better part of a day and a night making transfers and eating shitty food on airplanes and in airports.

Saved the best for last, he couldn't help thinking, his heart pounding when he spotted Mia's sandals on the top step. Of course, once she emerged from the airplane, once he got his first look at her pretty face and her shiny hair and the way her blouse clung to breasts he knew were warm and responsive and perfect, his pounding heart became the entire drum section of a high school marching band.

Will she look at me with longing and sadness? he wondered a little desperately. *Will there be anger in her eyes because she thinks I broke my promise and ruined our friendship by asking for more? Will she avoid my gaze altogether?*

Dumbfounded. That's what he was a second later, because when she started making her way across the beach, there wasn't sadness or anger in her amber eyes. She didn't avoid his gaze either. Quite the opposite, she looked straight at him and...*smiled.*

Not her closed-mouth grin. But her mega-watter. The smile that melted his brains so he stood blinking at her in stupefaction.

"I'm just gonna leave the luggage here for y'all!" Larry called, tossing out overnight bags and suitcases from the cargo hold.

"Thanks for the ride, Larry!" Alex waved.

And then, suddenly, the new arrivals were there, mingling with the gathered group. Cami nodded and said, "Good to see you again" to those she'd met in Key West after their rescue, and she shook the hands of everyone she was meeting for the first time. Alex hugged everyone, and Mason did as usual and simply stood there, mute, his only indication that he'd been gone for two weeks the chin-lift he gave to the crew.

As for Mia? She shuffled through the sand until she was standing right beside Romeo. Then, stupefying him further, she grabbed his hand and laced her fingers through his.

What the fuck is happening? He continued to blink at her. *Is this her way of saying she still wants to be friends? Or is it her way of telling me there will always be a place for me in her heart even if I'm not in her life? That our one night together will have to last me a lifetime? Or...has she changed her mind about giving us a chance?*

That last idea had the marching band that was his heart screeching to a cacophonous halt. He opened his mouth. But yeah. He still didn't have the first clue what to say, and so nothing but silence slipped through his lips.

Then, he lost his chance to say anything because Larry cranked over his plane's engine, and it was too noisy to talk for the sixty seconds it took Larry to reverse the aircraft into the lagoon and then throttle up to take off.

As soon as the plane was far enough away to make conversation possible, LT thwarted Romeo further by demanding of Mason and Alex, "Okay. We're all here and the suspense has been killin' us. Is it in the water? Please tell us it's in the water."

"It's in the water." Alex shoved her glasses higher on the bridge of her freckled nose. Then she made a face and added, "Well, sort of."

LT pulled his aviator sunglasses down the bridge of his nose, his eyes pinned on Alex. "Elaborate please."

After fishing a slip of paper out of her shorts, Alex carefully unfolded it and then cleared her throat to read aloud. "At the tip of the island's barrier reef, beneath the rock and the coral, there you will find the *Santa Cristina's* bounty."

Mia squeezed Romeo's hand and, not for the first time, he thought about how perfectly her palm seemed to fit inside his own. But when he glanced down at her, he found she'd stopped smiling up at him and was instead looking out to the tip of the reef, where the waves were allowed to roll toward the island unencumbered.

"It's been under our noses the entire time," Doc whispered, his toothpick hanging drunkenly from his slack mouth as he shook his head in disbelief.

"We're burnin' daylight," LT declared. "Let's get suited up and get ourselves out to Wayfarer II." He hitched his stubbled chin toward the salvage ship anchored beyond the reef. "At the very least, we can start sectionin' off the search area and puttin' the underwater metal detectors to good use."

"I hate to be the bearer of bad news, but you might want to hold off on that," Cami said.

As one, the group turned to stare at the lawyer. Doc was the one to demand, "What? *Why?*"

Cami grimaced. "Because I'm not sure if the reef counts as land or sea. And until I can find out the answer to that, it's best if you don't touch *anything*."

"Are you telling us two inches of exposed rock and coral might be all that's standing between us being able to claim the treasures we've been after for months and *not* being able to claim them?" Doc demanded.

"I know it's shitty." There was frustration in Cami's voice. "I *know* it is. But I didn't write the laws. I just interpret them and argue them for my clients. I'm asking you all to give me time. Even if the reef *is* considered land, in which case the federal government will claim the rights to what's beneath it, maybe there's a loophole. But, like I said, I need time to do some digging."

LT chuckled and lifted his gaze heavenward. "I swear, fate really does laugh at our endeavors."

"Don't lose faith yet," Olivia encouraged, wrapping an arm around his waist.

"Your profession sucks ass." Doc scowled at Cami.

"So you remind me every chance you get," Cami countered. "But has anyone ever stopped and told you that a good place to shove your opinions is straight up your own ass? Or, even better, how about you give that whole *if you can't say anything nice, don't say anything at all* thing a shot? I bet your life would be rosier and it'd probably wipe the dour expression off your face."

"Oh!" Doc feigned astonishment. "I didn't realize you were an expert on my life. Please continue while I take notes. What?" He pointed at Cami's face. "What's that look for? Why are you smiling?"

"I'm plotting your death."

Everyone glanced back and forth between Doc and

Cami like they were watching a tennis match. Everyone except Romeo.

He only had eyes for Mia.

And he didn't take them off her face when he called, "Hey, LT? I take it we have the rest of the day off?"

"Sounds like," he heard LT mutter unhappily.

Mia stopped watching the Doc and Cami show and lifted her lioness eyes to meet his gaze. She proved herself to be the *true* mind reader then, because the words hinged on *his* tongue came out of *her* pretty mouth.

"We need to talk."

CHAPTER 29

12:44 PM...

Is the sun brighter? The sky bluer? The wind sweeter?

Mia sat on the end of the long pier that stretched into the blue lagoon on Wayfarer Island and thought for sure the answer to all the above was...*yes*. That, or she'd lived under a psychological storm cloud for so long she'd forgotten what it was to truly appreciate the glory of a perfect day.

To make things even better? Spiro "Romeo" Delgado sat beside her, his hand fitting around hers like a glove. And all the reasons she'd had for holding herself back from him were gone.

Flushed down the toilet.

Thrown out the window.

Turned to dust by what she'd learned in that interrogation room in Miami.

She needed to tell him about it. Tell him *all* about it. Trouble was, there was so much of it—a lifetime's worth—

that she was having trouble figuring out where to start.

She decided to begin with something easy. "How are you feeling?" She studied his profile as he watched a pod of dolphins plowing through the surf near the reef. He *looked* good. *Better* than good in green board shorts and a white T-shirt that emphasized his tan and assured her his hospital pallor was long gone. "How's the pain?"

He narrowed his eyes as he scanned her face. "Good. Except for when I take a deep breath. Then it feels like someone jabbed me with a hot poker. Which sucks because part of my PT is to take deep breaths." He scratched his goatee and chuckled. "But as Doc likes to point out way too often, and with way too much sadistic glee, *no pain, no gain.*"

This was what had drawn her to him from the beginning. This easiness. This comfort. This sense of safety.

He'd never pushed her or made demands of her. He was always perfectly patient, waiting for her to be the one to poke her head out of her hard, protective shell.

And because she felt comfortable and safe around him, she didn't think it'd hurt anything if she teased him. Just a little. Just to take the edge off her nervousness. "Deep breaths hurt, huh? I guess that means blow jobs are out of the question for a while."

He smiled. She'd known he would smile, and still it pierced her heart like a harpoon fired from a speargun. He was such a beautiful man. Inside and out. When he smiled, both facets of his beauty shined through.

And he's mine, she thought with no small amount of wonder. Then she was hit with a terrible notion. *Unless he no longer wants me. Unless I blew my chance.*

Of course, his next words put her at ease. "Oh, don't say that. I'm *more* than happy to push past the pain."

She giggled and shook her head. "Men. Sometimes I think the world could be ending and you wouldn't notice so long as someone was polishing your knob."

"But that's the whole point," he countered. "The *perfect* time to have my knob polished is when the world is ending. I mean, what a way to go, right?"

They both laughed then. But he sobered first, and his melting-chocolate eyes caught and held hers. "So..." he said tentatively. "You want to explain what this"—he lifted their joined hands—"is about? After you ran out of my hospital room, I thought you might not get within ten feet of me ever again."

He didn't try to hide the hurt and confusion in his face when he talked about their last conversation. When she'd run out on him like a...*yellow-bellied coward*, in the parlance of Granny Susan.

Knowing she'd caused him even a *moment* of pain had a lump forming in her throat. "It's hard to stay away from someone who is as much a part of you as the blood in your veins and the air in your lungs," she admitted quietly. "Plus, I don't *want* to stay away."

The wind ran loving fingers through his hair, tussling it around his face. It was the only thing that moved on him because he'd gone statue still, as if he thought any movement might cause her to turn tail and run.

And why wouldn't he think that? You've given him every reason to believe you're exactly that kind of flight risk.

"What's changed?" he asked softly.

"*Everything.* And I'm so sorry!" she blurted, the lump in her throat making room for her heart to sit beside it. "I'm so sorry for leaving you alone in the hospital. For anything I said to hurt you. I wish I could take it all back."

She swallowed the tears that burned the back of her nose. "My only excuse is that I was scared. Scared of what I felt for you. Scared of what you felt for me. But mostly I was scared of who I was. Scared that if I *told* you who I was it'd change the way you felt about me."

"And you're...not scared now?" His words came slowly, as if he picked them carefully.

"No." She shook her head. "Because I'm *not* who I thought I was." She frowned. "Or maybe it's more correct to say I'm not *what* I thought I was. You remember when you asked me why I've never considered marriage?"

"You told me it was because you didn't have the first clue how to make a relationship work long-term."

"That's only a small part of the truth," she admitted. "The *bigger* part is that even though I don't have the first clue how to make a relationship work long-term, I felt...I still *feel* certain that one sure way to make it *not* work is to begin it with a lie. Even a lie by omission. And I couldn't stomach the thought of revealing myself to anyone. Especially not to someone like you. Someone so open and outgoing and virtuous and good and...all the things I'm not. Or..." She shook her head. "All the things I *thought* I wasn't."

"Mia." He turned toward her and grabbed both her hands. His callused fingertips rubbed against her palms, and she shivered slightly at the memory of them rubbing against *other* parts of her. "I'm sorry. I'm really trying to follow along here. But I'm having trouble—"

"I thought I was a *murderer*," she exclaimed. "I thought I'd killed my baby brother."

His chin jerked back. "Didn't you tell me your brother killed *himself?*"

She nodded, trying to arrange her thoughts into some sort of coherent order so that she could lay it all out comprehensibly for him. After a couple of seconds, she gave up on the endeavor and simply said, "I'm going to ramble a bit here." When she saw him blink, she amended her statement. "Or I'm going to ramble *more*. But just stick with me, okay? I swear I'll do my best to try to make everything clear by the time I get to the end."

He made a rolling motion with his hand.

She nodded gratefully. And then she told him. *Everything.*

About always feeling responsible for Andy's illness, because even though she'd only been seven years old at the time of the overdose, and even though her mother had *said* the pills were candy, she'd known they weren't. She told him how that guilt had led to her developing a strong sense of responsibility toward her brother, which had, in turn, led her to taking on the role of Andy's guardian—maybe not *legally*, but literally and unmistakably. She told him about how anything Andy had ever asked for, she'd gotten for him. About how whatever Andy had ever asked her to do, she'd done.

"I would drop everything for him," she said. "It didn't matter what I was doing or where I was, if Andy called, I was there." She closed her eyes, because she still had trouble admitting this next part. "Except for the night of my twenty-first birthday."

Romeo was a man of his word. He didn't coax her to continue when she lapsed into silence. Instead, he simply sat beside her. Strong. Patient. *Good.*

Everything she'd never dared to dream she could have.

"He called me that evening," she said quietly, keeping her eyes shut. "Said he wanted me to come over to Mom and Dad's. Said he had exciting news to share. He sounded a little manic, but not nearly as bad as he had at other times, so I didn't worry. I told him I couldn't come over because friends from college were taking me out on the town for some twenty-first birthday fun. I promised him I'd come over the next day and we could talk then."

She opened her eyes and watched the pod of dolphins frolic, their humped backs curling through the air as they

357

jumped the waves that grew taller as they rolled toward the reef. "But I never saw him again." Despite her best efforts, the words came out little more than a breath of wind. "He took his life that night."

Will it ever get easier to say that aloud?

An anvil attached itself to her heart, dragging the organ down from her throat and causing it to *thud* into the bottom of her stomach.

"I always thought...*if only.* If only I'd come when he called, if only I'd done my duty by him, if only I'd been a little less selfish that night, I could've stopped him." She could tell Romeo had something to say about that because he opened his mouth, but she lifted a hand and quickly continued. "And all that guilt and self-loathing, all that shame and self-recrimination made me a coward. It made me run. Run away from Chicago because the city reminded me of my brother. Run away from friendships because I didn't feel I deserved anyone's understanding or companionship. Run from job to job because I didn't feel I deserved a home. Run away from relationships because I didn't feel I deserved love."

"Mia—" he said, and she blurted the rest of it before he could sidetrack her.

"But I'm *tired* of running. I'm asking for your friendship and understanding. I'm asking for your love. I'm asking you to be my home, Spiro."

She bit her lip, waiting for him to answer. When he didn't, she realized he was waiting for her to give him the go ahead. "I'm done. Please say something," she said shakily.

"Yes," he replied simply. "To all of that."

She hadn't realized she'd been worried about his answer until she heard it. The wave of relief that washed over her was tsunami-level. She choked on a loud, watery-sounding sob.

Her arms were around his neck in the next instant. When

he grunted, she remembered he was still recovering from a *gunshot wound to the chest! Dear god!* And she quickly pulled back. "I'm so sorry." She wiped the tears from her cheeks, wincing as her eyes pinged down to the outline of the bandage visible beneath his T-shirt.

"Never apologize for hugging me, woman." His voice was gruff, as if he was battling to keep his emotions in check. "I just want to make sure we're on the same page. You love me and you want to try for forever. Is that right?" She could see the hesitation in his eyes, as if he was afraid to hope too much.

Another watery sob escaped her. She hated that she'd ever given him a reason to doubt her. And she vowed then and there to never do anything to ever make him doubt her again. "Yes. That's what I'm saying."

His eyes grew overly bright until one lone tear slipped from the corner of his eye and traveled down his tan cheek. "Thank *god.*"

This time *he* was the one to throw his arms around *her*. And for long moments, they stayed that way. Not kissing. Not caressing. Just hugging.

Hugging like friends.

Hugging like lovers.

Hugging like two people who hadn't gotten enough hugs in life.

When he finally pulled back, he cleared his throat and wiped the wetness from his face. "So *what* changed?" he asked again. "Why can you tell me all of this now, but you couldn't tell me that night in the hospital?"

She blinked and realized she'd somehow skipped over the part where she revealed she *wasn't* the one responsible for the overdose or Andy's mental illness or his suicide. She'd left out the most important piece and yet he still wanted her. Still *loved* her.

Things got *really* soggy then. *She* got really soggy.

We're talking ugly crying. Red face. Full-body sobs. Probably a little snot.

She wasn't sure how she got there, but suddenly she was in his lap. He rocked her gently and smoothed her hair, murmuring soft words in Spanish as she cried her eyes and her heart out.

Even though she wasn't the monster she'd always thought she was, she still wasn't sure she deserved this man. This man who was so generous and forgiving. This man who was so kind and compassionate.

I may not deserve him, she thought, *but I'm going to try the rest of my life,* work *the rest of my life, to be worthy of him.*

It took her a long time to run dry. But eventually—*thankfully*—she did. And even though she knew her face was a mess, she pushed back so she could see his eyes when she told him, "Thank you. Thank you for loving me even though I haven't even told you that I'm *not* the one responsible for what happened."

He frowned. "I know you're not. I mean, I don't *care* if you say you knew your mother's pills weren't candy. You were seven, and she *told* you they were. And since you aren't to blame for the overdose, how could you possibly be blamed for your brother's illness? And since you aren't to blame for his illness, how could you possibly be blamed for his death?"

He grabbed her face, his gaze holding on to hers with magnetic force. "You know when I told you that you deal with trauma by feeling responsible for it?" She nodded. "Well, I'd like to double down on that."

"You're right." She sniffed, wiping a hand under her nose. "And maybe I'll be able to work on that now that I know it was my mother. It was *all* my mother."

When a line appeared between his eyebrows, she

told him about her reclaimed memories of the night of the fundraiser. About her mother throwing away Andy's suicide letter. About everything. And that time, she managed not to leave anything out.

"Andy lived for me long after he'd stopped wanting to live," she whispered. "And I dedicated my life to him. But all his anguish and suffering can be laid at my mother's feet. I'm not the monster. *She* is."

When she was done, he simply stared at her. Then he pulled her in for another hug and whispered in her ear. "My poor, sweet *cariña*. I am so sorry for everything you've suffered."

She gave him a trembling smile. But what it lacked in stability, it made up for in pure, unfettered joy. "Don't feel sorry for me. I'm happier than I've ever been. *Freer* than I've ever been. Because now I know I can have you."

His smile was soft, deepening his dimples just the tiniest bit. "I love you, Mia Ennis." She knew she would never tire of hearing that phrase on his lips. "I fell in love with the way you spoke to me without ever saying a word."

CHAPTER 30

8:37 PM...

Romeo lay on his back, staring at the silvery stars flashing and winking in the black sky. The ocean breeze was cool on his skin. The smell of Mia's expensive lotion tunneled up his nose. And her voice was as erotic as her tongue in his ear as she finished the last of *In Darkness and Dreams*.

"Lazarus watched through the window as the sky to the east began to pinken with the rising sun," she read softly, lying on her belly on the blanket they'd spread out on the secluded beach at the back of the island. The little flashlight she used to illuminate the pages combined with the moonlight to make her pale skin luminesce. "The magical pull of the day-sleep dragged at his eyelids and weighed down his limbs. He didn't have much time before he was lost to slumber. Just enough time to brush a strand of hair behind Ursula's ear. Just enough time to give her one last kiss. Just enough time to think, *An eternity by her side isn't nearly long enough.*"

Mia sighed as she closed the book. Flicking off the flashlight, she snuggled next to him and pillowed her head on his shoulder. Her soft, feminine heat wrapped around him, and her breath was warm on his neck when she said, "I love how P.J. Warren always ends her books at happily-ever-after."

He considered what she said. "Oh, I don't know. I think the *really* good stuff, all the big and little things that make life so sweet, probably happens *after* the characters ride off into the sunset."

Mia pushed up on her elbow so she could smile down into his face. This time, he didn't stop himself from drowning in her golden gaze. He was looking forward to a lifetime sinking further and further still.

Emphasis on lifetime, he thought.

"Let's put that to the test, what do you think?" she asked.

"I think that's the best idea you've had yet. Except maybe..."

He let his sentence dangle, knowing she wouldn't be able to resist asking, "Except maybe what?"

"Except for maybe that thing you mentioned earlier about a blow job."

She laughed, that sparkling, musical laugh that filled him with joy. He cupped her face in his hand. "Promise me you'll do that for the rest of our lives."

She stuck her tongue in her cheek and quirked a brow. "What? Give you blow jobs."

"No." He shook his head. "Laugh. It's my favorite thing in the whole wide world. Your smile comes in at a close second."

She turned her head to drop a warm kiss into the center

of his palm. "I promise to laugh for the rest of our lives if you promise to always look at me the way you're looking at me right now."

"Deal." He told her, and then wiggled his eyebrows. "Now, let's seal it with a kiss, eh?"

"Let's seal it with *more* than a kiss," she countered, pressing her lips to his.

And for the next two hours, that's exactly what they did.

EPILOGUE

July 17th, 1624...

*F*ive...

Bartolome had lost five men in the span of less than a day to the nameless, faceless illness. More were sick and growing sicker by the minute since what little food they ate, and what little water they were able to drink, immediately exited their bodies by one means or another.

Bartolome was no longer in the role of capitán. *He, along with Rosario, had donned the mantles of caretakers, doing their best to nurse the weak and the ill.*

Ten men writhed on their bedrolls in various stages of distress and decline. Five more had begun to show symptoms, complaining of dry mouths and fatigue and—

"Capitán!" Rosario shouted from across the dirty clearing. "Come see!"

Bartolome turned away from wiping Alvaro's brow and was across the campsite and squatting next to Rosario within moments.

"Look." Rosario pointed down a poor dying sailor named Diego. "See his color? He appears to have taken a bath in indigo ink."

At first, Bartolome thought Rosario was seeing things. The leaves of the overhead trees played tricks with the morning light. But then...no.

Bartolome saw it.

A slight bluish hue stained poor Diego's skin.

Bartolome gasped and jerked to a stand.

"Capitán?" Rosario squinted up at him.

"I know this." Bartolome's blood ran cold with dread. "'Tis something I saw when I sailed through the East."

"What evil is it?" Rosario swallowed convulsively, his eyes wide with fear.

Bartolome shook his head even as his scalp prickled. "The locals called it moryxy. But to most others 'tis simply referred to as the blue death. Quick! We must dump the water!"

"What?" Rosario was on his feet in an instant and racing beside Bartolome as he marched with purpose toward the four water barrels positioned in the shade of a palm. "Sir! We cannot! We will die of thirst!"

"They are already dying of thirst." Bartolome flung an arm toward the writhing men. "'Tis the water that is killing them."

For the first time, Rosario did not jump at Bartolome's command. Instead, the midshipman stood watching, a hand over his mouth, horror in his eyes, as Bartolome tipped over one rain barrel after the other until every drop of drinking water they had soaked into the sand.

Wails of disbelief and anger arose from the sick men, but Bartolome turned a deaf ear.

"We must roll the barrels to the beach, scrub them with

sand and salt water, and then pray for rain," he said.

But even as he pressed his hands against the rough wooden slats of one barrel and began to move it along the trail they'd worn through the undergrowth, he knew the endeavor was likely futile.

As so it is, *he thought,* that we have reached the beginning of the end...

Coming June 2022!

DEAD
IN THE
WATER

THE DEEP SIX • Book 6

JULIE ANN WALKER

CHAPTER 1

Present Day
6:35 PM...

Have you ever had the urge to tell someone to shut up even when they weren't talking?"

Dalton "Doc" Simmons frowned at Cami; the toothpick caught between his teeth pointed at the floor. "What the hell? I'm just standing here."

"And silently calling me dirty names. I can *feel* you doing it even if I can't *hear* you." Her lips pursed. Lips that were plush, full, and painted a rich, velvety red. "Which is so much worse," she added. "Because then when I call you out for silently calling me dirty names, it makes me sound crazy." She narrowed her eyes. Eyes that were dark, heavily lashed, and tilted up at the corners, making her look like she knew a delicious secret.

Hands down, Camilla D'Angelo was the most beautiful woman Doc had ever met.

Not that he put a whole heck of a lot of stock in beauty.

After all, the Hope Diamond was said to be one of the most dazzling gems ever cut, but everyone who'd ever owned it had died a mysterious death. Beauty had a way of hiding what was sinister.

And okay, he wasn't saying *Cami*'s loveliness came with a curse or some sort of deep-seated moral turpitude. But he *was* saying she was a *lawyer*, so…

"But maybe that's your goal. To make me sound crazy." She tapped a ruby-red fingertip on her chin contemplatively. "You'd love to see me wrapped in a straitjacket. Admit it."

"I'll admit no such thing." He shook his head, noting how his blood bubbled with pleasure.

Trading barbs with Cami was…*stimulating*. Maybe because she was the only woman whose mouth he'd ever been tempted to simultaneously kiss and tape shut.

Although, having once done that first thing, he wasn't stupid enough to attempt it again. Not because it hadn't been good, but because it'd been *too* good. A kiss that'd gone past his lips to sink into a space he'd purposefully kept empty.

An alarming kiss. A dangerous kiss.

A kiss that will not be repeated.

"I wouldn't wish the indignity of a straitjacket on anyone," he assured her. "I'm a firm believer in bodily autonomy. So if it's looking like you're heading toward some sort of unwilling confinement, please know I'll put you out of your misery and smother you with a pillow first."

Her mouth flattened into a straight line. "What a gentleman."

"I like to think so." He inclined his head regally.

He wouldn't have thought it possible, but her mouth flattened further, until her red lips disappeared completely. "Apparently, when it comes to sarcasm you're tone deaf."

"Oh, no. I picked up what you were laying down. I was just being magnanimous and ignoring it." She opened her mouth to come back at him with something scathing, no doubt, but he cut her off by adding, "But since you brought it up, let's address it." He checked his watch. "By my count, that was two hours of stonewalling silence before you opened the conversation back up with sarcasm. It's like we've been married for ten years or something."

She shoved a fisted hand on her hip. "You could only dream of being so lucky. And those two hours of stonewalling silence were a direct result of you accusing me of purposefully making your job harder than it has to be." A fascinating wash of pink stained her high cheekbones. She enjoyed their linguistic tussles as much as he did. "You've called me a witch before, but surely you don't think I'm capable of conjuring up a storm."

Now both her hands were fisted on her hips as she stood with her legs slightly apart to counter the movement of the decking beneath her feet. The *Wayfarer II* was a large vessel, with a J-frame crane attached to the aft section and a HIAB hydraulic loader on the bow that kept the ship equally weighted in the water. But the approaching hurricane was beginning to rile the seas around the vessel, making it bob slightly.

"I never called you a witch." His brow puckered as his teeth and tongue worked the fraying end of the toothpick. A psych major would probably accuse him of having an oral fixation. But Doc would argue his affinity for the wooden sticks was simply habit. One he'd picked up from his old man. "I said you were *witchy*," he clarified. "There's a difference. And I *know* you're not responsible for the storm. But you *are* responsible for us having to wait until the reef was submerged before retrieving the treasure."

Her smooth brow puckered with frustration. "The *law* is responsible for that. Not me."

Admiralty Law, the salvor's best friend, stated it was

finders keepers when it came to recovered goods within state or federal waters. Unfortunately, Captain Bartolome Vargas had removed the treasure from the wreck of the *Santa Cristina* and hidden it beneath the reef that protected Wayfarer Island's lagoon from the ravages of the open ocean.

A reef was considered "waters" so long as it was submerged. But if a speck of it peeked above the waves? Well, then it was considered land.

Admiralty Law didn't apply to land.

"Instead of busting my balls over how tough the last day has been, you should be thanking me for finding the loophole that allows you to keep all of this to yourself instead of having to share it with Uncle Sam or the state of Florida," Cami continued, throwing out a lithe arm to indicate the treasure that lay piled atop the tables in the ship's computer room.

One tabletop held a collection of conglomerates, which was what happened to silver coins when they came into contact with seawater. Corrosion and other maritime accretions fused the currency together into rocky looking wads. But Doc knew as soon as they were electronically cleaned, the pieces of eight—coins like the one that hung on a chain around his neck—would be revealed.

Another table was mounded with doubloons. Unlike silver, gold wasn't affected by its time in the ocean. The doubloons glinted and winked under the artificial light as if they'd been minted the day before.

Then there was a small tabletop displaying swords and daggers, each ceremonial and encrusted with gems. A larger table held religious artifacts, all ornamental and heavily bejeweled. And still another was heaped with uncut emeralds that'd been mined from Columbia nearly four hundred years ago.

Truly, the immenseness of the *Santa Cristina*'s treasure was a mindboggling sight to behold. And that wasn't counting the gold bullion and the silver ingots the Deep Six crew had already cataloged and packed away in straw-lined boxes that were now stacked against the walls of the ship's engine room.

For the first few hours, when Doc and his former SEAL Team members and current Deep Six Salvage partners had hauled up the gems and coins and artifacts from where Captain Vargas had hidden them, he'd marveled at each new piece of wealth. Like a kid at a banner Christmas, he'd been agog at the glittering hoard.

But as the treasure trove grew, he began to feel an overwhelming sense of surrealism.

Like, how could any of this be real? How could he, Dalton Simmons, a poor kid from Nowhere, Montana, be a one-sixth owner of a lost treasure estimated to be worth nearly a half a billion dollars?

And yet…it *was* real. The sparkling jewels and precious metals sitting heavily upon the tabletops around him attested to that. Which meant he was officially a millionaire.

Not just a millionaire. A *multimillionaire*.

Thanks to Cami and her legal wrangling.

Ugh. It rankled to have to admit it. And yet, he heard himself saying dutifully, "Thank you for finding the loophole that allows us to keep all this." One corner of her mouth hitched up, but it fell into a straight line again when he added, "I just would've liked the loophole better if hadn't meant we had to wait for a king tide smack-dab in the middle of hurricane season."

She shook her head. "All you had to do was wait for a king tide. The fact that the next one happened to occur in the middle of hurricane season didn't have anything to do with me. It was bad luck."

"Not true." He lifted a finger. "There was a king tide earlier in the year, but we missed it while you were pouring over precedent."

"Wildly obscure precedent that I would stress, *again*, is the reason you're able to keep all this. Now"—she pointed toward the hallway—"you see that door? For the love of god, do me a favor and go find out what's on the other side of it."

He felt a chuckle rumbling around in his chest, but he suppressed it with a deep breath. "For the love of god, huh? I thought you told me you weren't religious."

"I wasn't before I met you. But now I've taken to getting down on my knees and praying nightly for you to go mute."

He allowed one corner of his mouth to lift into a languid, flirtatious smile.

Her eyes narrowed with suspicion. "What? What's that look for?"

"I'm imagining you down on your knees."

She gasped and left her mouth hanging open long after the sound escaped her lips.

Camilla D' Angelo gave as good as she got when it came to oral arguments—thanks to all the practice her career provided her, no doubt. But he'd learned he could beat her at her own game when he tossed in a little sexual innuendo. Or rather, not just beat her at her own game, but stop her dead in her tracks.

It was fascinating the way she blinked and sputtered and blushed to the roots of her sleek, black hair when he hinted at anything carnal.

"Oh!" She stomped her foot, annoyed as ever that he'd rendered her momentarily speechless. "You are the most *aggravating*—"

"Children!" Romeo yelled in exasperation. "I'm trying to count my riches like Scrooge McDuck, and your arguing is ruining the experience for me!"

"Here, here," Uncle John seconded from his seat at the emerald table. He had a jeweler's loupe plugged into one eye, making him look like a Borg off *Star Trek*. Although, his Earnest Hemingway hair and salty seadog beard went a long way toward ruining the sci-fi effect.

Before Doc could respond, the sound of bare feet slapping against the metal decking had him turning toward the computer room's open door. The remaining four members of the Deep Six crew, all still wearing their wetsuits and leaving wet footprints behind, shuffled into the room.

"Water's startin' to kick up out there," Leo "The Lion" Anderson, their former lieutenant and the current head of their salvage operation, said as he folded a fresh stick of Big Red gum into his mouth. Glancing around the room, he asked in his slow, Southern drawl, "Where's my wife?"

"In the galley making cupcakes to have for dessert after Bran's lasagnas," Cami informed him before turning her attention to Brando "Bran" Pallidino. "By the way, I took the lasagnas out of the oven fifteen minutes ago. Just like you said."

Bran scrubbed a hand through his dripping, wavy brown hair and nodded his thanks. Before he could say anything, however, a larger than average wave rolled beneath the ship.

"Erp." Cami lifted a hand to her mouth, her skin paling instantly when the vessel bobbed like a cork. But she was quick to drop her fingers and make a face at Bran as soon as the salvage ship steadied itself. "Sorry. I promise that me nearly losing my cookies has nothing to do with your lasagnas. They look and smell delicious."

Doc crossed his arms over his chest and leveled a censorious look on her. "You didn't take that Dramamine pill I gave you, did you?"

"First of all," she bristled, "you may be *a* doctor, but you're not *my* doctor. And second of all, Dramamine makes me sleepy. I didn't want to nap my way through all of this." Again, she threw out an arm to indicate the treasure.

"Has no one ever told you that you are *the* most stubborn woman to ever pull on a pair of pants?"

"Oh my god!" Her chin jutted out. "*You're* calling *me* stubborn? Ever been told that those who live in glass houses shouldn't throw stones?"

LT sighed heavily—LT was the nickname everyone used for Leo; it was a nod to his former rank—and asked Romeo, "Have they been at it like this all afternoon?" Before Romeo could reply, LT shook his head. "Never mind. It doesn't matter. We got more important things to deal with than the ongoin' animosity between our attorney and our resident malcontent."

"Hey!" Doc objected, snatching the toothpick from his mouth. But LT ignored him by turning to Bran and adding, "Go grab everyone and bring 'em here, Brando. We need all hands on deck for this discussion, seein' as how our decision on what to do next is gonna affect us all."

LT's statement had Doc narrowing his eyes. "I take it you weren't able to finish."

LT shook his head, causing water droplets to drip from the ends of his sun-streaked hair. "But let's wait to talk about it 'til we got everyone."

Doc recognized his former commanding officer's tone.

It was the same one LT had used the time their extraction site had been compromised after they'd carried out a surprise dawn attack on the AQAP headquarters in Yemen's Bayda Province. They'd been stuck behind enemy lines for sixteen hours with gun-toting tangos hot on their trail before a gutsy SH-60 Seahawk helicopter pilot had flown through hostile airspace to pull them out. It was the same tone LT had used *numerous* times when they'd found themselves all the way in harm's way, in the place where the metal meets the meat. And hearing that tone now made Doc's stomach sink.

Of their own accord, his eyes tracked over to Cami. She,

too, had picked up on the ominous ring in LT's voice, and the expression on her face pretty much mirrored everything Doc was feeling. He was hit by the oddest urge to throw a comforting arm around her shoulders and assure her that no matter what, everything would be okay.

Then again, maybe the urge wasn't all that odd. The truth was, as much as she riled him, he *liked* her.

Liked her swift mind and her sharp tongue. Liked the ornery sparkle in her eyes that always made him smile. Liked the way her laugh sounded like pure delight. Liked the graceful determination in her step that spoke of a woman who knew who she was, where she was going, and how she was going to get there all on her own, *thank you very much*.

In fact, were it not for her chosen profession, he could've imagined them becoming friends. The kind of friends to feed each other heaping helpings of shit on the reg, of course. But friends all the same.

And in the eternal words of OMC, he thought, *how bizarre*.

With the exception of the wives and girlfriends of his teammates and partners—who didn't really count because they *were* the wives and girlfriends of his teammate and partners, and therefore off-limits—he'd only ever been friends with one other woman.

The woman.

His woman.

And Jesus hopscotching Christ, what did it mean that he found himself thinking that, if things were different, Cami could hold a similar title?

Thankfully, he didn't have time to answer that question before the computer room began to fill with people.

LT's wife, Olivia, was still wearing the apron LT had gotten her for her birthday. Considering she was a former CIA agent, as comfortable carrying a loaded weapon as she was wearing a wire to a meeting with international weapons dealers, to say it was incongruous to see her looking like Betty Crocker was an understatement. But ever since Oliva had bugged out of the Agency, married LT, and joined them on their hunt for the *Santa Cristina*, she'd embraced domesticity.

Bran's wife, the miniscule Maddy, looped an arm around Bran's waist and smiled up at him radiantly when he bent to drop a loud, smacking kiss on her temple.

Chrissy and Wolf found a spot beside Uncle John at the emerald table. Chrissy's diving skills were as good as any Navy SEAL's. So she'd been helping the others haul up the treasure. Her ponytail was still wet from being down at the dive site, and Doc watched as Wolf absently twisted the damp, blond rope around his fingers.

Mia Ennis, the brilliant marine archeologist they'd brought on to oversee the excavation of the ship and the treasure, went to sit on Romeo's lap. The couple was still in the honeymoon phase of their relationship, and Doc had to refrain from groaning when they made googly eyes at each other.

Alexandra Merriweather, the historian they'd hired to study the old documents relating to the Spanish fleet, broke a strawberry Pop-Tart in two and handed half to Mason. The only person Doc had ever met who snacked more than Mason was Alex. And considering the woman was only five feet tall and barely weighed a buck ten soaking wet, he couldn't help but wonder where she put all those calories.

Peas in a pod, he thought as he watched Alex shove her tortoiseshell glasses higher on the bridge of her nose so she could grin up at her fiancé. Or maybe it was more apt to say Mason and Alex were two sides of the same coin. Because as chatty as Alex was, that's how closed-mouthed Mason was.

Glancing around the room then, Doc came to a startling

realization.

I'm the last man standing. The only member of my former SEAL Team who isn't head over heels in L.O.V.E.

Of course, that was because he'd been there, done that.

And lost it all.

As happened anytime his past reared its ugly head, he felt the terrible void that lived in the center of chest yawn wide. Felt himself falling into it, traveling back in time to a dirt road. To a pair of wide blue eyes. To the girl he'd loved since the eighth grade.

Lifting his right arm, he ran a reverent finger over the delicate flower tattooed on the inside of his wrist. He'd gotten the ink when he was eighteen years old, the day after he proposed. The day after she said yes.

But just like his memories of her, the tattoo was beginning to fade. The flower growing fuzzy around the edges. No longer bright and pure.

And that hurts worst of all.

It made him feel untrue. *Unfaithful.*

"Sorry! I got stuck in the bathroom. That door lock is like a jigsaw puzzle with pieces that don't quite fit." The last and newest member of their merry band of misfits burst into the computer room, the sides of her windbreaker flapping like a drunken bird.

Her name was Dana Levine and she worked for the FMC—the Federal Maritime Commission. Cami had insisted on bringing Dana on to bear witness to the salvage since, according to Cami, *"We need a Fed who will swear under oath that you guys didn't touch so much as a single coin of that treasure while the top of the reef was exposed."*

Glad for the distraction from the melancholy turn of his thoughts, Doc watched Dana hastily slip past LT and plop into a chair next to the table that held the conglomerates. She'd been on the deck all day and her wild, windblown hair and slightly sunburned nose attested to the diligence with which she'd taken on the role of witness.

Doc would guess her to be somewhere in her mid-fifties. Her bouncy blond curls were interspersed with threads of gray, and there were laugh lines at the corners of her cornflower-blue eyes.

He'd taken an instant liking to Dana. Not only because she was the ticket to him and his partners keeping the treasure, but also because her sweet, ready smile and the gentle way she had of talking reminded him of Lily. Just a little.

Lily...

His wife's name echoed inside the confines of his skull and caused the chasm inside him to fill with a familiar ache.

"Okay. Now that everyone's here, it's time to talk turkey." LT's voice rang with military authority even though they'd waved their goodbyes to the Navy more than two years earlier. "We thought we were gonna be able to finish this evenin', but that didn't happen."

Doc had pulled the early morning shift at the dive site, so he knew just how much work was involved in bringing up the treasure. Knew all about spending hours waving a handheld metal detector over the seabed, waiting for the blinking light to indicate whether he'd found ferrous or non-ferrous metals. Knew how tedious the sectioning off and gridding of the area could be, because even though the treasure had been removed from the *Santa Cristina*, it still had to be excavated in an archeological manner. Knew how slow and painstaking the process was of carefully attaching the treasure to lift bags—the vinyl-coated nylon satchels—that did the hard work of floating the riches to the surface.

And that was all before the approaching hurricane had begun to stir up the ocean around the salvage site.

He wasn't surprised his partners hadn't managed to haul up the last of the booty before the sun set. But he *was* surprised to hear LT add, "And to make matters worse, looks like Julia is going to hit us after all."

The hairs on Doc's arms lifted in warning. He tugged on his ear. "I thought the meteorologists said she was only going to skim us with her outer edges."

"Apparently she changed her mind and changed directions." LT made a face. "New projections say she'll smack us head-on before turnin' to make landfall somewhere around New Orleans."

"Fuck," Mason muttered. The man was a born and raised Bostonian. When he *did* deign to speak, it was a safe bet the F-bomb would be involved.

"She's currently a Category 2, but they're estimatin' she'll be a 3 by the time she reaches us," LT continued, and Doc heard his molars creak when he gritted his teeth together.

As a bona fide landlubber, he'd never gotten completely comfortable with the tropical storms that crashed through the Straits of Florida on a yearly basis. Luckily, in the time he'd lived on Wayfarer Island, the biggest hurricane he'd had to weather had topped out at a Category 2.

Even then, he'd thought the beach house was going to blow down.

He shuddered to remember how the rain hadn't fallen from the sky so much as it'd been flung through the air like tiny, watery missiles that'd pummeled his exposed skin. How his hair had whipped around so violently that it's stung when it made contact with his face.

"How much time do we have?" Bran asked, his arm tightening around his wife's shoulders.

"We'll probably start feelin' the winds of her leading edges around noon tomorrow," LT said.

"Which gives us tomorrow morning to finish bringing up what's left of the loot." Bran's concerned expression cleared. "Bada bing, bada boom. Easy peasy."

Bran was a New Jerseyan through and through and couldn't help sounding like an extra off *The Sopranos*.

LT's jaw muscles worked hard against the gum in his mouth. He used a hand to indicate the ship around him. "There's no way we'll be able to outrun the hurricane in *Wayfarer II* if we wait to leave until the storm is almost on top us. She's not fast enough. We'll hafta anchor her on the leeward side of the island and cross our fingers she rides out the storm."

"Um." Alex raised her hand, her freckled nose wrinkling. "Is that really the best idea? I mean, what if she sinks? The treasure will go down with her." She frowned. "Not that we couldn't salvage it again, of course. But for the love of all that's holy, what a pain in the ass."

"Which is why I say we should sail her to Key West tonight." LT's drawl always grew more pronounced when he was keyed up and working through a problem.

"And leave what's left of the treasure behind?" One pitch-black eyebrow winged up Wolf's forehead. "I know we were thinkin' we got all but about one, maybe two percent of it up today. But two percent of half a billion dollars is still ten million. Are we really okay lettin' the storm come in and scatter ten million benjis across the ocean floor?"

Whereas LT had grown up in New Orleans and spoke with the elongated vowels of the South, Wolf had a twang that was right out of an old Western, thanks to having spent his formative years on a reservation in northeast Oklahoma.

LT pinned a look on Mia. "You got everything cataloged and recorded at the site for the state, yeah? Everything you need to finish the paperwork?"

Mia nodded and the movement caused a lock of strawberry-blond hair to fall into her face. Romeo casually, almost absently, brushed it behind her ear. "The actual hands-on archeological part of my job is finished," she assured LT.

"All that's left is to photograph the final pieces once you've brough them up."

LT ran a finger under his chin. After a couple of seconds, he declared, "Then I volunteer to stay behind and salvage what's left tomorrow mornin'. I'll load it into Uncle John's catamaran and head west. The sailboat is faster than *Wayfarer II*. I'll sail out of the path of the storm and hang out in calm water until it passes. Then we can all meet back here in two days. Three days tops."

Doc opened his mouth to tell LT there was no way in hell he was letting him stay back to finish salvaging the treasure alone, but Dana beat him to the punch by asking, "Will the tide still be covering the reef tomorrow morning?"

"Accordin' to the charts it will," LT assured her. "Plus, Julia will be pushin' the ocean ahead of her. So we should be good to go."

"I'll need to stay to make sure of that, of course," Dana said.

"I'm stayin' too," Uncle John piped up. He was dressed in his standard getup of baggy cargo shorts and a Hawaiian shirt that was bright enough to blind a person. "I'm better at sailin' the cat than you are anyway."

When LT opened his mouth to argue, Uncle John—who was technically only LT's biological uncle, but who held the honorary title when it came to the rest of them—lifted a wide, callused hand. "My mind's made up, boy. And you know better than to argue with me once that's happened."

LT snapped his mouth shut, but a muscle ticked in his jaw. It was obvious he wished to finish the job himself. But as Doc's father had been so fond of saying, *You can wish in one hand and shit in the other, and just see which one fills up faster.*

"I'm staying too," Doc told LT, making sure his tone brooked no argument at the same time he shoved the toothpick back into his mouth. "It'll go faster tomorrow with both of us working."

"And as your lawyer," Cami interjected, "I'm duty-bound to stay until the very last coin is recovered."

"I'm staying if you're staying," Olivia told LT.

"No." LT shook his head, staring down at his dark-haired wife. "I want you safe in Key West."

Oliva arched an imperious-looking eyebrow. "Safe? The way you tell it, there's no danger. We'll be long gone before Julia hits, right?"

"It's settled then," Doc declared with a decisive nod. "The six of us will stay here and finish the job while everyone else makes sure the salvage ship and the rest of the treasure is hell and gone out of Julia's path."

"Please say we have time to eat before heading to Key West." Alex's Kewpie doll mouth was pursed into a bow. "I'm starving."

"I swear you must have a hollow leg," Chrissy harrumphed.

"Jealous?" Alex wiggled her eyebrows.

"*Yes*," Chrissy declared. But the heat in her voice didn't match the twinkle in her eyes. Chrissy and Alex had become fast friends in the months they'd been working with the Deep Six crew. Probably because they were cut from the same cloth. Both strong-willed. Both independent. Both crazy in love with a former fighting man. "Because if I ate half of what you do, I'd weight six hundred pounds."

Alex shook her head. "Not necessarily. I read this interesting article recently about metabolism that said—"

A font of information. That was Alexandra Merriweather. She chattered on about the article as everyone shuffled out of the computer room, headed down to the galley where Bran's famous lasagnas awaited them.

Doc was the last one through the computer room's door,

but his flip-flops skidded to a halt on the metal decking when he saw Cami standing in the hallway, her head cocked as she stared at him.

"What?" he demanded, ignoring how his heart was suddenly thudding against his rib cage.

"I'm wondering why you didn't try to talk me out of staying," she said. "You and me, stuck on a sailboat for two, maybe three days? I figured you'd consider that only slightly more appealing than a long walk through the seventh circle of hell."

"Now, normally that would be true," he told her.

"But?" she pressed when he didn't immediately go on.

"But I reckon I can pass the time by telling you the latest batch of lawyer jokes I found on the internet. And you'll be too seasick to stop me." He wiggled his eyebrows and the end of the toothpick at the same time.

He expected her to snap and snarl at him. So he was a little surprised when her wide mouth stretched into a toothy smile.

Apprehension had his chin jerking back. "What are you grinning about?"

She fluttered her thick lashes. "Oh, I'm just plotting all the ways I could end you while we're out on that little sailboat in the middle of nowhere."

As she turned and sauntered down the hall, her hips swishing dramatically, he got the distinct impression the approaching storm was the very *least* of his worries.

MORE BOOKS BY
JULIE ANN WALKER

In Moonlight and Memories:
In Moonlight and Memories: Volume One
In Moonlight and Memories: Volume Two
In Moonlight and Memories: Volume Three

Black Knights Inc.:
Hell on Wheels
In Rides Trouble
Rev It Up
Thrill Ride
Born Wild
Hell for Leather
Full Throttle
Too Hard to Handle
Wild Ride
Fuel for Fire
Hot Pursuit
Built to Last

The Deep Six:
Hot as Hell
Hell or High Water
Devil and the Deep
Ride the Tide
Deeper than the Ocean

ABOUT THE AUTHOR

A New York Times and USA Today bestselling author, Julie loves to travel the world looking for views to compete with her deadlines. And if those views happen to come with a blue sky and sunshine? All the better! When she's not writing, Julie enjoys camping, hiking, cycling, fishing, cooking, petting every dog that walks by her, and…reading, of course!

Be sure to sign up for Julie's occasional newsletter at:

www.julieannwalker.com

To learn more about Julie, visit her website or follow her all over social media:

Facebook: www.facebook.com/julieannwalkerauthor

Instagram: @julieannwalker_author

TikTok: @julieannwalker_author

Twitter: @JAWalker_author

ACKNOWLEDGMENTS

Big hugs and big thanks to my friends and family. Lord knows we've all been put through the ringer the last couple of years. I couldn't ask for a better group of people to belong to. Love you all to pieces!

Kudos to Joyce Lamb for enjoying Mia and Romeo, and Doc and Cami as much as I did. Thank you for helping me polish up the story to make it shine!

A loud shout-out to all the folks who do the unsung work of getting a book into readers' hands. Marlene Roberts, proofer extraordinaire, Amanda Carlson, writer and friend who took on the job of formatting for me because I'm all thumbs when it comes to technology, and Erin Dameron-Hill for the drool-worthy cover.

Made in United States
North Haven, CT
30 May 2023

37162379R00243